WHERE TH...

New York Times bestselling author
FERN MICHAELS's
The Journey

Still hurting twelve years after being left at the altar, wilderness guide Maggie Harper is about to make the most difficult trek of her life: back to the man who abandoned her.

New York Times **bestselling author**
JANET DAILEY's
Heading Home

Seeking peace and emotional healing at her family's ranch, Kate Summers is wary of her rugged new neighbor, Josh Reynolds—and tries to still the yearnings of her lonely, broken heart.

New York Times **bestselling author**
SHARON SALA's
The Return of Walker Lee

Walker Lee should never have let Carrie Ann Wainwright go—and now he's coming back to win the love of the high-spirited Texas gal all over again.

And
DEBORAH BEDFORD's
Rockabye Inn

Returning to her hotel after the accident that stole her memory, innkeeper Anna Burden discovers shattering truths and healing passion in the arms of a handsome stranger.

FERN
MICHAELS
JANET
DAILEY
SHARON SALA
DEBORAH BEDFORD

Homecoming

AVON BOOKS

An Imprint of HarperCollins*Publishers*

This book was originally published in mass market by HarperCollins Paperbacks in March 1997.

"The Return of Walker Lee" was originally published by Sharon Sala, writing under the pseudonym Dinah McCall.

AVON BOOKS
An Imprint of HarperCollins*Publishers*
10 East 53rd Street
New York, New York 10022-5299

"The Journey" copyright © 1997 by Fern Michaels; "Heading Home" copyright © 1997 by Janet Dailey; "The Return of Walker Lee" copyright © 1997 by Sharon Sala; "Rockabye Inn" copyright © 1997 by Deborah Bedford
ISBN: 978-0-06-108508-6
ISBN-10: 0-06-108508-1
www.avonromance.com

First Avon Books paperback printing: May 2007
First HarperCollins paperback printing: March 1997

Avon Trademark Reg. U.S. Pat. Off. and in Other Countries, Marca Registrada, Hecho en U.S.A.
Harpercollins® is a registered trademark of HarperCollins Publishers.

Printed in the U.S.A.

10   9

Contents

The Journey

Fern Michaels

One

Maggie Osborne Harper set her bags down on the polished floor. Her own personal, lonely homecoming. Home being this snug, cozy cabin in Wyoming. Her real home, if you could call a condo in sunny Florida home, was her secondary place of residence, a place to go to when the snows came and Ozzie Conklin's Survival Camp shut down for three long months.

She hated Florida, hated the two-bedroom condos in Fort Lauderdale, hated the green-and-yellow decor, but most of all she hated the crowds of sun birds and the noise that blanketed the area during the winter months.

This was the time of year when, on returning to the cabin, she did a thirty-minute stint of soul-searching. She kicked her bags to the side of the door and headed for the small efficiency kitchen, where she stoked the wood-burning stove and made a strong pot of tea. The fire in the monster fireplace in the living room was blazing, thanks to Lulu, Ozzie's wife. She could curl up with her mug of tea and think about either the year ahead or past years. Usually, she thought about the past, because she still felt bitter and wounded even though it was twelve years since Matt Star had left her standing at the altar without so much as a, Look, this isn't working for me, or a, So long. Marriage isn't in my cards. Not to mention the loss of the thirty-five thousand dollars her parents had paid for the wedding.

Probably the hardest thing to remember, but she brought it to the forefront of her mind each time she returned to Wyoming, were the pitying looks on her parents' and friends' faces. Dumped on her wedding day at the proverbial altar. A girl never got over something like that. At least this girl didn't. She'd tried; she'd even gotten married for three whole weeks before she called it quits. Licking her wounds, she'd returned to college in Pennsylvania and got her degree in forestry, an unlikely profession for someone like her, who preferred the fast-track life sprinkled with glitz and glamour. After graduation, she'd sent out applications by the dozen and taken the first offer that came in, Ozzie Conklin's Survival Camp for men and women who needed to prove they had what it took to survive in the wilderness and to become a man or woman of the '90s.

In a way, she'd stacked the deck when she sent out her applications. She'd remembered Matt talking about the time he took Ozzie's survival course when he was fifteen, the course that earned him his cap, the cap he said he was wearing to the wedding, the cap he ate with, slept with, and was never without. It had been Matt's choice for their honeymoon, and she'd gone along with it. All she cared about was seeing Matt happy. What was it he'd said? Oh, yes, If we go to Ozzie's camp it will be like a homecoming for me. "Me" meant him.

Instead, she'd been the one to follow through and, to her knowledge, Matt Star had never been back. So much for homecomings and passion-filled nights under the stars.

She'd put Matt's name on her application as the person who'd recommended the camp. She'd come out here the day after Ozzie called to offer her the job, and she'd been here ever since.

Matt Star, neighbor, childhood friend, teenage friend, and then lover. God, how she'd loved him. So much so that she used to make herself sick at the mere thought he might not show up for a date. He always did, though; Matt was a man of his word. Until the day of the wedding. Matt, at the age of twenty, was a legend in his own time.

Today, Matt Star headed up Digi-Star, the largest software company in the country, second only to Bill Gates's Microsoft. Matt was a billionaire several times over. He was still as handsome as ever in a rugged kind of way. Just last week, she'd seen a pictorial article in the Sunday section of the *Miami Herald*. She'd even clipped the article so she could torture herself occasionally by looking at it.

Enough of the past! Maggie poured herself a second cup of tea and switched her thoughts to the future—a future that was so iffy she'd filed an application in the Everglades in case Ozzie was forced to file for bankruptcy this year. Ozzie and Lulu owed her and every other trail guide six months of back pay. She wondered if the others would return the way she had. She'd work for Ozzie for nothing as long as he fed her and let her stay in the cabin. She owed Ozzie and Lulu. Big time. It was going to be interesting to see if the others felt the same way. She'd know by supper time, which was three short hours away.

Maggie stirred in her nest of pillows, her tea cup empty. Time to get on with the business of living. She threw a log on the fire, poked at it, watched the flames dance upward. She'd sat with Matt in front of many a fire, their arms around each other, telling one another what they saw in the flames. Matt's visions were always so much more interesting than hers. What was he doing? Right now, this very minute? Did he ever think of her? What did he think and feel the day he sent her parents the check for $35,000 to cover the wedding he'd walked out on? Surely a small measure of guilt.

Her parents had died that same year, one after the other, in the space of eight months. She'd sold their small house on the Intercoastal, taken the $35,000 and the money from the sale of the house, and paid for the two-bedroom highrise condo on Highway A1A that was fully furnished.

Enough already! The past was as dead as yesterday's newspapers. Twelve years was too long to dwell on things that weren't meant to be.

Maggie turned when she heard wild scratching on her door. She thrust it open and was propelled backward until she landed on the couch, one hundred and ten pounds of dog on top of her.

"Buzz!" She tussled with the chocolate Labrador who was licking her face and neck and trying to crawl under her sweater. "Guess that means you missed me. Guess what, I missed you, too. Next time you're going with me. If that fancy condo association won't let you in, we're moving. So there! I brought you the biggest bone Publix had in the meat department. I even cooked it and it stunk up my luggage, but I didn't care. Go get it. It's in the duffel."

She watched in amazement as the dog worked the

zipper with his teeth, found the Baggie, pawed it open, sniffed it, and then carried it over to the fire-place, where he proceeded to chew it, one eye and one ear cocked in Maggie's direction to make sure she wasn't going anywhere.

Maggie loved the rough, two-room cabin with its chintz draperies, worn flowered furniture, homemade rugs and heavy quilts, all made by Lulu during the winter months. The space heaters were Ozzie's contri-bution, as well as the ceiling-high stack of firewood. She crossed her fingers and said a prayer that Ozzie would find a way to pay his bills and keep the camp going. If there was a way, Lulu would find it.

Buzz was a streak of darkness as he raced to the door, his tail wagging ninety miles to the minute. "Yo! Anyone here?"

"Annie, you're back! Welcome home!" Maggie said throwing her arms around her best friend. "I thought you said—"

"Yeah, yeah, yeah. I got a good job this winter tend-ing bar in the Catskills and managed to save enough to see me through till next year. I had to come back because I love those two cantankerous curmudgeons. Did you hear anything? I put on seven pounds. Can you tell?" It was all said in one long, breathless streak of sound.

Maggie eyed the pudgy, freckled face young woman, six years her junior. Annie was an eternal optimist. Maggie suspected she slept with a smile on her face. She was smiling now as she cuddled with Buzz by the fire.

"So, tell me, did you meet any men this winter?" The devilish glint in Annie's eyes made Maggie laugh.

"Yep, two very spry eighty-year-olds who were

looking for a nurse to take care of them. I wasn't looking. How about you?"

"At least two dozen. Not one ounce of marriage material in either one of them. I had a lot of fun, though. I hate to mention this, Maggie, but you're thirty-three. Your biological clock is starting to tick. I can hear it! By the way, I saw—I clipped this article out of the *Times* on Sunday. It's about that guy you almost married. If you don't want it—"

"I don't. I saw it." Maggie's voice turned flat and hard.

"Ooooh-kay. I signed up two guys for April 15th. I even got deposits for Ozzie. One of them has potential. I think you might even like him, Maggie. He's an architect and he was an Olympic skier a few years ago. A nice guy, and he's got money. His hair is thinning a tad, and he needs to lose a few pounds around the middle, but the guy is sterling. He *wants* to get married. Now, how often do you hear a guy admit to *that*?"

"What's really wrong with him?"

"He makes a lot of noise when he eats. He has this jaw problem."

Maggie tossed a pillow in Annie's direction. "I'm not interested, thank you. I'll find my own man. Then maybe I won't. I might opt for old-maid status."

"Get real, Maggie. You're a one-man woman. I know it, you know it, everyone in this camp knows it. You're letting the best years of your life slide by. Hiding here in this place isn't your answer. When was the last time you had a real date? Never mind trying to think. It was so long ago you can't remember. When was the last time you bought a pretty dress and got all gussied up? Twelve years ago," she said answering herself. "By the way, I like that new hairdo—and is that sunglitz I see on those sheared strands? You did meet someone! I want to hear everything."

Maggie flushed. "I did not meet anyone. I went for a haircut and this guy talked me into the sunglitz. I have to admit I like it. It's a great wash and wear cut. I brought the stuff with me in case you want me to do yours. I have a feeling we're going to have lots of spare time this year."

"My God, Maggie, what will we do if Ozzie—?"

"I don't want to think about it, Annie. Ten years is a long time to work in one place. It becomes a home. I filled out an application with the Everglades Park Service. You know, just in case. I'll hang in here till the last second. I want you to know that."

"Me, too. If it comes to that, I'm willing to relocate if you want a roommate."

Maggie nodded.

"What do you suppose Lulu is making for dinner? First night back is always special. Take your best guess," Annie said.

"If the larder is full, a big venison roast with potatoes and carrots, fresh bread, coleslaw, and peach cobbler. If things are tight, Spam or tuna, as in Lulu's Special Surprise. Frozen Twinkies with grape jelly on top for dessert. If everyone comes, it won't matter what we're having. God, Annie, I hope they all show."

"They will. The guys are as loyal to Ozzie and Lulu as you and me. I tried calling Harry and Gus before I left this morning, but their phones were disconnected. I think that means they're on their way. Ben called me to wish me a happy new year and he said he was coming back. I think we can count on Sophie and Mickey. The only two I'm not sure about are Kevin and Ross. Is that pretty much how you see it?"

"I'd say so. I don't think Tiny will be back. He said he was going to have to take care of his dad because of some back surgery. Nine out of ten isn't bad. The flip side to that is Tiny might show up later, when things are more settled with his father. We are a loyal group."

"Cross your fingers that things work out. I don't want to see Ozzie go under. Oh, I see you unpacked your cap."

Maggie's features hardened. "I goddamn well earned every thread in that cap. This cap is what lets me know I am who I am." She fingered the embroidered lettering that said "Lulu's Bait Shack." In a defiant gesture of something she couldn't define, Maggie jammed the khaki-colored baseball cap on her head.

"I didn't mean . . . everyone knows the story of those two baseball caps. Let's drop it, okay?"

"Good idea. Let's check out the other cabins and see who else arrived. Maybe Lulu can use some help in the kitchen."

Annie watched as Maggie removed the baseball cap and hung it on a hook jutting out from the corner of the fireplace. "I hate you, Matt Star, even though I don't know you," Annie muttered under her breath. "I wish you sleepless nights for the rest of your life for what you did to Maggie."

Two

Three thousand miles away in a suite of plush corporate offices, Matt Star, shining CEO of Digi-Star, propped his feet on top of his glass-topped desk. He pushed his baseball cap, which said, "Lulu's Bait Shack," farther back on his head. He eyed the hole in the knee of his jeans, which, to him, seemed to match the size of the hole in his right sneaker. He finger-combed the springy curls on top of his head with his left hand while his right hand traced intricate invisible patterns on a manila envelope that was marked "Personal" and had been hand-delivered at three o'clock that afternoon. It was now ten minutes past ten P.M.

The contents of the envelope intrigued him.

A challenge?

A mission?

The homecoming he'd put off for more years than he cared to remember?

All of the above?

The man who was a legend in his own time, the man Wall Street said was snapping at Bill Gates's heels, felt like crying. All because of the envelope in his hand. At 3:10 that afternoon, after he'd read the contents of the envelope, he realized he'd conquered all his worlds. He was on top, and when you were on top, there was no place else to go but down. He knew he could stay on top if he wanted to. But what was the point?

Better to move on now, by his own choice.

He was thirty-five and he'd done it all—the Himalaya thing, he'd almost gotten married, the Everest thing, he'd shot the most dangerous rapids in the world, almost got married, gone big-game hunting in Africa, almost got married, finished first in his class at college, gotten his MBA, almost got married, became a media darling, started up Digi-Star on a shoestring, gone on the big board, almost got married, was a billionaire ten times over. He wiggled his big toe until it popped out of the hole of his sneaker. The sight pleased him. These days, very few things in his life pleased him. Plain and simple. There was no one to share all these things with. By his own choice. And it was the wrong choice, one of the very few mistakes he'd made in his life.

He should be married now with kids, a boy and a girl. He should have a dog and a cat, maybe a bird that sang in the morning. A house in the mountains and one at the shore. He should have a wife waiting at the door when he got home, at two in the morning, at three. If he had a family, he'd go home to dinner and a noisy house with the dogs barking and the kids wailing. He didn't have any of that. What he did have was the house in the mountains decorated by some cross-eyed yuppie. He should have learned his lesson with that decorating fiasco, but he'd gone ahead and allowed the yuppie to decorate the shore house. It, too, was a horror. He didn't go to either place anymore.

Instead, he stayed in his apartment at the Dakota in Manhattan or went to Stamford on the weekends. Hell, he had houses everywhere—Maui, St. Croix, Gstaad, Paris, Hong Kong—and he rarely ever saw them. They were empty, unwelcoming structures that cried for a family—a family he didn't have. His eyes started to burn.

He should have married Maggie. Walking out on her had been the biggest mistake of his life, a mistake he thought about every day of his life. Twice he'd tried to find her so he could explain something he didn't understand himself. With all the resources at his disposal, he knew he could find her if he really wanted to. And say what? Hey, I'm sorry. I hope I didn't ruin your life. I paid your family back for the wedding. Well, la-de-da. Big deal. Like that really made it more palatable. Maggie was probably married now with kids of her own. She had the house with the kids and the animals and a husband who came home for dinner. Maggie with the laughing eyes. Maggie with a heart full of love for him. Then, not now. Now, someone else was probably receiving that love, love that should be his.

Son of a fucking bitch! he thought.

Matt's eyes burned again as he got up from his desk to stare out at the New York skyline. The baseball cap he was never without was suddenly in his hands. As far as he knew, there were only two in existence, and he had one of them. Handmade by Lulu, who twenty years ago had her own bait and tackle shop. Given to him by Lulu and Ozzie for a job well done. The proudest moment of his life—and there were many proud moments—was when Ozzie put the cap on his head and said, "Today, son, you earned my respect, and I'm proud to call you my friend. The day you come back here to take on Big Red will be the day you become a man." And what had he done to earn that respect? He'd climbed down a mountain, putting his own life at risk, to save a young girl who'd slipped over the edge of a rocky precipice. He'd carried her twenty miles on a litter. She was married now, with five children. Every year, she sent him a Christmas card with a picture of her family and a five-pound box of homemade cookies she said the kids made. Twenty years of gratitude and the best cookies he ever ate was worthy of the five college funds he'd set up for Susie Jensen's kids. He wasn't going to think about Big Red and that man crap.

"Jesus, Matt, are you still here? You need to get a life, my friend." Long years of familiarity allowed Marcus Collins to say whatever he pleased to Matt, who never took his bluntness the wrong way. "It's almost eleven o'clock. Is something wrong?"

"I guess it depends on your point of view, Marcus. Yes, I know it's after eleven, which makes me wonder what you're doing here."

"I hate going home to an empty house. Julie took the kids to her mother's for Easter break. It gives me time to play catch-up. Before you ask, they took the dog and the cat with them. Betsy can't sleep unless Tiger is at the foot of her bed."

"Maybe that's what I need, an animal to sleep with. Jesus, I can't remember when I had a good night's sleep."

"Why don't you take a vacation, Matt? I can handle things here. Did something happen I don't know about? You seem kind of jittery to me."

"I managed to work my big toe through the hole in my sneaker. That's a happening, don't you think?"

"It's right up there. What's in the envelope? Since I'm your right hand, shouldn't I know?"

"I guess you could say it's my past, my present, and possibly my future. Tell me something, Marcus. The truth now, and don't stop to think before you answer. I'm going to ask the question and I want your answer lickety-split."

"Okay."

"Can you run this company?"

"Damn straight I can. I had the best teacher in the world: you. Why?"

"You asked me what was in this messengered envelope. See for yourself. Want a beer?"

"Sure. The Chinese I ordered should get here any minute."

"You ordered Chinese at this time of night?"

"Yeah, I said I was you. Sam Chin said he'd make it special and bring it right over. Best time to eat Chinese is the witching hour. Ah, I see now. So, what's the game plan?"

Matt eyed his friend of thirty years. He was the one person in the whole world next to Maggie that he would trust with his kids—if he had kids—and his money. Marcus was a warm, caring, unflappable friend who'd go to the wall for him if need be. He was pudgy, with a thinning hairline and merry blue eyes. It was his infectious smile that endeared him to everyone in the company. Marcus never made a statement he couldn't back up, and he was that rare person who followed through on every single thing that happened during the course of a day. Matt knew he'd been offered jobs paying three times the money he was paying him, but Marcus was loyal, saying only, "You're paying me more than I'm worth plus stock options, so that has to make me wonder what those other guys want from me."

"Ah, our food is here. Pine nut chicken, chow mein,

fried rice, ribs, and egg rolls. Dig in, Matt, and tell me what we're going to do."

Matt grimaced. "Ozzie and Lulu are in financial trouble. This information, as you can see, was sent anonymously. I ran a financial check and it's true. If Ozzie doesn't have a good year, he's out of business. The camp is his and Lulu's life. When he met her, she owned a bait and tackle shop that was very profitable. She gave it up to go with him into the wilderness to set up his survival camp. I guess the past five years or so he just managed his payroll. Lulu can make do with almost nothing, so I have to assume it's been tough. Now, I could step in and offer to lend him money, but he'd refuse. I could buy the camp and let him run it, but he'd refuse that, too. Ozzie is a proud man. I was a snot-nosed, arrogant fifteen-year-old when my old man shipped me off to Ozzie's camp. Whatever I am today is because of Ozzie.

"I've been sitting here thinking all evening. Tell me what you think. I'm going to sign up all our department heads for Ozzie's survival course. That goes for you, too, Marcus. We'll bounce the calls off the satellite so Lulu won't know where they're coming from. I'll give him a good year so he can put some money aside in case next year isn't as good. He's got ten guides who take out twelve people for two weeks each at five grand a clip. His first course starts a week from tomorrow and he goes until the snow comes, usually around the end of October, sometimes till the end of November. This year is his and Lulu's twenty-fifth year in business. They deserve to be successful. No one should have to worry about scrounging for money in their old age. I'm not going to let it happen. We'll stagger the department heads so the company is covered. If I go, that means I have to deal with Big Red. Do you think it will work? Pick your time, Marcus."

"Of course it will work. Everything you touch works. As you know, I'm not the outdoor type. I can't swim either. I get blisters when I hike. I hate wood smoke. It burns my eyes. I get poison ivy when the wind blows. I'm allergic to mosquitoes and I don't have the foggiest idea of how to rub two sticks together to make a fire. Do you want to rethink this, Matt? I gotta tell you, old buddy, that guy Ozzie messed with your head back then. You're a man. This business and your bank balance says so. You don't need to do that homecoming thing. Why can't I stay here and mind the store?"

"What if I said it's a requirement to taking over this company?"

"Then I'll do it. Jesus, I hate beef jerky."

Matt dusted his hands. "Let's do it! You start bouncing those calls. I'll make some direct calls and send some telegrams and faxes. We can't screw this up, Marcus. It's too important."

Marcus stared at his friend. The light of battle was in Matt's eyes. It had been years since he'd seen him this excited. The man had a mission, and the homecoming part of the deal didn't seem to be bothering him too much. Now, if he could find a way to locate Maggie Osborne, things just might get even better for his best friend.

"This is like the old days when we pulled all-nighters. A lot of years ago. Don't forget the photographer is coming at eight in the morning. High Tech Man of the Year three years running. You should be proud of that, Matt."

Being Man of the Year was the last thing in the world Matt Star was interested in. He was already on the phone with his list of potential clients for Ozzie Conklin. When the photographer showed up in the morning, Marcus knew Matt's big toe would be sticking out of his sneaker. He would pose for the photographer because he'd given his word, but the pose would be next to his beat-up pickup truck, and his baseball cap would be tilted at just the right angle so everyone could see the words "Lulu's Bait Shack" clearly. Knowing Matt as he did, he knew he'd have his sneaker with the hole in the toe positioned just right so it, too, was clear in the photograph. Matt Star was a what-you-see-is-what-you-get kind of guy.

The two-hundred-pound bell on the Conklins' back porch bonged to life, one bong, two, and then three earsplitting sounds. The disaster bell, as the guides referred to it, had only rung three times in twenty-five years. It was a sound to be taken seriously. The guides, one by one, hurtled from their bunks, grabbing slippers, boots, and robes for the mad dash to the main building. Buzz howled as he streaked past Maggie and Annie, who were in a dead heat, breathless from their effort to reach the main cabin.

"Breakfast's ready," Lulu said.

"There's no emergency. I want everyone to sit. Sit. I have good news. Wonderful news!" Ozzie said pointing to a pile of papers at the end of the kitchen table.

"It's four o'clock in the morning," someone said.

"I thought someone died," Annie said.

Ozzie Conklin was a big, grizzled man whose hands were bigger than ham hocks. He was barrel-chested, with no waist line and short stubby legs. His curly white hair ran into his beard, which Lulu kept trimmed and matched his eyebrows to perfection. On more than one occasion, Ozzie had posed for Santa Claus pictures in town. One of his proudest possessions was a red suit that Lulu made for him one year when they were snow bound.

"We're in business, gang. The reservations have been coming in so fast my fax machine got jammed up. Lulu can't keep up with the telephone calls, and Western Union has been here four times during the night. You aren't going to believe this, but I've had to turn some people down." The ham hock hands slammed down on the kitchen table. "What do you all make of this?"

"We've had so many direct deposits Ozzie is going to give all of you your back pay today. We're solvent, so it's steak and eggs for breakfast and steak again this evening." Lulu's tired face was so happy. Maggie hugged her.

"Did you advertise or did someone recommend us?" Annie asked.

"Lulu and I don't know what happened. The reservations are coming in from all over in groups, not just one at a time. I called Tiny this morning and offered to pay for a male nurse for his father if he agreed to come back. He'll be here late tonight. If I had four more guides, this place would be set for the next five years. God's smiling on all of us this year. You're all getting a bonus, too. Lulu and me, we've been thinking maybe we'd each take a group. Some seniors group. Got two dozen of them coming a week from tomorrow. If it looks like it isn't working, we'll refund. Whatcha think?"

"I say go for it. A hundred and twenty grand is too good to pass up," Maggie said. The others agreed.

The ham hocks slapped at the table again. "Hear that, Lulu?" Ozzie bellowed. "We're going out again!

It's gonna be like old times. Wish I knew what was happening. I hope I ain't dreaming."

"The fax is jammed again," Lulu called from the makeshift office on the other side of the kitchen. "Sixteen reservations, all with direct deposits. What should I do, Ozzie?"

Ozzie scurried into the office, his face gleeful.

"This is the first time in ten years that Ozzie is turning people away. I hate to see that. Are any of you guys comfortable with a larger group? Let's say we take out fifteen each, that's only three more people a trip. It translates into thirty reservations for Ozzie. We could throw in an extra day or something," Annie said.

"Each trip? Are there that many reservations?" Maggie asked nervously.

"Do you have a problem with that?" Annie asked.

"In a manner of speaking. Think about it. Last week we were eating Spam and there were only six reservations. All of a sudden this place is overbooked. Ozzie never had a direct deposit in his life. It occurs to me to wonder if someone is setting him up. For what I don't know. Admit it. This is very strange."

Annie stared off into space, a smile working at the corners of her mouth.

"Let's not look for trouble. Ozzie will finally get to pay off his mortgage, he's going to have money for his retirement years, he can buy Moon Mountain now if he wants to, Lulu will get a new dress and will be able to hire a real cook, and we get our back pay plus a bonus. So we work our butts off. Hell, we were doing that anyway," Mickey said. "The god of good fortune is finally smiling on the Conklins. Let's just be happy it's working out for everyone. And, don't for one minute forget the happy smiles on their faces when we agreed they could handle two parties of senior citizens."

"Okay, okay. What you said is true, but I still think something isn't . . . right. It's my opinion and I'm entitled to it," Maggie said with an edge to her voice.

The Conklins were back with stacks of reservations in their hands, their faces full of elation.

"I'll help with the scheduling," Annie volunteered. "You guys can finish clearing those boulders from the snake trail before you go on to the Big Red course. I finished posting the warning signs late yesterday, so my time is free unless you need me for the Big Red. You all know I can't handle that bridge over the gorge. It gives me the splats."

Ozzie motioned the crew to follow him to the office, where he pulled down a tattered wall map. Each guide had a color assigned to him that matched a course up and down the mountain. Maggie had chosen red early on. She looked now at the course she would be responsible for. When she'd left in October, the trails and steep mountain paths had been in excellent shape. The bridge over the gorge had been stable. However, as Ozzie pointed out each year, winter played havoc with the mountains, particularly the gorge. "We have six days until the first parties arrive. Get cracking, guys, and be careful. When you get back Lulu and Annie will have a working schedule we're all comfortable with. I'm going into town to give Jeff Culpepper a deposit on Moon Mountain." He smacked his hands gleefully. Lulu smiled indulgently.

To Maggie's eye, it looked as if Annie had a secret she wasn't sharing. She shrugged off the feeling as she headed back to her cabin to dress for the day. An hour into the mountain climb, a headache started to pound behind her eyes, a sure sign that something wasn't quite right within her peaceful world.

* * *

This past week, they had worked as a group on one course each day to ready it for the first climb of the season. Today, they were to work on the Big Red course, the most dangerous climb of them all.

Maggie eyed the gorge now and the rickety bridge that spanned it. Her Achilles heel. Her stomach started to churn as she approached the small platform that led directly onto the bridge. Her eyes were wary as she looked around for the new log whose weight would test the spindly bridge; a log representing five adults weighing in at 1,000 pounds.

The ritual each year was the same. The red course was hers. The red armband was hers. The red ribbon tied to the bridge said she was the first one to walk the bridge each spring. She never hesitated. To do so would mean she was acknowledging her fear. Fear of any kind was not permitted, according to Ozzie. Either you cut it or you didn't. When one agreed to take on the responsibility of other lives, it became serious business.

She checked the nylon rope on her belt, tested the slack, checked the knot on a massive tree at the edge of the small platform. Her job was to check for cracks in the wood, wear and tear on the nylon mesh that served as side closures for the bridge. She hated this bridge almost as much as she hated Florida and Matt Star. She thought she could smell her own fear as she tentatively stepped onto the bridge. Her stomach lurched as the bridge started to sway. Her suede gloves gripped the mesh railing as she moved along, her eyes seeking and searching. A half mile to go.

"Don't look down, Maggie!" one of the guides shouted. What an asinine thing to say. She had to look down, otherwise, she wouldn't be able to tell if there were cracks in the base or on the foot treads. Next year, she was going to ask for the yellow pussycat course. With a red piece of chalk, she made large X's on the slats that needed to be replaced. Finished, she heaved a sigh loud enough to be heard on the other side of the bridge. Now, all she had to do was make her way back to the platform, where she'd choose a new tree to be cut and shorn of its limbs, at which point it would be tied with nylon rope and dragged from one end of the bridge to the other. Tonight she would have nightmares. The headache continued to hammer behind her eyes.

It was after eight when the group sat down to supper. Maggie did her best to join in the lively chatter, but she was bone-tired, her eyes closing from time to time. She managed to congratulate Ozzie on his contract for Moon Mountain, lapped up Lulu's famous peach pie, accepted her assignments for the year, and then headed back to her cabin for a hot bath and bed. It was always this way on final inspection day out on the course. She knew from long years of habit that she would wake around three in the morning, prop herself up in bed, and read the applications, going first to the last question on the form: What do you hope to gain from this experience? Someday she was going to write a book about the responses. Someday, she was going to do a lot of things. Someday, she was going to write a letter to Matt Star and tell him off for breaking her heart.

Someday.

Three

Matt Star shuffled Ozzie Conklin's confirmation slips on his desk. He'd pulled it off, and no one except Marcus and him were the wiser for his efforts. Ozzie was set, if not for life, for a very long time. He felt as if he had accomplished a monumental task.

He leaned back in his ergonomic chair to prop his feet on the desk. He was delighted to see the hole in the toe of his sneaker was bigger than it was last week. Maybe he needed to start wearing socks.

"Matt?"

"It's me. You know, Marcus, some people contemplate their belly button, I contemplate my big toe. Why do you suppose that is?"

"Beats me. Digi-Star is behind you, right? You get an anonymous letter and suddenly the company is passé. I've heard of mercurial people, but, Matt, this is a billion-dollar company. Thousands of people depend on it for a living. How can you walk away from it without a backward glance?"

"You walk away. Just because I'm good at this business doesn't mean I have to love it or even like it. It was a goal. I met that goal and now it's time to move on."

"Would you be doing this if you didn't get that anonymous letter?"

"Eventually."

"After you get done playing Mr. Bountiful, what are you going to do?"

"Maybe I'll sign on with Ozzie. I've certainly got the attire for the job. You better than anyone should know I'm not the suit type, and these walls close in on me. I don't like this office. I hate canned air. I like open windows. I think I'll go fishing. Want to come along?"

"Who's going to watch over things if we go fishing?" Marcus demanded.

"When you're in authority, you delegate. I guess you're trying to tell me I'm irresponsible, eh? You know what, Marcus, this goddamn company runs itself because I had the good sense to hire the best of the best. We, as in you and me, could go fishing five days a week and no one would even know. The back of my truck is so full of gadgets that I want to puke. For instance, I have beepers, I have pagers, I have laptops, portable fax machines, portable this and portable that. For years I've been hoping someone would steal the damn stuff. So far, no takers. If you don't want to go fishing, then I'm going out and get a dog. A man's dog, a best friend."

"Matt—"

"I'm not me anymore, Marcus. Where did that person who used to be me go?"

"Locate Maggie and you'll find out where the old Matt is. And you need to forget that safety crap Ozzie Osborne put in your head about where that cockamamie course is concerned. You need to lay it to rest once and for all. Don't think walking out of here is going to do it any more than fishing or getting a dog is going to do it. You need to yank out those guts of yours and stare it all down and then make decisions. You can't be a free spirit forever. The time always comes when you have to take responsibility for your actions."

"That's all bullshit and you know it."

Marcus laughed. "It sounded good. The part about Maggie is right on though."

"I'll give you that one. So, are we going fishing or not?"

"I'm your man. Let me issue a few orders and I'll meet you at the elevator."

On the ride down in Matt's private elevator, Matt said, "Should we get the dog before or after we go fishing?"

"Hell, let's get it first. A man's dog, right? What kind—a Shepherd? a Golden Retriever? or maybe a Lab?"

"I want a big dog that no one else wants. Let's head for the island and the pound. I'm gonna call him Duke, or Spike, something manly."

"Sounds good."

Two hours later, Matt shook his head in disgust. "How can they not have a big dog? People adopted all the animals over Easter. That's good. At least I think it is."

"Mister, we do have one dog. It came in this morning," a young girl of fifteen or so said. "I'll get her for you. Wait here. She really needs a home. Her owner died last week and his heirs didn't want her. She's not quite a year old, but she's had all her shots and everything. I gave her a bath a little while ago, so she's nice and clean. It's just seven dollars. Now, you wait right here."

"She? She means a her."

"Look at it this way, females don't lift their legs, and

the truth is they are more protective of their owners. That's a documented fact," Marcus said knowledgeably.

"Here she is. Isn't she the most precious thing? She's a three-pound teacup Yorkie and her name is Gracie," the girl said thrusting the shaking dog into Matt's hands.

"What—Now wait—Oh, Jesus, she's licking my face. I wanted a big dog. This powder puff is—"

"Ferocious," the young girl said.

"She's shaking. What does that mean?" Matt demanded.

"It means she's scared. The only person she knew was the owner and he passed away. The people that brought her here said she sat next to him for a whole day until the super came to check on the old man. That means she's loyal. She likes you. She didn't lick me at all. It's only seven dollars, mister. If you take her, I can close up and go home. I'll even give you a bag of dog food."

"Is she going to get *any* bigger?"

"No. You shouldn't be so picky. This dog needs a home. She's clean and pretty and she's had all her shots. She's a good watch dog and already she likes you. What more do you want, mister? I'll give her to you. How's that?"

"Yeah, how's that?" Marcus said reaching for his billfold. "I can see she adores you. She won't take up much room on your bed. She'll probably curl right up against your neck and you'll end up finally sleeping like a baby. We'll take her," he said forcefully. "Don't say I never gave you a gift."

"I don't know if I can handle this."

"You're whining, Matt. The dog needs a home. You want a dog. Enough said."

"Gracie?"

"It was probably the old guy's dead wife's name. People get sentimental when they get old. Hold her tight so she bonds with you. I'll drive. They make these little canvas bags with mesh windows for small dogs. You'll be able to take Gracie with you when you take Ozzie's survival course. What's three more pounds? By this time tomorrow you are going to be in love with that little dog. Trust me. So where do you want to go fishing?"

"I don't. I have things to do now. I have to get gear, food, blankets. I don't have time to go fishing. I'll probably never have time to do anything, ever again. I can see it now. I'm going to be married to this dog. You're right. She loves me." The soft tone of his voice and the pleasure in it did not go unnoticed by Marcus.

"I'll drop you off at the pet store, circle the block, and come back for you. It's a good thing we have the truck." Marcus guffawed.

Matt was standing on the curb, Gracie's gear piled high at his feet, when Marcus pulled to a stop. Gracie's head peeped out of Matt's oversize safari shirt pocket. "I spent $480 for this gear and I didn't even get any food because it looked like rabbit poop. I'm not giving her that!"

"God forbid," Marcus said. "What *is* this stuff?"

"Everything she needs. Treats, vitamins, toys, four beds, one for every room she'll be in—you know, she might wet one—pee-pee papers, toothbrush, paste, a carry bag, an orthopedic fleece mat, a leash, a collar, raincoats, boots, hat. I just got one of everything," Matt said, his eyes wild. "Her heart's beating real fast. I can feel it."

"She needs to feel *your* heart. That will make her feel safe. She's asleep. Too much excitement. You might have to put a clock in her bed so she thinks it's her mother. Of course, if she sleeps with you, you won't have to do that."

His eyes still wild, Matt said, "They loved her in the pet store. Everyone wanted to hold her. I didn't let them. I didn't want her getting strange germs."

"Makes sense. Guess you want to go home now, huh?"

"Yeah, I have to feed her and brush her teeth. They get a plaque buildup. Some smart-ass in there told me I should take her to get her nails done."

"You gotta do that once a month."

"Shut up, Marcus. I don't want to hear anymore. Take the truck back to the garage and I'll pick it up in the morning."

"Bye, Gracie," Marcus said with a straight face. "See you tomorrow, Matt."

"Yeah, see you tomorrow."

Inside his spacious apartment, Matt dumped the dog's gear in the foyer. He bellowed for his housekeeper. "See this stuff? Place it where it will do the most good. I got a dog! Her name is Gracie. We need some food, maybe chicken livers mixed with something. Some water, too. I got some special dishes and there's a decal to paste on her bowl." Matt's voice was so strangled-sounding he barely recognized it as his own.

"Where?" Agnes, the housekeeper, said.

"Here." Matt lifted the little dog from his oversized pocket. She opened her eyes to stare adoringly at her new owner. Matt could feel his heart start to melt. This little bundle was dependent on him. Him. No one else. His shoulders straightened. "This is my dog and I'll take care of her. You don't have to do anything where she's concerned. Is that understood? Do we have chicken livers?"

"In the freezer; they need to be thawed. I would have thought, Mr. Star, that a big dog would be more your style."

"I love this dog," Matt said vehemently. "She's mine. I'm going to put her down now. I have pee-pee papers to put by the door, if I can find them." Gracie couldn't wait. She piddled next to Matt's shoe. She yipped softly.

"She wants your approval. Say, Good girl, Gracie," the housekeeper said.

The wild look was back in Matt's eyes. "Good girl, Gracie." The little dog pawed at his pant leg. Matt picked her up. "See. She loves me, too."

"I see that," the housekeeper said.

"I'll be in my office. If anyone calls take a message and say I'm on a business trip and you don't know when I'll be back."

Matt's home office was Spartan: a desk, a swivel chair, and two deep easy chairs flanking the desk. A bank of ugly filing cabinets rested under the triple windows. There were no floor lamps, no plants, no pictures on the walls. The room had a temporary look and feel to it.

Matt placed one of the small dog beds next to his chair. He unwrapped toys and chewies. Gracie watched, sniffing each new item. He filled the small water bowl from the adjoining lavatory. "You're set, Gracie." Gracie yipped, her short tail wagging furiously. Matt picked her up. Gracie licked the tip of his nose. Matt smiled and smiled.

"Guess you like my pocket best. Go to sleep. I have

some work to do." The little dog snuggled deeper into Matt's pocket, her tiny ears sticking out over the flap.

Matt shuffled through the applications on his desk. He hadn't filled out his own yet. If he filled it out, if he faxed it to Ozzie, he was making a commitment to truly walk away from Digi-Star. Turning the reins over to Marcus, his second in command, meant he could return to resume his position in the company at some point in the future. The details had all been taken care of by his attorney. He wasn't selling out, he was simply moving on.

He would be going backward in a sense, starting over. Trying to find out if he was a man or not. In order to start over, one had to go back to the original starting point. Ozzie's words rang in his ears, even now, twenty-five years later. *"You can do whatever you set your mind to, son. All you have to do is make a commitment the way Lulu and I did."* The only problem was, Ozzie hadn't said what he was to do after it all came into being. Ride it out, give it up, move on, hunker down? Be miserable? What the hell did he want?

"I want a goddamn reason to get up in the morning is what I want!" Gracie's head jerked out of his pocket, soft mewling sounds coming from her mouth. Matt lifted her out and cuddled her, his eyes burning unmercifully.

"You know what, Gracie," Matt whispered. "I'm a stand-up guy except for one area of my life. That one time when I—It haunts me. Maggie Osborne haunts me. I should have done something, made it right. Maggie was the best thing that ever happened to me and I screwed it up. I'm going to find her and give her the chance to tell me off. Maybe I can do something for her and her family. I know money can't buy forgiveness, but maybe it can buy her some comfort, give her and her family some security. I can do it anonymously so she won't know it's from me. I need her to get in my face and tell me how much she hates me. I need to apologize. Me. I need to do that, Gracie. I'm going to do it, too. I'm going to hire a private detective. There, that's a commitment. You know what I like about you, Gracie, you listen and you don't talk back."

Five minutes later, Matt had the investigative department of Digi-Star on the line. He gave his password and listened to the respect creep into the investigator's voice. "This is what I want you to do. I'm going to fax you all the information I have when I hang up. I want a report ASAP. As soon as you get anything fax it to me here."

He'd followed through just the way Marcus did.

Matt barely noticed his housekeeper as she set his afternoon coffee on the corner of his desk. He heard rather than saw her place a small dish with mashed-up chicken livers on the floor. Gracie noticed and leaped to the floor to gobble it all down. While Gracie licked the bowl, Matt finished filling out the reservation form for Ozzie's survival camp. He grinned from ear to ear when he filled out the line that said Matt and Gracie Star would arrive on May 10th. The fax went over the wire at the same moment his bank transferred $5,000 for his reservation. In his opinion, he was paid in full for the course.

Matt buzzed his housekeeper. "Pack me a bag and have the garage bring the Rover up. I'm taking Gracie to Stamford. I've got green grass up there. Call maintenance and have them lug her stuff down to the lobby. I don't know when I'll be back. Load up on the chicken livers and pack them in ice. Then call Marcus and tell him I'm going to Connecticut. If any faxes come in, send them on. Check this machine on the hour. I don't know how long I'll be staying.

"We're on the move, Gracie. I've been a mover and a shaker all my life and I don't see that changing, so you'll have to get used to it. In you go," he said as he opened the flap of his breast pocket. "I have this feeling things are finally going to work out for me. I think you are the second-best thing that ever happened to me."

Four

$\mathcal{A}$nnie ripped the incoming reservation from the fax machine at the same moment the phone rang. Her eyes almost popped from her head as she read the signature on the reservation and heard the bank teller inform her that a $5,000 deposit covering half of Mr. and Mrs. Star's registration had been credited to Ozzie's account. The remaining $5,000 was to be paid when the couple signed in on arrival. Her well-meaning anonymous letter was working so well Matt Star and his wife, Gracie, were coming to Wyoming. "This is not good," she muttered under her breath.

"Was that another reservation?" Lulu called from the kitchen.

"Yeah, but we're full up. I'm going to send it back and call the bank to refund the money. Is that okay with you, Lulu?"

"You could put him on a waiting list in case someone cancels out. It will be a last-minute thing. Call him and see if he's agreeable to it. Where's he from?"

"New York. He'll probably show up in a three-piece suit and wingtips. I'm going to do it now, Lulu."

"Make sure the bank gives you a confirmation number when they redirect his deposit. Have them fax it."

Annie did as instructed, her heart pumping wildly. Sweat dripped from her forehead. "This will teach me to mind my own business," she mumbled to herself. Damn, what if the guy showed up with his wife anyway? A wife hadn't entered her thoughts at all. The article in the paper hadn't mentioned a wife. It hadn't said Matt Star was a bachelor, either. Her head dropped to her hands. Was she the only one here who knew where all the reservations were coming from? She'd created a monster, and now the monster wasn't going to be allowed to participate. If everything she read about Matt Star was true, he and Gracie would show up on the 10th of May. He'd bump two of his people and send them packing. God, now what was she supposed to do? Fess up? Get fired for her efforts? Lose Maggie's friendship for sticking her nose where it didn't belong? Maybe she should call Matt Star and tell him the truth. Truth was good. Did she have the guts? Hell, no, she didn't.

"Lulu, I have a really bad stomachache. I'm going back to the cabin for a little while. All the paperwork is filed. The bank gave me a confirmation number. I put it with all the bank records."

"I can handle things, Annie. Thanks for helping out. Do you want some Pepto?"

"I have some." Annie folded the Star application and stuck it in the back pocket of her jeans. "I'll be back later."

Annie was so deep in thought she almost fainted when Maggie clapped her on the back. Buzz circled her feet, woofing softly. "You look funny. Is anything wrong?" Maggie asked.

"That's funny, I was going to say the same thing to you. You crossed the gorge, didn't you? To answer your question, those two hot dogs I had for lunch aren't sitting too well in my stomach."

"Yeah, I did. Take some Pepto. I think I got a really good group the first trip out. Four women and eleven men. Late thirties, early forties. Not one of them has ever gone camping, so the rules won't be too hard for them to accept. The part I like best is seeing their firstday outfits. Especially the women in their designer clothes and Gucci shoes. The second thing I like is watching them shoulder the thirty-five-pound backpack, and the third thing is taking out the candy and goodies and dumping them in one big pile. Pounds and pounds of chocolate. I finally figured out that's why Lulu puts on so much weight. She eats it all. She doesn't share with Ozzie, either. I'm babbling here, Annie. Is something wrong? I've had this feeling something isn't right since the day you got here. If you want to talk about it, you know where to find me. Buzz did well on the bridge."

Annie bent down to hug the big dog. "You're lucky to have this dog, Maggie. Dogs always seem to foresee trouble before we do. If any of those guys get frisky on the course, Buzz will take care of things."

"I don't need Buzz to do that, but you're right. How's business? Are the reservations still coming in? I still can't figure it out. I suppose Ozzie's explanation of word of mouth really does work."

Annie started to walk away. "Some reservations came in today, but Lulu told me to send them back. The waiting list is too long as it is. See you at supper."

"C'mon, Buzz, let's take a run around the compound."

The Lab raced off, Maggie on his heels. When the run was over, Maggie headed for the cabin, where she made a strong pot of tea and then laced it with brandy. "I did it. I crossed the bridge. You sensed my fear, didn't you? Good boy," she said hugging the dog. "I don't think the others know how that bridge petrifies me. I didn't start to shake, though, until I was on the other side. This is the last year for the Big Red course. I know I say that every year and every year I back down. This time I mean it." Buzz snuggled onto Maggie's lap. "Maybe we need to move on, Buzz. Ozzie's going to be okay. He'll be able to pay top dollar for guides. We stayed through the bad times, but I don't have a life and I'm not getting any younger. Annie was right about that. I've been thinking a lot about this, and what I came up with is I'm going to write Matt Star a letter in care of his company and I'm going to tell him exactly what I think of him. Once that's behind me, I'll follow through on that application I filed with the Everglades Park Service. Or, maybe I'll head north and see what they have to offer at some of the national parks. I'll sell that shitty condo, bank the money, get a little interest, buy a motor home, and we'll live on the road. I say that every year, too. Obviously, you're tired of hearing it, too," Maggie said, tweaking the sleeping dog's ears.

Maggie leaned back into the softness of the worn sofa. She sipped at the tea as she mentally began to compose the letter she was finally going to write to Matt Star, twelve years after the fact. With the way her luck was running, he probably wouldn't even remember her. She wondered if he married along the way and what kind of woman he chose. Men as rich and good-looking as Matt Star would be fair game for every woman on the prowl. Did he succumb to some woman's wiles? The article hadn't said if he was married or not. Matt probably wanted it that way to protect his family. Did he have children that looked like him? The thought was so painful, Maggie slid out from under Buzz's heavy body. On her feet, she took great gasping breaths. *Do it now! Go to the main cabin, switch on the computer and write the letter. Now!* her mind ordered.

Maggie didn't stop to think beyond the word "letter." Her face grim, she headed for the main cabin, her thoughts ricocheting inside her head. Whatever came out first was what went on the paper. She was not going to redo it, she was not going to struggle for just the right words, she was going to—what she was going to do was rip him to shreds. Then she was going to send him back his $35,000. She was calling the bank to tap her equity loan.

Sparks blazed in Maggie's eyes as she stomped into the kitchen of the main cabin. "I need to use the computer, Lulu. Can I borrow the jeep to run into town? I need to send something by Federal Express."

"Of course, Maggie. You know you don't have to ask. Is something wrong?"

"Yes. No. I don't know. What I do know is I have to do this. Twelve years is long enough. I guess the time was never right. I know you don't understand. That's okay. I understand."

"This, whatever this is, will it bring the smile back to your face, honey?"

"God, Lulu, I hope so. I want my life back. Don't pay any attention to me; I'm simply mumbling so I won't change my mind."

•

"Want some coffee and cookies? I baked them fresh this afternoon."

"Sure, Lulu. Make them to go, though. What I have to do won't take me very long."

Maggie was as good as her word. Ten minutes later, she was galloping out of the kitchen, letter in one hand, coffee and cookies in the other.

From time to time, Maggie eyed the letter on the seat next to her. It was a short, blunt, brutal letter. It was going to her bank to be included with the cashier's check. At the last second, she'd scratched a note to the loan officer telling him not to give out her address. Tomorrow morning at ten o'clock, the bank would receive her letter. Since she'd applied for an equity loan and been approved three years ago, she had only to tap it.

"And that's the end of you, Mr. Star," Maggie said as she exited the small Federal Express office.

On the ride back to camp, Maggie was stunned to realize she didn't feel one bit better. If anything, she felt worse. Tears dripped from her eyes. Now it was over. She'd given back the money for the wedding. She'd written the final letter.

Closure.

Her new life was starting this very minute.

Lulu was right. She needed to smile more often. She needed to laugh out loud. She needed to start living.

The only thing she had to worry about now was the Big Red course and the bridge over the gorge. She could handle it. She *would* handle it. Hadn't she just done the hardest thing in the world? Nothing could compare to that decision, not even the bridge over the gorge.

The jeep ground to a halt in the middle of the road. Did she tell the loan officer to use the name Osborne or Harper? She couldn't remember. She turned the jeep around and headed back to town. This was as good a time as any to take back her maiden name. Why in the world she'd kept the name Harper after only three weeks of marriage was something she'd never understand. The best answer she could come up with was she was simply too lazy to change things back. Her new life demanded she become Maggie Osborne again.

It was dark and past the supper hour when Maggie returned to the compound, a smile on her face. "Am I in time for dessert?"

"I saved a plate for you. It's warming in the oven. Did you get all your business taken care of?"

"I certainly did. Any leftovers for Buzz?"

"His plate is warming in the oven along with yours. He's been sitting on the back steps waiting for you."

"Where is everyone?" Maggie asked as she dug into her meatloaf.

"Annie went into town. She said she had some long distance calls to make. Some of the boys went with her and the others are watching television with Ozzie. If you don't need me, Maggie, I'm going upstairs to do some sewing."

"I'm fine. I'll clean up. Thanks, Lulu, for not asking questions. Someday when it doesn't hurt so much, I'll tell you all about it."

"I know, honey. I didn't get to be this old without my share of heartache." She leaned over the table to whisper in Maggie's ear, "Sometimes I still dream about that drifter who sweet-talked me and got me into his bed. Some things stay with you forever, honey."

Maggie nodded, her eyes filling with tears.

The kitchen cleaned, their after-supper walk over,

Maggie went back to her cabin. "We have one more thing to do, Buzz. We're going to make a fire and burn all that stuff that's been cluttering up my trunk. When we finish, there won't be a single trace that Matt Star was ever in my life. Not even a smidgin of a trace." There were no tears with this declaration.

Five

Unaware of what was going on in Wyoming, Matt Star settled Gracie in her new bed at the side of his king-size bed. He filled up the small area with a plush teddy bear the same size as Gracie, along with a few toys. His heart leaped up into his chest when he saw the way the little dog looked at him. Gracie allowed him to cover her. "I feel like a new father. It's kind of a nice feeling, Gracie. Good night."

He was dozing off when he heard the scratching and knew immediately what the sound was: Gracie looking for traction so she could jump up on the bed. He found himself grinning as he fumbled for the light switch. "Ah, I see what the problem is. You want up, but you want your teddy and the blanket, too. C'mere." The little dog ran to the side of the bed and leaped into his waiting arms. "Find your spot," Matt said, reaching down for the teddy bear and blanket. He found his eyes starting to burn again when Gracie snuggled under his chin. "This is good," Matt mumbled as his eyes closed wearily. "Just me and you, kid."

Two days later, Matt was romping in the front yard when Marcus swerved into his driveway. "Whatever it is, I don't want to hear it. You're carrying something and my gut tells me it's a problem. Get in your car, buddy, and head back to town. I'm serious. Can't you see me and Gracie are bonding? I love this dog. I mean I *really* love her. It's the best present you ever gave me. Want some coffee, a beer, a late lunch?"

"No. This isn't business. This is personal. The damn letter didn't say it was personal. How was I supposed to know? It was from some bank in Florida. I didn't want to call you with it, so I decided to bring it. You need to read this. Maybe I will have some coffee after all. I can make it myself. I'll be in the kitchen if you want to, you know, talk."

"Why should a letter from a bank in Florida be personal? We get letters from banks all over the country every day of the week. I thought you said you could take care of the company."

"I can. I will. I do. This, I can't handle."

The sound of the screen door slamming behind Marcus sounded ominous to Matt.

Matt sat down on the steps. He stared at the bright colors on the Federal Express envelope. He didn't personally know an Edwin Blevins at the Sun Bank. Aside from the fact that the air bill was typed, the envelope offered no other clue as to the contents. He found Marcus's attitude strange, since the air bill wasn't marked personal. "So, open the damn envelope already!"

Another envelope with his name written on the front. He studied the writing, certain he'd seen it before. He pulled out the single sheet of note paper. He found himself rearing back when he read the signature, Maggie Osborne. His heart took on an extra beat as his stomach started to churn. In seven seconds, he had the letter committed to memory.

Dear Matt,

I've wanted to write this letter for twelve years and now it's finally time.

What you did to me was not only unconscionable but unforgivable as well. How dare you play with my life the way you did? How dare you make love to me, swear undying love, ask me to marry you and then leave me standing at the altar? I deserved better from you. No self-respecting man would act in such a manner, which makes you a lowlife in my eyes. All you had to do was call me, Matt. I might not have liked what you had to say, but I would have tried to understand. You lied to me, and if there's one thing in this world I hate, it's a liar. I don't care if you are a CEO of a big company. All that tells me is you must have stepped on many people to get where you are. Whatever is best for Matt Star and the hell with everyone else is your credo. Well, guess what, your day is coming. The day always comes when one's misdeeds surface to be dealt with. Love and devotion are not emotions to be trampled and stomped on. I loved you, Matt, with all my heart and you broke my heart. I cannot forgive you for that. I do not wish you well. What I wish for you is every torment known to man and more.

Enclosed is a bank check for the $35,000 you gave to my parents. I don't want anything from you. This money is only a reminder of what a piece of scum you are.

Maggie Osborne

Matt's hands shook so badly he could barely fit the letter back into the envelope. He felt dizzy, disoriented. His shoulders started to shake. Marcus's comforting hand on his shoulder made them shake all the more.

"This is a tough one, Matt. Why now, twelve years later?"

"Maybe it took her that long to save up the money," Matt said hoarsely. "Jesus, I feel like I've been kicked in the gut."

"You have been."

"You know, Marcus, I called the investigative department and told them to locate her. A day doesn't go by that I don't think about her."

"Why didn't you do something about it?"

"Shame. No guts. I didn't want to see how badly I hurt her. That man crap Ozzie dished out to me . . . it was all part of it. At the time I was young and— She's right, I should have called her or told her face to face. I couldn't face her. If I hadn't done what I did there is every possibility Digi-Star would be just a thought and neither one of us would be sitting here on these steps. Everything happens for a reason. She must really hate my guts after all these years."

"I think it's safe to say that," Marcus said gently. "Is there anything I can do?"

"Nope. I guess my torment is about to begin. Thanks for coming up, Marcus. Go back to the city. I have some thinking to do."

"Call me if you need me."

"Yeah, sure."

Marcus watched through the rearview mirror as Matt picked Gracie up to cuddle next to his cheek. Poor dumb bastard.

A long time later, Matt walked into the house. His fax machine was whirring. Check it or not? He shrugged.

His eyes turned murderous when he saw his canceled reservation and the accompanying note. "We'll goddamn well see about that!" Maybe it was time to trade on his name and reputation and call Ozzie or Lulu direct. Nobody turned down Matt Star.

The Federal Express envelope in his hand felt hot.

Matt was a whirlwind then. He dialed the investigative offices with his right hand, barking orders to the voice on the other end of the line while his left hand dialed Ozzie Conklin's number in Wyoming on a second phone. He barked again, louder this time, demanding to speak to either Ozzie or Lulu. "Who is this?" he demanded.

"My name is Annie. Whom should I say is calling?"

"Matt Star is calling from New York. Now, put Ozzie or Lulu on the phone or you'll be unemployed tomorrow." He was aghast at the threat. He'd never threatened anyone in his entire life.

"Mr. Star— I-I'll get him. Hold on."

"Matt, boy, is it really you? I'll be a son of a gun. Lulu, it's Matt Star. Lulu wants to know if you still have that cap we gave you."

"Sure do, Ozzie, I'm never without it. Listen, I sent in a reservation and it was sent back canceled. Are you that busy? I'd really like to come out and take the course again. I think I'm ready for Big Red now."

"Matt, our doors are always open to you. You come ahead anytime you want. We'll fit you in and Lulu will make you that blackberry pie you liked so much. Don't you go worrying about your deposit. The girl, she don't know who you are. Otherwise she wouldn't have sent back the reservation. How are you, Matt? Me and Lulu, we follow your career. That's somethin' the way you started up that company. Didn't I tell you you could do whatever you set your mind to?"

"Yes, you did, Ozzie, and I'm grateful every day of my life that I followed your advice. I'll see you around the tenth of May, if that's okay."

"You said you wanted Big Red? Do ya think you're up to Big Red?"

"I can't tell you how often I dreamed about that course. I'd sure as hell like to give it a try. Sign me up. You said if I passed it I'd be a man. It's time to find out, Ozzie."

"I'll have Annie sign you on as soon as I hang up. Big Red has the best guide going. Hope you can handle it. Big Red ain't for wimps, Matt. If you only want to go as far as the gorge, that's somethin' else. Harper cracks the whip, and she won't care who you are. You do it her way or it's no way. You gonna abide by the rules."

"A woman guide on Big Red! I'll follow the rules and I want the full course."

"Good thing because you have to sign a paper releasing the camp of all liability when you go out on Big Red. My lawyers tell me I have to do all that crap. Guess you know a thing or two about that."

"Sure do. Nice talking to you, Ozzie. Give my regards to Lulu. I'll see you on the tenth."

On the morning of May 9th, Annie stumbled her way toward the main house. It was four-thirty in the morning, but the kitchen, as well as the back porch, was well lighted. It was time to talk to Lulu about her well-meaning meddling.

The kitchen was fragrant with the smell of frying bacon and baking cinnamon rolls even though breakfast wasn't served until five-thirty. Breakfast was the same every morning: scrambled eggs, bacon, flapjacks, toast, gallons of coffee and orange juice, along with

Lulu's homemade crab apple preserves. Apple dumplings in sweet cream were served with the last pot of coffee. Lulu took it as a personal insult if even a crumb remained.

"Lulu, I need to talk to you, woman to woman."

"Then let's go into the office. Ozzie went into town for the paper. I don't know whom I worry about most, you or Maggie. It's time to tell me what it is. Start at the beginning."

The words rushed out of Annie's mouth like ricocheting bullets. When she wound down, tears dripping down her cheeks, Lulu just stared at her. "Ozzie and me, we never knew the man's name that left Maggie standing at the altar. It's hard to believe it was Matt. Ozzie adored that boy. We won't mention all those reservations. It's hardly important compared to Maggie meeting up with Matt."

"He's married to someone named Gracie. He's bringing her. It's going to . . . do something to Maggie. He signed up for Big Red. He'll be here tonight, maybe even late this afternoon. Maggie is the only one qualified to take a party out on Big Red. What's she going to do when you give her her roster after breakfast?"

"She'll act like the professional she is," Lulu said. There was no conviction in the older woman's voice.

"Switch courses. I can sit this one out. Let her take her party out on the Blue Course."

"If we do that we're both meddling. My instinct is to let things take a natural course. Maggie made some decisions in her life last month. I don't know what they were and she didn't want to talk about it. She did take back her maiden name because she told Ozzie just last week to make her check out to Osborne instead of Harper. I heard him on the phone with Matt and he referred to Maggie as Harper. That tells me

Matt doesn't know she's his guide and Maggie doesn't know he's taking the course. God acts in mysterious ways, Annie. Perhaps this is supposed to happen, just the way you were supposed to write that anonymous letter to Matt."

"But he's married. I don't think Maggie can handle a wife."

"She won't have a choice. It's the way it is," Lulu said.

"Are you saying it's business as usual?"

"That's what I'm saying. Don't sell Maggie short, Annie."

"I'm not. I just don't want her hurt all over again. This is all my fault. I meant well. In a million years I never thought it would come to this. I just wanted to get some business for you and Ozzie. If Maggie is finally moving forward with her life, my meddling might set her back."

"Maggie isn't going to fall apart. She'll handle it and she might even get some pleasure out of making Matt dance to her way of doing things. I can use some help with the home fries."

Annie stared at the older woman. Lulu hadn't fired her. Things were the same as they were an hour ago, but now Lulu knew what was going on. Annie felt a little better with that knowledge.

The day before each wilderness trek was what the guides called "blitzkrieg day." The guides compared notes, courses, and rosters, and mapped out shortcuts to each other's course in case of an emergency. Gear was checked and double-checked. If one course was proving too difficult for a particular guest, then he or she was traded down to a course less strenuous with a minimum of wasted time. The day started off with

Lulu's famous breakfast and picked up speed from that point on. It was also payday.

Normally, each guide was responsible for picking up his or her own guests in the ancient bus. Today, though, Lulu was doing the chauffeuring because she had a dental and a hair appointment in town.

"I'm all set," Maggie said as she carried her dishes to the sink. "I'll catch up with you all later. I'm going up to the gorge to check the bridge one last time this morning. One of the mesh sections tore lose yesterday. I have to be honest and tell you Buzz spotted it before I did."

"Is it bad?"

"Bad enough to cause me concern. The bridge lists at that point. If someone lost their footing or slipped they could slide right through it. I'll fix it."

"Do you need any help?" Annie asked.

"If I have a problem I'll send up a flare, or else I'll send Buzz back. Where's my roster? Never mind. I'll get it later."

"Maggie, let's go into town for an early dinner and movie this evening," Annie said, a tremor in her voice.

"Sure. Is four-thirty okay?"

"I'll be ready."

Annie was the last to leave. "Covering all the bases, eh?" Lulu said.

"I just don't want her meeting up with Mr. Star cold. Give her the roster as we're leaving. I'll be driving, so she can . . . react, and I'll be the only one to see how she takes it."

"I guess that makes sense, but all it does is delay the inevitable. Not to mention a sleepless night."

"I'll worry about that later. Do you know what time he's arriving?"

"A fax came in late last night saying the airport

shuttle would get him to town around five-thirty if his flight's on time. The barbecue will be over by seven-thirty. Orientation is scheduled for eight-fifteen. If you think Maggie can't handle it, I'll take over."

"You just might have to do that, Lulu. I can clean up if you want to go to town early."

"Ozzie always cleans up on blitzkrieg day. Stop worrying, Annie. You meant well."

Annie nodded.

"My adrenaline is pumping, Annie," Maggie said as she met up with her friend in the middle of the compound. "Guess that means this is an extra-special trek. Annie, did I ever thank you for being such a good friend? Probably not. I was locked up in my own little world for so long I . . . Thanks for being my friend. I feel so good today. That terrible bridge doesn't even scare me anymore. See you later."

Maggie whistled for Buzz, who leaped down the back steps with a roll of white paper and a small bag between his teeth. "Ah, the roster," Maggie said sticking it in her hip pocket. "I'll look at it later when we finish the bridge. A Hershey bar for you and an apple for me," Maggie said peering into the paper sack. "Ozzie must like you this morning. Let's go."

It was two o'clock when Maggie walked off the bridge over the gorge. She poured water into a small tin bowl for Buzz from her backpack, swigging the rest from the bottle. "Here's your Hershey bar. Don't litter now."

Maggie leaned back against a monstrous tree trunk. How many times in the past ten years had she done this exact same thing? Hundreds probably. Until today, though, she'd always been jittery. It was strange how calm she felt, how peaceful. "It was clearing all that baggage out of my life, Buzz. My shoulders are lighter. I made decisions I know I can live with. Life is looking good these days. Now, let's see whom we are going to be taking out on Big Red tomorrow.

"Hmmnn, Alvin and Kate Dennison, James Walker, Calvin Connors, Nancy and Susan Palmer. They must be sisters. Mike Sayers, Pete Nelson, Carlos Ramos, Matt and Gracie Star, Andy Greer, Alice Fontaine." *Matt and Gracie Star.* Maggie's heart thundered in her chest. A blanket of dizziness settled over her and her heart threatened to pound right out of her chest. Her frenzied fingers ripped at the rolled-up reservations. She'd recognize his scrawled penmanship anywhere. She tried to dig herself into the ground, her back grinding into the tree behind her.

Somebody must be playing a trick on her. Who? Annie was the only one who knew about Matt. Annie would never play such a cruel trick on her. Blevins at the Sun Bank? Bankers were like doctors. They didn't divulge clients' personal information. Maybe Matt didn't know she was here. Maybe. He was just . . . what? Taking time off from his billion-dollar company to go out on Big Red? With his wife. Matt and Gracie Star. Not a girlfriend, a wife. Maybe it was her letter and the check that spurred him to come here. It probably pissed him off, and he was going to show her. Show her what? That he was this big tycoon and her little check of $35,000 was a drip in a very big bucket. He probably chewed up the letter and spit it out. He'd remember, though. This was his payback for her mean-spirited letter and check.

"It should be my payback, not his. I should damn well leave him stranded on the bridge with his heart thumping in his chest the way mine thumped when

I was left alone at the altar with 300 people staring at me. Matt's afraid of heights," she said to Buzz, who was nuzzling her neck.

Maggie looked at the oversize watch on her wrist. In a few hours she was finally going to see him, at the orientation. This wasn't the past; this was a brand new day, and she was a totally different person than she was twelve years ago. Matt would be a totally different person, too. Now he was married. "I can handle this. I can really handle this. I know I can handle this." Buzz backed up, his front paws digging into the ground. "I'm telling you. I can handle this. Matt Star is just someone I used to know. Time to head back to camp." Buzz barked his approval as Maggie threw her apple core into the gorge.

On the way back to camp, Maggie ran the article she'd read in the Sunday paper over and over in her mind. She was one step ahead of Matt—she knew what he looked like, whereas her appearance was going to be a complete surprise. These days, she was well rounded, her hair was fashionable, and she already had a light tan from being outdoors. Her last trip up the mountain, just weeks ago, had every guy in her group hitting on her. "Your loss, Matt Star," Maggie muttered.

Promptly at four o'clock, Annie and Lulu walked out onto the front porch to wait for Maggie. She watched her friend cross the compound, her stomach tied in knots. "Here she comes. She must have cut through to the Green Course to get here so quickly. She doesn't look like she knows," Annie whispered to Lulu, who was busy fluffing her beehive hairdo. "How come you and Ozzie switched and he's picking up Mr. Star?"

"I didn't want to mess up my new do."

"Oh. I'll see you at the orientation."

Engine running, Annie backed the jeep up to Maggie's cabin and blew the horn. Maggie came out dressed in freshly pressed khaki slacks and a pale blue shirt that showed off her light tan. Annie noticed she wore eye makeup and rouge, and her lips were glossy. Makeup was good. "So, did you get the bridge fixed?"

"Yep."

"So, what's new?"

"If that's your way of asking me if I read the roster, the answer is yes, I read it, and yes, I know Matt Star and his wife are going out with me tomorrow on Big Red. My question to you is, when did you find out?"

"Maggie, I sent back his reservation, but then Mr. Star called Ozzie direct. I didn't say anything because I didn't want to see you hurting all over again. You seem to have a handle on everything these days."

"That's because I finally sent him back the $35,000 he paid my parents for the wedding. I also had my loan officer at the bank mail him a letter at the same time. I finally told him off. I got it all out. That must be why he's coming here. I suspect he knows I'm here, but I'm not sure. I guess he just wants to drive the knife in farther. Guess what, I have the edge. Matt Star has a fear of heights that's worse than my own. I'm talking real fear here. He can't even stand on a chair without getting dizzy. I'm going to make him go over the bridge first. By himself. That's my pound of flesh. After that I don't give a hoot what he does."

"I love it!" Annie gurgled. "What if he chickens out and won't cross it?"

"Then he looks like a loser in front of the group. Matt Star, CEO of Digi-Star, afraid to cross a bridge. You know someone in the group will sell that story to the tabloids for five grand. Matt always said he didn't have a bone of fear in his body. We'll see. Something happened to him on a bad climb a long time ago and that's why he has his fear of heights. He never told me what it was, though. I did hear rumors that one of his buddies died and Matt couldn't do anything to save him."

"You're okay with this then?"

"I don't know if okay is the right term. I can handle it. I have to handle it because I don't have any other choice. He's going to leave and I have to get on with my life. I made up my mind that this is my last year. As much as I love this place, and I do love it, I know I have to move on. I can't keep having these homecomings every year. I'm going to get a life if it's the last thing I do. We're here. Let's do ribs and shrimp."

"Sounds good to me. Maggie, just out of curiosity, what do you think Mr. Star will do when he sees you're his guide?"

"I have no idea. If I had to guess I'd say after the initial shock, if he doesn't know it's me, he'll shake my hand and say, nice to see you again, Maggie. This is my wife, Gracie. I'll say something stupid and we'll get on with it. I can handle it, Annie. This is my turf we're on. What time is he due in?"

"Five-thirty I think. We better get moving."

"I'd say so."

"You look good, Maggie. Really good."

"Thanks for that, Annie."

"Maggie, I have something to tell you."

"Can it wait till we're in the restaurant? I can see Ozzie pacing over by the bus stop."

"Sure it can wait."

"Ozzie, it's good to see you!" Matt said as he bear-hugged the man standing in front of him. "It's been a long time. How's business? God, this air smells good."

"It's good to see you, too. Where's your wife, son?"

"What wife?"

"Your reservation said Matt and Gracie Star. Who's Gracie and where is she?"

"Right here," Matt said as he unzipped his green canvas shoulder bag. Gracie yipped.

"A dog! I'll be goldarned. Now if that ain't somethin'. I seen jack rabbits bigger than her."

"She's a killer dog, Ozzie. Nobody gets within a foot of me."

"I picked you for a Doberman or a Shepherd man, not an itty-bitty little dog like this. Lulu is gonna love her. Next thing you know she'll be wantin' one. Let's go, son. You are a sight for sore eyes. Lulu is gonna purely love that cap on your head. Looks like maybe you might be needin' a newer model."

"Never happen, Ozzie. Is everything still the same, barbecue and then orientation? How many in my group?"

"Yep. Twelve in the group. We've been scheduling fifteen to a group because business is so good, but only twelve qualify for Big Red. I thought this would be my last year for sure, but then things turned around in a matter of days. I think it would have killed Lulu if we lost the camp."

"If you ever need a partner or if you want to take a long vacation let me know. I'm fed up with the corporate world. I can see myself living out here."

"If you love it so much how come you never came back?" Ozzie asked bluntly.

"Because I'm stupid. Life got in the way. I thought I had things to do and places to go, worlds to conquer, that kind of thing. I made some mistakes along the way that can't be made right. I guess what I'm trying to say is it's time for me to get back to the basics. This seemed like a good place to start. Time to see if I'm a man or not. I feel, Ozzie, like this is . . . a homecoming. Who ever it was that said you can't go home again didn't know what he was talking about. I'm home. End of story."

"How come a fine man like you that's so rich never got married?"

"I almost did once, but I managed to screw that up really quick. Never met anyone who could compare to her. It's me and Gracie."

"You better watch out for Lulu. Once she finds out you ain't married she'll be parading every single female she knows in front of you. We got a couple of guides you might be interested in, particularly the once taking you out to Big Red."

"No matchmaking, Ozzie. I'm not here to find a wife. I think I'm here to find myself, if that makes sense. Jesus, I forgot how beautiful it is here. God must have been in a kind mood when he created this place."

"Just about everyone who comes here says the same thing. Well, we're home. There's Lulu waiting on the steps. Make sure you mention her new hairdo. Women like that kind of thing."

"Gotcha," Matt laughed as he ran toward Lulu to hug her, Gracie on his heels.

"Lulu, this is Gracie."

"Mercy. Gracie's a dog! Did you hear that, Ozzie? Matt ain't married. That makes things— What it does is— Don't pay me no mind. Everything's just fine. Just pure peachy. Oh, my, I have so much to do. I'll see you later."

"Now, if that don't beat all. She couldn't wait for you to get here and there she goes running off. You didn't mention her hair, son. Can't imagine why she didn't want to pick up that dog? Never could figure women out."

"Don't even try. Whoa, what's that?" Matt asked as a dark brown streak flashed past him.

"That's Buzz. He belongs to one of our guides. Now, would you look at that! He likes your dog. Looks like she likes him, too."

Matt watched as the little Yorkie ran circles around the confused Labrador, who tried to catch her, to no avail. In the time it took Matt to blink twice, Gracie backed up and ran toward Buzz to leap on his back. The Lab tried to shake her loose, but Gracie held on, yipping and yowling. When she had enough, she leaped to the ground, panting. Like the gentleman he was, Buzz led her to his water bowl on the front porch of the cabin. He waited for her to drink before he dropped his own head to the bowl.

"He's in love." Ozzie guffawed.

"Looks like Gracie is smitten, too. I don't think she ever saw another dog, at least while I've had her. Do you think it's okay for me to leave her out here while I shower and change?"

"Sure. Buzz will watch out for her. That's some fancy hair ribbon you got in her hair. Makes her look taller." Ozzie guffawed again.

"The groomer put it on her. I tried to take it out, but Gracie wouldn't let me. She's a girl dog. Girl dogs wear ribbons. Don't think for one minute I'm embarrassed, because I'm not." Ozzie just laughed. And laughed.

The camp bustled as the hundred and fifty-five guests milled around the long food tables manned by Lulu and four of her women friends from town. Ozzie was in charge of the barbecue pit with four of the guides. The food was plain, but plentiful. Thick ribeye steaks, potatoes, gravy, coleslaw, a mountain of green salad, pans of chicory-flavored beans, homemade bread, and blackberry pies were the fare. Matt ate like it was his last meal. He watched in amusement as Buzz carried tidbits of meat to where Gracie was hiding because she was frightened of all the people and noise. When she was finished eating, Buzz licked at Gracie's whiskers to clean her off. Matt's amusement turned to sadness when he wondered why humans couldn't be as open and trusting as these two animals meeting for the first time.

Satisfied that Gracie was safe, Matt meandered over to the small group of people wearing red armbands. He introduced himself and shook hands.

"What happens if we get blisters from all the hiking?" one of the women asked.

"You live with it, and you don't even want to think about taking your boots off or you won't get them back on," someone said.

"You're supposed to get them wet and wear them that way for twelve hours so the boots will mold to your feet," someone else said.

"I can hardly lift that backpack."

"You lift weights. Are you telling me you can't lug thirty-five pounds on your back? Didn't you people read the brochure?" a balding man demanded.

Everyone admitted they'd read the brochure, but didn't pay much attention to the instructions.

Matt stepped to the front of the small group. He lowered his voice to a harsh whisper. "Is this the way you run my goddamn company? If it is, you're all out of a job. You were told to read the brochure and follow the instructions. Each and every one of you signed a paper saying you were qualified to make this trip. You all work out, you run, you jog, you eat properly. What the hell is the problem? I have no patience for this. One whimper, one whine, and I'll make sure you never get another job in your field.

"Is there anything I've said that you don't understand?" At what point did he turn into this tyrant, Matt wondered. What in the hell was wrong with him?

"Understood," the group said as one.

"Good. Go get your gear and bring it out here. Everything you brought will be inspected. Don't even think about trying to smuggle something into your pack that doesn't belong there. For the next two weeks you live off the land. It's almost eight o'clock and orientation starts promptly."

Matt followed his own advice and headed for his cabin to assemble his gear. He felt uneasy when he thought about what the guide would say when she saw Gracie and the dog food packets he would be carrying. Maybe he'd better check it out with Ozzie now, before he made a fool of himself.

"I'm planning to take Gracie on the trip, Ozzie. It occurs to me I should have said something earlier," Matt said, cornering the old man near the spring house.

"Don't see a problem with that. Buzz goes. It's some pretty rough terrain. You'll probably be carrying her most of the way. You sent a check for her deposit along with yours, so how could I turn her away? Did you give Lulu the balance? If you didn't, do it now, son. That way your guide can't have no comeback. Git my point."

"Yes, sir."

Matt raced back to his cabin, scribbled out a check for $5,000, pocketed it, and then raced to where he saw Lulu gabbing with her friends.

"Lulu, in all the excitement of seeing you and Ozzie I forgot to give you the balance of my payment. I think your hair is very becoming, Lulu."

Lulu put the check in her apron pocket. "Did Ozzie tell you to say that?" she asked suspiciously.

"Nope. You're one of the prettiest ladies here." He realized as he walked away that he sincerely meant the words.

The bell on the back porch sounded promptly at eight o'clock. A moment later, floodlights lit up the compound. The guides, all wearing colored armbands, headed for their assigned group, also wearing matching armbands. Matt stretched his neck to see the paragon who was going to lead his group through the Big Red course.

He knew his heart stopped beating because he grew so light-headed he thought he was going to pass out. He reached out to a scrubby bush to hang onto for support. The pounding in his head matched the pounding in his heart when he heard her voice.

"Hi. I'm Maggie Osborne and I'll be your guide this trip. According to your papers, you're all qualified to do the Big Red course. I hope none of you fibbed. If you did, this is your last chance to back out. No? Okay. I'm going to call your name, and when I do, step forward. It's best if we're on a first-name basis. I'm Maggie. I have a degree in forestry, and I've been a survival guide on this course for the past ten years, in case you're wondering what my qualifications are. I'm also the only guide to ever work the Big Red course. As I call your name, step forward, form a straight line, and empty your pack. If there's a crumb that doesn't belong, it goes. Mike Sayers, Pete Nelson, Carlos Ramos, Matt and Gracie Star, Mark Forbes." Maggie raised her eyes from the clipboard. She literally froze as her eyes locked with Matt's. He was taller than she remembered, just as muscular, just as handsome. *Please, God, let me handle this. Please, don't let me fall apart.*

Matt sucked in his breath. How did Maggie get to be so beautiful? Tough, from the looks of things.

Shapely. Oh, yes. His breath exploded in a loud sigh. Maggie Osborne. Never in a million years would he have thought he would find her like this, out in the wilderness, in the middle of nowhere. He looked around for Gracie. He spotted her curled up next to Buzz under one of the picnic tables. Gracie was going to be the true test. His heart was still hammering in his chest as he watched the members of his group empty their packs.

"Matt and Gracie Star. Dump it out, Matt. Let's see what you have? Gracie Star," she said.

Matt whistled shrilly. "Gracie!" he bellowed. The Yorkie sprinted toward Matt, to everyone's amusement. Buzz barked angrily when Gracie leaped into Matt's arms.

"Down, Buzz. Down. Sit." It was an iron command the Labrador ignored. He wanted Gracie. The confusion she felt was registered on Maggie's face. Gracie was a dog, not Matt's wife. Her anger kicked in again.

His eyes on Maggie's flushed face, Matt lowered the little dog to the ground. Buzz picked her up by the scruff of the neck and trotted off. "This is Gracie's gear," he said, tossing the green canvas bag on the ground. "It has five packets of dog food and a small tin water dish. This is my gear."

Maggie's heart pumped furiously. Take a stand now or later? In her life she'd never been this flustered. He wasn't supposed to be this good-looking. His hair should be thinning or something. He was laughing at her. She could see it in his eyes. He was uneasy, though; she could see that in his eyes, too. There was no Mrs. Star. The thought left her giddy. She looked in the direction of the dogs. Buzz had never disobeyed her. He'd been trained by a professional. Did she dare call him and have him ignore her? "The hairball stays behind, Mr. Star." The title sounded obscene even to her own ears.

"Gracie is not a hairball. She's a dog, and she goes with me. I paid for her," Matt said quietly. He was in her face, just an inch away. He could kiss her if he wanted to. She smelled wonderful, all powdery and flowery. He stared her down.

"It doesn't work that way, Mr. Star."

"Yes, it does. I paid for her. I'm responsible for her. I'll carry her if the going gets rough. Why don't we put it to a vote or ask Ozzie."

Maggie's voice took on the quality of chilled milk. "Yes, why don't we do that. What do you all think?"

"Let him bring her," the group said.

"Ozzie! Would you please come over here. Mr. Star wants to bring his dog with him. The course is dangerous enough without that, that powder puff. This is not a good thing, Ozzie."

"He paid for her, Maggie. Do any of you object?" Ozzie asked the group.

"They all agreed," Matt said. "She won't be a problem. I don't think your dog will go unless Gracie goes. I think they bonded earlier. Of course, I could be wrong," he said generously. So Maggie was the other recipient of Lulu's cap. He eyed it now. If anything, hers looked more worn, more used. The thought pleased him.

"Bonded?" The blank look on Maggie's face brought a smile to Matt's face.

"Yeah." Matt lowered his voice to a whisper. "Maggie, let's talk. Out here in the open, after the others leave, or in one of our cabins. I need to—"

"I'm not interested in what you *need*, Mr. Star." Her voice dropped to below frost level.

"Maggie, I'm sorry. I know it's just a word. Can we talk like two civilized human beings? Your letter pretty much said it all, but I imagine you have more to say. I have a lot to say. Let's clear the air before we go out on the course. You're responsible for all our lives and I want to make sure your judgment isn't impaired. These are my people, but then I suspect you already know that. We'll go out in the bushes, have a knock-down-drag-out-fight, call names, and then put it behind us. You're angry. I can see it in your eyes, in your face. I won't let you take us out on that course until we deal with it. If you refuse, I'll have to go to Ozzie. I don't want to do that, but I will not allow you to endanger our lives."

"You must have a very low opinion of me, Matt. I would never do something like that. I'm not a fool. All right, ten o'clock by the spring house."

"Okay, Maggie."

I am a fool for agreeing to this, Maggie thought. Matt was right, though, she couldn't go out on the course with all this bottled-up anger. But would telling him off, would name calling erase the hurt, the anger? Unlikely.

"Is something wrong? Jeez, it's just a little dog. We can take turns carrying her if that will speed things up. Four o'clock will be here before we know it. I for one would like to get this show on the road," the bald-headed man said.

Maggie dug her heels into the ground. "Since you're so eager, Mr. Sadler, you're in charge of piling up the goodies. The Cheese Doodles, the Kit Kat bars, and the gum drops go in the pile. Don't miss anything. Now, repack your gear and I'll see you in the dining room promptly at four o'clock. We have thirty minutes for breakfast. You have an extra ten minutes for bathroom privileges before we start our hike. Do any of you have any questions?"

"How long is the day?"

"We make camp at six o'clock. If there are no other questions, I'll say good night."

"The lady is no pussycat. I hope she knows her stuff," the balding man said.

There was a small amount of good-natured joking tinged with apprehension as the group packed their gear to head for the dormitory-style cabins.

Matt watched as Maggie whistled for Buzz, who totally ignored her. He tried doing the same thing, but Gracie turned a deaf ear. He went over to the picnic table to scoop her up into his arms. Maggie tugged at Buzz's collar. The Lab growled and Gracie whined.

"I told you that hairball was going to be a problem," Maggie snapped.

"Your dog instigated this. He's in love. My dog is merely enjoying his attentions. I think it's called companionship. Your dog is going to howl and yowl all night long. My dog is going to cry and whine. Shall we leave them to their own devices or make an issue of it?"

He was too close. Maggie drew a deep breath. He smelled like the piney forest after a heavy rain. All clean and woodsy. "I don't like your dog any more than I like you, Mr. Star. Let's make sure we understand that little fact. In this case, though, you're probably right. Don't read anything into that statement that isn't there. Another thing, *Mr.* Star—don't try pulling rank on me out here. I don't care if you do own the second-largest software company in the country. This is my turf and you're just another customer who thinks a survival course will turn him into a man overnight. You're wrong, and you have some nerve wearing that hat."

"That's funny, I was going to say the same thing to you. I got it all figured out now. You came here to hide out. You are hiding out, aren't you? You don't have the guts to face the real world. Look. I was young and stupid. I admit it. I should have handled it better, but I didn't. I did show up. On time no less. Then I turned tail and ran. I had my tux on, the whole thing. I came back two hours later, after I got done being sick. All the guests were gone."

"That's probably the biggest damn lie you ever told, Matt Star."

"Oh yeah, well, try this one on for size, Miss Know-It-All. You were sitting on the church steps with your mother and maid of honor. You were bawling your eyes out. I saw you put your heel through your wedding veil. I was prepared to go through with the wedding because I loved you. You know what, I think I still love you. I even heard your mother say I was a dreamer, a drifter, and would never amount to anything. Your father came up and said if he ever found me he was going to kick my ass all the way to New York City. He said other things that were less flattering than what your mother said. I took off again. I never did return that tux."

"I thought we were going to discuss this at ten o'clock." Every word he said was true. Her insides started to churn. Another minute and she was going to upchuck her dinner. "Ten o'clock by the spring house." She ran then, twelve years of demons on her heels.

Annie was waiting for her inside the cabin. "Are you okay, Maggie? Did you make him squirm? What did he do when he saw you? I hope he turned green."

"Oh, Annie. He looks the same. Older, of course. My heart—I thought it was going to hammer right out of my chest. He smelled the way he always smelled, you know, like the woods after a good rain. He was right in my face. There is no Mrs. Star. Gracie is a tiny little dog. I was absolutely giddy when I realized that. God, he can still make me crazy. He told me he came back the day of the wedding. He said things . . . It has to be true because he said he saw and heard things that really happened. He said he came back because he loved me and thinks he *still* loves me. It's a crock. He said he's worried that I'm too emotional to be taking this party out on Big Red."

"What are you going to do?"

"Meet him at the spring house in"—Maggie looked at her watch—"in twenty-five minutes. He needs to talk to me. Do you get that 'need' part?"

"You both need to talk. You tell him off, he tells you off. You call him a few names to make yourself feel better. He'll call you a few. You tell him how much he hurt you and he'll tell you how much he's suffered. Then the two of you can lie to each other about how neither one of you cares for the other. I just want to leave you with one thought: He's never married. You tried it for three weeks for all the wrong reasons. You're free. He's free. The fact that he's never married tells me a lot. All you have to do is listen, Maggie. My mother always used to say it's not enough to listen, though. She said you have to *hear* the words. In the end it will be whatever you want it to be. Be open. It isn't often that people get a second chance. Don't blow it. See you in the morning."

Annie, the eternal optimist, Maggie thought.

At precisely two minutes to ten, Maggie crossed the compound toward the spring house. The flood lights were out now. The only light to guide her was a thin slice of silver moonlight. She could see his shadowy form, both dogs at his feet.

"Since this meeting was your idea, I suggest you get on with it. Four o'clock will be here before we know it." Her voice was colder than chipped ice.

"You aren't the old Maggie. You're so cold and distant. What happened to all that fire that used to burn in you?"

"That's a pretty stupid statement coming from you. I learned some hard lessons. I grew up."

"You grew up and then you shut down. I have eyes and ears. I also have a good memory. When was the last time you smiled or laughed? When was the last time you got out there and mingled?"

"Mingled? That's pretty funny. I was always a late bloomer. I can't shrug off things that are important to me. You goddamn well left me standing at the altar, Matt Star."

"Maggie, I tried to tell you in a hundred different ways, but you didn't hear me. My God, yes, I loved you. I wanted all the same things you wanted. I just didn't want them at that time. I tried telling you there were things I had to do, places I had to go. You said I could do them later. At the time I believed you, or I thought I did. You can't do the things I wanted to do when you're married, with responsibilities. I wanted you to finish college so you could be the person you were meant to be. You said you would finish when the time was right. You were in love with the idea of marriage. You wanted the house, the picket fence, the kids, the animals. I told you more than once neither one of us was truly ready. I know your mother pushed you into pushing me because she didn't like it that we were sleeping together. I can just imagine what she said after I bolted. Maggie, I didn't even have a job for God's sake. Do you remember what you said? You said, You're smart, Matt, you'll get a job. My dad can get you a job at the freight company. I'll work at the supermarket. I didn't want to work at the freight company and I sure as hell didn't want to work with your father. I told you that a dozen times, but you didn't hear me. I didn't want you working at the supermarket either. There's nothing wrong with that, but I knew you, you'd trench in, do that cooking, baking, and gardening thing and you wouldn't go back to school. I wanted more for us. All you wanted was the ring on your finger. That's how I saw it at the time. I did love you. A day didn't go by that I didn't think about you afterward. I wanted to find you a million different times. I just assumed you'd be married with a family because that was what you wanted."

"I wasn't that hard to find, Matt. If you were looking."

"See! See! You don't *hear* what I say. I didn't say I was looking. I said I assumed you were married with a family. The truth is I didn't have the guts to find you. I did put the company's investigative team on call to try and locate you, though. I'm turning the company over to Marcus as of October. That's the reason I came here. I want to start over. Gracie made me realize what I've been missing. This journey, and make no mistake, this is a journey for me, is for me to start over. I need to find out who I am. Back to the basics if you will."

"Because Annie wrote you that letter," Maggie snapped. She didn't like this conversation at all. Well, what had she expected?

"No. The letter just brought it to a head. I planned on coming out here this summer anyway. I decided not to wait after I got the anonymous letter. I'm sorry. I don't know about you, but I've said all I have to say. Unless, of course, you have stuff you want to get off your chest."

Maggie jammed her hands into the pockets of her slacks. Why couldn't she think about all the things she had on her chest, all the mean, ugly things she wanted to say? She felt wounded, battle-scarred, and she hadn't lifted a verbal finger. What he said was true. She had said all those things, done all those things. She should have gone to a shrink to talk it out. Instead, she'd burrowed in and convinced herself she was totally blameless. He was waiting now for her to say something hateful and vitriolic, something in character for her. If he had truly thought of her often over the years, how sad that all he had were such pitiful memories of her. All she wanted was to run to her dark cabin, lock the door, and hug Buzz so she could wail and cry. She would have to settle for a pillow now that Buzz was otherwise occupied.

"You broke my heart," Maggie said softly.

She walked away so quickly she didn't hear Matt's tortured response, "I know, but I never stopped loving you."

Six

Maggie pulled her rain gear out of the closet when she heard the unmistakable dripping sounds on the roof. She grimaced. An omen? She'd probably lose half her group before she got out of the compound. An early morning rain was always cold. The group would be cranky. Their pace would be slowed.

It would be different if she'd gotten a good night's sleep, which she hadn't. For most of the night, she'd lain in her bed staring at the ceiling. She'd gotten up twice to make instant coffee, knowing she wouldn't sleep for sure. She'd sat in the old armchair until after two when Buzz scratched at the door to come in, Gracie alongside him. She watched, a half smile tugging at her mouth as Buzz nudged the little dog closer to her legs. Maggie dropped to her haunches to fondle Gracie's ears.

"You did good, Buzz. This little cream puff would probably catch cold if she stayed out in the rain. I bet Matt has a raincoat for her. And a hat. She is cute. I guess you are lonely out here with just us humans. I never took the time to think about that, Buzz, and I'm sorry. I've made a lot of mistakes these past years. Pride has to be the deadliest sin of all. I'll try and make things right for myself. You, too. Is it okay if I pick her up?"

Buzz woofed his approval.

"Oh, she's like a little feather, and so warm and soft. She even smells like Matt. I think, little lady, you could melt anyone's heart. I see what Matt meant now. Come on, Buzz, there's room for all of us on this chair."

The dogs slept. Maggie stared into the dying embers of the fire.

Outside, in the dripping rain, Matt Star peered into the window. He felt a lump form deep in his throat when he saw Gracie cuddled in Maggie's arms. They were all warm and dry. Parting when the trip came to an end was going to be a bitch. How was he going to take Gracie away from Buzz? Unless, of course, Maggie agreed to part with Buzz, which didn't even bear thinking about. Maybe they could share custody. He could take both dogs six months of the year and she could have them the other six months. Like a marriage when it came to an end and provisions had to be made for the children. The thought was so unbearable, he ran, sloshing through the rain, back to his cabin.

There didn't seem to be much point in going back to bed. Instead, he dozed in the chair, one ear tuned to the rain and one eye trained on the clock. It would be just his luck to fall asleep and miss the four o'clock wake-up call.

When the bell sounded promptly at four o'clock, Matt donned his slicker. He stuffed Gracie's rain gear into one of the deep pockets before he trudged outside in the pouring rain to the dining cabin.

Babbling, complaining voices greeted him. It sounded like a revolt was in progress. Whatever it was, it stopped the moment he walked through the door.

"Eat hearty, ladies and gentlemen, because this is the last real food you're going to get until we return." Matt helped himself to three piping-hot cinnamon buns and a glass of orange juice. He was finishing the last of it when Maggie entered the cabin, Buzz at her side, Gracie in her pocket. She handed the little dog over. Buzz, he noticed, had a homemade slicker on that was tied under his belly. He whipped out Gracie's fashionable yellow rain gear to cheers. Buzz barked loudly.

"Single file, match my pace," Maggie said. Groans and moans followed her as the group filed out the door.

"It's cold, it's wet, and it's miserable. If you keep up the pace you'll stay warm. It's a waste of energy to grumble and complain. This is an all-day rain, so get used to it. The forecast for tomorrow is the same," Maggie said.

Maggie was like a nimble-footed mountain goat as she scaled the rough terrain, Buzz at her side.

Three hours into the bone-crushing climb, Matt realized how out of shape he was. Racquetball once a week with Marcus was no preparation for this torture. By nightfall he would have shin splints, and he could feel the blisters beginning to form on the heels of his feet. Rain dripped from his hat down his back. He cursed at his own discomfort. Maggie continued to climb, shouting encouragement to those lagging behind. When she called a halt at eleven o'clock for lunch, Matt heaved a sigh of relief. Dried currants, apricots, and a stick of beef jerky.

Gracie woofed softly. Matt set her on the ground. She peed and immediately ran to Maggie and Buzz. In an attempt to make conversation, Matt said, "I guess Buzz is an experienced guide, huh?"

"I brought him with me from the time he was seven months old. He's surefooted and he's got the hang of the bridge. I've had to send him back for help several times. He's a part of the team. Ozzie calls him the team mascot. By the way, that was a nice thing you did for Ozzie." This last was said grudgingly.

"Does he suspect?"

"No. Lulu wants to retire and go to Hawaii. She says that every winter. Every summer she says she's going to die here because this is her slice of heaven. They aren't getting any younger. Ozzie is seventy-nine and Lulu is seventy-seven. Lunch is over!" she called.

"Do you think he'd sell out to me? I'd make it worth his while, and they could stay on if they wanted to."

Maggie stared at the man standing within arms' reach, the man she'd almost married. "I don't know. I'm leaving when the season ends. Annie is, too. Some of the guys were talking about leaving. No fringe benefits. Health insurance is prohibitive. None of us are getting any younger."

"We're having a civilized conversation. We're making progress."

"To what end?" Maggie said.

"To being friends. I'd like us to be friends, Maggie. I wish there was something I could do to make up for all the hurt I caused you."

"It's past. You know you can't unring the bell. I thought about all the things you said last night and you were right. Why don't we leave it at that?"

"Does that mean you forgive me?"

"No, that's not what it means. We're five minutes behind schedule," she called to the others.

"Well, then, what does it mean?" Matt persisted.

"It means you need to be quiet and pay attention to where you're walking or you're going to slide backwards. If you do that it will have a domino effect. Your people won't thank you."

"What happened to the soft side of Maggie Osborne?"

"It's gone. You robbed me of that. It doesn't matter whose fault it is, it's gone."

"I don't believe that for a minute. I bet if I kissed you, you'd melt."

"Don't count on it, and you won't get close enough to try, so forget it."

Matt babbled on, huffing and puffing as he did so. Maggie, he noticed, wasn't even breathing hard. He didn't know if he wanted to smack her or kiss her. He said so and was rewarded with a tinkly sounding laugh. He felt so encouraged by the sound he lost his footing and tumbled backward. He laughed when he realized she was right, again, as the others toppled over, rolling past the spot where they'd broken for lunch. A true domino spill.

"Now we're fifteen minutes behind schedule. It's double-time until we make up the time," Maggie said.

"What happened to, Is anyone hurt? Can I help?" Matt asked. Maggie didn't bother to reply.

"I hate this," someone said.

"My underwear is wet," someone else said.

A woman volunteered that she had a raging headache and was going to resign any second. Matt grinned as he did his best to catch up to Maggie. He could hear Gracie snoring lightly in his pocket.

By three o'clock, they were back on schedule. "I don't think I've ever been this tired, this exhilarated, in my entire life. I don't sleep well."

"Did you feel a need to share that with me, Matt?"

"Yes, I did. In case you haven't noticed, I'm trying to win you over."

She didn't mean to ask the question, but the word tumbled off her tongue. "Why?"

"I guess because I still love you."

The tinkly laugh sounded again. "You think! I'm insulted."

"I'm ready to get married now," Matt gasped.

"Really."

"Yes, really. Hell, we might as well get married. If we don't, we're going to fight over the dogs. Dogs have hearts, too, and they feel things. We can't separate them. I'll fight for custody. I'll win, too, because I have all this money to spend on lawyers. So, what do you say?"

"No. You rich people think you can do anything. You can't buy me or my dog."

"Does my money bother you?"

"No, you bother me. Shut up and walk faster. You're holding us up again. What's your problem?"

"You're my problem. I admire your stamina. I'm bushed. I admit it. So are the others. We're cold, we're wet, and we're tired."

"That sounds like a tired old song. You all agreed to follow the rules. We have two more hours to go before we break for the night. I want you all to see the gorge while it's still light so you'll know what you're up against in the morning."

"Wouldn't it be better for them to see it in the morning? If they see it now, they aren't going to be able to sleep. Fear is not a good tactic."

"Are you speaking for them or for yourself?"

"Both. I remember the gorge. I had nightmares for years about that bridge. Crossing it does not make you a man or a woman. Crossing it means you get to the other side with your adrenaline boiling over, so don't go giving me any bullshit about being manly or any of that other crap. Anyone who isn't afraid of that bridge is stark, raving crazy. You make that poor dog cross it, too, don't you? To prove what and to whom? I think I feel sorry for you, Maggie." Matt slowed until he was even with his group.

Ahead, Maggie wiped at the tears trickling down her cheeks. Damn, why was he always right? Why was she always wrong? More important, why was she suddenly experiencing the same feelings she'd experienced twelve years ago? Stick your neck out, Maggie, and someone will chop it off. Shut down, don't let him do a number on your head. He was going to walk away from here in two weeks, and she'd be right back to square one. She slowed her gait imperceptibly. She'd never been one to follow her own advice.

At six o'clock, Maggie called a halt as she looked at her sorry, miserable group.

"We're two hours behind schedule and there's no way we can make up the time, so we'll make camp. I think we'll all welcome a nice fire. It's relatively dry here, so if any of you want to make a pine bed, go ahead. If your sleeping gear is wet you might want to spread it out and put some pine needles on the top and on the bottom. Your dinner is in your provision pack. Follow the recommended ration. Living off the land is lean at this time of year, so be very frugal."

Where was Matt? Behind her? She could feel his eyes boring into her back as she cleared a spot to build the fire. She felt the cold and dampness then, knowing if Matt came up behind her and put his arms around her, she'd be hotter than any other fire she could build. "Twigs, Buzz. Time to work and then you get supper."

The Lab raced off, with Gracie close behind, her yellow slicker flapping in the breeze Buzz created. They both returned, Gracie with a stick no bigger than Maggie's little finger clamped between her teeth.

"This could take all night," Matt muttered. He marched off, returning with his arms full of half-dry twigs. He found himself laughing aloud when he saw Buzz drop twigs onto Gracie's pile. "You're a gentleman, Buzz, I'll give you that."

He patted the Lab and cuddled with Gracie for a few seconds before he started to build the fire. Maggie sat down next to the dogs.

"You look tired, Maggie."

"I was going to say the same thing to you. I hate to admit it, but you were right."

"About some things. Thanks for breaking here instead of the bridge. A thought did occur to me earlier. The heavy rain last night and today might have done some damage to the bridge. It definitely wouldn't be good for morale. I like your dog, Maggie."

"I like yours, too. When you leave, Buzz is going to go into a funk. Don't give me any of that talk about custody, either. Nice fire."

"I'd kill for a weenie."

"Me, too," Maggie said wearily.

They sat side by side on a damp log, both dogs at their sides.

"What happens tomorrow if my people balk at the bridge? I hate saying this, but I didn't think beyond getting everyone here for Ozzie. I don't even know if I can handle it myself. I feel . . . I feel like I did the day of the wedding. Is it your intention to make a fool of me when it's time to cross the gorge? Are you going to get off on seeing my people's reaction to my fright?"

"The thought crossed my mind. I won't humiliate you." In a rare burst of confidence she couldn't explain, Maggie said, "The bridge scares the hell out of me. I force myself to do it. That's why Lulu and Ozzie gave me this cap. No one else would take on Big Red. You know that saying, 'There's nothing to fear but fear itself.' It isn't true. I couldn't do it without Buzz. You're right about that, too. I'm going to send him back in the morning. I love him too much to put him in danger. I do stupid things sometimes, Matt."

"We all do, Maggie. I'll send Gracie with him. We can fashion some kind of a pocket or sack to his slicker. I think he can carry three pounds, don't you?"

"Absolutely. The only problem is, Buzz is trained to react to an emergency. He might balk at simply being sent back without just cause. We can all go back if it's what you want. Or we can alter our route and strike out for the Green Course first thing in the morning. Your call, Matt."

"Why don't we make it a group decision in the morning? I like it when you aren't being so hardnosed. Now you're more like the old Maggie I knew and loved."

"But not enough to marry me." Her voice was so sad that Matt reached for her hand.

"Not true. I think I backed out because I was afraid I would ruin what we did have. At that time in our lives I would have made a miserable husband and you would have smothered me in your efforts to make me happy. The timing wasn't right. Do you at least agree with that?"

"Yes."

"I can't hear you," Matt sing-songed.

"I guess we both made a mess of things."

"I'm willing to take half the blame. We're making progress here," Matt said, squeezing her hand.

Maggie smiled in the darkness. "I'll take the other half. What's it like being a billionaire?" Suddenly, she felt so good she wanted to sing.

"It doesn't bring happiness, if that's your next question. It gives you security and frees you from a lot of worries, but then it creates other worries. It's not a piece of cake. What's it like doing what you've been doing?"

"It's very rewarding. No one is ever the same after they take the course. I'm not just talking about Big Red, either. It's amazing to see how everyone pulls together and acts as a team. Knowing your life depends on a stranger is something to take seriously. It was good for me. I learned a lot about myself, and it was a place to lick my wounds. I did get married for three whole weeks, but I did it for all the wrong reasons. I was looking for another you, and he simply wasn't you. Annie says I'm a one-man woman."

"Marcus says the same thing about me. Do you think it's true, Maggie?"

Maggie smiled again in the darkness. "I suppose it's possible. Were you serious about giving up your company?"

"Yeah. Are you serious about leaving here?"

"Uh-huh."

"That means we're both more or less free. Maybe we could go in the same direction, wherever that journey might lead us. When I knew for sure that I was coming here I felt like I was taking a journey home. Does that sound silly? Guess so, by the look on your face.

Whatever, it's something to think about anyway. I don't want to break Gracie's heart the way I broke yours. Look at them. Gracie is cuddled under Buzz's front paws. He's taking care of her. He's taken on the responsibility. Last night he brought her food. Today he helped her do her share by putting some of his kindling on her pile. A person can learn a lot from animals. If you stop to analyze this whole thing, you have to consider that we both made a journey to get to this point in time. I don't know if I believe in divine providence and stuff like that, but somebody, somewhere, seems to be watching over us. What's your opinion?"

"I agree, but I'm too tired to think about it tonight. Each year when I came back here I thought about it as coming home. It isn't a silly thought at all. Good journeys always end up at home. If you're lucky, that is. As soon as everyone gets settled, I'm going to turn in. Tomorrow night, if the group votes to continue, we can stay in the line shack farther up the mountain. Your people will like that."

"Are you going to think about us, Maggie?"

Maggie felt her heart flutter in her chest. "There is no 'us,' Matt. There's you and there's me."

"There could be an 'us' if you'd open up all the way. It could be better than it was before. We're older, we're wiser, and now we have these two dogs to consider. I think we need to give someone else a chance at this fire. I'll say good night."

Maggie moved off in the darkness. She longed for Buzz's warm body as she did her best to get comfortable in her damp bedroll. She felt excited and confused as she played back her conversation with Matt. *Divine providence. A journey. Things can be better than before. Older and wiser.* He'd said all those things? A long, heartbreaking journey. She closed her eyes.

She woke once, when she felt a presence next to her.

"Oh, Buzz, you came back. I missed you. Where's Gracie?" she asked sleepily. Maggie felt a tiny tongue lick at her cheek. She was wide awake now, aware that the two dogs were with her. "Go to Matt, Buzz. He misses Gracie, too. It's okay. You came back. That's all I care about. Matt doesn't understand things like that. At least not yet."

She felt rather than saw the two dogs leave her side. In the quiet night, she heard Matt's loud sigh as a single tear rolled down her cheek. Everything was happening too fast. Her emotions were churning and swirling. She buried her face in the bedroll to smother the sounds of her sobs. Tomorrow was another day. A day Matt would use to try to play catch-up. The question was, did she want to play? *Yes. Yes. Yes.*

On the other side of the fire, Matt reached out to the two dogs. "So, you didn't desert me after all." He stroked the little dog, his touch soft and gentle. When Buzz whined, he held out one arm for the Lab, who dropped gracefully to the ground. The dog whimpered. "I know just how you feel, big fella. You don't know what to do. Neither do I. I gave it my best shot this evening. Tomorrow will tell the tale. It's all up to Maggie. Listen, big guy, I'm glad you brought Gracie back, but I think Maggie needs you. It's okay if you take Gracie with you. I won't ever take her away from you. That's a promise."

Matt was awestruck when the Lab smothered his face with his wet tongue. *He must understand,* he thought wildly. Jesus, and they said animals were dumb. He propped himself up on one elbow trying to see through the flames to where Maggie was sleeping. True love, his friend Marcus had once said, was putting the other person first. Marcus hadn't said anything about how bad the hurt would be, though. Tomorrow he was going to be a basket case if he didn't get some sleep.

Maggie woke knowing she'd overslept. She packed up her bedroll, threw more logs on the fire, and made coffee, the only luxury the course allowed. As the scent of the boiling coffee permeated the air, the group woke, one by one. She tried to hide her amusement at the grumbling. They were game, though, calling out to each other as they brushed their teeth and headed for the bushes.

"One cup each. Ten minutes and we're on our way. It's ten minutes past six. If you follow my pace, we'll be at the gorge by eight fifteen. At that time we'll make some decisions. It stopped raining and the temperature's rising. That means there's going to be some fog. Stay close and talk to the person in front of you. Do not, I repeat, do not, go off the path. These next two hours are going to be more difficult because the climb is almost straight up. Be careful."

The fire smothered and packed down, the group set off, with Maggie, Buzz, and Gracie in the lead. Matt was the last in line.

Maggie had handed him his coffee and even smiled. What did the smile mean?

Word came down the line. The gorge was just ten minutes away. Matt sucked in his breath. He settled Lulu's cap more firmly on his head.

Ten minutes later, Matt pulled up short as he stared at the bridge and the fog surrounding it. For the life of him, he couldn't figure out why there would be fog this high up the mountain. The term low-lying fog meant fog was low, by one's foot or eye level. He could feel his heart thundering in his chest. Would the fog dissipate or burn off? If so, when? Hours from now? Tomorrow?

"This is Big Red. This part of the course is the hardest. We're going to take our twenty-minute break now. I want you all to look at that bridge very carefully. It won't be a cakewalk. I want each one of you to walk to the edge and look down. If any of you think you can't handle it, say so. We can alter our course and strike out for either the Blue or Green Course. The decision will be yours. I want you to know that I personally checked the bridge the day before yesterday and it was fine. However, Mr. Star pointed out to me last evening that the heavy rains of yesterday and the night before might have damaged it. If it's your intention to continue, I'll go out and check it again. If you want to alter the course, we'll leave it as it is for now."

Matt already knew what his vote was going to be. "How long does fog like this last?"

"A few hours, all day. I always waited it out. Last year we had to wait three days, and then, when the group had a clear view of the gorge, they backed out. What's your vote?"

"No. Does that make me less a man in your eyes, Maggie?"

"No, it makes you a sensible man."

"What would be your vote, Maggie?"

"I don't vote. I get paid to do a job and I do it. You guys pay my salary, so I do what you say."

"I understand that, but if you did have a vote, what would it be?"

Maggie moved away. She hated the fog, feared it with a passion. "I told you, I don't vote. I think you should voice your vote first, Matt, in case some of your people think they have to prove something to you. Are you comfortable with that? And, are you comfortable with me telling your group we can go back if they think this isn't for them?"

"Yes and yes." A smile tugged at the corners of Maggie's mouth. For a split second, he really thought she was going to pat him on the head and say, "Good boy."

Maggie looked at her watch. "What's it going to be, ladies and gentlemen? We're going to do an aye and nay vote. Mr. Star will go first. Matt?"

"No." His voice rang clear in the mountain air and carried down into the gorge to rise and bounce back, making it sound like he voted five times.

"Eleven no and one yes. That's pretty unanimous. Second question, how many of you are in favor of switching courses as opposed to going back to camp? Mr. Star will vote first again. Matt?"

"Return to camp. Where's Gracie and Buzz?"

The fear in Matt's voice transferred itself to Maggie. "Oh, God, we took the vote and Buzz must have thought it was time to go out on the bridge. That's the routine. Don't call him. He might panic. I don't see Gracie."

"She'll follow him. She'll slip through!" The fear and anguish in his voice made the hackles on Maggie's neck stand on end.

"Buzz won't let that happen," Maggie called as she ran to the little platform before the bridge. Buzz was a quarter of the way across the bridge, Gracie next to him.

"Everyone keep quiet. Not a sound." The stark fear in her voice could be heard by everyone.

"Buzz. We're going back. Turn around and come back. Real slow, boy. We voted no, Buzz. Pick Gracie up and bring her back. Slow, Buzz. Come on, boy, you can do it. Oh, God, he's never turned around in the middle. He doesn't know how to do it. If he doesn't turn around, I have to let him cross and then go and get him. Come on, Buzz, easy does it. Gracie, good girl, do what Buzz does."

Even from where he was standing, Matt could see the little dog start to shake. Buzz seemed frozen to the slat boards.

"He's afraid," Maggie whispered. "I have to go get him."

"I'll go, Gracie's my dog."

"Buzz is my dog. You're afraid of heights, Matt. It's my job. I can do it. Once Buzz sees me pick up Gracie, he'll go on. I know my dog."

"I'm going. I think you're more afraid of this bridge than me. It's a long way to the other side and then you have to come back. That doesn't make any sense. I want you to stay here! That's an order." To his people, he said, "Keep her here."

Maggie started to cry just as Gracie's foot slipped. Buzz moved then, the bridge swaying crazily. "Her foot's caught, she can't move and he can't pick her up," someone said. Buzz howled, the most human, heart-breaking sound Matt had ever heard. "I'm coming, Buzz. Don't move! What's the command he recognizes?" Matt said, stepping off the platform.

"Stay."

"Stay, Buzz."

It was Idaho all over again. Fear rivered through Matt as he made his way, step by step, across the bridge. *Don't think about Daniel dying on that mountain climb.* This wasn't Idaho, this was Wyoming, and he could help those dogs. He couldn't help Daniel. His rope broke. *Don't think about Daniel, don't think about the gorge. Don't think about your fear. Think about those two dogs. Think about how warm and soft Gracie feels when you hold her. Think about how much Maggie loves Buzz.*

Fog swirled about him. He swiped at it, sweat dripping down his face. He swiped at it, too. "I'm coming, I'm coming," he said over and over. He could hear Gracie's whimpers and Buzz's heartbreaking howls. His foot slipped on the wet slats. He started to shake as the bridge started to sway. Buzz howled louder. "Shhhh, I'm coming. It's okay, boy."

Suddenly, the fog was thicker, more dense. He couldn't see anything, even the slats he was walking on. He moved gingerly, one hand on the mesh side, the other stretched in front of him. When he felt the big dog's head, he thought he was going to pass out with relief. Where was Gracie? He dropped to his haunches, his hands feeling the slats and the narrow opening. The moment he felt the trembling little body, he relaxed.

"I got her, Buzz." The bridge swayed again as he struggled with the slats to loosen Gracie's paw. She yipped, either with pain or pleasure. A moment later, she was secure inside his shirt. "Okay, Buzz, we're going home," he said reaching for the dog's collar. "Gently now, a quarter turn and you're headed back." He could feel the Lab's trembling body as Buzz obeyed him.

Fifteen minutes later, they were all back on solid ground. Another fifteen minutes passed before Matt had the stamina to get to his feet. Anger unlike anything he'd ever experienced, stampeded through him. "Maggie, get everyone together and let's head home. I've got some things to say to the man in charge of this goddamn bridge."

The group watched as Matt rummaged in his back-pack for his bowie knife. They all cheered and clapped when he cut the nylon ropes that held the bridge to the platform. "That's the end of that!" he said, dusting his hands together dramatically.

"I wanted to do that a hundred times," Maggie said, throwing her arms around Matt's neck. "We're going back. Let's do some double time so we get there faster. I'm personally going to cook us some weenies with all the trimmings. Listen, I'm proud of all of you."

"Let's go home!" Matt said.

"I second that," Maggie said, snuggling next to Matt. "Thanks for saving my dog."

"Thanks for trusting and believing in me. So what do you say—are we going to take that journey to-gether?"

"Are you sure, Matt, that you're ready this time?"

"He's ready, he's ready," the group chorused.

"I'll spread the mustard on those weenies," Matt said. He lowered his voice. "To answer your question, yes, I'm ready. I want 'us' more than I've ever wanted anything in my life."

"I'm ready this time, too. Where are we going, what are we going to do?"

"Let's rent a four-by-four and drive back to my place. I have a lot of loose ends to tie up. Then we can do whatever we want. After the wedding. Do you still have that dress?"

"Sure do. And it still fits. What happened to your tux?"

"I sold it for twenty bucks and lit out for Baja. I hated that cummerbund."

"So don't wear one."

"What about that veil you put your shoe through?"

"Guess you're going to have to buy me another one.

I love your dog, Matt. Do you know they slept with me last night? I kept sending them back to you, but they kept coming back. That's all they did all night long, back and forth. I thought you were lonely. Guess they like me best, huh?"

"Guess so. I don't remember you talking so much in the old days. If you'd shut up for five minutes, I'd kiss you."

"So do it already. All you do is talk about things. Action is what counts. I have to warn you. These lips can sizzle a steak right off a grill or, in this case, a weenie. Pucker up, Mr. Star."

He did.

"Ahhhh."

"Hmmmnn."

"I liked that. Do it again," Maggie said.

He did.

"Will we live happily ever after, Matt?"

"Count on it, Mrs. Soon-To-Be-Star. Count on it."

"What are you going to do when we get back to camp, Matt? How are you going to explain that bridge to Ozzie?"

"What bridge?" Matt hooted.

They were a sorry group as they straggled into the compound. Ozzie ran out of the office, his face a mixture of fright and anger. "What's wrong? Did something happen?"

"Damn right something's wrong and damn straight something happened. I cut your goddamn bridge and it's at the bottom of the gorge. You told me a lie, Ozzie. You told me if I had the courage to cross that stinking bridge I'd be a man. I tortured myself for years. Jesus Christ, I wish I could tell you how many nightmares I had over that thing. You were wrong.

What makes a man is having the good sense not to cross that rickety excuse for a bridge. I do not think I will ever forgive you for playing with Maggie's head to convince her crossing that stupid bridge was . . . whatever the hell you thought it was. Do you hear me, Ozzie? You were wrong. I'm the one who voted no. I'm the one who had the sense not to cross it. There was so much fog you couldn't see the other side. Buzz went out and Gracie followed him. Never again, Ozzie. This has nothing to do with my fear of heights, either. All these years you played on people's fears. I don't know how Maggie did it. I'm willing to pay for the bridge. I'm not willing to forgive you, though. I'm leaving and Maggie is going with me. My people from the Red Course will leave tomorrow. That's all I have to say."

"Son, wait."

"I'm not your son, Ozzie. For years I thought I was because my own father never had time for me. You took an interest in me and I bought into it. I'm giving this back. I think I used up my credit where this cap is concerned. When you start fresh, you start fresh, no baggage. This cap is baggage."

Maggie handed over her cap to Lulu before she linked her arm with Matt's. "We're going to walk into town as soon as I get my gear together."

"Like hell you are. I'm driving you," Lulu said. "I'd like to kiss both of you for cutting down that bridge. In fact, I'm going to do just that. After I do that I'm going to call Jake Myers to get that honeymoon suite of his ready for you. 'Course, he'll marry you first. Not a peep, Ozzie, or I'm going to Ha-why-ee. By myself."

"Married? So soon?" Maggie said, her voice flustered.

"We can do all the frills later," Matt said. "You know, the church, the get up, the whole ball of wax."

"You're my kind of guy, Matt Star," Maggie said, planting a big kiss on his cheek.

"And you're my kind of girl."

"Let the journey begin," Maggie said.

FERN MICHAELS

It truly boggles my mind that people are interested in reading my bio, since I consider myself such an ordinary person, whose job is writing books. I don't do anything exciting like bungee jumping or white-water rafting. Although I did go tent camping *once* with my five kids. Notice that the key word here is "once."

I am a southern transplant. I haven't reached the status of Southern Belle yet. However, I live in a restored southern plantation house in South Carolina surrounded by acres of hybrid camellias and azaleas. At one time, the grounds had slave quarters that Hurricane Hugo destroyed. I rebuilt it, and it's now my office. The old carriage house is now a guest house. I have a dozen 300-year-old angel oak trees with dripping Spanish moss. There are no words to tell you how peaceful it is to sit under the trees to read or edit manuscript pages on a warm spring or summer day. I even have a hammock. However, I got tired of falling out of it, so now I have a chair that is deliciously tufted and soft.

My real treasure, though, is my veranda. I have two delightful Charleston rockers and two swings (I get a lot of company). Wicker stands that came with the house are full of ferns and all the bright summer flowers. I love to sit there in the evening and listen to the crickets and bullfrogs. Sometimes, I try to count the stars, but usually give up by nine o'clock. A mallard duck stops by on occasion. She comes right to the front door and is partial to popcorn. A morning dove (my son and I saved her from a wild cat last year) made a nest in one of the ferns, laid five eggs, hatched them, and kept house for three weeks. She's gone now, but she'll be back next year.

I also have a real, honest-to-goodness ghost. (She came with the house, and we have some documentation on her.) Her name is Mary Margaret. At least twice a week, she stops all the clocks in the house at ten minutes past nine. She messes with my computer and leaves weird messages. (High energy, I'm told.) She hides pillows, rearranges my condiments, moves my dishes. *Somebody* walks around upstairs at night. So far, I consider her a "friendly," and she hasn't spooked me yet. (I always know when she's here because my dogs look like they're at a tennis match.)

I live alone with my five dogs: Fred, Gus, Harry, Maxie, and Rosie. They're all Yorkies. Each of my five children lives within walking distance. I have two grandchildren, who visit often. When I'm not writing, which isn't often, I'm at one of the day-care centers my children manage, rocking the babies.

What I do is a job. Fortunately for me, it's a job I love. I can't imagine ever doing anything else. I was thrilled to the tip of my toes last year when I was inducted into the Literary Hall of Fame in New Jersey. I was honored to be included with such notables as Mary Higgins Clark, Belva Plain, Thomas Fleming, and Peter Benchley. It left me breathless. I think it was one of the highlights of my career.

I'd like to share one last thing before I sign off here

to get back to work. Several fans sent me an enormous bucket of gumdrops to eat while I work. The note that came with the gumdrops said my writing was so sweet they wanted to give me more energy to write faster. I'm going to pop the lid and pick out all the orange ones first.

To all my readers, keep reading, and I'll keep writing.

Heading Home

Janet Dailey

One

The morning breeze rustled through the autumn-yellow leaves of the aspen. A few yards below the white-barked trees, a horse and rider picked their way along a trail that skirted the stand of trees tucked along a mountain slope in southwestern New Mexico.

Kate Summers rode with the ease of one born to the saddle. At twenty-five years old, she was tall and boy-slim, with a mane of auburn hair as bright as a copper penny.

A beauty she wasn't. Her features were too strong for that. But Kate Summers was far from plain. There was a sculpted purity to her profile: the strong chin, the clean jawline, and the prominent ridging of cheekbone. Yet, her looks didn't fall under the heading of exotic or striking, but rather that of a handsome woman with an innate strength and confidence that most men found uncomfortable. As a result, Kate had dated rarely. And her one fling with love had left her badly bruised and twice as wary.

But the memory of that episode was far from her

mind as she rode along the trail. Her thoughts were on something else entirely.

Legally, Kate was trespassing. The land she traveled was no longer part of the Summers Ranch. Her father had sold this particular section while she was away on the horse show circuit last winter. The parcel now belonged to a stranger by the name of Josh Reynolds.

She hadn't met him. More than that, she had no desire to meet the new owner of the canyon land she loved so much.

But it was fall roundup time, and a section of downed fence had been a clear reminder that cattle paid no attention to boundary lines. There was grass and water in the canyon. If any of their livestock had strayed onto Reynold's land, Kate was certain she would find them.

Just ahead, the trail made a sharp bend to round the mountain slope. When Kate made the turn, the rocky trail dipped to a level stretch of ground that reached all the way to the mouth of the canyon. The buckskin gelding pricked its ears, looking ahead with interest.

Tall cottonwood trees crowded the banks of the small stream that ambled across the grassy floor of the narrow canyon. Walls of craggy stone rose on either side, a-tumble with giant boulders and bristling with spruce, piñon, and pines. Seeing it all again, Kate was gripped by the familiar feeling that she was coming home.

Agriculturally speaking, the section of land Reynolds now owned had little value other than this area of grass and water. But, to Kate's mind, the rugged beauty of it couldn't be measured in worth.

Initially, the raw grandeur of the scene claimed the whole of her attention, and her heart ached a little more over the loss of it. Then she noticed the first change to its landscape—utility poles marching along the rutted track that led from the distant county highway to the canyon.

Riding closer, Kate saw more changes. The old holding pen had been repaired. The paleness of new wood railings and posts stood out in sharp contrast to the weathered darkness of the old. A shed had been added, with a lean-to that would provide shelter for the muscular gray horse lazing in the pen. There was a tidiness to the whole area, as well, the brush and debris had been cleared away and the tall weeds cut.

Sunlight glinted on something metal beneath the cottonwood trees—at a spot extremely near the ruins of the old hacienda that had so completely captured her imagination as a girl. Focusing on the sheen of metal, Kate recognized the shape of a travel trailer, roughly twenty-five feet long, parked under the shelter of the trees. Utility lines ran toward it.

She had a sick feeling in her stomach the instant she saw evidence that even more extensive clearing had been done around the trailer—and the site of the old hacienda. She reined her horse in, unwilling to ride close enough to see what the new owner had done to the ruins.

Range etiquette demanded that Kate approach the trailer and advise its occupant that she was looking for stray livestock on his land. But there was no vehicle parked by either the trailer or the pen, no sign of life.

"It doesn't look like anyone is home, does it?" she said to her horse.

Convincing herself, Kate veered away from the trailer and pointed the buckskin toward the meandering stream, lifting the horse into a jog-trot. She knew every inch of the canyon, and every place a stray might go, of which there were few. She would check those and leave, with no one the wiser for her having been there.

As they approached the tree-lined bank, the buckskin slowed to a walk of its own accord. At this time of the year, the water ran clear and shallow, barely more than an inch deep in places. The sound of it running over its gravel bed was a restful murmur that echoed the soft whisperings of the wind in the trees and invited pause.

When the buckskin paused along the bank and stretched its nose toward the water, Kate dismounted to let the horse drink and take a short break herself. She took off her hat and shook loose her long hair, letting it tumble about her shoulders, then hung her hat on the saddle horn and idly scanned the area between the stream and the canyon's side wall. But she saw no cattle.

The buckskin pawed at the water between drinks, seeming to take as much pleasure in splashing the water as he did drinking it. Kate smiled at the horse's antics and crouched down upstream. Slipping off the bandana around her neck, she dipped one end of it in the water and wiped some of the morning's trail grime from her face and neck.

"Mind telling me what you're doing on my land?" The hard challenge came from somewhere behind her.

Startled, Kate straightened in a whirling turn and stared in silent shock at the man standing a few feet away, a trio of none-too-friendly looking dogs at his feet. But her gaze was on the man. He was tall with narrow hips that emphasized the width of his shoulders. His shirt was unbuttoned and hung loose, revealing the glisten of perspiration on his skin and the washboard flatness of his stomach.

"Who are you?" Kate dragged her gaze up to the lean, tanned lines of his face. The sight of it was like a body blow. The man was drop-dead handsome.

"The owner," he snapped.

"You are Josh Reynolds." She was stunned and angry at the same time. She knew his kind. Too well.

"And who might you be?" Some of the hardness went out of his voice, but his sky-blue eyes continued to study her with close interest.

"Kate Summers," she stated with deliberate coolness.

His head lifted in faint surprise. "You're Bick Summer's daughter."

"Yes."

"You weren't here when I bought this place off your father last February," he recalled. "But I've heard a lot about you. Unfortunately, no one mentioned you have red hair."

His glance traveled over her auburn mane, a glint of more than passing interest in his eyes. When his mouth curved in a lazy smile guaranteed to curl a woman's toes, Kate was glad she was wearing boots. She would be damned if she would let Josh Reynolds see that he had any effect on her whatsoever.

"They probably didn't mention it because it isn't important." Kate had to fight the urge to snatch her hat off the saddle horn and jam it on her head.

"To them, maybe. But it would have given me a clue as to who you were," he said, then paused a beat, his smile taking on a rueful quality. "Sorry. I don't know where my manners went. I should be offering to put some coffee on at the trailer. Having neighbors stop by is new for me."

"This isn't a neighborly visit." Kate wanted that crystal-clear. "We're in the middle of fall gather. I noticed some downed fence and decided to see if any of our cattle had strayed over here. There wasn't any vehicle in sight, so I assumed no one was here."

"I was stringing fence in the canyon." He jerked a thumb over his shoulder.

Kate had an instant image of Josh Reynolds at work, shirtless, muscles rippling as he stretched wire. It was enough to touch off a disturbing shiver of awareness. To shake it, she looked beyond him and made out the vague shape of a vehicle parked twenty yards away, the bulk of it obscured by the intervening trees and brush.

"I haven't seen any Bar S stock around," he said, referring to the brand of the Summers Ranch. "And if any of your cattle had strayed into the canyon, my dogs would have let me know about it."

The smaller of the three dogs, a brindle tan with a smattering of dark, leopardlike spots on its back, left his side to approach Kate with a shy, tentative wag of his tail. She recognized the friendly overture for what it was and held out the back of her hand for the dog to sniff.

"They aren't much for watchdogs," she remarked, bending slightly to lightly scratch the dog's head when he indicated a willingness to be touched.

"I wouldn't say that. They definitely let me know you were here."

She caught the warm inflection in his voice, the kind that hinted he was glad they had met, the kind that suggested his interest might be more than friendly— the kind she had misread once before. It was not a mistake she would ever make again.

"That's all that counts, I guess." Avoiding his gaze, Kate reached for her hat. "It's time I got back to work and let you get back to yours."

"Speaking of work," he said. "I've been meaning to call your father, but maybe you can help me."

"With what?" She slipped on her hat, snagging the string under her chin.

"These ruins I found." He instantly had her undivided attention. "I uncovered what looks like an old stone floor."

"The courtyard," Kate murmured in surprise, stunned that it still existed. From the moment she had learned her father had sold the old Montoya property, she had been haunted by visions of the new owner bulldozing the ruins into a rubble pile and hauling it all away.

"A courtyard—is that what it is?" He frowned.

"That's what I always called it." Suddenly, she had to see it again. Leading the buckskin, she walked past Josh Reynolds and cut through the trees, drawn like a magnet to the site of the old hacienda and its flag-stoned terrace.

He fell in beside her. "I suspected that a house had once stood there."

"A hacienda, built out of adobe brick."

"How long ago? Do you know?"

"I'm not sure. Maybe a hundred years or more. I do know the hacienda was destroyed by fire when my grandfather was six years old. Not long after that, the Montoyas—the family that owned it—sold the land to my great-grandfather and moved away. To Texas, I think."

Her steps slowed when she neared the site. She dropped the reins, leaving the buckskin to graze, a sense of wonder stealing over her. For a moment, it was as if she had been transported back to the days of her childhood, when she had stood on almost the same spot and gazed at the flat stones laid out so closely and precisely.

Kate stepped onto them, placing each foot carefully, just as she had done long ago. She walked to the edge of a large, square area directly in the center of the terrace, where there were no stones, only dirt.

"I dug around a bit," Josh said from behind her, "but I could only find chunks of crumbled brick. There weren't any stones in that area at all."

"I know." Kate smiled. "That's the way I found it, too, when I cleared off the terrace. I decided that the Montoyas had a fountain here. It's the perfect spot for one, with the front door right over there."

She swung around to face the former site of the hacienda and received another surprise. No longer was it weed-choked and overgrown with brush. It had been cleared to bare dirt and crumbled walls, revealing the building's dimensions and a partial layout of its interior rooms.

"It's larger than I remember." Kate stepped over the remnants of an outer wall and into the house itself, completely unaware of the glow on her face—or the attention Josh Reynolds was paying to it. "When I was a little girl, you could still find pieces of charred vigas scattered around inside. You did a lot of work clearing away all the brush and debris. It must have taken you days to do this."

"Days and then some, considering I could only work at it whenever I had an hour or two to spare."

"Why did you do it?" It was suddenly imperative that Kate learn his reason.

"In the beginning it was sheer curiosity. I wanted to know what kind of structure had stood here. It didn't take me long to figure out it had once been a house. The more I studied the site, the more I knew it was an ideal location for a home. To be truthful, I don't fancy spending too many more months in that trailer," he said. "Once I knew I wanted to build here, I went ahead and cleared it off so I could start planning how I wanted the house laid out. Some of the floor plan is obvious, like the living room here, near the front door. But I can't decide if the kitchen should be on this side"—he pointed to the right—"or if the bedrooms should be there."

"I vote for the kitchen," Kate said. "You'll have morning light the minute the sun climbs over the canyon rim. And if you tuck it in the corner, you'll have a south breeze in the afternoons to cool the room."

"You would, wouldn't you?" He nodded thoughtfully.

"The bedrooms can go along the back of the house, with doors that open onto a rear patio, so you can sit outside in the evenings before you turn in and listen to the babble of the stream."

"How did you see all that so quickly?"

Kate laughed. "I have built this house a thousand times in my head."

His smile was wide and warm, carving lethally attractive grooves in his cheeks. "You have definitely had a head start on me. I'm only up to about twenty. Maybe you could give me a hand with the floor plan."

She seriously considered it for all of two seconds, then came sharply to her senses. She couldn't design the house of her dreams for someone else to live in. The mere thought of it made her ache.

"Sorry, but it's your house," Kate said with a quick, firm shake of her head. "You need to come up with your own ideas and build it the way you see it."

"I'm open to suggestions, just the same." There was that winning smile again, potently male.

Kate felt the pull of it and immediately turned away. "I'm afraid I'm too busy to spare the time." She walked toward her horse.

"If you change your mind, let me know."

"I'm not likely to change my mind," she told him and swung into the saddle, conscious of his curious gaze.

"Give my regards to your father," he added.

She gave a curt nod in answer and reined the buckskin around, touching a spur to it. In truth, she had no intention of mentioning this meeting to her father.

Two

Two days after her meeting with Josh Reynolds, Kate rode along the right flank of the gathered herd. The cattle were a Hereford/Brahma cross, bred for their toughness and adaptability to New Mexico's climate and terrain.

Saddle leather creaked as her fifty-year-old father, Bick Summers, rose in his stirrups and made a survey of the herd as if he expected trouble. "We're about a mile from the holding pens," he called to the other riders, raising his voice to make himself heard above the low rumble of hooves and occasional bellow from the herd. "As soon as we catch sight of the wing fence, that wily old horned devil will make a break for it and take her gang with her. She's stuck in the middle of the herd now. Let's bunch them up and try to keep her there."

Wasting no time with a verbal response, Kate pressed her horse closer to the herd to carry out his order. Automatically, she made a visual search to locate the notorious cow that had managed to evade capture for the last three years. She had one quick glimpse of a cow with a respectable set of horns and a distinctively jagged patch of brown splashed on her white face before the commotion began.

"Here she comes—your side, Kate!" Bick shouted the warning as the right side of the herd bulged.

With a touch of the rein and a squeeze of the legs, Kate sent the blood bay stallion beneath her straight toward the area. It erupted just as she reached it. A half-dozen animals broke from the herd, with the wily cow leading the charge.

The stallion changed directions in a flash and raced after the fleeing band. With the horse's speed and quickness, Kate was ahead of them within seconds. But when she tried to turn them and drive them back toward the herd, the cow hooked a horn at the stallion, forcing Kate to swing her mount out of reach.

For the first time, Kate questioned her decision to ride the prize-winning stallion, Cayenne Red, this morning. It was one thing to risk injuring his legs helling over broken ground the way they were, but quite another to expose the champion horse to the gore of a cow's horns.

Even as she heard her father shouting, "Let the devil go!" she crowded close and made one last attempt to turn the outlaw cow.

This time there was no idle swipe of a horn in warning, but a vicious and determined hook meant to inflict damage. Kate jerked the stallion away as the tip of the cow's horn raked his shoulder.

Immediately, she reined in the stallion and jumped from the saddle to determine the extent of the injury. Her heart lodged in her throat at the sight of bright red blood mixing with the sweat on his shoulder. But a closer look revealed that the raking horn had barely sliced the skin. To her relief, it was a minor scratch that would quickly heal.

Kate dragged in a deep, shaky breath and laid a soothing hand on the stallion's neck. "It's okay, big guy. No harm done, thank God." She added the last words in a soft undertone.

The bay stallion snorted and danced restively under her touch, still full of energy and eager to be on the move again. Kate obliged him by gathering up the reins and mounting.

In the saddle again, she threw a glance after the small band of renegade cattle. Now that they were no longer being pursued, they had slowed to a fast trot. Kate watched as the last of them dropped into a rocky draw. She swung the stallion around and rode back toward the herd.

It was noon time when the last of the cattle were driven into the holding pens and the crew took a break before the sorting process began. Kate led the stallion to the shady side of the horse trailer and rummaged through its storage compartment until she found a clean rag and tube of antiseptic salve.

As she started to wash the shoulder wound, her father came over to take his first look at the injury to the ranch's prize stallion. "Don't say it, Dad. I know I should have broke off pursuit as soon as the cow took her first swipe at us."

"It's my fault." Bick Summers yanked off his hat and ran his fingers through his prematurely silver hair in a gesture of self-disgust. "I knew that she-devil of a cow no longer had any respect for a horse. After the way she knocked Manny's horse down last spring, I was a fool to tell you to go after her—especially on Red." Bending closer, he inspected the wound. "Fortunately, it doesn't appear to be anything more serious than a scratch. If he wasn't so agile and lightning fast, it could have been a lot worse."

"But it wasn't." Kate refused to look on the dark side; the view was too scary and the memory of the heart-stopping moment when she first saw the blood was still too fresh.

She smeared a glob of antiseptic salve into the cut, more as a precaution than a necessity. The stallion never flinched, proof that the scratch was minor indeed.

"How is the big red one?" Manny Ortega walked toward them, each stride marked by the chink of his spurs.

Kate and her father turned as one to face the long-time employee of the Summers Ranch. For an instant, the resemblance between father and daughter was striking. Each had the same long, slender body, the same faint dusting of freckles across their faces, the same rich brown color of eyes, the same slope to the jawline, and the same tilt of the head.

"Red is fine, Manny." Kate smiled, and the differences between them became marked.

In contrast to her father's roughly hewn features, hers were finely sculpted, like her mother's. His lips were narrow and firm, while hers were soft and round, and his hair was starkly silver next to the dark copper shade of hers.

"*Bueno.* The big red one is too fine a horse to tangle with that devil-cow," Manny stated, bringing his short, stocky body to a halt.

"I couldn't agree more," Bick remarked somewhat grimly. "It's for damned sure something has to be done about that cow. Every time she gets away from a gather, she gets harder to handle in the next one."

"Sí." Manny nodded in quick agreement. "The devil-cow she takes more followers with her each time. Last spring she had only three. Now she makes outlaws out of two more."

Bick Summers stared in the direction of the distant rocky draw, his mouth tight with displeasure. "As soon as we finish this fall gather, we're going after her."

"I think we will not have much luck," Manny said with an idle shrug. "Maybe you should consider siccing Reynolds and his dogs on the devil-cow."

"Reynolds." Kate stiffened in instant resistance. "Do you mean the man who bought the old Montoya place?"

Detecting the faint challenge in her voice, Bick exchanged a quiet look with Manny.

"Sí, Josh Reynolds. He is the one I mean," Manny confirmed.

The sale of the Montoya place to Reynolds was a subject Bick Summers had come to avoid. It had been purely a business decision—and the right one as far as he was concerned. He had never once guessed that his daughter was so emotionally attached to that particular piece of the ranch's property.

Not that she had ever argued with him over his decision. He could have dealt with a display of temper. But Bick Summers didn't know how to handle her silence or the look of hurt in her eyes whenever the subject of the sale came up.

"Josh Reynolds is a good man and a hard worker," he stated, succumbing to the need to fill the sudden silence, a silence that somehow added to his vague feelings of guilt. "You should ride over there one afternoon and see the changes he's made to the old place."

"I have." She turned back to the stallion.

He gave her a stunned look. "When?"

"A couple days ago." She flipped up the stirrup to loosen the cinch a notch. "There was some fence down, so I rode over to see if any of our stock had strayed into the canyon."

"Then you must have seen the improvements he's made."

"I noticed them."

"Damn it, Kate, why have you taken this attitude?" Exasperation riddled his voice. "It isn't right for you to take it out on Reynolds because I sold him the Montoya place."

"I don't blame him for buying it, Dad. But I do think he was foolish." Finished with loosening the cinch, Kate made busy work of checking the rest of the saddle rigging. "We all know that one section of land will never support enough cattle or sheep for him to make a living off the place, and it isn't good for anything else."

Manny bobbed his head in a nod of agreement. "Everything you said about the Montoya place is true, but Reynolds does not depend on it for his living. He does many other things to bring in money."

"Is that right?" Her voice was coolly indifferent.

"*Sí.* He buys and sells horses. Does some breaking and training of them, too. Sometimes he hires out to do day work at the ranches around here. And he and his dogs are getting a reputation for catching outlaw cattle."

"Good for him," Kate retorted.

"He has cowdogs?" Bick Summers cast a questioning glance of surprise at Manny. "I hadn't heard that."

"*Sí.* At church last Sunday I saw Luis Gonzalez. He works up north for the Great Southern Cattle Company. They hired Reynolds to catch some cows that they had not been able to gather. Luis said it was a sight to behold to watch Reynolds and his dogs take care of the wild ones."

"Maybe I should talk to Reynolds about ours." A thoughtful frown creased Summers's forehead. "We had a couple cows get away during our gather up in the summer pasture. It's the second time for one of them."

"In my opinion we don't need any help catching cows that have turned into bunch-quitters." Kate lifted her chin with a hint of challenge. "But if you want to take pity on this Reynolds fellow and give him work when we could do the job ourselves, that's your decision. It's a terrible waste of money, though." She collected the stallion's reins. "Come on, big guy. Let's go get some water."

She led the stallion away, her shoulders stiffly squared in disapproval. Bick watched her for a moment, then looked away shaking his head in frustration.

"I swear, Manny, I don't know what has gotten into her lately. Ever since I sold that land. Hellfire, it was practically worthless ground, all rocks and canyon with little graze. That spring-fed creek was the best thing it had going for it."

Manny Ortega nodded in agreement, but made no comment. It would soon be twenty years that he had worked for Bick Summers. He had watched Kate grow up and seen her father's hair turn from a sorrel red to silver.

Ten years ago, he had stood behind them at the cemetery when Amy Summers was laid to rest. The epitaph on her gravestone read Beloved Wife and Mother, simple words that explained so clearly the grief the husband and daughter felt.

Raising a teen-aged girl alone had not been easy for Bick Summers. Those years had been confusing and uncertain times for both father and daughter.

On many occasions, Manny had listened silently while Bick vented his frustration, recognizing that it was an ear Bick wanted rather than advice. He suspected this time it was the same.

"This ranch has been in our family for four generations," Bick declared in growing irritation. "And over the years, the ranch has been bigger and it's been smaller. For the life of me, I can't understand why she is so upset with me for selling the Montoya place."

"But you forget all the times Kate played in the ruins of the old hacienda when she was a young girl," Manny offered the gentle reminder. "It was a place of dreams for her."

"She did love playing there, pretending those ruins were her house," he recalled. "It was one of the few times she acted like a girl instead of a tomboy. Maybe I didn't do a very good job of raising her without Amy around to show her the woman side of things."

"Kate is who she is. Your wife could not have made her into something different if she had lived. If you remember, Kate would never wear pink dresses with frilly ruffles. But she was no less girl, as she is no less a woman now."

"I guess not," Bick said, sighing. "She certainly isn't a little girl anymore. She gave away all her toys a long time ago. Which makes it all the harder for me to understand this attachment she has for the Montoya place."

"Ah, but it is never good to give away everything from our childhood," Manny said. "Too often, there is one we wish we would have kept. Me, I had a small wooden top that my uncle carved. To my regret, I no longer have it. I think Kate wishes she still had her playhouse in the ruins."

"Unfortunately, the property is sold. She needs to accept that."

"I think she has," Manny told him. "But in her heart, she still mourns the loss. Sadly, there is always turmoil when the head and the heart don't agree on a thing."

"And I'm caught in the backlash of it." Bick realized this even as his expression softened in new compassion and understanding for his daughter.

"You *and* Josh Reynolds are caught in it," Manny pointed out. "But life must go on.

"True." Bick nodded and glanced at the pens of milling cattle. "And we have a bunch of sorting to do before this day is through."

"And a devil-cow to catch," Manny reminded him. "Will you call in Josh Reynolds?"

"If that man and his dogs are as experienced at catching cows as potentially dangerous as that she-devil, you're damned right I will."

"Kate will not be happy about that."

"She probably won't. But I'm calling him tonight just the same."

Three

$\mathcal{A}$ dusty blue pickup with a trio of dogs riding in the back and a horse trailer in tow rolled into the main yard of the Summers Ranch. Kate threw a quick glance at it, tension coiling anew as the pickup pulled to a stop near the barn.

Josh Reynolds had arrived.

Kate jerked her gaze back to the saddled sorrel gelding and concentrated all her attention on buckling the rear cinch while her father and Manny went to greet the man stepping out of the truck. As soon as she finished, she led the horse to the stock trailer and handed the gelding over to Manny's son, Carlos, for loading. Turning, she faced the three men still standing by the blue pickup. After a split-second pause, she walked toward them.

As much as she wished her father had never hired Josh Reynolds to catch the bunch-quitters, it never occurred to Kate not to go along this morning. Avoiding disagreeable tasks had never been a part of her makeup.

And seeing Josh Reynolds again definitely fell under the category of disagreeable tasks.

He had his back to Kate, giving her a chance to look him over unobserved. He was dressed in typical ranch clothes, denim jacket and Levis. The spurs on his boots had blunt-tipped rowels, serviceable rather than fancy, and his jeans showed the fading of wear, as did the dark cowboy hat he wore.

Search as she might, Kate couldn't find fault with him.

Her father saw Kate first and nodded in her direction, saying to Josh Reynolds, "I don't believe you've met my daughter, Kate."

"As a matter of fact, I have," he interrupted smoothly and turned to greet her, smiling warmly. "Hello, Kate. Good to see you again."

She truly thought she was prepared to come face to face with Josh Reynolds again. She had definitely remembered how ruggedly handsome he was. But she had forgotten the impact he had on her senses—the instant leap of her pulse, the delicious little tinglings all through her body, and the husky sound of his voice that was so irritatingly sexy. It was a dangerous mistake.

"When did the two of you meet?" Her father looked at her with a questioning frown.

"A couple days ago, when I stopped by the canyon to check for strays." Kate focused on her father and did her best to ignore the man beside her. Her best proved to be very poor. "I told you about it."

"You didn't say anything about meeting Josh."

She raised one shoulder in a vague shrug. "You didn't ask."

One of the dogs in the back of the pickup whined for attention. Kate pivoted toward it, seizing on the distraction. Her father did the same.

"Manny told us you worked with dogs." Bick Summers studied the short-haired dogs with broad, hound-like heads. Two were brindle in color, with a dark, leopardlike spotting. The third dog was a speckled black and tan. "Catahoulas, aren't they?"

"That's right," Josh confirmed. "You could say they are more in the line of law enforcers than they are herding dogs."

"Is that right?" Kate barely managed to contain a smile when the brindle dog that had made friends with her at the canyon draped itself over the side of the pickup bed and wiggled with excitement at seeing her again.

Law enforcer indeed, she thought and walked over to give the dog a pat. It went wild with ecstasy at her touch and pushed closer, trying to lick her face. Laughing, she dodged its long tongue.

"I'm glad to see you again, too," Kate declared. "What's your name anyway?"

"I call him Trooper," Josh said. "He's a young dog, a few days short of a year old and still with some puppy in him."

"I can tell." Kate kept her attention riveted on the dog and tried to block out the closeness of its owner.

After a brief hesitation, Josh Reynolds leaned over and firmly pushed the young dog back onto the truck bed, ordering it to stay. Crushed by the command, the dog sank back on its haunches and gave Kate a woe-begone look that tugged at her heart.

"It's okay, Trooper." As she started to give the dog a reassuring pat, Josh Reynolds laid a restraining hand on her arm, checking the movement.

"If you don't mind, I would rather you didn't pet him," he said. "I want Trooper to concentrate on the job he has to do today, and not go looking for attention. Young dogs can be easily sidetracked sometimes."

"He is your dog, Mr. Reynolds." Kate stepped back, stung by his inference that she was somehow interfering. "But it's been my experience that animals respond better to kindness and praise."

"They usually do. But I want to be the one doing the praising," he replied, gently but firmly putting Kate in her place.

"As I said, he's your dog." Abruptly, she turned on her heel, throwing over her shoulder, "The horses are all loaded. We can leave whenever you're ready."

Bick Summers watched his daughter walk away. "I'm sorry about that, Reynolds. She isn't usually so rude."

"I'm glad to hear it." Wryness tugged at one corner of his mouth, his expression turning thoughtful as he gazed after her. Then he pulled his glance around to Bick. "I'm ready to go after that devil-cow of yours if you are."

Bick nodded that he was. "Manny here thinks he saw the cow and her bunch shortly after dawn near the east fence line. We'll check that area first," he said. "Fall in behind us and we'll lead the way."

"Will do." He turned toward his truck.

"I will ride with you," Manny said.

"Be my guest." Josh waved him toward the pickup's passenger side while Bick Summers headed after his daughter.

An hour later, Manny's sharp eyes spotted the renegade cow and her followers grazing in a grassy hollow a short distance from the fence line. The alert cow took immediate note of their arrival and watched until the first saddled horse emerged from the trailers. Then, with lofty disdain, the cow went back to grazing.

Kate led her sorrel gelding off to the side and stopped to tighten the saddle cinch. Down the way, Josh Reynolds unloaded a big gray gelding from his double-horse trailer. Kate automatically ran an appraising glance over the animal and found a lot to like about the big gray horse—which was more than she could say for its owner.

The thought brought an instant attack of conscience. In all honesty, she could find little to dislike about Josh Reynolds—not his looks or the way he treated his dogs, not the extensive work he'd done in the canyon or his rescue of the ruins. That's what scared her.

Her gaze strayed toward the dogs still waiting in the back end of the pickup. There was an air of tension about them, their whole attention glued to Josh Reynolds as they watched his every move. As he started to cinch up his saddle, he finally glanced their way. All three dogs quivered in anticipation.

"Cap, Sarge, Trooper, out." A hand signal accompanied the command. "It's time to go to work."

The dogs bounded from the truck in an explosion of energy. For a moment they milled around him, then cast about, checking out the new scents. The instant Josh Reynolds swung into the saddle, the dogs were back, ranging alongside him as he trotted his horse forward to join the rest of the group.

Kate jerked her attention back to her task and hurriedly secured the trailing end of the latigo in its keeper. With reins in hand, she unhooked the stirrup from the saddle horn and let it drop. As she prepared to mount, young Trooper ran up to her, panting a happy greeting.

Hesitating, Kate looked down at the dog, then up, locking eyes with its handsome owner. Something sizzled in the air between them, touching off tremors of awareness through her.

Irritated by her reaction to the man, she fought back with the only weapon she had on hand. She reached down and gave the dog a good scratching behind the ears, murmuring little sounds of approval to it. The dog responded with tail-wagging delight and danced about her legs when she drew her hand away.

Careful to avoid any eye contact with Josh Reynolds, Kate mounted her horse. Once in the saddle, she gave him a cool, sideways glance.

"It isn't my fault you have such a friendly dog," she said.

His mouth curved in the smallest of smiles. "With luck, some of it will rub off on you."

With amusement still edging his mouth, he touched a heel to the gray and rode up to join her father, leaving Kate with the uncomfortable knowledge that she had been duly chastised. Worse than that, she had deserved it. And it wasn't like her to behave like a spiteful child.

Once everyone was mounted, they set out after the renegade cow. Her father and Josh Reynolds took the lead. Kate lagged behind, still battling with her conscience.

But there was no getting around it; she knew what she had to do.

She kicked the sorrel into a lope and rode to the front, drawing rein alongside Josh Reynolds. Her father took one look at her face and discreetly slowed his horse, falling back to give Kate a measure of privacy. She stared straight ahead, the words sticking in her throat.

"Beautiful morning, isn't it?" Josh observed with a sincerity in his voice that startled Kate into taking notice of the world around her.

There was a clarity to the morning air that made colors and shapes stand out sharply. Ahead, the southernmost mountains of the Mogollon Range towered above a desert floor dotted with yucca and cholla cactus, newly greened from last week's rain. Over it all was the incredible blue sweep of sky.

Drinking in the invigorating sight of it, Kate smiled. "It is very beautiful."

"At least we agree on that if nothing else," he said with a trace of drollness that snapped her back to the business at hand.

"Look—" She paused to choose her words. "Perhaps I was out of line earlier."

"Perhaps?" he mocked.

Furious with him, Kate resorted to sarcasm. "Whatever you do, don't make this easy."

"I won't." His eyes glinted with amusement. "I've always believed that if you have to eat humble pie, you might as well take a big slice of it."

"All right." Maybe if she hadn't been choking on her portion, she would have had the grace to smile. As it was, the discovery that Josh Reynolds had a sense of humor only made it harder to swallow. "I was wrong to criticize your training methods."

"Especially when you don't know what they are," he added, then smiled. "Your apology is accepted, Kate."

She hesitated, then plunged ahead with the rest of it, needing to lay it all out. "You might as well know that I wasn't in favor of hiring you. As far as I'm concerned, we could have brought these bunch-quitters in without the help of you and your dogs."

"No doubt you could have, after considerable wear and tear on both horses and riders. My dogs will spare you all that and do it in half the time it would have taken you."

"We'll see," Kate replied, not totally convinced.

He slanted her a look, a gleam of lively interest in his blue eyes. "I'll tell you what, I'll make you a friendly wager." She went cold at his words. "I'll bet my dogs can bring that renegade cow and her bunch all the way to the pens before the first loop is thrown on her. If they don't, I'll buy you the biggest steak dinner around."

"And if they do?" She looked straight ahead, gripped by an awful sense of déjà vu.

"You'll buy me dinner," he answered with a lazy grin. "So what do you say—is it a bet?"

"No."

"Why not? Don't you like the odds?"

"I don't like the game." She reined her horse away and circled around to the rear of the group, memories flooding back of another "friendly" wager two years ago that had ultimately led to heartbreak.

Dinner had been the stakes that time, too, when Cody Jones had bet Kate that he would score higher in the reining class than she would on Cayenne Red. Kate had won the bet and lost her heart to the blond-haired, brown-eyed cowboy with incredibly sexy good looks.

She was convinced that no woman could have fallen harder than she had—or been so blind to the fact that the man was a natural-born flirt. His smiles, the gleam in his eyes, the long talks over coffee, the natural way his arm slid around her shoulders, the few quick kisses, none of it had meant anything to him. Their accidental meetings on the show circuit had been just that—accidental. He hadn't changed his schedule in order to compete in the same shows with her like she'd thought.

For an entire month, Kate had lived in a dream

world of her own making, believing that Cody Jones was pursuing her, reading things into his every action to support that belief.

All of it had come crashing down when she ran into Cody with some Texas rodeo queen who could have passed for a Dallas Cowboy cheerleader. He had introduced the girl as his fiancée. The news had nearly killed her.

"Look!" Manny called out. "The devil-cow knows we are coming for her. There she goes."

Caught up in her own black thoughts, Kate had almost forgotten about the cow they hunted. But there the outlaw was, about a half mile ahead of them, trotting off with her band in the opposite direction, heading for rougher country that would make pursuit difficult.

Josh Reynolds noticed it at the same time. He whistled to his dogs and sent them after the cattle with a sweep of his arm. To Kate's surprise, he reined in and watched the three dogs streak toward the cows.

"Aren't you going after them?" She pulled up her own horse, as did the others.

He shook his head. "Not yet. It's better to let the dogs give the cows a lesson in speed limits. Once they come to an understanding, it will be time for us to move in."

"Understanding" wasn't the word Kate would have used to describe the ensuing confrontation. It looked more like a war to her, full of churned-up dust and considerable barking and bellowing while the two sides battled it out.

The Catahoula dogs were not the typical get-behind-and-nip-at-the-heels kind of cowdogs. They attacked the cattle from the front, forcing them to slow down and bunch up.

When the action had lost most of its fury, Josh signaled they could move in. Fanning out, they rode closer and maneuvered into position to drive the bunch-quitters to the holding pens two miles away.

Again, they stopped while the dogs foiled another bovine attempt at escape. Then they moved out, pushing the renegade cow and her small gang toward the pens.

Each time the cows shifted into a trot or tried to make a break for it, the dogs were in their faces, slowing them, turning them, and bunching them up again.

Kate noticed that Trooper was in the thick of it every time. If, as Josh had said, this was a learning experience for the young dog, then he was definitely a star pupil.

Things went well, with few serious incidents until they were within a half mile of the wing fences that funneled into the holding pens. As soon as the renegade cow caught sight of them, she made her stand.

Mad with fury, she charged the dogs, hooking her horns at whichever one was closest. The dogs darted, dodged, and danced out of reach, while giving little ground. When her scatter-gun technique met with little success, the cow zeroed in on a target.

With dismay, Kate saw that it was Trooper. Off to her left, she heard Josh say in a low, earnest voice, "Get him out of there, Cap."

As if hearing the command, the older, spotted-tan dog rushed in, but the maddened cow wouldn't be distracted. Twice young Trooper narrowly eluded the twisting horns. The third time the cow rolled him.

Out of the corner of her eye, Kate saw Josh shake out his lariat. But the young dog was on his feet in a flash and attacked the cow with a vengeance, driving her back.

"Good job, Trooper!" Kate cried, instinctively cheering him on.

At the sound of her voice, the young dog swung his head to look her way, his tail wagging. The cow was instantly on him. There was a yelp of pain.

Horrified, Kate saw the cow fling the dog in the air. Then her view was blocked by Josh Reynolds as he spurred his gray horse forward, swinging his rope.

Suddenly, everything went into fast-forward. As Josh's lariat settled over the cow's horns and he turned off, dallying the rope, her father and Manny raced in and stacked two more loops on top of his. With the cow trapped between the three ropes, they took off at a canter for the pens while Carlos hurried the remainder of the cow's gang after them. Kate galloped up to check on Trooper.

The dog lay motionless on the rocky ground, one front leg bent at an unnatural angle. Blood flowed from a deep and ugly gash that ran from his chest halfway back to his haunches, slicing through veins and muscles. There was a moment when Kate first knelt beside him that she thought he was dead. Then she heard a low, extremely faint moan.

He was alive.

"You'll make it, Trooper. Just hang in there," she murmured, her glance running in concern to the bloodstained sand beneath him.

Realizing that she had to check the bleeding, Kate yanked the wild rag from around her neck and jammed it into the long wound. But there wasn't nearly enough material to do the job. Hurriedly, she shrugged out of her denim jacket and peeled off her chambray shirt, then wadded up the shirt and stretched it the length of the gash, pressing it in.

The dog whimpered once, sharply, as she applied

pressure along the rib cage area. Worried that he might have broken ribs, possibly even punctured a lung, Kate paused and moved to the dog's head. But there was no bloody froth coming from his nostrils. She took that as a positive sign even though she knew it didn't mean he didn't have other internal injuries.

She ran a trembling hand lightly over the dog's broad forehead. "I'm sorry, Trooper. It's my fault. If I hadn't—" A lump filled her throat, choking off the rest of the words.

In her mind, she could still see that moment frozen in time when the dog had turned in response to her voice. But remembering that wouldn't help Trooper now.

Swiping at a tear that slipped onto her cheek, Kate turned back to recheck the wound and see what else she could do for him. The makeshift compression bandage seemed to be doing the trick.

Shock was her only remaining concern. She draped her jacket over the dog to keep him warm and carefully tucked in the sides. Suddenly, there was nothing left to do.

Kate shifted around and gently cradled the dog's head on her lap. She shivered once, conscious of both the air's lingering coolness against her bare skin and the scant coverage her sports bra offered. It was an awareness that grew moments later, when Josh Reynolds galloped up.

Part of her objected to the fact that, with her athletically slim build, he would clearly see that she wasn't the type of woman men lusted after. Still, Kate refused to make any attempt to cover her front.

He was out of the saddle before the big gray horse came to a stop. "How bad is it?"

He hesitated only a split second before kneeling

beside the dog. But it was long enough for his sweeping glance to assess the bareness of her top—and the smallness of her breasts.

Kate told herself she didn't care. It was the dog that mattered. "Be careful. He has a broken front leg and a deep, ugly tear on his side." But Josh had already lifted her jacket to see that for himself. "I think I managed to get the worst of the bleeding stopped, but it will need stitching."

"I can see that," he said, making his own examination of the dog.

"He might have some broken ribs, too."

He handed back her jacket. "You'll need this," he said and pulled off his own coat to wrap around the dog.

Her father joined them. The other two dogs were with him. The large, leopard-spotted female trotted over to Trooper, sniffed him, and whined anxiously.

"It's okay, Cap," Josh spoke softly to the dog. "Your boy will be fine."

"How bad is it?" Bick Summers asked.

"I need to get him to the vet." With the greatest of care, Josh scooped the dog into the cradle of his arms and stood up, turning toward his horse.

After hastily buttoning her jacket, Kate hurried over to the big gray and held the horse's head while Josh mounted with the dog in his arms.

"I'm coming with you," she said and went to retrieve her own horse.

"I have a cell phone in the pickup. I'll call Doc Petersen and let him know you're coming in," her father volunteered.

Four

$\mathcal{K}$ate cradled Trooper in her arms, trying to absorb the bouncing and jostling caused by the rough, uneven grade the pickup traveled on. Josh was behind the wheel, his gaze fixed on the road ahead.

The silence in the cab was heavy, like a weight that pressed down harder with every passing minute. But Kate made no attempt to break it until they had reached the relative smoothness of the highway.

"I want you to know I am fully aware that I'm the reason Trooper got hurt," she said. "I'm sorry. Truly sorry."

His expression never lost its look of tight-lipped hardness. If anything, it turned a little grimmer.

"Maybe now you understand why I didn't want you fooling with him." There was a faint snap to his voice. "Pups are naturally affectionate. Part of training a young dog is teaching him the difference between work and play. It isn't like he's being taught to flush pheasant or quail. His job is to catch feral cattle. That's risky business. He has to have his wits about him because distractions can be dangerous. Praise is given *only* when the job is done."

"I had that coming." Like him, Kate looked straight ahead.

"Forget it," he said, and expelled a long breath, releasing tension. "I know you didn't want this to happen any more than I did."

"I didn't deliberately call out to him." Kate looked down at the dog in her arms, then worked a hand free to stroke his head. "It's just that when I saw the way he went for that cow after she had rolled him, I was so impressed that the words just popped out."

A faint smile touched his mouth as Josh glanced at the dog. "You can't question his courage."

"He's a fighter," Kate agreed.

They lapsed into silence again. This time, it was a comfortable one, now that the air was cleared between them.

When they arrived at the animal clinic, Josh took Trooper from Kate and carried him inside. Velma Petersen, the vet's wife, escorted them straight to the treatment area in the rear of the clinic, where her husband waited. Doc Petersen was a tall man of Scandinavian descent, with strong, muscled arms and kind hands.

"Put him here on the table," he directed with barely a glance at either of them. "Tangled with the wrong cow, did ya, boy?" he murmured, stepping in to remove the denim jacket when Josh placed Trooper on the table. "I've done that a time or two." After a quick, cursory look at the extent of the dog's injuries, the vet flicked a glance at his wife. "You might as well take these two back to the waiting room and get them some coffee. This will take a while."

After they returned to the reception area, Josh offered to drive Kate back to the ranch. She refused.

"If you don't mind, I would rather stay. I feel responsible for what happened," she explained, "and I'd like to wait and make sure Trooper is all right."

Josh didn't object.

A long two hours later, they were summoned to the vet's private office at the back. Kate nervously wiped her suddenly sweaty palms on the sides of her jeans.

Doc Petersen greeted them with a broad smile. "Sorry you had to wait so long. We got the X-rays and tests in short order, but it took considerable amount of time sewing up that wound. You have one lucky dog there, Mr. Reynolds. A half inch more, and he likely would have bled to death before you got him here. As it is, he lost a lot of blood."

"He's going to be okay, isn't he?" Kate asked, a fine tension threading her nerves.

"Barring any complications, he should be," the vet answered and swiveled his chair to face an X-ray clipped on a lighted viewing screen. "Let me show you his other injuries. As you can see here, there are fractures of both the right ulna and radius, mid-shaft. Luckily, both are what we call 'green-stick' fractures with minimal displacement of the bones. Which allowed us to put a cast on the leg. And here," he slapped up another X-ray, "we have fractures to three ribs. Fortunately, they are stable, as well. Which brings me to the good news. I do see evidence that the lungs have suffered some contusions, but there is no evidence that a lung has been punctured."

He swung back to face them. "To play it safe, we have strapped the ribs to restrict movement and to prevent a lung from accidentally getting punctured.

Otherwise, I think we have succeeded in stabilizing his condition. Currently he's getting a blood transfusion and we have loaded him up with antibiotics. Naturally, we are keeping him sedated against the pain—"

Josh interrupted, "When do you think I will be able to take him home?"

"I'd like to keep him under observation for at least another twenty-four hours. In trauma cases there is always the risk the animal could go into shock. When that happens, sometimes minutes count," the vet explained, then paused. "When you do take him home, you'll need to keep him confined. I don't want him moving around any more than necessary until those fractured ribs have a chance to heal—not that he will feel much like moving. And you'll need to keep a close eye on him during the first few days." Like Kate, the vet observed Josh's sudden, troubled frown. "Is that a problem?"

"I had promised Ken Miller that I'd give him a hand out at the Box Six," Josh explained.

Only last week, Ken Miller had stopped by the Summers Ranch asking if her father knew who he could get to string some fence for him. Josh had obviously hired out to do the job. Now he might lose it.

Kate couldn't let that happen, not when she was responsible for his dog being hurt in the first place.

"I could take care of Trooper," she volunteered. "At least until he's well enough to be left on his own."

"Thanks, but it isn't necessary," Josh said with a brief, sideways glance at her.

"Probably not," Kate agreed. "But if you have work to do and I have the free time to look after him, it's the logical solution."

"I know," he said, and hesitated a minute longer, then finally accepted her offer.

The following afternoon, Kate collected Trooper from the vet's and took him back to the ranch. With Manny's help, she carried the dog into the low, rambling ranch house, where she had an area fixed up for him in a corner of the big, spacious kitchen. As soon as she had the dog settled in his temporary quarters, she called Josh Reynolds and left a brief message on his recorder telling him she had picked up the dog, that Trooper was weak and woozy, but otherwise fine.

Along about seven-thirty that night, there was a knock at the back door, startling Kate. Only strangers knocked at doors in their part of the country. She was halfway to the door before she guessed the identity of their visitor.

Sure enough, when she opened the door, there stood Josh Reynolds. Kate knew at once that he had come straight from the job. The dust and sweat of a day's work still clung to his clothes and skin, and little lines of fatigue were etched around his chiseled features.

None of it lessened the impact of him. If anything, the haggard look enhanced the maleness about him, giving it power and punch.

"Hello." His mouth curved in a tired smile that still packed enough voltage to send a tingle all the way down to her toes—and set off alarm bells in her head. "I thought I'd stop and check on Trooper."

"Of course. Come in." Kate swung the door wide and retreated well into the kitchen, her mind racing.

Why on earth hadn't it occurred to her that Josh would come to see his dog? Why had she been so foolish as to assume he would be satisfied with mere progress reports left on his answering machine? She certainly hadn't bargained for this.

"I fixed a place for him over here in the corner," she said, walking over to the area.

Josh removed his hat upon entering and followed her to the corner alcove next to the stone fireplace. An old wooden storage bench penned the dog in. Trooper lay on the other side of it sprawled on an old blanket, his eyes closed, his rib area strapped with tape, a lightweight cast on his front leg. A thick, gauze dressing covered the long wound on his side. Josh stepped over the bench and crouched down beside his dog while Kate looked on.

"Hey, Trooper. How you doin', fella?" Josh stroked a gentle hand over the dog's head.

The familiar sound of his voice roused the dog from his drugged stupor. He whined a weak greeting and feebly tried to wag his tail.

Josh smiled at the effort. "Not feeling too perky, are you, fella?"

"He's still pretty doped up, too," Kate explained stiffly.

To her relief, her father chose that moment to walk into the kitchen. "I thought I heard—" He saw Josh and broke off the sentence. "It was you at the door, was it? I figured you would stop by to check on your dog. Have you got time for a cup of coffee?" he asked, then glanced at Kate. "There's still some in the pot, isn't there?"

She wanted to say no, but the coffeemaker's glass carafe was still half full—and clearly visible to Josh Reynolds.

Reluctantly, Kate admitted, "Yes, I think so."

"Good. Pour us a couple cups, will you? How do you like yours, Josh? Black or with cream and sugar?"

"Black is fine." Josh gave the dog a final pat, then joined Kate's father at the kitchen table.

As simply and naturally as that, the pattern was set. Every night for the next four nights, Josh arrived at the ranch somewhere around seven o'clock, spent a little time with Trooper, then drank coffee with her father and talked ranch talk—cattle prices, range conditions, weather, and business woes.

Invariably, her father had drawn Kate into their conversations, as well. Too often, she had caught herself enjoying them and promptly reminded herself that men like Josh Reynolds were easy to like.

Too easy. Which was where the danger lay.

When seven o'clock rolled around on the fifth night, Kate found herself listening for the sound of his pickup. Annoyed with such foolishness, she instantly snatched up the dish towel and began drying the dinner dishes stacked in the draining rack. She was even more annoyed when she recognized the distinctive rumble of his vehicle and tensed up.

Her father got up from the table and walked to the window. "Josh is here. You might as well pour him a cup of coffee."

"Aren't you jumping the gun a little?" Kate suggested coolly. "You don't even know whether he's going to stay. He could have other plans tonight."

"Other plans?" Bick turned to stare at her, taken aback by the idea.

His reaction made it clear that he was looking forward to visiting with Josh, that he enjoyed his company. Just for a moment, Kate was irritated by that. And a little jealous.

"Yes, other plans." She slipped the dried plate onto the stack in the cupboard and reached for another one. "I mean, for all you know, he could have a date tonight."

"That's possible, I suppose," her father conceded.

From outside came the metal sound of a truck door closing, followed by the crunch of footsteps along the path to the back door. Over in the corner, Trooper struggled to his feet and fixed his gaze on the door, a faint whine of anticipation coming from him. When Josh walked in, the whine turned into an excited yelp of welcome.

Kate nodded briefly to Josh and immediately went back to drying the dinner dishes, struck again by the way he had of dominating a room with his presence. Every time he walked in, the big kitchen seemed to shrink in size. She should have gotten used to it by now, but she hadn't.

After exchanging greetings with her father, Josh went over to see Trooper. As always, Kate softened a little whenever she saw the two of them together. There was never any doubt the affection between them was mutual. She certainly couldn't fault Josh Reynolds on that score.

"Have you got time for coffee?" her father asked when Josh finally left the dog's corner.

"Always, if you already have some made."

"Sure do." He nodded and signaled to Kate to bring two cups to the table. "I would have had a cup waiting for you when you came in, but Kate didn't think I should. She thought you might have a date tonight."

Right at that moment, Kate could have cheerfully hit her father.

"Is that right?" Josh gave her a long, interested look. "Well, as it happens, I don't."

"To be honest, that surprises me some," her father replied and gave Kate an absent smile of thanks when she set his cup of coffee in front of him. "A good-looking guy like you, I would have thought women would fall like flies around you."

"I don't know," Josh murmured skeptically and glanced at Kate, his eyes twinkling and a smile deepening the corners of his mouth. "Kate has managed to stay on her feet around me without any difficulty."

"More's the pity," her father grumbled.

She definitely wanted to hit him.

"Ignore him," she told Josh, throwing a glare at her father. "If he had his way, he would marry me off to the first man who came along."

"And why not?" her father demanded, his head lifting in challenge. "It's time you were married and raising me some grandchildren. And don't go accusing me of being chauvinistic. It's right and natural for me to want you to know the kind of happiness your mother and I shared."

"Fine, but I'll do the picking and the looking myself, thank you very much." The instant Kate heard the anger in her voice, she knew she had made a mistake.

Her father frequently delighted in baiting her. Judging by the mischievous glint in his eye, this was one of those occasions.

He cupped a hand to the side of his mouth and whispered loudly to Josh, "In case you didn't notice, she's mad. Of course, it doesn't take much to rile Kate sometimes."

"I guess the temper goes with the red hair and freckles." Josh grinned at her over the rim of his coffee cup, his eyes twinkling with the same teasing light that her father had.

There was one thing that Kate was particularly sensitive about, and that was her freckles. With the greatest of difficulty, she managed not to react. Instead, she channeled all her anger into a saccharine smile.

"We have some homemade apple pie left from dinner. Would you like a slice?" She directed the question to Josh.

"I think she's trying to change the subject, don't you, Josh?" her father said behind his hand.

"No doubt about it, but it's good change." His smile held both approval and admiration. "And I would like a slice of that pie, thank you."

She went to the counter and retrieved a dessert plate from the cupboard. "How about you, Dad? Do you have room for another piece?"

"A small one."

Kate dished up two large slices of pie and carried them to the table along with a pair of forks. "Who wants a scoop of vanilla ice cream on theirs?"

"Not me." Josh picked up a fork and dug into the pie.

"Me either. But I would like a warm-up on my coffee." Her father pointed to his half-full cup.

Kate carried the glass pot to the table and filled his cup, then walked around to Josh's chair and topped off his cup. But he was too intent on the pie to notice, consuming it with an obvious relish and not stopping until the plate was slicked clean. He leaned back in his chair, his mouth curving in satisfaction.

"I can't remember the last time I had homemade apple pie," he declared to Kate. "It was absolutely delicious."

"The compliment belongs to him." She nodded to her father. "He's the pie-maker in this household."

"That's true enough," Bick acknowledged. "Kate unfortunately takes after her mother. Amy never could make a decent pie. Her crusts always ended up tasting like thick cardboard." The telephone rang, and he pushed his chair back from the table and stood. "That's probably Austin calling me back. I'll catch it in the office."

When he left the kitchen, Kate busied herself with clearing away the pie dishes. At the sink, she turned on the water and began rinsing the crumbs from the plates.

A chair leg scraped across the tiled kitchen floor. The sound was followed by footsteps approaching the sink. A second later, Josh Reynolds filled her side vision, a coffee cup in his hand. He leaned against the counter and took a sip of his coffee.

"These last few nights have been damned pleasant," he remarked. "I've bounced around most of my life, never staying in any one place long enough to get closely acquainted with anyone. I guess that's why I have genuinely enjoyed coming over here and spending my evenings with you and your dad."

From the odd bits of information Josh had revealed about his past, Kate had gathered that it had been a rootless existence. His father had been from Wyoming, his mother from Oklahoma, and Josh had been born in Arizona. She had gotten the impression that his father had made a habit of drifting from job to job and place to place. Josh had apparently done the same once he went out on his own. Until he bought the old Montoya place, that is.

The thought of him owning it suddenly set her teeth on edge while twisting her heart at the same time. The combination made her abrupt with him.

"After tonight, it will all end." The plates and forks clattered together as she stacked them in the sink.

"Why's that?" Josh eyed her curiously.

"Because"—Kate moistened the dish rag before

turning off the water—"Trooper is well enough that you can take him home tomorrow. Which means there will be no reason for you to come here anymore."

For a moment Josh said nothing and simply looked at her long and hard. "Your shoulders must get very tired at the end of the day," he said at last.

"What? Why?" She frowned in bewilderment.

"From carrying that big chip around," he replied smoothly. "Or is it only there when I'm around?"

"I don't know what you mean," Kate declared none too convincingly and immediately set to work wiping off the kitchen counter with a vigor that the nearly spotless counter didn't warrant.

"Not much, you don't," he mocked. "Sometimes you have been about as friendly as a cactus around me."

"Then maybe you should back off," she suggested.

"Maybe I would if I hadn't seen glimpses of someone who's strong and compassionate, honest and easygoing. Which makes me curious why you're different with me."

"I think you forget, I barely know you." She continued to wipe the kitchen counter, pretending to give it her full attention even though she was rapidly running out of areas to clean.

"And you don't want to get to know me either, do you?" he said, then reminded her, "We are neighbors, remember."

"Maybe we should leave it at that." Kate threw him a cool smile and walked back to the sink to rinse out the dishrag.

He studied her closely. "You have made up your mind not to like me, haven't you?" Confronted with the truth, Kate started to turn away, but Josh reached out and caught her arm, stopping her. "Why?"

The warmth of his hand penetrated the sleeve of

her blouse, heating her skin and touching off a host of new sensations. For an instant Kate was unnerved by this purely physical reaction to him. Pride insisted that she not reveal it to him.

"Who knows why personalities clash sometimes? It just happens." She feigned a shrug of indifference and freed her arm from his touch. "Call it bad chemistry, if you like."

"Chemistry is as good a description as any." But there was a trace of amusement in his voice that suggested Josh was talking about something else.

Kate ignored it. "What time do you want to pick Trooper up tomorrow?"

"Would mid-morning be all right? Say, around ten?"

"That's fine." She nodded with deliberate coolness.

He studied her for another long second, then lifted his cup and drained the last of the coffee before setting the empty cup in the sink.

"I'll see you tomorrow at ten." He headed for the door. "Tell your father I'll catch him another time."

Caught off guard by his sudden departure, Kate managed a rather stunned, "I will." Then Josh was out the door.

When it clicked shut behind him, Trooper whined in protest and tried to climb over the wooden bench, clunking his cast on the wooden seat. Kate hurried over and gently but firmly pushed him back into his corner pen, then crawled over the bench to comfort him. Whimpering, he watched the door.

"It's okay, Trooper," she murmured, loosely circling an arm around his neck and rubbing his ears. "He'll be back tomorrow to take you home. You'll like that, won't you?"

He barked once, as if he understood every word she said. Kate laughed.

"You are a smart little rascal. I'm going to miss you." Her smile turned a little sad. "But you won't miss me at all, will you?"

Trooper whined and butted his head against her face, giving her cheek a long swipe with his tongue. "You clown." Smiling, Kate pushed his nose away, but she unexpectedly had a lump in her throat.

Kate made sure she said her good-byes to Trooper before ten o'clock arrived. It was difficult. She hadn't guessed how difficult it would be. But then she had never suspected she would become so attached to the dog in just five short days. But that was precisely what had happened.

When she heard Josh drive in, Kate hurriedly double-checked to be certain all of Trooper's various pills and ointments were in the sack she had set aside for Josh to take with him. Satisfied that it was all there, she turned to face the door when it opened.

She was so intent on not showing any emotion that she didn't notice the plastic bag Josh carried when he walked in. It was emblazoned with the name of a local store.

"This is yours." He held it out to her.

"Mine?" At first Kate assumed that he meant she had left it somewhere.

She took the bag and looked inside, trying to remember the last time she had been in Graf's Store and what she might have purchased. Inside was a long-sleeved, white blouse of dress cotton. She knew at once she hadn't bought it.

"What's this?" She looked at Josh for an explanation.

"It's to replace the one that was ruined when Trooper got hurt."

"You didn't have to do this," Kate protested, fully aware that this blouse was much more expensive than the one that had been ruined.

"Yes, I did," he stated and walked past her straight to his dog. "Come on, fella. We're ready to go home."

Kate barely had time to hand over Trooper's medications before Josh was out the door and gone. She had braced herself for something painfully long and drawn out. But it was over almost before it began.

Suddenly, she was alone in the kitchen. A very empty kitchen.

Five

Sunset splashed vivid streaks of fuschia and crimson across the western horizon, tinting the landscape as Bick Summers swung the ranch pickup into the parking lot of Trudy's Cafe. There were few vehicles in the lot, enabling him to park near the door.

"It doesn't look like Trudy has many customers." Kate opened the truck's passenger door.

"I expect business is slow on weeknights." Her father climbed out the driver's side.

Together, they went into the restaurant and seated themselves in an empty booth by the window. A waitress came by and slid a pair of menus toward them.

"I'm glad we're eating out tonight." Kate opened hers and studied the specials. "I honestly didn't feel like cooking."

"We needed a break in the routine. The house has been too quiet lately," her father stated. "I have to be honest—I didn't realize how much I enjoyed visiting with Josh Reynolds until he stopped coming over. It kinda surprises me that he hasn't been by."

"He's probably been busy." Kate kept her head down, conscious of a funny little ache inside.

"According to Manny, Josh bought a half dozen head of horses the other day. From the sounds of it, he got quite a bargain on them, too. Manny said a couple of them were on the sour side. Probably had some bad riders on them," Bick said as he perused his menu. "Josh figures he can turn them around and sell them for a handy profit. In the meantime, Manny heard that he's over at Austin's helping to re-roof his barn."

"How on earth does Manny learn everybody's business around here?" Kate shook her head in amazement.

"He's the biggest gossip in the county, that's how." Her father grinned.

"Heaven knows, he certainly has his sources," she agreed, then asked with forced idleness, "Manny didn't happen to ask Josh how Trooper is, did he?"

"He didn't say, so I guess not," her father replied, then added with a thoughtful look, "You know, I miss having that dog around. It's been awhile since we had one in the house—not since you were a little girl."

"Dogs can be a lot of company." Kate pushed her menu aside. "I'm surprised Josh hasn't let us know about Trooper's progress. You would have thought he would."

"Maybe he figured if you really cared, you would call and find out for yourself."

Kate cared, but she wasn't about to call Josh Reynolds to get an update on the dog.

Fortunately, the waitress came to take their order, and the subject was conveniently dropped.

Later, over coffee, her father remarked, "I think I'll run over to Austin's tomorrow morning and take another look at the young bull he's been trying to convince me to buy. Want to ride along?"

And run into Josh Reynolds? No, thanks, Kate thought.

"I'd better not," she said instead. "I haven't worked Red for a couple days. I need to ride him tomorrow."

"Afraid of seeing Josh again?" her father teased.

"I'm not of afraid of anyone," Kate retorted. "And certainly not Mr. High, Wide, and Handsome."

Her father shrugged, a little too innocently. "If you say so."

The autumn-yellow leaves of the aspen trees shimmered in the morning sunlight like newly minted gold, their slender trunks a splash of white against the mountain slope. The big red stallion snorted and eyed them in brief suspicion, then proceeded along the trail to the canyon.

As always when she approached the site of the old Montoya place, Kate was gripped by the feeling she was coming home. For a second time since she started out, she almost turned around, but she could hear her father's voice chiding her for being a coward. It goaded her on, reminding her that Josh would be gone this morning and Trooper would be there alone.

Which was why she was riding over familiar ground, tension coiling her nerves tighter and tighter the closer she got to the canyon entrance.

When the trail leveled out, the stallion pushed at the bit, rested now from his canter across the grassy foothills and eager to stretch his legs again. Kate firmly held him to a walk while her eyes drank in the sight of her beloved canyon.

The stallion tossed his head and whinnied at the two horses in the pen. As their heads jerked around, a dog barked an alarm. It was Trooper. Kate recognized his voice instantly.

It seemed to be coming from somewhere near the trailer. Pushing her misgivings aside, Kate rode toward the area.

She found Trooper in a kennel with a short, fenced run that had been erected near the trailer's tongue. His barking turned into excited yelps of greeting the instant he recognized her. The tape was gone from his rib area, and the wound to his side looked almost completely healed.

Dismounting, Kate dropped the stallion's reins and walked over to the kennel. Trooper crowded close to the run's gate and did his best to bounce up and down, despite his hobbling cast.

"Did you think I had forgotten about you?" She smiled when he whined anxiously. "I didn't."

To Trooper's delight, she unlatched the gate and stepped into the run, crouching down to return his exuberant greeting. He was all over her, washing her face with wet kisses and whining with happiness.

"I missed you, too, Trooper," she declared huskily.

He licked her face again, making her laugh despite the welling of tears in her eyes. In defense, she caught his broad head between her hands and held it away.

"I don't have to ask how you're getting along, do I?" Her heart melted at the look of utter adoration in his eyes. "You are a regular bundle of energy. I bet you can hardly wait until that cast comes off. But it won't be for awhile, you know."

The dog whined an answer, then pulled his head away to look down the rutted lane, his hound ears pricking.

"What do you see?" Kate glanced that way, as well,

and stiffened in dismay at the sight of the blue pickup traveling toward them.

Josh Reynolds was behind the wheel.

Instinct told her to run, but pride kept her rooted in place. She didn't stand up until the pickup rolled to a stop beside the travel trailer. Her pulse leaped crazily when Josh stepped out of the cab.

It had been a week since Kate had seen him last. As impossible as it seemed, he looked more devastatingly handsome than before.

"This is a surprise." The warm pitch of his voice was like a caress.

Awareness shivered through her as his gaze briefly locked with hers. Then he turned and signaled to the two Catahoula dogs riding in the back of the pickup. They jumped out and glanced indifferently at Kate and the stallion, then trotted over to the trailer and noisily lapped at the water in the pail beside the steps.

Kate finally found her voice. "I stopped by to see how Trooper was doing."

"So I guessed." He walked over and unlatched the kennel gate, letting Trooper out, then reached down to pat the dog's head.

"I understood you were over to Austin's place, re-roofing his barn."

"Or you wouldn't have stopped by, right?" His smile took some of the sting out of his idle challenge, but not all.

"Probably not." Kate refused to sound defensive. "Red needed some exercise, and I thought the ride over here would give him a good workout. I guess you finished up your work over at Austin's?"

"This morning," he confirmed with a nod, then strolled over to the ground-hitched stallion. "This must be Cayenne Red. I've heard a lot about him."

"All of it is true." Leaving the kennel, Kate walked over to the horse that was her pride and joy, confident that Josh wouldn't be able to find a single fault with him. "Red has brought home a pile of trophies, with more to come now that he's had some experience."

"Then you plan on taking him back on the show circuit?" Josh glanced at her curiously.

"This winter, yes. But we'll be hitting only big shows," she explained. "If Red does as well as I think he will, we'll retire him to stud next spring."

"Will you stand him yourself?"

"Or lease him to a breeder." Kate shrugged to indicate the decision hadn't been made. "We've already had some offers."

"I can believe that." He ran an admiring eye over the stallion, then glanced at Kate. "Can I offer you a cup of coffee? It won't take a minute to put some on."

"No, thanks," she refused quickly. "It's time I started back to the ranch. I only stopped—"

Josh broke in, finishing the sentence for her, "—to see how Trooper is." Hearing his name, the dog limped over to him, the cast on his front leg giving him an awkward gait. "You can see for yourself that he's healing fast. The cast slows him down a bit. Which is just as well, or he would probably take off after the first rabbit he saw and open up his wound."

"By the time that cast comes off, there won't be much danger of that happening."

"No, there shouldn't." His gaze traveled over her face. "By chance have you given any more thought to helping out with my house plans? I really would like to hear more of your ideas."

"Sorry, I'm still not interested." Kate glanced toward the ruins, stabbed by the thought that the house of her dreams might be built on the site and she would never live in it. Resentment flared anew that Josh now owned the canyon. "Why did you buy the Montoya place?" she demanded in sudden irritation. "You do realize that you'll never be able to make a living off it. You'll always have to take outside work to support yourself."

He looked at her for a long second before answering. "In time, I hope to get a permit to graze cattle on federal land. Until then, it's a beginning."

"A beginning of what?" Now that she had gone on the attack, Kate continued with it, and struggled inwardly with her own sense of confusion. "Of working yourself to death trying to hang on to it?"

"Maybe that, too," he conceded. "But for me it's the beginning of a real home, something permanent that doesn't roll on wheels, a place for a man to stretch and grow." The line of his mouth tilted in a crooked smile. "I don't expect that's something you could understand. You and your family have lived in the same place for generations, maybe even in the same house. That's something I can't even imagine. I've always lived a tumbleweed life and never called anywhere home until now."

"But why now? And why here? Why not somewhere else? Texas? Arizona? Colorado?"

"The truth?" he challenged, locking eyes with her.

Kate sensed at once that he was about to relate something personal and private. She wasn't sure she wanted to hear it, but it was too late. Her mouth was already saying, "Yes, the truth."

"My mother died six years ago. A neighbor finally tracked me down three weeks later. By the time I got there, the county had already buried her. I remember standing at her grave thinking that all she had ever wanted was a home and family around her, but my father was always looking for greener grass. It hit me then that I was turning out to be just like him, going wherever the urge took me and never saving a dollar. The worst of it was that I always envied people like you, and talked about settling down somewhere and sinking in roots. I told myself that I hadn't found the perfect spot yet. Hell, I was young still, only twenty-five. I had plenty of time left. But I knew it was all an excuse. If I really wanted a piece of land to call my own, I would have been saving every dime I could. In short, I took a good look at myself and I didn't like what I saw. So I set about changing it. It took me six years of working and saving, but I got together enough money to make a down payment on some land."

Six years. Kate had to admire the commitment and determination that had taken, aware that a man of lesser character would have given up. Yet he still hadn't answered her initial question.

"But why New Mexico? Why here?"

"Because my mother is buried in Silver City. A couple of years ago, I had my father's remains moved from Tucson to the grave beside hers. I always planned to find a place close by. This land fits the bill."

His words moved her more than she wanted. "Your mother would be proud of you." A tightness gripped her throat, giving a huskiness to her voice.

"I think maybe she would be." He nodded in quiet satisfaction, then looked in the direction of the ruins. "But that's one more reason why I'm determined to get a house built. Are you sure you won't reconsider helping with the layout? We could have dinner tomorrow night and discuss it then," he suggested with an easy smile.

Kate felt her resistance melting under the warmth of it and immediately resisted it. "There's nothing to discuss."

"Maybe, and maybe not, but we can have dinner and find out."

Her eyes narrowed in sudden suspicion. "Did my father put you up to this?"

One eyebrow lifted in amused surprise. "No. Does he usually arrange dates for you?"

"Of course not," she denied, briefly rattled by his question. "It's just that he likes you. And he doesn't understand—" Kate stopped before she said more than she wanted to.

But Josh didn't let her get away with that. "Just what is it that he doesn't understand?"

Furious that she had left herself open for that, she reined in her anger and replied smoothly, "That I don't happen to be your type of woman."

"Really?" There went that eyebrow again. "And just what is my type?"

"Oh, for heaven's sake!" Kate muttered in exasperation. "We both know I look like everybody's big sister. I am definitely not the type men go ga-ga over."

"Ga-ga?" He grinned at her choice of words, infuriating her even further.

"Go ahead and laugh," she snapped. "But the fact is that I'm not some curvaceous beauty."

"Isn't there a saying about small packages?" Josh prompted.

"Yes, but there is nothing about tall, slender ones."

"Isn't that what florists send long-stemmed roses in?" he countered. "Of course, the thorns are usually removed."

"That's very flattering, but I know the way men see me."

"Then the men you've known have obviously been immune to the fire in your hair and the freckles on your nose." His glance ran over both, an admiring light in his eyes.

"Leave my freckles out of this," Kate declared, his reference to them striking a sensitive nerve.

"Why? I like your freckles." His fingertips skimmed the freckled area on her nose and cheek before she even noticed his hand lifting. "They give you a fresh and sexy, sun-kissed look."

Sexy! Kate was stunned. No one had ever described her as sexy before. Certainly Cody Jones never had. Jolted back to reality by that memory, Kate angled her chin a little higher.

"Save your smooth talk for someone who will buy it," she told him. "You're wasting it on me."

"That wasn't a line, Kate."

"Right. And wolves don't howl," she mocked, then said, "Look, I know what you're trying to do."

"You do, huh?"

"Yes, I do." But, for the life of her, Kate suddenly couldn't think what it was. He was standing too close, closer than she realized. And his hand was on her waist. When had that gotten there? She plunged on, unnerved and determined not to show it. "I have met men like you before."

"You have, huh?" There was that hint of challenge again.

She met it. "Yes, I have. This is nothing but a game to you. We both know you aren't really interested in me."

"Is that right?" he murmured.

"Yes," she said right back.

"You seem to know a lot about the way I think."

Her smile was a little dry and a little smug. "No offense, but it isn't hard."

"Really," he murmured again. There was a lazy, hooded look in his eyes as their gaze drifted to her lips. "Then maybe you can tell me what I'm thinking now?"

Kate knew the answer in a flash. "You're thinking about kissing me."

But there was no sense of triumph, only stunned surprise at the sight of his head tipping toward her.

"That is the first time you've been right," he said an instant before his mouth settled onto hers.

All coherent thought was lost to her as her breath quickened and her pulse took an answering leap. There was no controlling it, not the kiss nor her response to it. It was something to savor and explore, like the astonishing pleasure she felt—and the even more astonishing greed.

The kiss ended without ever ending at all as his mouth cruised along her cheek to the sensitive lobe of her ear, creating delicious shivers over her skin.

"Sisters don't kiss like that." His voice vibrated through her, husky and soft, echoing the same disturbance that Kate felt. Then he was back investigating a corner of her mouth, his breath heating her lips. "Do you know what I'm thinking now?"

"No." Her answer was a breathy sound, and Kate struggled to surface from the haze of sensation.

"I'm thinking"—he rubbed his mouth over the curves of her lips—"that kissing you could become a very enjoyable habit."

She couldn't check the murmur of satisfaction that escaped when he kissed her again. But it brought a return of sanity, fragile though it was. Still, it was enough for Kate to marshall sufficient strength to push herself away from him. His hands tightened only briefly, then released her, letting her draw away.

"Do you know what I'm thinking now, Kate?" he asked quietly.

She threw her head up, pride cloaking her. "You're thinking that I'm leaving now. And you would be right."

Careful to conceal her haste, Kate caught up the stallion's reins and led him ahead a couple steps. As she looped the reins around the horse's neck and prepared to mount, Trooper hobbled over to her, his tail wagging. Kate hesitated, then bent down and rubbed his ears in a rough, brief caress, conscious all the while of Josh's watchful gaze on her.

"Take care of yourself, Trooper," she said and straightened.

When she slipped a toe in the stirrup, the dog barked once. Kate glanced at him as she grabbed the saddle-horn. Trooper whined hopefully.

"He doesn't want you to leave," Josh observed. "He likes you."

"I like him." Kate swung into the saddle.

"You know the old saying." Josh walked over to stand next to Trooper. "Love my dog, love me."

"You have it backwards," she told him.

"Do I?" He smiled lazily.

She reined the stallion away from the trailer and touched a heel to his side. The horse broke into a lope. Behind her, Trooper barked in protest.

But Kate was too shaken by the kiss to look back. She had never felt that way the few times Cody had kissed her. She was afraid of what that meant, afraid that it would only take a little push and she would find herself falling in love with Josh Reynolds.

Only a fool made the same mistake twice.

Six

During a routine check of the pasture tanks the next day, Kate discovered one of them was nearly dry. The cause turned out to be a problem with the float. She spent the better part of the afternoon hanging half-upside down in the tank, fixing it.

Being handy with a wrench had proved useful to her on more than one occasion.

When Kate pulled into the ranch yard, she was ready for a shower. She spotted her father halfway to the house carrying a wire basket with a dozen eggs in it. He waited for her, and together they walked toward the back door.

The strident ring of the telephone greeted them when they entered the kitchen. "I'll get it." Kate hurried over to the wall-mounted phone and picked up the receiver. "Summers Ranch."

"Hello, Kate. It's Josh."

The sound of his voice touched off the vivid memory of yesterday's kiss. Kate gripped the phone a little tighter and struggled to block out the little curlings of remembered heat. "What is it you want, Josh?" she asked, striving to sound cool and indifferent. "If you're calling to repeat your invitation to dinner, the answer is still no."

The instant she said that, Kate regretted it, as her father snapped his head around, a sudden gleam lighting his eyes. Kate was torn between slamming the phone back on the hook and hitting him with it.

"That's not why I phoned," Josh said. "It's Trooper. He's come up missing."

"What?" She instantly gave Josh her full and undivided attention. "When? How?"

"I don't know. I went into town around noon to pick up some feed and run a few errands. He was in the pen when I left. But when I got back an hour ago, the pen was empty and the gate was open. I thought—" He bit off the rest of it, then added, somewhat wearily, "Never mind what I thought. Maybe I didn't have the gate latched tight and he went after a rabbit."

"With that cast on his leg?" Kate was skeptical.

"I suppose I should have said that maybe he might have *tried* to go after a rabbit," Josh conceded. "Anyway, he probably just wandered out of earshot. I'll go look around some more. Sorry I bothered you."

"No problem. Let me know when you find him, would you?" she asked, none too certain that was wise.

"Sure," he said and hung up.

Automatically, Kate replaced the receiver on its cradle. No matter how much she tried to convince herself that there was no reason to be worried about the missing dog, she was.

"So, Josh asked you out for a date, did he?" her father remarked, looking quite pleased. "How come you haven't mentioned that?"

"It wasn't important." It certainly wasn't now. "Trooper is missing."

"Missing?" He frowned.

Kate repeated what Josh had told her, and concluded with, "Josh thinks he has simply wandered somewhere."

Her father nodded in agreement. "Probably out checking his territory. Dogs do that all the time. It's part of being a dog, I expect. He'll probably come wandering in along about dark, tired and hungry."

"Probably." But her mind kept saying, *What if he didn't?*

"You're worried about Trooper, aren't you?"

Kate started to deny it, then encountered her father's knowing look and sighed in concern. "Every time I think about Trooper wandering back into the canyon and climbing up into those rocks with that cast . . ." She let the sentence trail off.

"Personally, I think Trooper has more sense than to get himself in that situation." Her father carried the wire basket to the sink to wash the eggs.

"I hope so."

"It seems to me"—His sideways glance made a quick, appraising sweep of her—"that instead of sitting around here fretting and stewing, you ought to go over and help look for the dog. Two pairs of eyes and ears are always better than one."

There was logic in his suggestion, but Kate had noticed that telltale glint in his eye.

"You'd like me to do that, wouldn't you?" she challenged in irritation. "You're thinking that by me spending more time with Josh, I'll start to like him."

Little did he know that she already liked Josh. Now she had to guard against falling in love with him.

"Who said anything about Josh?" Her father frowned in a marvelous show of innocence. "I was talking about looking for Trooper."

"Right, and beef is a thousand dollars a pound, too," Kate said, showing her disbelief.

"Don't get me wrong," her father said. "If the other happened as well, that would be all right, too."

"Too bad, because I don't want to ever lay eyes on Josh again," she flashed.

"So you are going to just sit around here and do nothing while that poor dog is out wandering around with that broken leg." Her father gave her a sad-eyed look of disappointment.

Kate glared in return. "You plan to keep this up, don't you? You won't stop until I go look for Trooper."

"Are you going?" His mouth held the beginnings of a grin, matching the hopeful twinkle in his eyes.

She continued to glare at him for another long second, then spun away. "Yes."

As the crow flies, the old Montoya place was close to three miles from the ranch. By gravel road and highway, it was closer to fifteen miles. Kate made it there in eighteen minutes flat, the heaviness of her foot doing wonders for her temper.

Josh was at the old holding pen, throwing a saddle on his big gray horse when Kate roared up the lane in the ranch pickup, gravel popping under her tires. The truck fishtailed to a stop near the pens. A scant second later, Kate piled out of the cab.

"You haven't found Trooper yet, have you?" She knew what his answer would be. She had known from the moment she saw him at the pen.

"No," Josh confirmed. "I was just saddling Gringo to

ride back in the canyon and see if I could find any sign of him." He proceeded to cinch the saddle on the gray.

"I came to help you look," Kate explained.

"Thanks." His smile was quick and warm with gratitude, like the glance he sent her.

Both snatched at her breath, but she managed to control her reaction. She was here to look for Trooper; that was her sole reason for coming.

"I haven't checked along the creek yet," he said. "It isn't deep enough to worry about this time of year, but he might have gotten his cast wedged between some rocks. 'Course, if that happened, you would think he would have raised a ruckus before now."

"You would think so," Kate agreed. "But I'll look anyway. It's a place to start."

Kate headed for the stream on foot while Josh mounted up and rode into the canyon, accompanied by his other two dogs. The banks of the stream were weed-choked, in places rocky and strewn with cottonwood and willow trees. Kate worked her way along it, intermittently calling for Trooper and pausing to listen for an answering yelp or whine.

Nothing.

At last she reached the spot where the stream made its stair-stepped descent down a canyon wall. She picked her way around boulders and loose rock chunks, climbing until she reached an area that only a mountain goat could negotiate. Which effectively eliminated a dog with a broken leg. Discouraged, Kate turned around and headed back down.

Drumming hooves sounded above the gurgling chortle of water over a small rock fall as she reached the relative flatness of the canyon floor. A fragile hope sprang up when Kate saw Josh cantering the gray horse across the grassy meadow toward her. But his expression told her everything before he reined.

"I came up empty." He rested an arm on the saddle horn and pushed his hat to the back of his head. An absent frown creased his forehead as his gaze idly swept the boulders behind. "How about you?"

"The same."

Swiveling at the hips, he glanced back in the direction of the trailer, better than a half mile away and hidden from view by the sheltering shadows of the cottonwoods. "Maybe he's made it home already."

"Maybe." Kate didn't hold out much hope of that.

"I guess we might as well find out," he said somewhat grimly and turned, holding out his arm to her. "Hop aboard."

She hesitated only an instant before common sense and a concern for Trooper overrode her desire to avoid any physical contact with Josh. It was a long walk back to the trailer, but only a short ride. She grabbed his arm and agilely swung up behind the saddle cantle.

"All set?" he asked after she had rocked from side to side a couple of times to get herself properly adjusted on the saddle's rear jockey.

"Ready." She nodded, extremely conscious of the strong back and wide set of shoulders directly in front of her.

He sent the horse forward and immediately lifted the gray into an easy-riding lope. Kate had an unerring sense of balance on a horse. She could have easily ridden without holding on. But, seemingly of their own accord, her hands reached forward and settled on the points of his hips. She was forced to admit, if only to herself, that she welcomed the excuse to touch him.

The long shadows cast by the canyon wall stretched

over them, enclosing them in a false darkness. Kate glanced at the sky, for the first time noticing the lateness of the hour.

Day was fading rapidly. The soft lavender hues that bathed the land seemed to compress the light that remained, making the things close by appear brighter and more vivid while the distant trees and canyon wall seemed to lose their shape and merge together.

"It's almost dark," she said to Josh, needing to break the land's spell and the feeling that they were the only two people in the world.

"I know."

"Has Trooper ever run off like this before?"

"No, never. A time or two he has taken off after a rabbit, but he has always come back right away." He slowed the horse to a walk when they reached the stand of trees.

Kate peered around his shoulder to search the thickening shadows for an advance glimpse of Trooper. But the dog wasn't waiting by the camper-trailer or his kennel.

"He isn't here," she said when Josh reined in.

"No." He swung a leg over the front of the saddle and jumped to the ground, then turned to help her down.

Ignoring his outstretched hands, Kate slid off the horse unaided. Turning, she cast an anxious glance at the sky's fading light. "What now?"

"It's too dark to keep looking," Josh stated. "We don't have much choice but to wait and see if Trooper shows up on his own tonight."

"But if he's out there alone and the coyotes find him—" Kate shuddered, breaking off the chilling thought.

"Trooper is tougher than you might think." His

mouth curved in an easy smile of assurance. "He could handle a pack of coyotes with one arm tied behind his back—or a cast on his leg."

Kate smiled briefly in return, then glanced again into the gathering darkness. "Where do you suppose he is?"

"I gave up trying to figure that out about an hour ago," Josh replied, a wryness in his voice.

"Could he have tried to follow you when you went to town earlier?" she wondered.

"It's possible, but I would have noticed him along the road when I came back."

"You might have missed him." She wished now that she hadn't driven so fast getting there, but it hadn't occurred to her that Trooper might be somewhere along the highway.

"Maybe, but Cap and Sarge wouldn't have." He indicated the two dogs now sprawled on the ground near the trailer's metal steps.

"I—" A telephone rang inside the trailer, and Kate jumped, startled by the harsh sound of it.

"Here." Josh pushed the reins into her hands. "I'll be right back."

In two long strides, he reached the trailer door and stepped inside, flipping on a light. It spilled through the side window, illuminating a long, rectangular patch of ground and stopping just short of Kate's feet. The gray horse nosed her arm, distracting her as Josh disappeared from view.

The telephone jangled loudly again, then stopped abruptly in mid-ring, indicating that Josh had picked up the receiver. She heard his voice, but it was pitched low, making most of the words inaudible.

Less than a minute later, he came out of the trailer. "That was your dad on the phone," he announced. "He called to tell us to stop looking for Trooper. He found him."

"Is he—"

"Trooper's fine."

"Where did he find him?"

"He didn't say and I didn't ask. I figured we could find out the details when we got there."

Kate was the first to arrive at the ranch, but Josh pulled into the yard right behind her. When she reached the back door, she heard Trooper whining and scratching at the other side. He launched himself at her the minute she walked in.

"Trooper, you rascal." She knelt down to return his exuberant greeting. "Don't you know we have been searching everywhere for you?"

"He's been hobbling all over the house trying to find you." Her father sat at the kitchen table.

"You have, have you?" she said to the dog as Josh walked in. Trooper instantly switched his attention to his master. Kate stood up. "Where did you find him, Dad?"

"Manny spotted him on the other side of Gila River about a mile from the house. He was looking for a place to cross, I guess. So Manny loaded him in the truck and brought him here."

"You mean that he came all the way from Josh's place to here?" She looked at the dog in amazement.

Josh chuckled and ruffled the dog's fur. "You got lonesome all by yourself and decided to visit your girlfriend, did you, fella?" He glanced at Kate and smiled, his eyes crinkling at the corners in a way that had her pulse speeding up. "Can't say as I blame you."

"But how did he know where we live?"

"If you can come up with the answer to that question," her father said, "you'll be bringing home the Nobel Prize in biology. Until you do, that's something only Trooper knows."

"His cast looks battered and worn, but otherwise he seems to be okay," Josh remarked after checking the dog over. "So what do you say, boy? Are you ready to go home?"

Trooper whined and sank to the floor, as if collapsing in exhaustion.

"There's no need for you to rush off," her father said. "I've got chili cooking on the stove. Why don't you stay and have supper with us?"

Josh glanced briefly at Kate, a soft, speculative light in his eyes. Pleasure shivered through her even as she wanted to scream at her father for issuing the invitation. She didn't want Josh to stay.

Liar, a little voice said.

"Thanks, I'd like that," Josh replied.

"Good. We have that settled now." Her father rubbed his hands together in satisfaction. "Kate, how about making some of that good Mexican cornbread to go with my chili?"

An hour later, Kate stacked the dirty supper dishes in the sink while Josh and her father sat at the table, drinking coffee and talking cattle business. Trooper was stretched in his old corner of the kitchen, snoring a noisy accompaniment to their conversation.

Leaving the dirty dishes to wash later, she picked up the coffeepot and carried it to the table. "How about a warm-up?"

Her father pushed his cup toward her, but Josh placed a hand over the top of his. "I'll pass, thanks," he said. "It's time I was heading home. Unfortunately, I still have evening chores to do."

"I don't think Trooper will be happy to hear that." Her father looked at the snoring dog and smiled. "He kinda gives new meaning to the expression 'dog-tired,' doesn't he?"

"He does that." Josh rose from his chair and walked over to the corner. "Come on, Trooper. Let's go home."

The dog awakened with a little grunt, then raised his head to give Josh a sleepy-eyed look, his tail thumping the floor twice.

"Come on." Josh slapped his leg in a summoning command. "We're leaving now."

Grunting again, the dog roused himself and started to get up, then groaned and sagged back to the floor as if he was too sore and weary to move.

Kate laughed softly at the sight. "Something tells me that you'll have to carry him to the truck."

"Something tells me you're right." Smiling, Josh crouched down and scooped the young dog up in his arms. Trooper twisted his head around to stretch his nose along Josh's upper arm and sighed in contentment, closing his eyes.

"You are one spoiled dog, Trooper." Kate shook her head in amusement.

"I wonder how he got that way?" Josh murmured, glancing her way.

Rather than discuss that point, Kate switched subjects. "I'll get the door for you." She shoved the coffee-pot back on its burner before walking to the back door and holding it open for him.

"If you don't mind, I could use some help getting him in my truck," Josh said as he maneuvered past her.

"Sure."

She followed him outside and held the door again while he laid Trooper on the passenger seat. The minute she closed the truck door, the dog sat up and poked his head out the open window, whining anxiously at her.

"Can't leave without saying goodbye, is that it, fella?" Kate stepped closer and affectionately rubbed him behind his droopy hound ears.

His long tongue took a swipe at her ear. Obligingly, Kate turned her head and allowed Trooper to bestow one of his wet kisses on her cheek.

"That's enough now." She drew back and wiped the back of her hand across her cheek. "You take care of yourself," she told the dog. "And don't pull any more crazy stunts like you did today, okay?"

Trooper whined an answer.

"Sometimes I think he understands every word I say." Smiling, Kate turned away, then instantly froze when she found herself face to face with Josh.

"My turn," he said simply and reached out, gathering her into his arms.

Despite all the alarm bells going off in her head, it felt completely right to Kate, completely natural that they should come together like this, mouth to mouth and body to body. It was more than odd; it was crazy, she told herself even as she gave herself up to the warm, demanding pressure of his kiss and the slow, molding stroke of his hands.

Every touch, every taste added to the dazzling assault on her senses. Over and over again, Kate reminded herself that blood couldn't heat, bones couldn't melt, but that's what it felt like in his arms.

When at last the kiss ended in a slow parting of lips, Kate stepped back on quivering legs, needing to put distance between them, and desperately needing to feel solid ground beneath her feet. Even then she was conscious of the hard, quick strike of her heart-beat and the aching shortness of her breathing.

"Kate," he said her name in a soft, husky voice that invited her back into his arms.

She wanted to go back.

The instant she realized that, she was furious with herself. She threw her head back, taking her anger out on him. "Why do men like you always have to make conquests out of every woman you meet?"

The warm, lazy blue of his eyes turned suddenly cool and hard. "Men like *me*? Just what is that supposed to mean?" he asked tightly.

"As if you didn't know," she muttered in disgust.

"No, I don't. Why don't you enlighten me?"

"Look, we both know you aren't really interested in me," Kate began in a burst of impatience.

"We both know that, do we?" he said grimly. "And just where did you get the idea that you are so unattractive to a man?"

"What?" she snapped, stung by the question. "For your information, I happen to think I am very attractive in my own way. But I'm not stupid. I know I don't have the sexy looks or classic beauty that men like you prefer."

"There is that 'men like you' again." He studied her with narrowed eyes. "You do realize that you are guilty of the very thing you are so quick to accuse others of doing?"

"Really?" She lifted her head a little higher. "And what exactly is that?"

"Judging by appearances," he stated and immediately turned on his heel to walk around to the driver's side of his pickup.

Stunned into silence, Kate could only stand and

watch as he drove out of the yard. The longer his words echoed through her mind, the more uncomfortable she became with the ring of truth they carried.

"Kate, are you out there?" her father called from the kitchen doorway.

"Coming." She turned and headed back toward the house.

"I was beginning to think you had left with Josh," he said when she walked in the door. "What were you doing out there all this time?"

"Thinking." She crossed to the sink, intending to wash the dishes, then stopped and turned back to face her father. "Can I ask you a question, Dad?"

"Fire away."

"What's your opinion of Josh?"

"My opinion?" His eyebrow shot up in surprise. "I like him, that's my opinion."

"I know you do, but I meant, what kind of man is he?"

"Well, let's see." Bick Summers paused to collect his thoughts. "He's honest, dependable, hardworking. He's got a good head on his shoulders and he knows the ins and outs of the ranch business. At the same time, he isn't above asking for advice. He has dreams, but he doesn't walk around with his head in the clouds. He knows he has to build a solid foundation under those dreams if he wants them to come true. And he can tell a good joke," he concluded.

"What about his looks?" Kate asked.

"What has that got to do with it?" He drew his head back with a frown. "His looks don't tell you what kind of man he is." He paused and studied Kate a little closer. "Don't tell me you've been holding his looks against him?"

"Maybe I have," she admitted and turned back to the sink.

Privately, she faced the truth that she had been quick to judge Josh simply because he was every bit as handsome as Cody Jones had been. There had been no other reason.

Seven

$\mathcal{K}$ate held the bay stallion's halter rope and idly rubbed his forehead while Manny hammered a nail into the horse's new shoe and through the outside of its hoof wall. More shoe nails were gripped between his teeth, but they didn't interfere with his ability to talk.

"I saw Josh Reynolds the other day." Manny paused to pluck another nail from his mouth. "He sold three of his horses to a buyer from the East. He got a bundle of money for them, too."

"Did Josh tell you that?" Kate felt sharp twinges of guilt at the mention of his name.

A dozen times in the last three days, she had picked up the phone to call him, aware that she owed him an apology. But every time she stopped because she didn't know what to say after she apologized.

"No. My cousin's sister told me, the one that works at the bank," Manny explained. "She notarized the bill of sale for the horses. But Josh, he told me that the buyer can sell those same horses in the East for two or three times what he paid Josh for them." Another nail went in, and the hammer tapped on metal again. "We have some jugheads here that say your father should send his horses out East to sell."

Catching a movement in her side vision, Kate glanced around and saw her father approaching, the sound of his footsteps masked by the shoer's hammer. "Here comes Dad. Why don't you suggest that to him?"

Manny looked around, then bent to his task again, muttering in Spanish.

"Are you about finished there?" her father asked with unusual brusqueness.

"Almost. Why? What's up?" She eyed him curiously.

"Josh just called," he said. Kate couldn't check the shiver of excitement she felt. "He wants us to keep watch for Trooper. He's run off again."

"When?"

"Not much more than two hours ago, he thought," her father replied, then explained. "Josh went to pick up some late calves he bought. When he got back, Trooper was gone. Josh figures that Trooper is headed our way again."

"I hope so. That will make it a lot easier to find him. Here." She handed him the stallion's halter rope. "You hold Red. I'll go look for Trooper."

Manny straightened from his hunched-over shoeing position. "He will probably come the same way he did before," he told Kate, then went on to describe the exact spot where he had found the dog the last time.

But there was no sign of Trooper when Kate reached the bank of the Gila River. She stopped the truck and let the motor idle while she scanned the immediate area.

Nothing stirred.

Taking a chance, she aimed the pickup in the general direction of Josh's place and drove toward it. A half mile from the river bank, she spotted Trooper hopping along on three legs, making good time in spite of the cast. Angling the truck toward him, she drove closer and stopped when he did.

"Hey, Trooper!" She swung down from the cab. "Come here, boy."

He gave an excited bark of recognition and hopped faster, talking to her all the way in a growling whine. Laughing, Kate wrapped her arms around him and hugged his wiggling body close to her.

"You wonderful, crazy dog, I love you." She laughed some more when he tried to wash her face with kisses. Kate pushed his nose away and stood up. "Come on. Let's go tell Josh that you're all right."

She half pushed and half lifted the dog into the cab of the pickup, then climbed in after him. He rode beside her, leaning against her shoulder and panting happily the whole way back.

The first blush of sunset dusted the underbellies of the sky's puffy clouds a soft pink when Kate drove into the yard. Her father was at the corrals, throwing hay to the horses.

She honked and waved to him. "I found Trooper!" she yelled out the window, then pointed toward the house. "I'm going to call Josh."

Her father lifted a hand, acknowledging that he understood, and Kate continued toward the house. When the pickup rolled to a stop near the back door, Trooper whined with excitement and tried to climb over her in his eagerness to get out. She pushed the dog back and stepped out, then helped him down.

Tail wagging, Trooper took off for the house at a fast hobble, then waited impatiently at the back steps for Kate. The minute she opened the door, he bulled his way in ahead of her.

"Josh needs to give you some lessons in manners.

It's supposed to be ladies first, Trooper," she chided, and went straight to the phone. He answered on the fifth ring. "Josh, it's Kate," she said. "Trooper is here, safe and sound."

"Good. I thought he would go there."

"If you like, I can run him over to your place."

"Don't bother." His voice sounded flat and slightly grim.

"It's no bother," Kate assured him.

"No, I meant that it's a waste of time. He would only slip off again and head back there the first chance he got. You might as well keep him."

Stunned by his announcement, Kate couldn't believe what she was hearing. "But—Trooper is your dog."

"It's obvious he has decided otherwise," Josh stated, his tone curt and final.

"You can't be sure of that," she protested. "Once you get him home—"

"Home is where the heart is, Kate," Josh interrupted. "And his heart is with you. Even you must recognize that."

"I think you're being a bit rash. We need to talk about this first. Why don't I come over? I wanted to apologize anyway for the things I—"

Too late, Kate realized that she was talking to a dead phone. Josh had hung up.

In a daze, she lowered the receiver and held it loosely in both hands, her mind racing in circles. She was still holding the phone when her father walked in. Trooper limped over to greet him.

"Did you talk to Josh?" he asked, stooping to pat the dog's head.

"Yes." She quickly put the phone back on its hook.

"When is he coming over, did he say?" Bick shrugged out of his jacket and hung it on a wall peg by the door.

"He won't be over." She clasped her hands together, tightly lacing her fingers in agitation. "He said we should keep Trooper. Permanently."

"What?" Her father frowned his surprise.

"I know. That was my reaction, too." She tugged her hands apart and lifted them in a gesture of hopeless confusion. "But Josh said that if he took him back, Trooper would only run away again, that he wants to be with us."

"Josh has a point there."

"I know he does, but—" She stopped, a heavy sigh breaking from her.

"But what?" her father prompted.

Confused and uncertain of the answer, Kate shook her head. "I don't know. It just doesn't feel right somehow."

"Trooper doesn't think so. Look at him." Her father motioned toward the dog. "He's made himself at home."

Turning, Kate saw the dog lying in his old corner, his head resting across the lightweight cast on his leg, his bright eyes watching her every move. His tail slapped the floor a couple times.

"Whether it feels right or not, I think you'd better go into town tomorrow morning and pick up some dog food," her father said.

Trooper woofed a quick agreement, drawing a faint smile from Kate.

"That's your vote, too, is it?" she murmured. "I guess I'm outnumbered."

On the way back from town the next morning, Kate kept an uneasy eye on the thunderheads that towered like white, craggy cliffs above the southern Mogollon Mountains. The black-bellied clouds filled the western sky with a quiet menace. Darting tongues of lightning flicked along the dark edges of them.

The air blowing through the open windows of the pickup felt heavy, laden with electricity. As Kate neared the ranch, the wind arrived in advance of the storm, blowing up clouds of dust and buffeting the truck with a force that tugged at the steering wheel.

When she reached the ranchyard, Kate paused long enough to poke through the grocery sacks until she found the one with the perishables. As she ran for the house, clutching the paper sack in her arms, the first fat drops of rain pelted down, raising puffs of dust across the dry ground.

The wind whipped the door from her grasp and banged it against the house. She managed to grab it again and dart inside, pulling it shut behind her.

"Whew!" she said with a gusty exhalation and threw a glance at her father, who was sitting at the table. "That is some storm blowing in."

"Sounds like we could be in for a regular gully-washer," he agreed.

Kate walked toward the kitchen counter and lifted the sack onto it. Outside, the rain fell faster, turning into a deluge that drummed against the windows. Listening to it, Kate pulled the milk and cheese from the sack and carried them to the refrigerator.

Her glance strayed toward the empty corner by the fireplace.

"Where is Trooper?" she asked curiously. "Did the storm scare him into hiding?"

"Trooper?" her father repeated with a note of surprise. "What do you mean? Isn't he with you?"

Kate swung around, feeling the first glimmer of alarm. "No, I left him here. He was sitting by the back door when I drove out. You don't think—" She stopped, her gaze slicing toward the door. "He wouldn't have—"

It seemed too impossible to voice.

"He's probably down at the barn waiting out the rain." Her father didn't sound any more convinced of that than Kate was.

"I'd better go look for him." Moving, she grabbed her yellow slicker off the wall hook and pulled it on, quickly fastening it and throwing the hood over her head. "Maybe you'd better call Josh, just in case."

She yanked the door open and plunged outside.

The rain fell in a sheeting downpour that hid the barn and outbuildings behind a thick veil of precipitation. Cupping her hands to her mouth, Kate called for the dog, but the driving rain drowned out the sound of her voice.

She splashed across the ranchyard toward the barn and ducked inside, calling again. Her only answer was the hammer of rain on the barn's tin roof. Kate dashed back outside and checked the other buildings, her anxiety growing.

There was no sign of Trooper anywhere.

Hunching her shoulders against the downpour, she ran back to the house. Inside, she pushed her hood off and shook her head.

"I couldn't find him," she told her father. "Did you get hold of Josh?"

"No, I couldn't get through. Our phone is working, but the storm must have knocked out a line near his place."

Kate hesitated only a second, then raised her hood again and turned toward the door. "I'm going over there."

"Be careful," her father called after her.

Eight

The rain fell in torrents. The pickup's windshield wipers rhythmically slapped back and forth, uselessly chasing waves of water. Kate slowed the truck to a crawl, but she still couldn't see more than a few feet in front of her.

Tension twisted her neck and shoulder muscles into knots. She flexed her fingers, trying to loosen their death grip on the steering wheel. Lightning splintered the air in her side vision. An instant later came the reverberating boom of thunder.

"Kate Summers," she muttered to herself. "You are insane to be out in this storm all because of a dumb dog."

The pickup slipped and slithered along the rutted lane leading to the canyon. At least Kate hoped it was the lane. For all she knew, she could be traveling across country.

A large, dark mass suddenly loomed in front of the truck. Kate hit the brakes, and the pickup skated to a sideways stop. Through the sheeting rain, she managed to make out the shape of a huge tree limb blocking her path.

She sat there for a long minute studying the situation and trying to decide whether she should attempt to drive around it and possibly get stuck. Reason reminded her that a limb this large could only have come from one of the ancient cottonwoods that grew near the canyon's mouth.

Which meant Josh's camper had to be close by.

On that thought, Kate switched off the motor and dragged the slicker's hood over her head, then stepped out of the truck. Bowing her head against the downbeating rain, she splashed around the fallen limb and slogged forward, muddy water pulling at her boots with each step she took.

At last the trailer's distinctive shape became visible ahead of her. Kate trotted the last few yards to the camper and pounded on the door. The instant it swung open, she scrambled inside, tossing back the hood, her slicker streaming water. Josh stared at her, scowling in disbelief.

"Kate, what the hell are you doing out in this storm?" he exploded a second later.

"I have asked myself that question a dozen times the last few miles." She shook her dripping fingers and paused, conscious of the water squelching in her boots. "It's Trooper. He's gone again," she said and rushed to explain. "I had to go into town this morning. I know I should have shut him in the house. But I never thought . . . It never occurred to me . . . You haven't seen him, have you?"

"No, I haven't." Irritation made his voice clipped and hard. "You'd better get that coat off. It will be a miracle if you aren't soaked to the skin under it."

"We tried to call you." She fumbled with the buttons, her wet fingers losing their grip on the equally wet and slick material. Impatiently, Josh reached in to help her. "But your phone is out. There's a big limb lying across the road. It probably took your line down when it fell."

"I heard it crash about thirty minutes ago. It knocked out the power, as well as the telephone." He dragged the coat off her shoulders and held it while Kate freed her arms. Folding it, he turned and headed toward the shadowed dimness in the rear, the trailer rocking a little with each heavy stride. "I'll hang this in the shower for you."

The drumming rain on the camper roof muffled his voice. Without the layering of the slicker, the damp cool seeped in. Kate shivered and rubbed her arms to generate some warmth.

Her face was wet from the spray of rain, and the collar of her white blouse and its surrounding material were soaked. But it was the cold, numb sensation in her feet that demanded attention. Kate leaned against the side of the trailer and lifted a leg to pull the first boot off. The floor vibrated, signaling Josh's return.

"Sit down." He waved her toward the sofa that occupied one end of the trailer.

The minute Kate sank onto its cushion, Josh was on one knee in front of her, tugging at a boot. Water spilled from it when he pulled it free. Her sock was equally saturated. Josh peeled it off, as well, and laid it in a sodden heap next to the boot.

"I'm surprised your teeth aren't chattering." His voice still had that irritated edge to it as he shifted to the other boot.

"They are thinking about it," she admitted. "It didn't feel that cold outside."

"It never does when you're dry." When the second boot and sock hit the floor, Josh pushed himself to his feet, grabbing her hand and pulling her with him. "Come on. Let's see if we can't get you dried off." He pointed her toward the back of the trailer. "You'll find some towels in the bathroom, the first door on your right."

He gave her a small push in that direction, then followed a step behind. When Kate reached the door to the compact bathroom, Josh shouldered his way around her and continued toward the small bedroom at the trailer's rear. She barely had time to grab a thick terry towel before he came back and maneuvered by her again, making her very aware of the trailer's cramped quarters.

"You'll need to get out of that wet blouse," he told her. "There's a sweatshirt on the bed you can wear. And a heavy pair of socks, too. Your feet felt like ice."

Kate walked toward the bedroom while Josh busied himself in the trailer's small galley kitchen. Below the pounding rain, she caught the sound of water roaring in the canyon's stream.

"Where do you think Trooper is?" She raised her voice to make herself heard above the storm's din.

"Probably holed up somewhere." Pans clattered. "That dog happens to have more sense than you do."

"He also happens to have a broken leg and a cumbersome cast on it." Kate shrugged out of the blouse and hooked it on a closet doorknob, then reached for the sweatshirt, pulled it over her head, and poked her arms into the sleeves.

"He can take care of himself. I swear you care more about that dog than you would a child."

"That's not true." Temper simmering, she plopped on the bed and tugged on the first sock. "If a child was out in this storm, I'd still be out there searching instead of in here taking off half my clothes."

"Now there's an interesting picture." Amusement warmed his voice.

"Very funny," Kate muttered, her thoughts instantly turning to the flatness of her chest as she pulled on the last sock.

"What did you say?"

"Nothing." She stood up, and the sweatshirt's long sleeves slipped down, covering up her hands. Immediately, she shoved them up to her elbows and headed back toward the front of the trailer.

Josh was at the small stove stirring something in a pan. "I'm heating up some milk for cocoa," he said, giving her a once-over when she appeared. "I thought you could use a cup."

"Sure." As she started to move past him, she stepped on the floppy toe of a too-long sock and pitched forward.

A spoon clattered to the floor as his arm snaked out, catching her around the middle and checking her headlong fall. In the next second, Kate found herself pressed against his side, from muscled shoulder to leg. Her pulse skittered and took off at a wild pace.

"Are you okay?" His face was close. Too close.

"I'm fine." She felt weak at the knees and knew it wasn't from the near fall. She tried to bring her hands up and push herself a step back, but they were lost again in the sleeves of his sweatshirt. "It's your clothes. They're too large."

"They are kinda big." Josh didn't loosen his hold

on her. Instead, his hand began an experimental slide over her back while his gaze traveled over her face, an awareness of her darkening his eyes. "Why is it that women so often look sexy in men's clothes, I wonder?"

"I wouldn't know." Suddenly uncertain of herself, Kate lowered her gaze to the collar of his shirt.

"That's right. I forgot," he murmured, a hint of grimness entering his voice. "You don't think you can look sexy, do you?"

His comment harkened back to the disagreement they had had the other night outside her house. Not that Kate had needed it. She had been nagged by the memory of it, and her subsequent conversation with her father, ever since.

"Josh, I have to talk to you about something." She kept her gaze fixed to his collar.

"Oh?" His tone was hardly encouraging.

"The things you said the other night," she began, determined to get it off her conscience. "You were right. I have been guilty of judging by appearances and I regret that."

"Regrets can be difficult to live with." He shifted his position, squaring around to face her more directly, their bodies brushing.

"They can," Kate agreed, a slightly breathless catch in her voice. "Anyway, I was wrong. I'm sorry. I should have known better."

"Tell me something." He hooked a fingertip under her chin and tilted it up, forcing her to meet his eyes. "Do you always admit when you're wrong?"

"Of course." It never occurred to her to do otherwise. "I don't always like it, but—"

"I knew you were a rare woman," he broke in,

then brought his mouth down in a claiming kiss.

There was demand in it, and the growing heat of passion. This time Kate didn't question it. Instead, she wrapped her arms around his neck, dangling sleeves and all, and matched him, demand for demand.

She loved him. It was a terrifying thought. Yet, oddly enough, as afraid as she was of loving him, Kate felt a calming sense of rightness about it, too. For all the fire and magic, she knew there was something here that was solid and strong, something that could not only endure, but also grow.

At last, he dragged his mouth from hers and buried it in the damp edges of the hair near her ear. "And I thought I would have some convincing to do," Josh murmured, breathing as raggedly as she was.

She pulled in a deep, happy breath, then stiffened, catching an acrid scent. "Josh, I smell something burning."

"What?" He glanced over his shoulder and swore, instantly releasing her to turn to the propane stove and rescue the pan of milk that was boiling over. "You can forget about a cup of cocoa." He set the pan in the sink. "I just scorched the last of the milk."

"I'll survive without it." She hugged her arms around her, feeling positively aglow with happiness.

Josh glanced at her and forgot all about the pan. "Kate." He took a step back toward her.

There was a thump on the trailer steps, followed by an anxious, whining howl. Kate swung toward the sound. "It's Trooper. He made it here through the storm."

She stumbled over her socks trying to get to the door. Josh reached it first, pushing it open and hauling the rain-drenched dog inside the trailer. Whining and wiggling with joy, Trooper strained to lick Josh's face.

"Look at his cast," Kate said. "It's covered with mud."

Trooper swung his head around, a look of surprise in his eyes at the sight of her. With an excited yelp, he plunged toward her.

"Look out. He's soaking wet," Josh warned too late, as Kate tried to hold the dog back and failed. "I'll go get some towels."

When Josh headed for the rear of the trailer, Trooper started after him, then stopped and proceeded to vigorously shake himself off, spraying water in all directions.

Kate saw it coming and threw up her arms, uselessly protesting, "Trooper, no!"

Josh came back with the towels. "I picked a good time to get these, didn't I?" he said, eyes twinkling.

"Lucky you." She wiped at the scattered drops of water on her face.

"Not lucky. Smart." He handed her a towel.

Together they wrapped the dog up and began rubbing him dry. Trooper sat happily through it all, drinking in the attention.

"His wound is bleeding," Kate murmured in concern.

Josh examined it. "I think it's just from the scab coming off." He took some alcohol from one of the cupboards and cleaned the area thoroughly, then applied an antiseptic salve. "That should take care of it."

"You do realize that Trooper has a serious problem." Kate fondled the dog's head, watching while Josh finished tending to the wound.

"What's that?" He screwed the cap back on the tube of salve.

"He can't make up his mind which one of us he wants to be with," she said. "He's going to wear himself out going back and forth."

"There's a solution to that."

"There is?" When she looked at Josh, her heart did a little flip.

"You and I could fall in love and get married."

"I suppose we could, but don't you think that's a bit drastic?" She fought to keep a casual note in her voice.

"Probably. But the idea appeals to me. How about you?" His smile was crooked, matching the lightness in his voice, but the look in his eyes was dead-serious.

"It's a bit quick, don't you think?" Kate replied, feeling strangely light and breathless, yet blissfully happy at the same time, as if she had finally come home. "We haven't known each other very long."

"How much longer do you think it would take? One week? Two weeks?"

She laughed a little giddily. "This is crazy. People don't get married because of a dog."

"There's a house we both want to build. And I'll bet if we put our heads together, we can come up with another reason," Josh suggested and cupped a hand behind her neck, drawing her lips to meet his.

JANET DAILEY

Janet Dailey is among the world's bestselling authors. She has written more than ninety novels and lives in Branson, Missouri.

The Return of
Walker Lee

Sharon Sala

Like the song goes, my heroes have always been cowboys, so I'm dedicating this story to them.

As a young girl, I was held hostage until the very last page by Zane Grey's stories about the Old West and the men on horseback who conquered it. As I grew older, Louis L'Amour became my author of choice. Now, as a writer myself, I find I'm drawn to creating the same type of heroes for my stories: men with indomitable spirits and never-say-die attitudes. Tough, hard men who know when to be gentle.

To the cowboys.

Prologue

Speed-limit signs were an insult to a man like Walker Lee. Thirty years before, his mother had given birth to him in less than four hours, and it seemed as if he'd been in a hurry ever since. Some people said the way he rodeoed, he must even be in a hurry to die.

But those people didn't know the real Walker Lee. They'd never known the lonely little boy from Spurlock, Texas who'd been born on the wrong side of a blanket and on the wrong side of the tracks. They only knew the death-defying charmer he'd become.

When Walker was eighteen years old, his mother had gotten on a bus and never bothered to come back. Her abandonment only reinforced a lesson he had learned early on: Never let them know you care, and never let them see you cry. Only once had he broken that rule, and the act itself had nearly broken him.

Carrie Ann Wainright had turned him upside down and sideways before he'd gotten the guts to cut himself loose. Ten years had come and gone since the night he'd walked out of her life. But now circumstance and a longing for something he refused to name had set Walker back on a path toward the only home he'd ever known.

Walker Lee entered the city limits of Spurlock, Texas just as the digital clock on his dashboard clicked over to three in the morning. As he drove through town, not even the assurance that everyone of consequence should be sound asleep in their beds could ease the knot in Walker's belly. And neither the money in his pocket or the new three-quarter-ton, extend-a-cab pickup he was driving could stop the flood of painful memories. The house he'd grown up in had burned to the ground years before, yet, when he passed Concord Street, the urge to turn left was strong.

As he drove past the football field, everything he'd accomplished during the past ten years seemed worthless compared to the pain this town and its inhabitants had put him through. He rolled to a stop at the fifty-yard line with his gut in a knot. Even though the field was in darkness, in his mind's eye, the ceremony that had marked the end of his and Carrie's relationship was as vivid now as it had been all those years ago.

The loudspeaker had squealed, "Ladies and gentlemen, I give you Spurlock High's new homecoming queen, Caroline Wainright."

Walker blinked, and the image disappeared, although he still remembered the hurt and rage he'd felt when Sammy Wayne Alcott set the crown on Carrie's head then sealed her status with a long, passionate kiss that had left him stunned. Unable to believe Carrie would let anyone kiss her like that when she belonged to him, he walked out of the stadium as the crowd went into a frenzy.

Carrie was Walker's girl, had been for months, but only on the sly. Besides the fact that Walker was twenty to Carrie Ann's eighteen, he wasn't the kind of man good girls took home to mama.

A train whistle sounded at the two-mile crossing outside of town, yanking Walker out of the past. He glanced up, then around, making sure his presence was still undetected.

He looked away, his hands shaking. Obviously, the old memory had not faded, although he'd tried for years to convince himself he no longer cared. He was living proof that love, however fickle, could still hurt like hell.

He took his foot off the brake and accelerated slowly, moving past the high school toward the park, and then to the shallow creek meandering through the woods within. He gritted his teeth as he stared into the tree line, preparing himself for a jolt of pain. It came, and with it the urge to see for himself if their place looked the same.

He parked, then walked across the grass into the trees bordering the creek. A few steps farther, he walked up on the flat, overhanging rock that had been 'their' place. In the dark, the moss growing on the rock looked like spilled blood; an apt analogy to the love that had ended here so many years ago. His nostrils flared and he lifted his chin in a gesture of self-defense. Anger assailed him, and when it did, it was as fresh as it had been then.

"Please, Carrie, let me talk to your folks."

Carrie's eyes widened in fear.

Cursing beneath his breath, he looked away. Frustration with the situation made him angry. He was unaware Carrie's parents were already suspicious. He had no way of knowing her father had made subtle threats as to what would happen to that Lee boy and his job if Carrie was messing around with him. He didn't know it was shame, not fear, that colored the expression on her face.

"You don't understand," she said. "My father could make trouble for you in more ways than one."

Walker's eyes glittered in anger. "I'm not afraid of your father, or anyone else."

Carrie shook her head. "Look, we can't talk to my parents and that's that."

Walker's expression stilled. He'd never heard such finality in her voice before.

"But I love you, Carrie."

Her voice shook. "I love you, too."

A cold smile centered on his face as he remembered the way she'd melted into Sammy Wayne Alcott's arms only hours earlier.

"Those are only words, Carrie. Sometimes words aren't enough."

Walker turned away and missed seeing the panic on Carrie's face. In spite of the love he felt for her, he was pulling away from the conditions under which they'd been meeting. He might be poor, but he had more pride than most.

He'd known from the start of their relationship her parents might never approve of him, but he'd expected Carrie to give him the chance to try. He owned nothing, had nothing, not even a clue to the man who'd fathered him, but he was willing to change. For Carrie Ann, he would do anything.

He flinched as her fingers caressed his forearm, the plea in her voice breaking his heart.

"Please, Walker, just give me a little more time to figure something out."

He almost sneered. "Like what? Time's not going to change who I am."

She clutched at him in desperation. "I know, I know, but maybe—"

"Maybe nothing, Carrie. For once, why don't you be honest with yourself? I think you're ashamed of me."

"No! You're wrong!" she cried and tried to throw herself into his arms. He pushed her away.

She started to cry. "Oh God, Walker, don't do this to us."

He reacted with anger.

"I'm not doing anything. You're the one who's been calling the shots."

"Only for your protection," Carrie argued. "How can you believe I'd be so shallow?"

"Maybe because you hide me from everyone in your life who matters."

Carrie bit her lip and looked away. She couldn't argue with the truth. She did hide how she felt about him, but for his benefit, not hers.

Walker grabbed her by the arm, forcing her to look at him again. "Listen to me, girl. We're through sneaking around." His voice softened as he cupped her cheek. "I want to marry you. I thought you wanted the same thing."

Carrie panicked. Marry? Oh, God!

"Carrie?"

"What?"

"I'm waiting."

Resolve settled as Carrie accepted full blame for the impossible situation they were in. She loved him without caution, yet didn't have the guts to tell the world. There must be a way to get through this, but for now, the only way she knew to prove her love to Walker was to show him.

"Walker . . ."

"What?"

"You don't have to wait any longer."

Carrie took him by the hand and pulled him down beside her on the flat, mossy rock. The water from the creek below

flowed gently over the meandering bed, creating an indis-
tinct melody by which to make love.

Walker cursed beneath his breath. Carrie had taken
from him time and time again, and all he'd asked in
return was a little respect. Even then, after what they'd
shared, she hadn't been strong enough to give him
what he'd asked. That night had been the last straw in
their fragile affair.

He picked up a stick and flung it far and hard. It
clattered through some bushes on the other side of
the creek, but Walker didn't stay to see where it
landed. He was already on his way back to his truck.

Mad at himself for letting old emotions get the best
of him, he put the truck into gear and drove on, only
to come face to face with the tall, white water tower on
the south side of town. Once again, he hit the brakes
and shoved the gears into park. Leaning forward, he
rested his forearms on the steering wheel and stared
up through the windshield at the broad, white face of
the towering tank. The attached ladder on the side
was 156 steps high. He clearly remembered counting
them as he'd climbed with paint bucket and brush in
hand.

Bits of rust showed through the paint, an indication
of the time that had passed, as well as the lack of care
a tiny, one-horse town like Spurlock had given to its
upkeep.

He stared, trying to remember exactly where he
had painted the words "Walker Loves Carrie." Maybe
just a little to the right of that star-shaped rusty spot,
but he wasn't sure. What he did remember was the
wrenching pain that came in knowing it was the first
and only time their names would be publicly linked.

Headlights from an oncoming car swept his vehicle. He squinted against the glare and put the truck in gear. It was time to leave.

Tonight's visit might have been foolhardy, but it had been necessary for his peace of mind. The next time he drove into Spurlock, he'd come in true Walker Lee style. Then he'd give the town's tight-assed citizens something to talk about.

He drove away, leaving Spurlock and its ghosts to the dark. But as fast as he drove and as hard as he tried, he couldn't outrun the memory of the girl he'd left behind.

One

"*For* God's sake, Carrie, *The Weekly Spur* does not run condom ads. Call Mildred Cook and tell her to put something else on sale at her pharmacy besides rubbers, or the entire congregation of the Southern Baptist Church will be picketing my paper."

Carrie Wainright looked up from her computer. The blank expression on her face told Ansel Charles she hadn't heard a word he'd been saying.

Lost in the story on which she was working, the only thing Carrie heard her boss say was something about the paper being picketed.

"Who's picketing the paper?" she asked.

Ansel waved her back to the keyboard.

"Never mind, I'll do it myself. I swear I think Mildred does this on purpose just to get my dander up."

"Does what?" Carrie asked.

Ansel held up the ad. Even though she was across the room, the wording on the ad was impossible to miss: "Give your mate something to remember you by." The brand name of the condoms, as well as the price per box, was blatantly portrayed beneath the slogan.

Carrie grinned.

"It's not funny," Ansel muttered and popped a handful of M&M's into his mouth before he picked up the phone.

It wasn't polite to eat and talk at the same time, but he didn't give a damn. It had been exactly four days, eleven hours and twenty-four minutes since he'd had his last cigarette. Between the nicotine he longed for and Mildred Cook's persistence in trying his patience, he was beginning to fear there wasn't enough chocolate in Texas to keep him off the smokes.

Carrie looked back at the screen before her. Being the only reporter on *The Weekly Spur* had its good points, as well as its bad. Today, the bad ones were taking the forefront.

A headache hovered. Life had played a cruel joke on Caroline by allowing her to fall in love with the wrong man; a man who'd run out on her years ago. Every now and then, fate was still getting in its chuckles just to remind her she was not, and never had been, the one in control.

She read the words she'd just typed, editing as she went along. Although it was difficult, she tried not to think of the text.

Mr. and Mrs. Junior Bettis were proudly announcing the birth of their first child.

Carrie frowned. Once she'd been engaged to Junior Bettis. She sighed. That had been the first of her fool-hardy attempts to forget Walker Lee. That engagement had lasted exactly four months, after which time she'd come to the painful conclusion that Junior's kisses were too wet and his hands were too dry.

Her shoulders slumped as she stared at the screen.

As a child, and then as a teenager, Carrie Wainright had been good at everything. As an adult, she had yet to get anything right. *Junior Bettis moved on. Why the hell can't I?*

Hours earlier, she'd been putting together what passed as the paper's society page. There, in black and white and grinning like a raccoon eating ripe persimmons, was Mark Wyatt and his new little bride. About a year and a half after Junior had come and gone, Carrie had accepted Mark Wyatt's engagement ring. That relationship lasted an entire six weeks before Carrie called it off, as well. There hadn't been anything really wrong with Mark Wyatt other than the fact his hair wasn't as black and his eyes weren't as blue as Walker Lee's. Carrie's sigh deepened. In all fairness to Mark, and every other man who'd come and gone, there would never be but one Walker Lee.

The bell over the door jingled. Carrie glanced up at the man entering the newspaper office.

When Jerry James leaned over the counter and winked in her direction, she grinned politely then looked away, wishing his smile was a bit more off center, like . . .

She blinked. What was wrong with her? Walker Lee was long gone. Had been for years. For weeks after he'd disappeared, she'd waited like a child for Christmas, expecting a letter, a card, anything that would tell her where he'd gone. It hadn't come—and neither had Walker. He'd obviously forgotten her, and, except for the occasional rude reminder, she managed to keep Walker Lee in her past, where he belonged.

"Hey, Carrie, you're looking pretty today."

She acknowledged the compliment with an uncomfortable thank you.

Ansel arched an eyebrow and grinned. She glared

back at him as if to say what was going on was none of his business.

Because he was boss, Ansel waved her toward the counter. "Carrie, Mildred put me on hold. Get Jerry's ad for me, will you?"

Carrie glared. Ansel had done that on purpose. He was always trying to match her up with every single male who came along. She didn't know why he was so set on fixing her up. He'd been divorced for three years. If he wanted to meddle with romance, he should be worrying about his own love life, not hers. Besides, she was perfectly satisfied with her life the way it was.

Carrie got up from her chair and went to the counter. "Morning, Jerry. Let's see what's on special."

He slid his ad toward her. When she reached for it, he caught her hand instead, plying her with his megawatt smile. He lowered his voice.

"How about me and dinner tonight at eight?"

Carrie pretended she didn't hear while she scanned the ad for mistakes. At thirty-three, Jerry James's hair was starting to thin. And a slight roll of fat sagged over his belt, an early indication of what the ensuing years were going to leave behind.

When Jerry didn't get the response he wanted from Carrie, he returned to the ad in question.

"Pork is on special, and twenty-pound bags of potatoes are half-price with a ten-dollar purchase."

"That's good," Carrie said.

Jerry couldn't resist adding. "Business is good, too. I'm thinking of expanding the store and adding a deli, just like those city stores have."

"That's great," Carrie said, feigning great interest as she tossed the ad on Ansel's desk. Without waiting for her boss's response, she added, "Ansel, I'm going to lunch," and left the room, eager to escape Jerry James's pursuit.

She yanked her car door open and slammed herself inside, ignoring the heat from the sweltering interior as it sucked the breath from her lungs and seared the backs of her legs. When she started the car, she rolled down the windows instead of turning on the air conditioner. It wouldn't have time to get cool before she drove the mile and a half home.

The day was a typical late August scorcher. The sky was clear—too clear. Sky-blue had faded to a near-white, and the pastures on the neighboring ranches were in desperate need of rain. Yet, by the time she cleared the city limits of Spurlock, she was in a better frame of mind.

Thinking of the jug of sun tea in her refrigerator was enough to put a small smile on her face. There was probably enough pot roast left from Sunday dinner to make herself a sandwich. Having settled that, Carrie began to relax even more.

Wynonna's latest hit was playing on Carrie's favorite country station. She turned up the volume, letting the wind play hell with her hair while she sang along. The short, chocolate-colored curls framing her face were a far cry from the style she used to wear. It had been short for years, ever since she'd cut it off in a youthful gesture of defiance at Walker's absence. He'd liked it long, but he hadn't liked her enough to stay. A quarter of a mile from home, she noticed a new billboard had been installed on the old Ainsley place.

"Labor Day Rodeo!!"

Carrie sat up straighter in her seat and slowed down to read the dates: "August 31 and September 1 & 2."

" 'Three fun-filled days in Spurlock,' " she repeated, reading the rest of the sign aloud. Then she grinned, thinking of the lack of amenities in the small Texas town. "That might be hard to come by."

She drove past, wondering what organization had sponsored the event. Spurlock's population hardly warranted anything as vast as a professional rodeo, complete with silver buckles and the prize money the sign on the billboard promised.

By the time she got to her house, her curiosity was in high gear. She dashed outside to turn on the sprinkler in the flower bed, then ate her lunch in absent-minded fashion, planning the piece Ansel was bound to want written about the event.

Just as she was emptying the dishwasher, the mailman honked. Carrie dried her hands on her pants and dashed out the door. It was Truman Beggs's signal when her mail wouldn't fit in the box.

"Looks like your mom sent you a package," Truman said, handing Carrie an oversized box, as well as a handful of mail.

Carrie noted the Florida postmark and the Wainright name on the return address.

"Looks like," she agreed, and took what he handed her.

"Looks like we're gonna have ourselves a rodeo in town," Truman added.

Carrie nodded. It seemed Truman wasn't ready to leave.

"Yes, I saw the billboard on my way home," she said.

"Looks like it's gonna be quite a shindig."

Carrie grinned. "You're probably right."

"Looks like old Ansel oughta do a write-up on it. We ain't had ourselves a rodeo in town in quite a spell."

Carrie stifled her amusement. "I'll tell Ansel you said so."

Truman nodded, satisfied that he'd gotten his point across.

"You do that," he said as he eased off the brake. His Jeep was already rolling when he yelled out one last comment. "Tell your mother I said hello when you talk to her next."

Carrie ran back to the house with a lighter step. A package from her mother, no matter what the reason, was always fun. Carl Wainright, her father, had died during her junior year in college. Soon after, her mother, Susan, had moved to Florida to be near her sisters, and Carrie had learned to be satisfied with her mother's yearly holiday visits.

She dropped the mail on the kitchen table and went to get a knife. She opened the box in haste, and then her excitement slowly died. The items she took from inside, one by one, were like ghosts from her past.

A high school yearbook from her senior year of school.

The rhinestone tiara with which she'd been crowned homecoming queen.

A framed 8 x 10 black-and-white picture of Sammy Wayne Alcott jamming his tongue down her throat while she stood helpless beneath his onslaught, clutching at the crown on her head to keep it from falling. A dozen roses dangled from her hand.

She took a deep breath, remembering the shock of his unexpected behavior. Only afterwards had she learned it had been part of a bet, but it was too late then to undo what Sammy Wayne had done to Walker Lee's heart.

She looked up, staring blindly at a spider web in the corner of the ceiling. Just what she needed today. A reminder of her last night with Walker Lee.

An envelope was taped to the inside of the box.

Carrie took it out, wondering what her mother could possibly have to say that hadn't already been said by the return of these items.

Carrie darling,

Your aunt Mimi and I were cleaning out the garage the other day and I ran across some of your old treasures. I'm so short of storage space and I know you'll want to keep these. Such wonderful reminders of a happy time!

Which reminds me, have you gone out with that nice Jerry James yet? He's quite a catch, you know, although far be it from me to tell you what to do. I told your aunt Mimi I was sure you had good reason for breaking your other two engagements, although you've never seen fit to mention them to me.

At any rate, you know I only want what's best for you. Try to remember I'm not getting any younger. Mavis Childers (you remember Mavis. She and her second husband Dewey own all those dry cleaners in Ft. Lauderdale) has a new grandson. Her fourth. Write soon. I miss you.

Love, Mom

Carrie crumpled the letter and tossed it in the trash. Just more of the same quiet coercion. Get married to someone suitable. Have babies. Send pictures. She'd been getting this less-than-subtle third degree about her personal life for years. It was a little hard to explain why Junior Bettis and Mark Wyatt hadn't made the grade when her mother had never known about Walker Lee, or that he had set a standard for her no man since had been able to meet.

She stared down at the picture, then turned it face down on the table and glanced at the clock. No time to dwell on the past. She had to get back to work. A spray of water suddenly splattered the glass on her storm door.

"The flower bed!" she said, and hurried outside to turn off the water.

Droplets hung heavily on the fragile petals and leaves of her pansies. The brief watering left a fresh-washed scent in the air, although it had been weeks since Spurlock had last seen a rain. She knelt, picking at weeds and tossing out tiny sticks and leaves that had blown into the bed, then rose reluctantly. It was past time to get back to work.

As she drove toward town, the feeling of escape she'd had earlier was gone, and she knew it was all because of the old mementos her mother had sent. For the first time in years, she felt out of control. It was the same feeling she'd had when first seeing Walker Lee's message to the world on the water tower in the middle of town. She hadn't understood then, and still didn't now, why someone would announce such a fact to the entire world and then walk out of her life as if she just didn't matter anymore.

The rodeo was the talk of the town. By quitting time, even Ansel was getting into the excitement. The promoter for the Professional Rodeo Cowboys Association had placed a full-page ad in *The Weekly Spur* with Ansel's promise of coverage of the entire three-day event. Carrie might be at a loss as to the direction her life was going, but she knew where her job would take her, at least for the next few days: the rodeo.

Without fail, Ansel Charles spent every evening at the Sunset Home for the Elderly where his ninety-four-year-old mother resided, clinging to life with the tenacity of a ten-year-old. The fact that she rarely recognized her only son's face was immaterial to Ansel. He fed her supper every evening, whether she wanted it or not, and then read the same chapter of the Bible to her over and over until she went to sleep. There was something calming about the first book of Genesis to LucyBee Charles. Ansel figured it had to do with God creating the world, but he wasn't really sure. However, it hardly mattered. Getting LucyBee to sleep each night without a fuss was what counted.

Since Ansel's routine was always the same, it meant Carrie would have to be the on-the-spot reporter for each night's events. Even though she wasn't a die-hard rodeo fan, the assignment seemed exciting.

And she had to admit it would be a relief to cover something besides weddings and baby showers. She was a bit tired of fielding her old friends' snide remarks about her unwed state. Even though every other female in her graduating class had married, some more than once, being twenty-eight didn't exactly put her out of the running. She had plenty of time to find Mr. Right. She refused to admit that there was a distinct possibility that Mr. Right had already come and gone. Surely to God, Walker Lee wasn't the only man on earth who could make her hear bells.

"Don't forget your camera," Ansel said as Carrie headed for the door.

"Got it." She held it up by the strap to prove her point.

Ansel nodded approvingly. "Get me a great action shot and tomorrow's headline is yours."

Carrie's grin was a little wry. "I'm your only reporter. The headline is always mine."

Ansel popped a handful of M&M's into his mouth,

chewing around his words. "Don't be so damned cocky. Never know when that might change."

She made sure not to slam the door behind her.

There were more people on the portable bleachers set up at the rodeo grounds than Carrie had seen in one place in years. Last year, Spurlock High's football team had made state Class A finals, and even that hadn't prompted this kind of turnout. She got out of her car with the camera dangling around her neck and a notepad and tape recorder stuffed into the oversized bag on her shoulder.

Carrie was a woman who came prepared for everything. Settling herself in the center about midway up the bleachers, she ran her fingers through the curls bordering her face, absently ruffling the style, and sat back to enjoy the sights.

As with most rodeos, it began with the Grand Entry. The local roundup club, as well as the rodeo contestants, rode into the arena, two by two, led by a gray-haired cowboy riding a prancing Appaloosa. He carried the American flag, his head held high, while a pretty young girl on a Palomino horse rode beside him.

Carrie recognized the girl. She was Wallace Hillman's youngest daughter, Carletta, who was also the newly elected princess of the Spurlock Roundup Club. From the way her opulent curves were crammed into fringed and rhinestoned, powder-blue satin pants and shirt, Carrie figured Carletta would be lucky to make it around the ring without bursting out of her suit.

The announcer's voice resonated as he asked everyone to stand for the national anthem, and because Carrie was juggling camera and bag, she missed seeing a certain dark-haired cowboy on a high-stepping bay circle past where she was seated. By the time she got her camera up for a shot of Carletta Hillman's shiny blue satin, the national anthem was already playing.

The camera dangled from Carrie's neck as she focused her attention on the stars and stripes waving in the evening breeze. By the time the crowd sat back down, Carletta Hillman was gone.

Carrie sighed in frustration, reminding herself the night was young. There would be plenty of opportunities for other shots.

And so there were. An hour into the events, the air was thick with dust and the ripe, unmistakable scent of fresh manure as the contestants came and went.

Carrie watched the timed events with absent interest, especially the bulldogging, wondering what would possess a man to want to earn his living by jumping from a charging horse onto the back of a wild steer, then wrestling it to the ground. Calf roping made only a little more sense, considering the fact that the calves were smaller, and that the cowboy had to rope it first before dismounting and tying three of its four legs together in split-second time.

She made notes, visited with people on either side of her, and laughed along with everyone else as the rodeo clowns did their bit toward entertaining the crowd while making sure the participants stayed safe. It wasn't until the rough stock events began that she actually sat up and took serious notice.

One after another, young men in wide-brimmed Stetsons and flashy MoBetta shirts came out of the chutes on the bare backs of bulls. Big bulls, crazy mad with anger and fear. Bulls with eyes that seemed to glow blood-red as they twisted and kicked, doing all they knew to dislodge the rider sticking fast to their backs.

Dust boiled as the rodeo clowns raced in and out of danger, giving each rider time to jump free of his ride and climb up the steel fences to safety. The crowd seemed to gasp in unison, then cheer in the same fashion as the daring young men came out of the gates, each hoping to make the eight-second ride and qualify in the money.

Carrie sat white-knuckled and grim-lipped, tasting dust and sensing the tension spreading throughout the crowd. The woman sitting to Carrie's right had introduced herself as Babe Raines, from Abilene, Texas, and had been giving Carrie a play-by-play of each event, right down to more information on the cowboys' personal lives than she really wanted to know.

A stunning woman of forty-something, Babe Raines wore her clothes and red hair with the aplomb of a person who liked herself. Her burgeoning breasts pushed at the yellow fabric on her tight western shirt, and her shapely bottom fit nicely into new black Rockies.

Carrie felt absolutely drab in plain Levis and her blue denim shirt. Even her gray Ropers looked bland compared to Babe's red and black high-top Justin boots.

Carrie glanced at her camera, checking the film left on the roll, when Babe suddenly elbowed her.

"Ooo-eee, Diablo Blanco is up next. I wonder who drew that mean S.O.B., pardon my French."

"Who's Diablo Blanco?"

Babe grinned. "Diablo is a what, not a who." She pointed toward the end of the arena. "That's the meanest damned bull on the circuit."

Carrie looked toward the holding pens, watching as the stockmen moved the next bull to be ridden into the chute. The animal Babe pointed out was a massive, grayish-white Brahma. It's long, flop ears drooped down toward the ground like dangling earrings, and the muscles on its back rippled as it walked.

Carrie shuddered, then turned to the woman in amazement. "How do you know all these animals and men?"

Babe grinned. "Honey, I oughta know. That's my stock these boys are ridin'. As for knowin' who they are, I been followin' rodeos since I was in diapers. My daddy was Blue Boy Smith, National All-Around World Champion three years in a row. But that was way back when, before Diablo Blanco's great-grandfather broke his back." The light in her eyes dimmed. "Six months later, my daddy took a gun and killed hisself."

"Oh, my," Carrie said. "I'm sorry."

Babe pointed toward the end of the arena as Carrie lifted the camera to her face. "Old news. Best save your prayers for the man who drew Diablo Blanco."

Out of curiosity, Carrie zoomed in on the rider's face as he was sliding into position, thinking to herself she would like to get three shots. One of the cowboy getting into position on the bull's back just before the gate was opened, another as bull and rider came out, and the last one, the outcome of the ride. Whether he landed in the dust or made the eight-second ride hardly mattered to Carrie. It was the sequence of shots that claimed her attention.

Then the man's face came into focus. Her finger froze in the act of adjusting the shutter speed, and she started to shake. Her mouth went dry. Her heart skipped a beat.

Dear, sweet God.

Unaware of Carrie's panic, Babe leaned forward,

squinting as she tried to adjust her eyesight to the distance. "There he is, climbing up the back of the chute now." Then her voice changed pitch, and Carrie heard a new note of panic in Babe Raines's voice. "Oh, Lord have mercy. He didn't tell me he was up tonight."

The announcer's voice ended the moment, and seconds later verified what Carrie had already seen.

"Ladies and gentlemen, coming out of chute number two on Diablo Blanco is Walker Lee, of Abilene. I heard through the grapevine he grew up right here in Spurlock, Texas, so say a prayer for your hometown boy, because this bull ain't never been rode."

Carrie snapped the first shot just before they opened the gate. The bull's bellow accompanied the roar of the crowd as man and animal came out in a spinning cloud of yellow dirt. Carrie's second shot came as the ton and a half of bunching muscle twisted itself in opposite directions. Six seconds into the ride, Diablo Blanco's head came up. The bellow that came out of the great bull's mouth stilled the crowd. For a brief, heart-stopping moment, the only sounds to be heard were the ragged snorts and breaths of Diablo Blanco and Walker Lee's groan as the great bull hooked him with a horn.

Babe Raines was on her feet, screaming out Walker Lee's name, as Carrie fainted.

Two

"Sugar! Sugar! Are you all right?"

Carrie opened her eyes, expecting to see her bedroom ceiling, not the night sky and seven strangers leaning over her body.

"Where . . . what . . . ?" The scent of dust filled her nostrils, and she remembered. Walker! She struggled to sit up as the bystanders went back to their seats.

"Take it easy, sugar," Babe said. "You fainted."

"Walker—Is he—?"

Babe laughed. "Lord, honey, as always, that man is fine. I swear to God he lives a charmed life. The bull throwed him a good twenty feet. He landed feet first and started running. The rodeo clowns did their part, too, you know. You missed one hell of a show."

Carrie grabbed her head and groaned. Babe took one look at the white line around Carrie's mouth and tried to shove her head between her knees.

"Don't pass out on me again."

Carrie pushed out of Babe's grasp and began reaching for her bag. "My camera, where is my camera?"

"Here." Babe dropped it in her lap. "But I don't think you should be moving just yet. I have a trailer nearby. Why don't you let me take you—"

The earth kept shifting beneath Carrie's feet. Walker. Walker. He had come back.

"I have to go," Carrie said and started making her way down the bleachers between the people. She couldn't—wouldn't—look toward the rodeo arena again. After all these years, Walker Lee had come back—but not to her.

It had taken Carrie the better part of the night to develop all the pictures she'd taken, as well as finish the write-up that would accompany them. By morning, her eyes were red and burning from lack of sleep, but she had to get them to the office. Ansel would be doing the front-page layout.

She downed what was left of her coffee, grimacing at the room-temperature brew. Without bothering to change from the shorts and T-shirt she'd put on last night after coming home from the rodeo, she headed for the door. At this point, she didn't care how she looked. All she wanted to do was get every remnant of Walker Lee out of her house and out of her life.

She slid into the car seat, wincing when the hot leather seared her bare legs.

Lord, it's not even eight o'clock and it's already too hot to breathe.

She drove out of the yard and onto the highway, choking with anger.

How dare you come back without letting me know?

Ten minutes later, she pulled into the parking lot behind *The Weekly Spur*. As she expected, Ansel was inside at the computer, doing the front-page cut and paste. He looked up when she dropped her story and the envelope of pictures on his desk.

"Here's your story. Don't ask me to go back to that rodeo again."

Ansel's eyes narrowed thoughtfully, then, without comment, he began to sift through the photos, his pleasure increasing with each one he examined. When he got to the ones Carrie had taken of Walker, he whistled softly.

"Man alive, Carrie, you outdid yourself. These are top quality. Did you get the cowboy's name?"

She laughed, but her voice was shaky and full of rage. "Use any of them you want, or throw the damned things away. Just know this, they're the only ones you're going to get out of me. If you don't like it, then fire me now, because I swear to God, I will not set foot out there again."

"What happened?"

She spun away. "Nothing that mattered."

His voice was deep with sarcasm. "Oh, obviously. I suppose that's why you're about to cry."

Halfway out the back door, she stopped, then turned. Her eyes were wide and tear-filled, her lips trembling, but there was an unfamiliar fire in her voice.

"I will not cry. He can't make me cry again," she said and walked out with no further explanation.

The frown on Ansel's face deepened. "He who?" Ansel shouted, but it was no use. She was already gone.

He sighed and reached for his shirt pocket, then remembered he'd given up smoking. In disgust, he reached for a handful of M&M's and popped them in his mouth, studying the pictures he'd picked out of the lot as he chewed. Intuitively, Carrie had zeroed in on the studied concentration on the cowboy's face as he settled himself in place on the bull's broad back.

The second shot in the series came seconds after bull and rider had come out of the gate. The camera caught the bull in a mid-air twist, its back feet up and kicking, its head all but dragging the ground as it tried to dislodge its rider. But it was the expression on the cowboy's face that interested Ansel the most. If he didn't know better, he would have sworn the man was grinning.

The last shot was photography at its best. Even though the black-and-white snapshot was one-dimensional, Ansel imagined he could almost feel the impact of hooves to ground, of body-jolting pain, of horn to flesh.

The bull's head was up and thrown as far back as it would go. A horn was hooked into the cowboy's shirt, and the cowboy was already in motion, his body half-on and half-off the bull.

Ansel swallowed the candy and reached for a second helping. This was first-class work. He had no way of knowing Carrie had snapped that shot by reflex only. She'd been passing out as the moment occurred.

Thoughtfully chewing chocolate, he turned toward the computer screen and started moving text by the stroke of keys. The notice about the Lion's Club supper was going to the second page whether Ed Cage liked it or not, and the story about Betty Jo Purvis's hair-pulling fight with Andrea Taft at the Little League baseball game was moving to page four. He figured Betty Jo wouldn't care. Her court date was coming up real soon. The less notoriety she got about her social faux pas, the happier she would be.

By noon, Ansel Charles went to press knowing he had a winner.

* * *

"Look at this," Babe said. She handed Walker the paper she'd just picked up in town. "You made the front page."

Walker kicked back, elevating his heels onto the coffee table inside the fifth-wheel travel trailer Babe insisted on pulling when he rodeoed within the state. He unfolded *The Weekly Spur*, intent on checking out the latest press, when something about her behavior made him look back at her instead. She was fidgeting. That was never a good sign.

"Want some more coffee?" she asked, pouring herself a cup.

He stared thoughtfully as Babe hefted the near-empty pot his way.

"No, thanks. I was just waiting for you to get back so we could go eat. Where have you been, anyway? It's way past noon."

Babe shrugged. "Oh, you know, sightseeing."

She wouldn't look him in the eye. Now he knew she'd been up to something.

"Yeah, right. Tell that to someone who didn't grow up in this one-horse town. There's nothing *to* see in Spurlock except tumbleweeds and blowing dust."

"Oh, I don't know about that," Babe said, lifting the up to her lips, then blowing gently before taking a sip.

Walker's eyes narrowed. When Babe got like this, she could be considered dangerous.

What the hell have you been up to?" The last time she'd been noncommittal about her whereabouts, he'd ended up in a fight for her honor . . . such as it was.

"Just read the damned paper and mind your own business," Babe muttered. "You're not old enough to be my keeper."

Walker grinned. "Could have fooled me."

She made a face and then turned her back.

His grin widened. He loved to get her riled. Her cheeks always turned as red as her hair.

Satisfied that, for the moment, he'd gotten all he was going to get out of her, his gaze dropped back to the paper in his lap.

"Ride 'em Cowboy" headlined the paper. Below, the series of photographs said it all.

"Oh, hell," he said, more to himself than to her. "That even looks scary to me."

Babe threw a potholder at his head and swore beneath her breath when she missed.

"You should have been watching from where I was sitting," she said. "Damn you, Walker Lee. You didn't tell me you were up the first night, or that you'd drawn that crazy bull."

His expression stilled as he looked at her. "And what would you have done if I had?"

"I don't know," she muttered. "But you should have told me."

He softened. "Babe, you're not only the best aunt a man ever had, but you're just about my best friend, too. You don't lie and you don't make excuses for who you are or what you do. But you can't live my life for me, and I quit needing a babysitter years ago."

She flushed, then looked away.

He frowned. Something was wrong; he could feel it. He went back to the paper, skimming the text with absent interest. It was the usual blow-by-blow description of events, but, to his surprise, the emotion written into the story was unusual. Curious, he glanced up at the byline, and then froze.

The blood drained from his face and he came out of his chair with the paper wadded in his hand.

Babe had a strong urge to run. Instead, she thrust out her chin, readying herself for the hell she was about to catch.

"What is the meaning of this?"

For the first time in her life, Babe Raines was almost afraid of her sister's only son.

"The meaning of what?"

Walker was so angry he didn't trust himself to speak. Instead, he flung the paper on the floor between them, his eyes a cold, hard blue as he spun and started for the door.

"Where are you going?" she cried.

"Out!"

"But—"

At the door, he paused, then turned. At that moment, Babe almost wished she could undo what had been done. But the notion passed, and with its passing came the realization she'd been right to meddle. He wouldn't be this mad if he still didn't care.

"But what, Aunt Babe? I told you I didn't want to be anywhere near this town if she was still in it."

"No! You asked me to find out if Carl Wainright's family still lived here. I did not lie. Carl Wainright is dead. His wife lives in Florida just like I told you. You never mentioned anyone else's name and you know it."

Anger darkened his eyes to a wild, stormy gray.

"But you knew I wouldn't have come if—"

"Why, Walker? Why are you still running? It's been ten years. For God's sake, make your peace with the past."

They locked gazes with a certainty that each was right and the other was wrong.

"You tricked me."

Babe glared. "Do you still love her?"

He staggered, unbalanced by the question. "That's none of your damn business."

"You should have seen her face when she recognized you."

Right then, the fight went out of him. He hated himself for asking, but he had to know.

"Why?"

"I thought she was going to cry."

He turned away. "Damn you, Babe, let it go."

"I'm not the one who's lost in the past."

He grabbed the doorknob. The room was closing in on him, an inch at a time. If he didn't get outside and get some air, he was going to make a world-class fool of himself.

"Walker!"

His aunt's strident warning was enough to give him pause. Even when he was maddest at her, he couldn't turn his back on the woman who'd all but saved his life. He turned, glaring at her from across the room.

"What?" he muttered.

"She's not married."

A swift jolt of relief was followed by a cold, bitter smile.

"Neither the hell am I."

He hit the door with the flat of his hand, and Babe played her last card.

"Walker Lee, don't you walk out on me! I'm not through talking."

Respect for the woman who'd become the mother he never had made him pause.

"There's more?" he said.

Sarcasm fairly rolled off his tongue, making Babe even more certain she'd been right about Walker carrying a torch for Carrie Wainright all along.

"When the bull hooked you"—all the anger in him died. He sensed what she was going to say before she spoke—"she fainted."

His vision of Babe began to blur. An ache the size of Dallas was building inside his chest that he didn't know how to handle. All he could think to do was run. But, this time, there was nowhere else to go. His voice was quiet, his demeanor that of a man who knows when he's been had.

"Damn you, Babe."

He walked out, shutting the door behind him with a quiet thump.

Babe slid to the floor where she was standing, thankful that she was still in one piece.

"Oh, Lord," she muttered and buried her face in her hands.

Walker meant everything to her. He was the son she'd never had, as well as the best friend a woman could want. But she'd watched him daring fate once too often to bear. He had to find a reason to care again or she'd wind up being the one who buried him.

The Weekly Spur was a sellout. The only other time that had happened was two years ago last March, when the motel on the outskirts of town caught fire. Ansel had arrived just behind the fire truck and snapped first-hand pictures of the mayor coming out of room 201 in his underwear with Donna June Carpitcher right behind him, carrying her shoes and his pants. After that issue, the mayor's wife filed for divorce and Donna June Carpitcher moved to Dumas.

Although this issue wasn't riddled with scandal, as the other one had been, Ansel suspected there was more behind Carrie Wainright's behavior than a dislike for cowboys and dust. He'd drawn his own conclusions after something Mildred Cook, at the pharmacy, said about good-for-nothing men and the women who loved them, and the angle at which Carrie was tilting her chin. He glanced across the room where she sat at her desk, working away at what would be next week's issue.

She'd appeared just after noon dressed for work, with a glint in her eye upon which he didn't care to comment, with no further explanation for her earlier behavior. She'd taken mute residence behind her desk, as if her life depended on it.

Ansel frowned and reached for the bowl of M&M's, then hesitated and picked up a pencil instead. If he didn't kick the habit soon, he feared he'd be waddling from the added weight.

The bell over the front door jingled. Both Carrie and her boss turned toward the sound. It was Mildred Cook, and she was all out of breath.

"Have you heard?" she gasped, then glanced over her shoulder.

"Heard what?" Ansel asked.

"He's back!" she announced and cast a nervous eye toward Carrie, who was starting to pale.

"Who's back?" Ansel asked.

Carrie could tell by the way Mildred was looking at her that she'd seen Walker Lee. After what Walker had written on the water tower before he left town, it hadn't taken long for everyone to figure out they'd been meeting on the sly. And everyone had quickly deduced she'd been dumped like last week's garbage when he never came back. The weeks of knowing leers she'd been subjected to were nothing compared to what she'd endured at the hands of people she'd believed were her friends. They began watching her waistline, certain that he'd left her pregnant. To their surprise and dismay, not only had Carrie's waistline remained trim, but she'd managed to keep her chin up, as well. Not even her father's ranting and raving had been able to daunt the face she'd turned to the world. It was only at night, when she was alone in her room, that she had been able to let go of her anger and pain. It had taken the better part of four years to get over the shock. But she'd never gotten over the rejection. Now everything she'd lived down was being stirred up again. She didn't know whether to curse the ground he walked on or jump for joy.

Carrie started toward the door. Through the windows, she could see cars slowing down on the streets as the drivers turned and gawked, and the people on the sidewalks were staring and pointing as if a parade was in progress.

God, give me strength.

Mildred cast a wary glance toward Carrie, then stepped aside as Carrie walked past her and out the door.

"What the hell is going on?" Ansel asked.

Mildred wrung her hands. "Poor thing," she muttered, watching as Caroline Wainright came to a sudden stop. She leaned closer to the window and then wrung her hands again. "Oh, my, oh, my! This is just awful!"

"What's awful?" Ansel asked, resisting the urge to shout.

Mildred turned and glared. "You men! You're all alike!" she shrieked and left as abruptly as she'd entered.

Ansel glared. Mildred hadn't been nice to him once since he and Sheila had gotten their divorce. It didn't seem to matter to Mildred that Sheila was the one who'd run away with the high school track coach from

Wichita Falls. Damn it all, but it seemed to him that a man just didn't have a snowball's chance in hell of getting any respect in a town full of independent Texas women.

Carrie looked up the street and fought the urge to run. Dear Lord, it was him! Coming down the middle of the sidewalk as if he owned the place. Her fingers curled into her palms, her nails digging into the tender flesh. He seemed taller. She supposed that was possible. He'd turned twenty only weeks before he'd left. He could have grown some more. Her eyes widened as she watched his body in motion, remembering what it felt like to lie in his arms. Hating herself for the weakness in her knees and the thunder in her heart, she lifted her chin, noting that some things never change. He still had the same cocky swagger.

Carrie's anger filled to overflowing as she started toward him. *How dare you come back to this town, but not to me!*

When Caroline Wainright walked out of the newspaper office and onto the street, Walker almost turned tail and ran. The hot Texas wind lifted the tail of her pink sundress, belling it out around her knees, then shamelessly plastering it to the shape of her body. It was all he could do to keep moving. She looked the same, and yet she did not. Her nose still tilted just the least little bit, her lips were still wide, but somehow fuller. The truth of it hit him as he moved past the barber shop. She wasn't a girl anymore. She was a woman, and so damn beautiful it made his teeth ache.

He kept remembering the feel of sliding into her tight, sweet warmth, of the way she'd gasped and then sighed in his ear, of the way she'd given as much as she'd taken. He'd been prepared for the teenage Carrie he'd remembered, but not a woman who seemed to be daring him to come any closer. The length of his stride increased. Walker Lee was a man who dared.

He thought he'd been prepared for this meeting, but when he got close enough to see the brown in her eyes turn black with emotion, he knew he'd been kidding himself.

They met in the middle of the sidewalk, beneath the green-and-white striped awning of B & B Videos. Carrie knew she was shaking and hated herself for the weakness. At the moment, words were impossible to speak. Her gaze raked his cold, handsome face, from the black Stetson pulled low on his forehead to the thrust of that stubborn jaw. His mouth was little more than a thin, grim line. His eyelids hooded, his eyes mere slits of blue.

In spite of the heat from the overhead sun, she felt cold, from the inside out. Doing the first thing that came to mind, she drew back her arm and laid a slap on the side of his face that popped like a Fourth of July firecracker.

Walker didn't know what he'd expected, but that definitely hadn't been it. She was furious, and, now that he looked back, he supposed he could understand why. What did surprise him was the surge of passion that swept through his body. In that moment, if they'd been anywhere except standing in full view of half the population of Spurlock, he would have given her a better reason to slap his face than what she already had.

As it was, he reacted in the only way he had left. He grabbed her by both arms and, before she could voice the objection he saw coming, he yanked her up against him and slanted a hard, angry kiss across her startled lips. In the moment between contact and lift-off, Walker realized he'd made a mistake. He'd wanted to punish her, not himself. But he was the one who would be suffering when he had to let her go. She smelled like strawberries and sunshine, and he'd never wanted to sink himself into a woman as badly as he did now.

For seconds, neither Walker or Carrie could do anything but savor the feel, but when Carrie groaned beneath his onslaught, Walker relented. It was the break she'd been waiting for.

She tore herself away from his kiss, telling herself she hated him and hating herself for the lie. She didn't hate him nearly enough for her own good.

"How dare you!" she said and started to take another swing at him.

Walker caught her hand in mid-air, and the look on his face stilled her notion.

"So, daddy's little girl has turned into a grown-up bitch."

"At least *I* grew up," Carrie snapped and had the satisfaction of watching him turn redder beneath the imprint she'd left on his face.

Anger shook his voice. "I thought you'd be long gone to bright lights and big cities. What the hell are you still doing in this one-horse town?"

To Carrie's credit, her voice never faltered. "Fool that I am, I was waiting for you."

Carrie turned on her heel and left Walker standing beneath the green-and-white awning. She'd heard herself say it, but she couldn't believe that it had come out of her mouth. All these years she'd convinced herself she'd stayed behind in Spurlock because she liked small-town living. She'd told herself that being a reporter for *The Weekly Spur* was a fulfilling and valuable asset to the community. But one look at her nemesis and she'd blurted out a truth she'd spent ten years ignoring.

Walker stood frozen to the spot. He'd heard it from her own lips and he still didn't believe it. But when she entered the newspaper office and slammed the door behind her so hard that the windows actually rattled, his nerves rattled right along with them.

Caroline had taken him by surprise. He'd been waiting for lies, but, so help him God, he'd heard the truth in her voice as clearly as if her hand had been on a Bible. And, in that moment, he realized what a terrible mistake he'd made by leaving her behind. What he should have done ten years ago was take her with him.

He stared at the door leading into the newspaper office. Caroline was less than fifty feet away, and here he stood, like a damned knot on a log, letting her walk out of his life like he'd walked out of hers before.

Something inside of him snapped. He yanked his hat even lower across his forehead and started after her. It was obvious by the blow she'd laid up the side of his head that she'd been saving up anger. Getting her back was bound to be a fight, but, by God, he was more than ready to give her one.

He burst through the door of the newspaper office before Carrie had time to go out the back.

Ansel looked up at the unexpected noise as Carrie pivoted.

"I know you!" Ansel said. "You're the cowboy who was on that bull."

Walker turned on the charm as he held out his hand. "Yes, sir, that I am."

Carrie gawked. What was he up to now?

"Well, now, that was quite a stunt," Ansel said. "I suppose you're thanking your lucky stars you're still in one piece."

"That would be about right," Walker said. "In fact, that's why I'm here. Your reporter did a damned good job on the piece she wrote for the paper. In fact, it's the best I've read in years."

Ansel beamed, unaware of the tension between Carrie and Walker Lee.

"Thank you kindly," he said. "Carrie has been with me for nearly six years now. Ever since I bought the paper, right, Carrie?"

Walker wouldn't look at her, but took comfort in the fact that she was still in the same room with him.

"I was wondering, since your reporter is so empathetic to the cowboy lifestyle, if you might be interested in getting an exclusive. I'm willing to be your guinea pig for the next two days, so to speak."

Ansel's interest was caught. "How so?"

Carrie was starting to panic. She tried to get Ansel's attention, but it was too riveted upon the dark-haired charmer who, for reasons known only to him, was lying through his teeth.

"If you were interested, I'd be willing to let Miss Wainright do a piece on me. You know, sort of follow me around until the rodeo's over. I'd answer any questions she asked. No holds barred. Since I'm the leading contender for the all-around title this year, I figured you might like the exclusive."

"Yes!"

"No!"

Their answers came simultaneously. Only then did Walker venture to look Caroline's way. There was a cold, tight-lipped smile on his face that didn't quite meet his eyes.

"What's wrong, Caroline? Still afraid to be seen with me?"

The old barb shamed her. The expression on his face was frozen, as if he was bracing himself for more of the same rejection she'd given him years ago. In spite of the time that had come and gone, it stunned her to know she still had the ability to hurt him. For that reason alone, she found herself giving in.

"Do you two know each other?" Ansel asked.

Walker held his breath, waiting for her to answer. When Carrie folded her hands in front of her like a naughty child, he had the oddest urge to put his arms around her and hold her. But he neither moved nor spoke. What happened now was up to her.

"We used to," Carrie finally answered. "But that was a long time ago."

Ansel beamed. "That's great! That makes this all the easier for both of you, right?"

Walker almost grinned. Easy? Hell. Riding Diablo Blanco had been easy. Waiting for Carrie to say yes was scaring him to death.

His voice deepened. "So, you'll do it?"

Carrie sighed. She'd known since last night that this meeting was inevitable. Somewhere between midnight last night and six this morning, she'd also realized that up until twenty-four hours ago, if Walker Lee had asked her, she would have quit everything she had for the chance to be with him again. But his homecoming hadn't been quite as she'd dreamed. He hadn't come riding into town on a big white horse to carry her away. He'd come back to Spurlock without so much as a by-your-leave, crawled on the back of a big white bull and done his best to get himself killed. Only he'd survived. What had died last night were Caroline's dreams.

She bit her lip, blinking slowly as she focused on the brown skin visible just below his chin, where the top snap of his white western shirt lay undone.

"I'm not afraid of being with you. I never was." *My fear was always for you.* Then she bit her lip and lifted her chin a bit higher before she said too much.

Walker frowned at the odd way Caroline phrased her answer. Once he thought he'd known everything there was to know about the girl, but he didn't know a damn thing about this woman who kept daring him to make another mistake.

"That remains to be seen," he drawled.

Carrie flushed with anger. "Just name the place," she said shortly.

"Fantastic!" Ansel crowed.

Thank God, Walker thought.

Carrie turned away, unwilling to let either man see her fear. She didn't know what scared her most, finding out that Walker didn't love her anymore, or finding out he did.

Three

It was hard to say who was more stunned—Carrie for having agreed to the idea or Walker that she'd done it. But now that it was set in motion, panic began to sift through Carrie's mind.

"When do you want to start?" he asked.

She looked away. It was more like where to start, not when. She wanted to know where he'd gone ten years ago, when he'd walked out of her life. How had he wound up with the rodeo, when he'd never even owned a horse? Was there a woman in his life now? Had there been? Her stomach churned. Was she strong enough to ask the questions? Even more importantly, was she woman enough to hear the answers?

"This was your big idea," she said shortly. "You name the time and place. I'll be there."

"The rodeo grounds. One hour."

Carrie nodded, then started out the back door.

"Hey, Caroline."

Mesmerized by his slow, sexy drawl and the way

he'd lingered on the last half of her name, she paused, but refused to turn around.

"Come prepared to get a little dirt on yourself."

Muttering beneath her breath, she reached for the doorknob. "It can't be more than what you left on me before."

Walker's face was suddenly devoid of expression. He pivoted and walked out the front door as she walked out the back. Both doors slammed in unison, leaving Ansel with nothing but the echoes of their anger. He reached for the M&M's.

Walker drove back to the rodeo grounds without remembering how he'd gotten there. When he parked and got out of his truck, he forgot what he'd meant to do. His mind was reeling from the impact of their meeting. Her anger was unexpected. He was the one who'd been wronged.

"I was waiting for you to come back."

He yanked off his Stetson and ran a shaky hand through his hair. *Damn!*

He looked up just as Babe poked her head out the door.

"I thought I heard someone drive up," she said. When he didn't respond, she moved out to the top step. "Walker, honey, are you all right?"

He turned without answering and walked away. Babe's hesitation was momentary as she came off the steps and followed him to the nearby barn where the riding horses were stabled. There, she found him currying her horse, Mink Coat, the one he'd ridden in the Grand Entry last night. His hat was hanging from a nearby hook, and he'd rolled his shirt sleeves up past his elbows. A strand of yellow-white straw was stuck to a hard brown muscle on his forearm while sweat rolled down his face and body, molding his shirt to his frame. Although he was taller than most, the hard pack of muscles in Walker Lee's chest and arms were evidence of what it took to hang on to a ride.

She leaned against the doorway, breathing a quiet sigh of relief. At least he was venting his anger by doing something useful, and, from the looks of her horse, he was enjoying the smooth, repetitive motion of brush to hide.

"Make sure you don't brush too hard. That's the only mink coat I'm likely to have."

Walker's hand paused in the middle of a downward motion as he glanced up.

"So, did you see her?" Babe asked.

He nodded without missing a stroke.

"And?" Babe prompted.

"And what?" Walker said.

Babe rolled her eyes and counted to ten. When Walker wanted to, he could provoke a preacher to lose his religion.

"What happened?" Babe asked.

He paused, and Babe saw him take a deep breath before resuming his task. Silence stretched between them, and then, to her relief, a small smile crooked the corner of his mouth.

"She slapped the hell out of me."

Babe hid a grin. "Someone needed to. Personally, I never had the guts."

He kept right on grooming the bay gelding, stroke after sensuous stroke, until the dark red hair on the horse began to shine.

"So . . ." Babe urged.

He set the curry comb aside, then ran a gentle hand down the stallion's forehead, brushing at his forelock and smoothing down his mane, although it was already tangle-free.

Out of nowhere, emotion swamped him, and he clutched at the mane with both fists. He looked up, then down, trying without success to focus on something besides her parting words. It was no use.

Get a little dirt on yourself . . . can't be more than you left on me . . . get a little dirt on yourself . . . can't be more than . . .

He pivoted, and the hurt in his eyes staggered Babe.

"Nothing has changed."

"How can you say that?" Babe asked. "You weren't gone long enough to settle ten years of bad blood between you two."

"She's not the kind of woman to waste words."

Babe snorted gently. "Oh, great! Two of a kind."

He had the grace to flush. "This is different. I have never—would never—say anything about her, or say anything to hurt her."

Babe wanted to hug him. Instead, she kept her distance until she was sure she'd been forgiven for interfering.

"You didn't have to say anything to hurt her, Walker. Your leaving said it all. If that had happened to me . . ."—she shrugged—"All I can say is, you're lucky all you got was a slap in the face."

He dropped the brush and stalked past her, grabbing his hat as he went and leaving her behind to shut the stable door. Babe hurried to catch up.

"Walker, wait!"

He spun, and the anger on his face stopped her from touching him.

"All I asked from her was respect."

"She caught hell when you left."

He stilled, searching through his anger for something socially acceptable to say. When the words came, his voice was quiet and tight with unleashed emotion.

"What do you mean?"

"Some woman named Mildred Cook, who runs the drugstore in town, said Carrie's old man tried to kick her out of the house. Said if it hadn't been for her mother, she would have been out on the street."

The water tower! "Walker Loves Carrie." The brim of his hat shaded the expression on his face as he looked down, bracing himself for the rest of Babe's story.

"That wasn't the worst," Babe said softly. "Mildred said Carrie's friends made bets behind her back as to how long it would take before she started to show. They were certain you'd gotten her pregnant then skipped town on her when you found out."

His head jerked up as if he'd been shot. "Son of a—! Those aren't friends."

Babe's smile was sympathetic. "Pretty typical, actually. Remember, she was still in high school. There is nothing as cruel as what one child can do to another."

"We damn sure weren't children," he muttered.

"You might not have been, but I'd venture to say, at seventeen, Carrie Wainright hadn't been all that grown up."

"Eighteen."

"What?" Babe asked.

"She turned eighteen two months before—"

Babe sighed. "Oh, Walker."

He glanced at his watch.

"Going somewhere?"

"No. Company's coming," he said, pointing to the car pulling up to the grounds beyond.

Babe turned. Her eyes widened with interest—and hope.

Considering the fact Caroline would be in their pockets for the next few days, he felt obliged to explain.

"She's doing an interview on me for the paper."

"But I thought she was mad at you."

For the first time since he'd come back, Walker grinned. It didn't amount to much, but it was sincere.

"Oh, hell, Babe, she's mad all right. As mad a woman as I've ever seen."

"Then how did you get her to—"

His grin widened as he watched Caroline getting out of her car.

"I dared her."

Babe groaned. "Lord have mercy."

Walker jammed his hat a little tighter on his head as he started toward Caroline's car. "I don't need mercy, darlin'. I need a miracle."

Carrie's heart was hammering against her rib cage like a wild bird caught in a trap. Twice on the way to the rodeo grounds to meet Walker she'd almost turned back, and each time she'd heard the hurt in his voice all over again. *"Still afraid to be seen with me . . . still afraid to be . . . still afraid?"*

My God, yes, she was afraid, but not for the reasons he believed. She was afraid of getting hurt all over again. Yes, Walker had come back, but he wouldn't stay, of that she was certain. And when he left this time, like Humpty Dumpty, she knew she wouldn't be able to put herself back together again. In spite of the overwhelming fear, she kept driving.

When she got to the rodeo grounds, she parked and got out, wondering where to start looking, but when she turned around, that problem solved itself. Walker Lee was heading toward her. Resisting the urge to check and see if her white T-shirt was still tucked in her jeans, she stood without moving, waiting for him to come to her.

Keep moving, Walker told himself. *It's not hard. One foot in front of the other.*

But it was almost impossible to be within touching distance of Caroline Wainright and not hold her. It would be so easy. Just reach out and—

He stopped a foot or so away from where she was standing. All he had to do was extend a hand and he'd be touching her face, yet, in spite of their physical proximity, they'd never been farther apart. He tried to tell himself the only thing they'd ever really had together was good sex. The rest of their relationship had been wrong from the start. No good ever came of hiding and lying and pretending.

She gave him back look for look, her gaze never wavering. The honesty in her behavior kept surprising him. If she was the person he'd thought her to be, then why didn't she show some guilt? Had he been that wrong?

Carrie shifted from one foot to the other, then lifted her hand, shading her eyes from the afternoon sun. She wanted to hate this man, and all she could do was remember stupid little things like the way he ate chocolate ice cream, scooping up a giant spoonful, then slipping it into his mouth, one slow bite after another until there was nothing left on the spoon but a shine. And slow dances. Walker Lee could spin her heart into knots with little more than a shift of body to body, moving in rhythm to a musical ache she'd be better off forgetting. She shuddered. Eating ice cream and dancing weren't the only things he liked to take his time about.

Oh, God, what am I doing here?

"Where's your hat?"

She blinked. The abrupt question was a rude about-face to the memories in which she'd been lost.

"I, uh . . ."

He jammed his Stetson on her head, trying to ignore the tumble of dark, chocolate-colored curls peeking out from beneath the brim.

Her hair used to hang halfway down her back. He used to wrap his hands in it when they—

He jerked and, for a moment, thought she'd slapped him all over again, but he was wrong. She hadn't moved. In fact, she seemed stunned by what he'd done.

And she was. Respite from the sun and heat was unexpected. As unexpected as the hat sitting on her head. The scent of him filled her senses. The smell of clean straw and honest sweat, of leather and man. Her gaze drifted to the breadth of his chest and the length of his arms, then to his hands. She closed her eyes and missed seeing him as he reached for her. When she looked back, Walker's hands were in his pockets and there was a frown on his face.

"I see you didn't bring anything to take notes, either," he said, noticing she carried no bag or purse. The question was rude, but it was all he could think of to put some psychological distance between them.

Her gaze was clear, her expression cool. "I have a good memory."

This time he felt the slap, although it was verbal.

"Yeah, I do, too."

He thought he saw tears in her eyes before she looked away and wished he'd kept his mouth shut. When she looked back, whatever Carrie had been about to say was obviously forgotten as she stared in sudden confusion at a point past his shoulder. He turned to look. Babe was trying to get past them and into their trailer without being noticed.

"Hey, Babe, come here!" he yelled, taking small satisfaction in the sudden flush that swept up her neck and face. She'd started this by meddling with something he'd told her in confidence. It was only fair she catch part of the hell he was in.

Carrie froze. She knew that woman, and by the way Walker was looking at her, they had more than a passing interest in each other. Heat came at her in waves. Her worst fear had come true. He didn't travel alone. *Just don't let me faint again.*

Babe Raines might be nervous, but the world would never know it. She lifted her forty-something chin, straightened her shoulders until her heavy breasts were high and proud, and swaggered toward Carrie and Walker as if she hadn't a care in the world. She was a woman in full bloom on the verge of shedding, proud of the few and faint wrinkles time had given her because she'd had a damn good time putting them there.

Every instinct Carrie had told her there was something strong between Babe and Walker. It was there in the familiarity of the way they looked at each other, the cocky smile on Walker's face as Babe slid an arm around his neck and planted an easy kiss near his ear.

She wanted to die.

"Caroline, this is my—"

"We've met," Carrie said shortly and then took a deep breath, trying to still the ache in her heart that had come out in her voice.

Babe grinned and held out her hand. It took everything Carrie had to meet the gesture.

"We sure have," Babe said. "Feeling better today?"

"Loads," Carrie said shortly.

Walker grinned, and at that moment, Carrie hated him for coming back.

"Hey, where are you going?" Walker asked as Babe started toward the trailer.

"To get in out of the heat. I've got some calls to make. Besides, I'm sure you two have plenty to talk about without me tagging along. Enjoy," she said and walked away.

"Don't drink up all of my tea," Walker warned, and when Babe pressed two fingers against the pout of her mouth, then slapped them against her rear, the "kiss my ass" gesture was impossible to misinterpret. He grinned. "Same to you, honey!" he yelled.

Carrie wanted to scream. Couldn't these two lovebirds wait until they were alone to play these kinds of games?

"Look," she said shortly. "It's obvious you two have things you need to do. I can come back later—or not at all, whichever appeals to you most."

Walker turned, surprised by the venom in her voice. He looked down at the face beneath his hat, past the wide black brim to the disapproving purse of Carrie's lips and the glare in her dark, brown eyes. If he didn't know better, he might think she was jealous.

"Known her long?" Carrie asked and could have kicked herself for asking.

Walker's eyebrows arched. By God, he was right! She was jealous.

"Yeah," he drawled and pivoted, heading toward the barns and the shade they offered. A few feet away, he paused and looked back. Carrie hadn't moved. "Are you coming?"

She jammed the hat a little tighter over her curls and started walking. He turned and led the way into the barns, thankful she couldn't see the smile on his face.

What surprised Carrie most was Walker's patience with fans who'd come early to the rodeo grounds in hopes of a picture with their favorite cowboy or an autographed program. And it was obvious from the way they flocked around him that he was sought-after. He signed autographs faithfully, on everything from the back of a teenager's shirt to a used grocery list. He posed for pictures, held crying babies, and even stood between a trio of giggling young things who'd coerced Carrie into snapping the shots. When she lifted their camera to her eye, a sick feeling of déjà vu swept over her. This was the way she'd seen him first—through the eye of a camera and risking his life on a ride she didn't understand. She snapped the shots without thinking, wondering if this day would ever end. Her shoulders slumped as she gave the camera back.

The young girl clutched it to her breast, her voice breathless with excitement that she'd gotten this close to Walker Lee.

"Oh, Walker, honey, I saw your ride last night. It's just too bad you drew that awful bull. Where will you go next, now that you're out of the money here?"

Carrie didn't hear his answer because the question had stunned her. Go? It was the first time she'd let herself consider what the day after tomorrow would mean in the grand scheme of things. Tomorrow night the rodeo would be over. That meant the day after Walker Lee would be moving on. Suddenly, she'd had all of the torment she could handle. She yanked Walker's hat from her head and thrust it into his hands before heading for her car. If she could just make it to the—

He caught her by the arm. "Caroline?"

Carrie paused. Her voice was trembling as she turned to face him. Slowly, as if moving too fast might cause her to come apart, she pulled away from his grasp.

"I have a question," she said.

He almost smiled. "Ask. I might have an answer."

"You used to call me Carrie. Why do you keep calling me Caroline?"

An odd expression crossed his face, as if he'd never realized what he'd been doing until she'd called him on it.

"I don't know. Maybe because, when I left, you were a girl, now you're a woman. I suppose the name suits you better."

She wouldn't let him see she cared. She turned away.

Walker reacted by grabbing her again. "Why are you leaving? I didn't think we were through."

She pulled out of his grasp. "That's just it, Walker, we were through before we started."

He started to panic. There were so many things he'd wanted to say, and all he'd done today was knowingly let a lie stand between them.

"Babe Raines is my aunt."

The words hit her in the stomach like a fist. She turned, gauging the truth of what he'd said by his expression. Shock swept through her, coupled with a rage she wouldn't have believed she could feel. When she finally got the sense to speak, her words were as harsh and ragged as her breath.

"You've been laughing at me."

"Now, Caroline, I wasn't really—"

For the second time in the same day, she delivered a slap to the side of Walker's face he wouldn't soon forget.

"Laugh about that," she said and left him holding his jaw as she stomped toward her car.

Rubbing his cheek, he watched her spinning out in a flurry of dirt and gravel and wondered how many more of these he could take before he forgot his manners.

Babe handed Walker a fresh, cold compress and dropped the other one he'd had on his face into the sink. He looked so miserable stretched out on the couch, and yet she'd never seen him more alive than she had today. Since he'd gotten out of bed, he'd been mad as hell, scared to death, then thoughtfully silent, and not once had he been forced to resort to challenging a four-footed animal to remind himself he was still alive.

"Packs a wallop, doesn't she?"

"Thank you and shut up," Walker said as he laid the cold towel on his face and closed his eyes while the roar of the crowd droned on outside their trailer.

"I think I'll go see what's happening out there," she said. "Since you're out of the money, I might actually enjoy watching the performances tonight."

Walker slid the compress down the side of his face, eyeing the serious expression on Babe's face.

"Why do you do it?" he asked.

"Do what, honey?"

"Contract stock for rodeos if you hate them so much?"

She laughed. "Oh, Lord, Walker. You *do* need a lesson in reading women. I don't hate rodeos, or cowboys, it's quite the contrary. I just don't like to watch someone I love trying to kill himself for no other reason than to feel an emotion."

He sat up straight, the compress sliding into his lap. "I don't do any such damned thing."

"Yes, you do. When you showed up on my doorstep ten years ago, the farthest thing from your mind was riding bulls or anything else connected with rodeos. You wanted a job, remember?"

"And you gave me one."

"But you weren't satisfied with that, were you? There wasn't enough risk involved, was there, Walker?" Babe knelt beside the couch, took the wet cloth off his lap, and cupped the side of his cheek. "Maybe you haven't admitted it to yourself, but I saw it for what it was." She bit her lip as rare tears spiked, threatening the perfectly applied mascara she was wearing. "Just before you ride, your face loses all expression, and that's normal, honey. You're concentrating on the ride. All good cowboys do it."

Walker got up and walked to the sink. Bracing himself with outspread arms, he stared into the drain, focusing on the dark, narrow opening. It would be a good place to hide, only he was too big and it was too small.

She got up and followed him. "But when you straddle a bull, your eyes get all wild, and you get a smile on your face that makes me sick inside. Whether you're ready to admit it or not, you don't ride because you like it. You're just betting with yourself as to whether you'll make it out the other side of the ride alive."

"Let it go, Aunt Babe."

She wrapped her arms around his waist, turning her cheek against the middle of his back. If he'd been her child instead of her sister's, she couldn't have loved him more. He was her rock, and she'd known for over a year she had to find a way to give him away.

"No, you let it go, Walker Lee. I'm not the one who sleeps with devils. I'm also not the one who tries to exorcise them by every dangerous stunt known to man. Make peace with your woman and your world. Make me a grandmother—or at least a grand aunt. I deserve that much, don't you think?"

Walker turned and opened his arms, pulling her close against him. "You deserve a swift kick in the butt," he said gently, kissing the red curls beneath his chin as she settled within his embrace. "As for babies . . . Hell, Babe, you must be crazy. She nearly broke my jaw just for coming home. Think what would happen if I tried anything like that."

Babe Raines pushed out of Walker's arms and poked a painted fingernail in the middle of his chest.

"No, darlin', *you* think what might happen if you tried."

Having said that, she slung her purse over her shoulder and blew him a good-bye kiss as she opened the door.

"Walker."

"Yes, ma'am?"

"I won't wait up."

There was a thoughtful expression on his face as she closed the door behind her. The longer he stood there, the stronger his conviction became. Babe was right. He wouldn't gain a damn thing by sitting here. And if he went to Carrie, the worst she could do was tell him to get lost, which was already impossible, since he'd been lost for the better part of the last ten years anyway.

Carrie had cried until her eyes were so swollen she could hardly blink, then she'd lain down on her back with a cold compress draped across her face and fallen asleep. She woke up with wet hair and water in her ears and the worst headache she'd ever had in her life.

She got up, stumbling in the dark as she made her way to the bathroom to toss the washcloth in the sink. While she'd been grieving for lost dreams, night had come to Spurlock, Texas.

Her clothes smelled like hay and horses, and her hair smelled like Walker's hat. She stripped, leaving her clothes in a pile on the floor, turned on the water, and stepped into the shower without waiting for it to get warm.

The cold needles of spray pierced the miasma into which she'd let herself sink. She ducked beneath the shower head and reached for the shampoo. Minutes later, she turned off the water and was reaching for a towel when someone knocked on her front door.

"Oh, shoot," she muttered, swiping the terry cloth across her body in haphazard fashion.

If her car weren't parked out front, and if she hadn't already turned on her bedroom light, she'd pretend she wasn't home. But her car wasn't in the garage, and she had turned on the light, and short of ignoring the fact that someone was at her door, which was impossible for a well-bred Texas woman to do, she had company whether she liked it or not.

"Just a minute!" she yelled and started grabbing at clean clothes in her closet, trying to pull them on over her damp body without much luck.

The knocks subsided, but the anticipation of unexpected company made her fumble even more.

She made it to the front door in clean white shorts and an oversized Dallas Cowboys T-shirt persistently clinging to body. Her feet were bare, her hair was a mass of wet, tousled curls, and her face was devoid of makeup. She opened the door and then took a quick step back, resisting the urge to slam the door in his face.

"Walker!"

He held up his hands in surrender. "Don't hit me again. I just want to talk."

The screen door stood between them, as impenetrable a boundary as a prison wall. He held his breath, trying not to stare at the way the soft fabric of the T-shirt clung to her breasts or at the swollen pout on her lips.

For the longest moment, Carrie stood with her hand on the latch, wondering if she had the guts to let him in. But there was a plea in his eyes, and the want in her was too strong to ignore. A long, defeated sigh slipped out from between her lips as she flipped the lock.

"Just to talk," she reminded him.

He came in and was at once reminded that he'd been inside her body more than once, but never inside her house.

"I was in the shower," she said. It was the only apology she was going to make for the way she looked.

He gritted his teeth and looked away, trying not to think of Carrie bare and wet, trying not to think of her any way at all.

"Have a seat," she said and breathed a quiet sigh of relief when he did as he was told. Somehow, Walker Lee looked bigger than life inside four walls. At that moment, she realized he'd never been in her house, nor she in his.

"This is weird," she said.

"What?"

"After all, I mean, considering the past, I, uh . . ." She took a deep breath and started over again. "Welcome to my home, Walker Lee."

Old wounds eased along with Walker's nerves. He nodded, then remembered his manners and yanked off his hat, fiddling with the brim for something to do.

Carrie reached for the hat, her palm connecting with the back of Walker's hand. He felt solid and warm, and she wanted to throw herself in his arms.

"May I?" she asked waiting for him to turn the Stetson loose.

You can do anything to me you damned well please. He let go, watching the sway of her backside as she walked across the room and hung it on a hook by the door. Wanting surged, followed by a deep-seated fear that he might want for the rest of his life but never get. He looked around at the room, absorbing the casual comfort of her home, then back at Carrie, wondering where her bedroom was and if she slept alone. He knew she wasn't married, but then neither was he, and he hadn't exactly become a monk. The idea rankled, and he quickly cast it aside, unwilling to consider that Caroline Wainright might have a lover.

"May I get you something to drink?" she asked.

There was a muscle twitching in his temple next to his left eye, and the red flush on his cheeks told her more than she needed to know about the state of Walker's mind.

Her question startled him out of his muse. "For God's sake, Caroline, sit down before I lose what little control I have left, okay?"

She sat. "You wanted to talk?"

He chewed on the edge of his lower lip, then thrust his hands through his hair before coming out of the chair. Carrie jerked, not certain what to expect. He began to pace.

"I'm sorry, Caroline."

"About what, and which time?"

He winced. The chill in her voice cut deep. "About causing you trouble with your father. About the gossip you had to endure because of me."

"Oh, that."

He turned, surprised by her matter-of-fact tone.

"Old news," she said.

He didn't know where to go next. There was something undone he didn't understand, but Carrie seemed in no mood to share the same confidences. Silence stretched out between them until, finally, she spoke.

"Walker?"

"What?"

"Why bulls?"

"Why not?"

The moment he said it, he regretted the flip way it had come out of his mouth, but, truth be told, he didn't know.

She looked away, but he could tell she was remembering.

"I didn't know it was you." Her hands started to shake. "The camera was in focus. I panned it up the walls of the chute, past the bull, to the rider. I don't remember anything after I saw your face except thinking God was very, very cruel to bring you back so I could watch you die."

He started toward her. "My God, Carrie, I'm not going to—"

"Don't!" she said, startled that he'd moved so close. She wasn't prepared for that. Not yet. Maybe never.

He stayed where he was, but with reluctance, then turned and stared out the window into the dark.

"Babe lied to me," he said.

Carrie frowned. This made even less sense than

the rest of this evening. What did his relationship with his aunt have to do with anything?

"She contracted the stock for this event, and even though it's a smaller rodeo than I usually enter, she knew I would want to compete. I found out where it was being held and balked. She asked why. I told her. That's when she told me your father was dead and your mother was in Florida. She let me believe you were there, too."

Carrie sat up straight. "Are you telling me you didn't know I was still in Spurlock?"

He spun, and the anger on his face was impossible to miss. "Why would I want to come back if you were still here? I'd had my nose rubbed in rejection once. I had no desire to come back and see you happily married to God knows who when you belonged to me." He took a deep breath, then managed a grin that didn't quite meet his usual cocky standards. "Really hangin' myself out to dry, aren't I?"

"You didn't come to see me because you didn't know I was here."

Walker stared. There was such satisfaction in Carrie's voice, although, for the life of him, he failed to see the logic.

"That's right."

She looked up at him. "You know, Walker, we should have talked more back then instead of making love. Things might not have been so confused."

"Oh, I don't know about that, Caroline. I can't once remember being deep inside you and wishing we were having a conversation instead."

At that moment, the flush on her face suited him well.

"Walker Lee, the things you say!" Carrie stuttered.

He grinned.

Time hung between them like an overripe apple clinging to a tree. One little push, just the right touch, and they'd fall into each other's arms just like that apple would fall from the branch. But neither moved and neither spoke, afraid too much had already been said and too many years had gone by to pick up where they'd left off.

Walker kicked at a spot on the carpet with the toe of his boot and cast a wary glance at her quiet profile. With all those curls and lack of artifice on her face, she looked like a little girl who'd been set in a corner to consider her sins. Walker knew only too well what some of them might be. He'd contributed to her downfall in more ways than one.

"Sorry about your father," he finally said for lack of anything else to say. "He died young."

She nodded. "Heart attack. Mother said he tried too hard."

There wasn't much Walker could think of to say that was positive about Carl Wainright except that he'd sired a beautiful daughter.

"He was a busy lawyer and that was a fact," he said.

"And there was the feed store, and the packing plant where you worked, too, remember? He had his hand in too many pies."

Walker turned from the window to stare at Carrie. "What did you say?"

"I said there was the feed store and the packing plant where you—"

"Your father owned the packing plant?"

Carrie looked surprised. "Why, yes, I thought you knew."

"It was Beaumont Cutting and Packing, not Wainright. Tiny Beaumont was the owner. He reminded us of that every other week, when he handed out our checks."

"No, Walker. Daddy bought it the year I started high school and installed Tiny as manager. I think Tiny was about to file for bankruptcy or something." Carrie shrugged. "It doesn't really matter. Daddy was your boss whether you knew it or not."

An odd expression settled on Walker's face. All these years and he'd been so damned certain the reason she wouldn't take him home to meet her family was that she'd been ashamed of him. What if, what if she'd been protecting him?

"Caroline?"

There was something in the tone of his voice that made her nervous. In self-defense, she took a couple of steps back.

"That night, if I'd asked you to come away with me, would you have gone?"

Sadness came swiftly, settling around her heart and twisting it until there was nothing left to do but give in to the pain. Tears came to her eyes as she walked across the room, lifted Walker's hat from the hook and opened the door. When she turned, there was a small, polite smile on her face that Walker didn't understand.

"Thank you for coming tonight, Walker Lee. You were right. This talk was long overdue."

Stunned, Walker took his hat. He'd never felt so dismissed in his life, and the shock of it was only a little less painful than his regret.

He paused on the threshold, afraid to leave, afraid she'd never let him come back. "Caroline, I—"

"I'll see you tomorrow," she said. "Give your aunt my regards."

He stepped back as she closed the door between them, the hat still dangling from his hand. He was all the way off the porch before what she'd said sank in.

Tomorrow! She said she'd see me tomorrow!

For tonight, it was enough to sleep on.

Four

Sunrise was easing into the day with caution when Carrie pulled up next to Walker's trailer at the rodeo arena. His pickup was sitting in a puddle. Recently washed, it gently mirrored his temporary home.

She glanced at herself in the rearview mirror before getting out of the car. Her eyes still had that sleepy look about them, although she'd done everything last night but sleep. She'd gone over every word that passed between them long after Walker left her house, and the one thing that kept coming back to her time and again, that eased her conscience was he hadn't come back to snub her. He'd truly thought she was gone.

She got out, sidestepping the puddle as she admired the pickup's sheen. Walker must not have slept any better than she did to be washing trucks before dawn, and she was certain it was Walker who'd done the washing. Somehow, she couldn't see Babe Raines and her long, painted nails doing anything so unnecessary. Babe was the kind of woman who saved herself for the things that mattered, the kind of woman who figured a good truck was a truck that got you where you were going, whether it was washed or not.

She started to knock when a piece of paper taped on the outside door fluttered in the early morning breeze, catching her attention.

Carrie,

I'm out until noon. Please go in. Walker is waiting for you.

Babe

Carrie hesitated and again started to knock, then reread the note and did as she'd been told. Cool air met her at the door. She walked inside, welcoming the shade, as well as the change in temperature. The latch clicked loudly in the silence as she shut the door behind her. She stood within the quiet, absorbing the intimacy in which Walker and Babe resided while on the road.

The aroma of fresh-brewed coffee filled the small room. A crumb-filled plate was on the cabinet near a sink of soapy water. Just like a man, she thought. Gets it all the way to the sink, but doesn't bother to put it in.

The smile on her face was a little bit sad. Even though Babe Raines was his aunt, Carrie envied her freedom to live with and love Walker Lee.

A stack of papers lay near a portable phone, an open notepad was nearby with times and dates slashed across the paper in bold, black writing. The hum of the window-unit air conditioner was a welcome buffer to the building heat outside the trailer.

Carrie dropped the note on a nearby table and turned to look out the window over the couch when Walker unexpectedly emerged from a nearby room, towel-drying his hair.

Water droplets still clung to his smooth, brown skin from the shower he'd just exited, and, except for a low-riding towel wrapped around his hips, he was as naked as the day he'd been born.

"Hey, Babe, I thought you were already—"

The words died on his lips.

All the color drained from Carrie's face as she fumbled for the note, choking on an explanation.

"Your aunt—the note—I did what she—" And then she looked past his face to his body, and everything she'd been trying to say slipped out of her mind.

"Oh, dear God."

Shocked, her purse slid from her shoulder unnoticed. Twice she tried to look away, and both times her gaze was drawn back to the pattern of scars that the last seven years of rodeos had left on him.

The moment she looked at his chest, Walker knew what had caused her reaction. He tossed aside the towel he was holding and tightened the one around his waist.

"Now, honey, it's not as bad as it looks."

Carrie reached out to touch the corrugated band of muscles on his belly, then pulled back in dismay at the thick, four-inch scar in the middle, remnants of a bout with a bull with no manners.

A breath slid out of Walker's lungs in a slow, helpless sigh. This day wasn't starting out as he'd planned.

Quiet tears filled her eyes.

He groaned. "For God's sake, Caroline, please don't cry." He took her hand and laid it on the center of his chest, pressing it firmly to his flesh. "See, I'm still in one piece. Almost good as new."

She shook her head and pulled away from his touch, only to be drawn back to a white, jagged scar high up on his shoulder. Suddenly, it was all too much. She covered her face with her hands.

Walker took her in his arms. "Ah, damn it, Caroline, I never meant for you to—"

She lifted her head, her eyes bright with unshed tears. "Why, Walker? Who were you trying to punish? Me, or yourself?"

His grasp was firm as he took her by the shoulders. "Stop it, Caroline! What's between us has nothing to do with punishment. It's about the last ten miserable years of my life and you know it!"

She closed her eyes, refusing to face the cost of his profession.

His voice lowered. "Damn you, Carrie, look at me! Don't turn away from me. Not now."

A small, choked sob stilled his anger. Regret came swiftly as he yanked his hands from her face and put them around her instead. He pulled her close, so close he could smell the after-bath baby powder she was so fond of using. So close that the ache she'd created in him could no longer be denied.

He laid his cheek against the crown of her head and rocked her where she stood. She felt so good in his arms, and this felt so right. To hell with what had come and gone. He wanted to make new memories with an old love.

"Darlin', if you're of a mind to deliver another slap, now's your chance, because I'm giving you fair warning. In about five seconds, I'm going to take you to bed."

Carrie looked up in quiet resignation. "No more war."

Right after that, her feet left the floor. He carried her into his bedroom, shutting the door behind him. The mattress gave at her back as he laid her down. With a flick of his hand, he undid the towel at his waist and tossed it aside.

"You've got on too many clothes," he said softly.

"That never used to stop you before."

A smile tilted the corner of his mouth as he crawled into bed and stretched out beside her. He smoothed his hand across the flat of her stomach then up beneath her T-shirt. Carrie shifted beneath his gentle caress, reaching for him as he cupped a breast.

"Easy does it, baby. You know I like to take things slow."

She closed her eyes and swallowed a sigh. She remembered that and a whole lot more about Walker Lee. She waited, anticipating what he'd remove first— her inhibitions, or her clothes. To her surprise, he did neither.

He rolled on top of her as mouth met mouth, his hard and demanding, hers soft and yielding. And then he lifted himself from her body, bracing himself above her so that he had a clear, perfect view of Carrie Wainright's face.

"Caroline . . ."

She waited.

"There's something I need to say before this goes any further."

Carrie found herself holding her breath. *Please God, don't let this be bad.*

"I love you, girl. I've loved you since the day I saw you, and time hasn't changed a thing." There was an earnest, almost resigned look on his face, as if even now he expected rejection. "I can't say I've been celibate over the last ten years and face myself in a mirror, but I *can* say the only time in my life I've made love to a woman was with you."

Sweet words from a sweet, sweet man. Carrie pulled him down to her, whispering softly against his ear as he enfolded her in his embrace.

"Walker, darling."

Need hammered at him from within like a bull slamming against a gate. Hard. Fast. Relentlessly. He tore his mouth from the pulse point at the base of her throat, trying to focus on the fact that she was still talking. The best he could manage was a small grunt that sounded a little bit like the word "what."

"I love you, too. Always have. Always will. Shamelessly. Desperately."

Walker buried his face against her breasts and, for a long, quiet moment, lay still.

"Thank you, God," he whispered.

"God isn't the fool who's giving you a second chance," Carrie said as she tugged off her clothes. "It's me. Don't make me regret my decision."

Walker tossed her shirt on the floor. "No, ma'am. I surely won't."

When she handed him her shorts, there was a light in his eyes that made her a little bit nervous. She smiled and slipped her arms back up around Walker Lee's neck, pulling him close.

"Walker Lee . . ."

"What is it, honey?"

She laid her cheek against his, whispering softly, for his ears only.

"I'm ready."

"Caroline?"

She shifted restlessly beneath the weight of his

body, wanting that hard, probing part of him deep inside her, where it belonged. "What?"

"Are we making love, or making babies?"

She wrapped her legs around his waist, urging him to follow her lead.

"I don't know," she whispered. "Surprise me."

He dozed, his head on her breast and his arm slung over her bare body, pinning her in place as firmly as a roped and tied calf. Carrie lay willingly beneath his weight as she thought about the man he'd become.

So strong. So gentle. So hurt.

Asleep, with his features stilled and that dominating light in his eyes at ease, he was more like the boy she remembered. Threading her fingers through his thick, black hair, she closed her eyes, reveling in the silky feel of it against her palm and marveling at the way it sprang back into place as her fingers passed through. She smiled. Even the hair on his head had a mind of its own.

His back was broad, his legs long and powerful.

The better to ride you with, my dear.

His voice echoed in Carrie's memory as she shivered, remembering the slow, teasing manner with which Walker Lee made love. She wondered if other women knew what it felt like to climax in the middle of a laugh, then hugged him close. She didn't really want to know.

Where did she go from here? Where did Walker expect her to go? Even scarier, were these only her expectations, or did he share them, as well?

The pattern of his breathing changed, and Carrie knew he was awake, yet the stillness with which he laid made her nervous. The relationship between them was virtually uncharted. The only thing in their entire lives they'd ever shared was love and sex. She hugged him close as fear settled next to her heart. It wasn't all she wanted. Not by a long shot.

His stomach growled. He lifted his head, looking at her with a delightful leer. She started to smile when he kissed her, sealing the motion in place. The kiss was as abrupt as what he did next. He grabbed her and rolled. She squealed in protest. When the bed stopped rocking, Walker was very much the one on top. He was back in control.

"Caroline, I'm starving. Either we make ourselves crazy all over again or get something to eat."

"What are my options?" she asked.

He grinned, riding the high that came from the knowledge that all he had to do was move a little bit to the right and he'd be so far gone.

"Too late," he whispered and thrust a knee between her legs and himself inside her.

Sweet heat enveloped him. He closed his eyes, concentrating on the feel of skin against skin and the small, breathless gasps Caroline made as he moved within her.

Sun spilled through a part in the curtain, heating a pencil-slim spot on the back of his leg. He opened his eyes and gazed down at the woman beneath him. Branded. That's what it felt like. An invisible brand on a wild cowboy's body, just like the mark she'd left on his heart.

"Carrie, my Carrie."

He'd whispered her name, but she heard it just the same. She looked up. A muscle clenched in his jaw as he paused, immobile above her. Trying to concentrate on something other than the fullness of him inside of her was impossible. She arched up to meet him, wanting that out-of-control feeling to take her away.

"Easy, easy, darlin'," he begged as a film of perspiration broke out across his forehead.

"Walker, please," Carrie whispered, her body trembling from want.

"Honey, I need to tell you—"

She came after him, cutting off whatever he'd been about to say with a beseeching kiss he couldn't refuse. The urge to let go and follow the surge of release pounding within him was impossible to ignore. He swept her up in his arms, laying claim to all there was of Carrie Ann.

They heard nothing but the blood rushing through their bodies, felt nothing but the hammer of flesh against flesh. Lost in the act of love, Walker took Carrie on the ride of her life. At the point of her ecstasy, when she lost all focus on everything but the waves of pleasure spilling out from within her, he came, shattering within her until there was nothing for him to do but lie weak and spent in her arms until the madness had passed.

"Oh, my gosh, it's almost noon. We've got to get out of this bed before your aunt gets back."

Walker made a grab for Carrie and missed as she lurched out of bed and onto the floor after her clothes.

He rolled over on his side and grinned as he watched her dressing.

"Hey, darlin', is there something you might be wantin' to tell me?"

"Like what?" she muttered as she pulled up panties and shorts in one even motion.

"You were real quick to shuck out of those clothes,

but you're even quicker at putting them on. You dress like you've been shot at in rose bushes before."

In lieu of more important issues, she ignored his less-than-subtle reference to a cheating woman going out the window ahead of an angry wife with a gun.

"I can't find my bra. What did you do with my bra?"

Shamelessly naked, he got out of bed and lifted a bit of lingerie from the light fixture over their heads.

"Is this what you're looking for?"

She snatched it out of his hand with a groan. She had one arm in and the other in motion when the sound of a car driving up outside sent her into a new fit of panic.

"Oh, Lord, what if that's your aunt Babe!"

Walker crawled back onto the bed and peered between the curtains.

"Yep, you're right. Babe's back."

She grabbed her T-shirt from the floor and yanked it over her head just as the front door opened.

"Got it on wrong-side-out," Walker drawled.

Carrie spun, her brown eyes wild, her hands shaking as she pointed.

"Get up. Get on some clothes, and, so help me, Hannah, if you embarrass me in front of your aunt, I will make you pay."

For a big man, Walker could move real fast when the urge to do so struck him. He wasn't sure just what damage a little thing like Caroline could do that a three-thousand-pound bull hadn't already tried, but he wasn't in the mood to test the theory.

They came out of the bedroom. Carrie's face was flushed, her hair a jumble, but her head was held high. Walker wore nothing but Levis and a carefully bland expression, but there were devils dancing in his eyes that no one could miss.

Babe grinned as Walker gave her a warning glare she chose to ignore.

"Well, now," she said.

"Aunt Babe . . ."

"Yes, Walker Lee."

He cocked his head toward Carrie, as if to remind Babe she was treading on touchy ground.

"If you don't mind, I'd as soon you kept what you're about to say to yourself."

Carrie dropped into the single chair and stared at a shadow in the corner where the wall and ceiling met.

Babe pursed her lips, then sighed. He was right. Why rattle the trap she'd so carefully set? She arched her eyebrows, pretending great injustice had been heaped upon her head.

"All I was going to say was I picked up your plane ticket. They changed your flight. You don't leave tonight after all." She glanced down at her watch. "In fact, if you don't get a move on, you're going to miss your flight altogether."

When Walker thrust his hands through his hair in quiet disgust, Babe figured she'd done something wrong. One look at Carrie Wainright's face and she knew she'd been right.

"Uh, if you two will excuse me for a bit, I've got to check and see if that blue eighteen-wheeler is fixed. I've got livestock to haul out of here tonight and a long way to go before morning."

She left the trailer as abruptly as she'd come.

Carrie kept staring at her hands, telling herself that, if she didn't blink or didn't move, what she'd heard would go away.

Walker knelt before her. "Look at me, honey."

She couldn't. Today had been too sweet. She wasn't

ready to turn loose of Walker Lee or face the truth of what she'd just heard.

He sighed. "That's what I was trying to tell you earlier."

She started to shake. He cursed softly, then lifted her out of the chair and sat back down with her in his lap.

"Caroline, sweetheart, I'm not running out on you." When she shuddered, he wrapped his arms around her and pulled her close. "Honey, you've got to remember, when I committed to this rodeo, I didn't know you were here. I'm already entered in one in Albuquerque, then, after that, Cheyenne. You could come with me, you know."

Carrie covered her face with her hands and shook her head, trying to block out the image of Diablo Blanco hooking him with a horn, of the scars on his body from other nights and other rides.

He laid his cheek against tousled curls, breathing in the scent of Carrie's shampoo and savoring the silken texture of her hair against his face.

"The season is almost over." His worry began to increase when she didn't respond. He took a deep breath, hoping she understood what he was going to say. "I'm not a quitter, Caroline."

She didn't want to hear this. She got off his lap. What she had to say came better from a distance.

Walker stood up, too. He didn't think he wanted to hear this sitting down.

"And I can't watch you die."

The calm, matter-of-fact tone in her voice frightened him more than if she'd been screaming with rage.

"What are you saying, Caroline?"

Her eyes closed in a slow, painful blink. When she opened them again, they were shimmering with unshed tears.

"I don't know, Walker. What do you want me to say?"

His composure broke as he reached for her. "That you'll be here when I get back."

She collapsed in his arms, her spirit broken. "If it takes you another ten years, don't expect me to be waiting."

"You just keep my place warm in your bed. I'll be back before you know it."

"Then what? Next year will be more of the same. I can't live like that, Walker. I want to make babies with a man who'll be around to watch them grow up."

He knew she was right, but he was right, too. He cupped her face in his hands and feathered a kiss across her mouth, drawing out the contact until she was swaying on her feet.

"Caroline, I promise on my honor and on our love that I'm coming back after you, and you better start packing, because the next time I leave, I'm taking you with me."

October
Spurlock, Texas

Keeping a secret in Spurlock was hopeless, and driving to Midland was silly. It was too far away and would only delay what would soon be obvious. Carrie entered the pharmacy with her head held high and handed Mildred Cook her prescription, daring her to comment.

Mildred glanced at the prescription, then arched an eyebrow and tried to stare Carrie down. Carrie's gaze remained steadfast, in spite of the anxiety she was feeling. Mildred turned away to fill the order, then, a few minutes later, she called out Carrie's name.

"Here's your medicine," Mildred said, handing Carrie a sack.

"Thank you very much," Carrie said and pivoted sharply.

In her haste to get out of the pharmacy, she accidentally knocked a rack of condoms off the pegboard wall.

Mildred hustled out from behind the counter and pushed Carrie aside. "Here now, let me do that," she said, grabbing the packets in handfuls and putting them back on the pegs.

"I'm sorry," Carrie said and handed Mildred a couple she'd picked up from the floor.

Mildred gave her an assessing stare. "Too late for these. I warrant."

Carrie met Mildred look for look. "Don't you dare pity me."

Mildred sniffed. "Wasn't about to." Then she winked. "I wouldn't have turned him down either, honey. Lord, but he did grow into something else, didn't he?"

Carrie nodded, hoping he managed to grow old, as well.

"I'll be going now. Sorry about the mess."

"Reckon he'll be back?"

Carrie paused at the end of the aisle, then kept on walking. What was there to say?

She went back to the newspaper office, put water in her coffee cup, and shook two pills out of the bottle

Mildred had given her just as Jerry James sauntered in with his weekly ad. She tossed the pills down her throat, chasing them with water.

Ansel was on the phone. That left Carrie to deal with Jerry. Ever since Walker's exit from her life last month, Jerry James had been pushing and pushing for a date. She was honest enough with herself to assume that Jerry, like everyone else in Spurlock, figured she'd been dumped again. Only Carrie knew she'd been the one who'd refused to go.

"Hey, sweet thang," Jerry drawled and grabbed at Carrie's hand as she reached for his ad. "How about you and me and—"

"Baby makes three?"

Jerry gawked. The smirk on his face melted like butter on a hot biscuit. His gaze went from her face to her belly. When he realized he was still holding her hand, he jerked away, unconsciously wiping his hand on the front of his shirt as he backed for the door.

Carrie wanted to hit him. Instead, she lowered her voice.

"Don't worry, you're safe. You can't make a girl pregnant by holding her hand, especially if the deed has already been done."

She had the satisfaction of seeing him flush before he stammered some excuse and disappeared.

Carrie sighed. Now she'd done it. Mildred knew, but she wouldn't have told. She considered her occupation within the realm of doctor/patient relationship. However, Jerry James wouldn't be that considerate. It would be all over town before dark that Walker Lee had "knocked her up." She didn't know why she'd said it, but she had, and now the truth was out in the open. It was just as well. Pretty soon, her belly would be out, too.

"What was wrong with Jerry?" Ansel asked as he took the ad from the counter and tossed it on his desk.

"I think I finally cooled his ardor."

Ansel grinned. "How did you do that?"

"Told him I was pregnant."

Ansel laughed, but, when Carrie didn't join in, he choked to a stop.

"You were kidding, right?"

"Nope."

He turned pale, then a slow, red flush moved up his neck to his face. "Damn it, I should have known better than to send you out to that rodeo, do a story on some—"

"Walker wanted me to go with him."

Now Ansel was the one gawking at Carrie. "Then why on earth didn't you go?"

"I can't watch him ride those bulls and he wasn't ready to quit."

Ansel sighed. He felt sorry for Carrie, but had to agree with Walker Lee. There were some things a man just had to do to face himself in a mirror.

"You gonna be all right?"

She smiled, but hers was not a happy face. "I have to be, don't I? Besides, there is one positive thing about this. Last night I called my mother and told her. Surprisingly, she seemed quite happy. She's been plaguing me for years to make her a grandmother. I guess she figured at my age, she couldn't be too choosy about how it happened."

That night, Carrie stood naked before her bedroom mirror, assessing herself with a judgmental eye and wondering how big a mistake she was making by not calling Walker Lee right now. She kept telling herself he had a right to know, that it wasn't fair to keep him in the dark. All she had to do was pick up the phone. She ran a hand over her stomach and then closed her eyes.

I'm not a quitter.

Guilt stilled her intent. If she called, he would come, of that she was certain. But would he ever forgive her, or himself, for not finishing what he'd started? She turned away from the mirror and reached for her robe.

Not tonight. She wouldn't call tonight.

November
Spurlock, Texas

The telephone was ringing when Carrie walked in the door. She tossed her purse on a chair as she raced to answer.

"Wainright residence."

"There's a plane ticket to Montana with your name on it and a cold spot in my bed."

She bit her lip and then took a deep breath to still the quaver in her voice.

"Hello, Walker Lee."

"Hello, darlin'. I miss you like hell."

"I miss you, too," Carrie said.

Walker sat on the side of the motel bed, staring at a cigarette burn on the rug. He talked to Carrie at least four times a week, and every time he called he heard misery in her voice.

"Where are you?" she asked.

"Cow Palace."

"In San Francisco?"

He grinned. "Last time I looked." When she didn't respond, he couldn't help but try again. "About that plane ticket—"

"When, Walker? When will it be over?"

The grin stilled, then disappeared as heartache moved back into its old, familiar place.

"Soon, honey, real soon."

Carrie rubbed her hand across the small but significant swell on her stomach. *Oh, Walker, don't let this baby get here before you do.*

"That's good. I really need you."

Sadness enveloped him. "I need you, too, Caroline."

Guilt overwhelmed her. Not for the first time, she began to wonder if she was the one who was wrong.

"I'll call you after I get to Montana."

"Call me after you ride, that way I'll know you're all right."

Her voice vibrated with fear. Walker closed his eyes and dropped back onto the bed with a defeated thump.

"Caroline, I love you so much I hurt. I hope you know that."

"But that kind of hurt won't kill you."

There wasn't much else he could say.

December
Spurlock, Texas

"Carrie, it's Babe. Answer the phone, damn it!"

Carrie exited the shower in the middle of the message recording on her machine and made a dive for the phone on the other side of her bed.

"I'm here!" Carrie gasped, afraid of what she was going to hear. Babe Raines had never called her before. "Walker, is he—?"

"Oh, hell, I'm sorry," Babe said. "I didn't realize what you'd think. He's fine. At least he is right now."

The flesh crawled on the back of Carrie's arms. In response, the tiny baby inside of her rolled, as if sensing its mother's unrest.

"What do you mean?" Carrie asked.

Babe downed the last of her gin and tonic. It was her third. It had taken two of them to get mad enough at Walker to even consider making this call, and by the time she'd poured the third, she had the phone in her hand.

"You know where we are, don't you?" Babe asked.

"Nevada. The national finals, right?"

Babe cursed, and all the blood drained from Carrie's face. "What's wrong?" Carrie asked.

"I thought I had it covered," Babe muttered. "I even sold that damned bull after we left Spurlock, you know."

"Bull? What bull?"

Babe picked up a shoe and threw it at the wall on the other side of the room. It hit with a thump, leaving a small, dirty stain on the paint.

"What would have been the odds of this happening again?" she muttered, and, not for the first time this evening, wished she hadn't stopped smoking.

Carrie knew enough to be scared, but as yet was uncertain as to what posed a threat. "What bull? What odds?"

"Diablo Blanco. Walker drew that damned bull again. He's up tomorrow night, and I've talked until I'm blue in the face and he won't listen."

"Dear Lord," Carrie whispered and pressed her fingers against her lips to keep from screaming. A *horn hooked the sleeve of his shirt as the crowd rose to their feet.* Carrie moved her hand across the swell in her stomach. "Babe, there's something you should know."

"I swear, I've said everything I know to talk him out of this ride and it isn't happening."

"Babe, listen to me!"

"It's not my fault," Babe muttered. "He was like this before I got him. I can't do a thing with him."

"I'm going to have a baby."

Babe Raines sat down where she was standing, ignoring the fact that there wasn't a chair within a good ten feet. It didn't matter. The floor was as good a place as anywhere when you needed to faint.

"What did you say?" she asked and cleared her throat, trying to get past the squeak. "Did you say you were—?"

"About four months gone."

Babe inhaled slowly, considering the impact this news could have on Walker Lee.

"He doesn't know, does he?"

Carrie closed her eyes as guilt ate at her. If only she'd told him earlier, maybe he would have changed his mind. But now, on the very last ride of the season, when everything hinged on winning the title, she couldn't tell him. That would be the lowest form of deceit. She rolled over, sitting up in bed. Her decision was made.

"No, he doesn't," Carrie said. "And you're not going to tell him, either."

Babe's mouth dropped. "But why? This could be the very thing to keep him off that bull."

"At what cost to our relationship?"

Babe wanted to cry. "Oh, hell, a woman with principles. Then what are we going to do?"

Carrie sat, listening to the silence. Loneliness enveloped her, but she knew what needed to be done.

"Give me your number," Carrie said. "I'll call you when I get to the airport."

"You're coming here? But I thought you wouldn't—"

"Babe, I don't care what you have to do to get it, just make sure I have a ticket for tomorrow night's performances."

Babe sat up and took notice. "But they've been sold out for months and months."

"Then use your wiles, woman," Carrie ordered as she scrambled off the bed.

Babe got to her feet, dusting at the seat of her pants. "My wiles are on the down side of forty, remember?"

"Then find someone on the down side of fifty who likes old movies and fine wine."

Babe started to grin. She'd known from the start that this was the woman for Walker Lee. "I don't know how I'll manage it, but by damn, you've got yourself a deal. If I've lost my touch, you can have my seat. Now here's my number."

Nevada was cold as hell. Tiny snowflakes drifted down from the sky as the plane taxied to a stop. Carrie reached for her carry-on bag, eager to get out. At least then she would be that much closer to Walker Lee. She exited the plane with the crowd, walking out of the portable tunnel and into the airport, only to hear someone shouting her name.

It was Babe, and Carrie could tell by the smile on her face and the silver-haired cowboy at her side that her wiles were still in perfect working order.

"Carrie, darling," Babe said and swept her into an exuberant hug before plastering a kiss on her cheek. "Welcome, welcome."

"Did you get the ticket?"

Babe winked and leaned down to whisper in Carrie's ear. "Honey, that's not the only thing I got."

Carrie grinned. She was going to love having this woman for a relative. "I don't have a place to stay," Carrie warned her. "The city is packed."

"You can stay at the hotel with Walker," Babe said. "He won't come back from the arena until after he rides. By that time, it won't matter."

Carrie paled as a sudden wave of exhaustion swept over her. Babe grabbed her by the arm and handed Carrie's bag to her escort.

"Here you go, sugar, carry this for her, will you? We've got to take real good care of this little lady. She's going to make me a grandmother, of sorts."

Sugar did as he was asked, tipping his hat as he did and offering Carrie his arm. She took it, and gratefully. She was going to need all the strength she had to get through this night. After that, and God willing, she was going to lean on her own man for a change.

Sound rolled from one side of the arena to the other like waves in an ocean, often times drowning out the sonorous tones of the announcer's voice as six different events came and went. Carrie's nerves were on edge. Ten riders into bullriding, and Walker still wasn't up.

She sat, white-lipped and sweating, praying for a miracle and hoping she hadn't waited too long to ask for it. Through the miracle of ingenious marketing and a little bit of greed, Babe sat beside her. She had walked up to the kid in the seat next to Carrie and handed him a hundred dollar bill and her ticket, then waited to see if he swallowed her bait.

The young man had taken both with a silly grin and moved on to the seat on the other side of the arena, a richer man than when he'd come in.

Not for the first time, Babe gave Carrie a nervous glance. If anything happened to her or that baby, Walker would never forgive her.

"Are you all right?" she asked.

"Ask me tomorrow."

Babe grinned. She liked this woman's grit. The announcer interrupted, and their attention was quickly diverted.

"Ladies and gentlemen, let's move to Walker Lee, who's sitting in the number-one slot for the all-around world champion. He hails from Abilene, Texas, and he'll be up on Diablo Blanco, owned by the Springerle brand. Hang on to your hats. This bull is a ton and a half of bad attitude that's never been rode."

The crowd stilled, sensing they might see history being made.

Carrie covered her belly. It was an odd but symbolic act, as if she didn't want the baby to see.

"Hang in there, honey," Babe said, although she wasn't nearly as calm as she sounded. Dread hung heavily on her shoulders. She turned toward the far end of the arena, watching as Walker appeared.

He came over the top of the chute from behind and then crawled into place atop the bull, ignoring the pain when Diablo Blanco slammed his leg against the gate.

"Hold him still!" someone shouted. Walker tugged at his gloves, making sure they were tight.

Carrie watched with a glassy-eyed stare, mentally going through the motions she knew he was making. He'd be settling on the bull's back until he found a spot that felt right and pulling on the heavily resined bull rope on which he would hold, wrapping it over and over around his glove until he and the rope were as much a part of that bull as its hide. He'd be yanking his hat down hard and licking the fingertips of his right glove and then pounding his fist into the rope wrapped around his left palm, then pulling at the brim of his hat again. He would repeat the steps over and over until something within him felt right. Only then would he give the nod. Only then would the gate come open, and the rest of Carrie Ann's life would come down to an eight-second ride.

And then, after all the waiting, it happened. The gate swung open and the bull came out. Twisting in different directions at once, Diablo Blanco aimed his hind legs at the chute from which he'd come, kicking up and out in a ballet of muscle and mass and trying for all he was worth to buck his rider into another area code.

One bone-jarring move after another, Walker clung to the ride until he saw spots before his eyes, as close to unconscious as a man could get and still be up-right. Determination and the need to stay in one piece kept him mounted, but he no longer heard the roar of the crowd or felt the pain. For Walker, the ride moved in slow motion.

The harsh, uneven grunts coming from Diablo Blanco's lungs.

The sound of pounding hooves hitting hard-packed dirt.

The smell of the animal's fear.

The feel of riding a bullet with no target in sight.

A flash of color caught the corner of his eye. It was a rodeo clown, waving him off. *My God,* he thought, re-alizing the buzzer must have already sounded. *I did it!* The eight-second eternity was over.

He came off the bull on instinct alone. When his feet hit the ground, he went to his knees, then grabbed for dirt as he pushed himself upright and started to run. He didn't have to look behind him to know the bull was at his back. The ground thundered beneath his feet as he ran.

The crowd roared as he made the fence. Only then did he look back to see rodeo clowns darting between him and the bull, diverting Diablo Blanco's attention and allowing the bull to take out what was left of its aggression on new targets. The crowd came to its feet when the bull was herded out of the arena.

"Go on, man, take your bow. You earned it," a cowboy urged, thumping Walker on the back as he came down from the fence.

In true cowboy fashion, Walker lifted his hat, holding it high above his head and turning in place, acknowledging their praise in a silent moment of truth. He looked for Babe, searching the crowd for her copper-colored hair and that electric blue suit she was going to wear. And then he saw her and grinned. She was jumping up and down and hugging the woman next to her as if—

Walker stopped. Caroline! She'd watched him ride, and from the look on her face, she'd survived the incident a hell of a lot better than he had. He forgot there was a rodeo going on. He forgot that several thousand people were about to watch him lay his heart at Caroline Wainright's feet.

When he started walking toward them, Carrie came out of her seat.

"You be careful," Babe said, as Carrie made her way to the end of the aisle, then started running down the steps. "Remember the baby!" But it was no use. The only thing on Carrie's mind was Walker Lee.

There was a light in his eyes impossible to mistake as he reached the side of the arena. He reached up as Carrie leaned down.

"You came."

"I couldn't let you do this alone."

He started to grin. "If I come up, are you gonna slap my face?"

"Only if you don't make an honest woman out of me, Walker Lee. I'm carrying your baby."

The grin slid sideways. Carrie watched his face as shock came and went, followed by joy.

The next thing she knew, he'd cleared the side of the arena and she was in his arms. Ignoring the crowd's cheers and applause, Walker claimed his woman with a slow, soul-searching kiss that rocked their world. She went limp in his arms, yielding to his power and the unspoken promise of a forever kind of love.

Walker was shaking as he lifted his head. He splayed his hand across the small swell of her belly, awed by the life they'd created. A crooked smile tilted the corner of his mouth.

"Still love me?" he whispered.

She nodded.

"Think you could stand to be a rancher's wife?"

She bit her lip, afraid to hope. "What about the bulls?"

He grinned. "What about 'em? I've just ridden the best there is. At this point, I see no sense in lowering my standards."

"You mean you quit?"

To the delight of the onlookers, he took the Stetson from his head and plopped it on hers, then scooped her off her feet and started walking toward an exit with a satisfied grin on his face.

"Only the bulls. As for you, my darlin' Caroline, I haven't even started."

SHARON SALA

New York Times bestselling author Sharon Sala has written more than sixty-five books that regularly hit all the bestseller lists. She's a five-time RITA® finalist, five-time winner of the National Reader's Choice Award, five-time winner of the Colorado Romance Writer's Award of Excellence, and many other industry awards too numerous to mention. During that time, she has captured the hearts of countless readers with her award-winning romances written under her own name, Sharon Sala, as well as her pseudonym, Dinah McCall. She was born and raised in rural Oklahoma and still calls the state her home. Being with her family is her ultimate joy, although her life has changed drastically from when she made her first sale, to the way it is now. Sharon claims it is her greatest satisfaction to create her stories, then share them with people who love to read.

Rockabye Inn

Deborah Bedford

One

$\mathcal{T}$he truck, an ancient Dodge smelling of dust and pipe tobacco, rattled up the high-country road at a deliberate, unhurried pace.

This afternoon in April, the sky shone shadowless and rich, a magic Alice-blue above the mountains. Wheatgrass had begun to poke its shaggy way through the upland snow and, all about, the vast, lace-edged sweep of sagebrush had exchanged winter's gray for a rebirth of smoky, gentle green.

To the left of the road at Fish Creek Ranch, a furry assemblage of white-faced Herefords followed hay trails, the cows nudging and browsing their way across the snow-crusted pastures. On the passenger side of the truck, Anna Burden peered low through the cracked windshield and decided she'd give anything—anything—for this scenery to seem familiar.

She sat with hands folded solidly together. For a long while, she hadn't spoken. The way curved steeply. Ahead, to the right stood a wooden placard marking their approach to Heck of a Hill Road. With a heavy grating of gears, they slowed, made a turn onto the narrow, tire-furrowed lane, jostled across a cattle-guard, and continued upward.

They began to pass residences set back from the street and hidden among the pines, a hodgepodge of the fashionable and the archaic: long-standing cabins with smoke curling from stone chimneys, contemporary ski houses with massive glass facades. "Which is it?" Anna asked.

"Just up here. To the left, with the log fenceposts. See, they've left the gate open for us."

She leaned forward, ridiculously expectant—and frightened. "Wouldn't they leave the gate open for everyone?"

"I suppose they would." Richard glanced pointedly at her across the front seat. "You always did."

"Oh." She settled back and became silent again as the truck drew up at the front of the house. She didn't move, even when he'd killed the engine and waited, his huge fingers, sun-browned and outdoor-hardened, splayed against the steering wheel. "Well." He looked straight at her then, meeting her fears with his intelligent gray eyes. "Home at last, then, aren't you?"

Oh, how Anna wished he hadn't posed it in the form of a question. "I guess." She stared out again at the immense log walls, the balusters with their knobby burls that, in the singular afternoon light, edged the stoop like swollen wooden knuckles. Above the front door, a sign swung from chains: "Welcome Home," it read, "to Rockabye Inn."

He asked her, "Are you ready for this?"

"I don't know."

Around the inn, plots of aged snow lay where eaves protected the ground from the sun. Water ran in eager rivulets across the rutted driveway. Despite the snow, a clump of yellow bells bloomed early, their butter-gold blossoms nodding beside the porch.

Yellow bells. She clenched the car door handle, listening to the dull, steady pulse of her own heart. She knew the flowers. Knew them without thinking. "I'll get that for you." Richard jumped out of the truck and came around.

"They're all inside, aren't they?" she asked after he'd opened the door. "They're afraid to come out."

"They're not afraid of you."

She tucked a strand of dark hair behind one ear. "They're afraid because I won't remember them."

"But you *will*, Anna. Soon, if not today." He took her hands in his huge, roughened ones. "I can promise you that. That's why I've brought you here."

"Is it so much of me, then?" She peered again at the peculiar old place. *Yellow bells*, she reminded herself. *Of all things, I remember the yellow bells.*

"Yes. Very much of you." Richard laughed indulgently and took the cap that lay across her knees. "Come on."

A yellow Labrador followed at their heels as they started toward the yard. Above the roof of the Rockabye Inn, the land began its ascension to the mountain, the white-bark pines and Douglas firs and rocks fiercely pointing skyward like cathedral spires. A chipmunk ribboned across the walk and paused to assess them, its tail a momentary question mark before it chittered and scurried out of the way. They stomped up onto the porch, and Richard hardly got the chance to knock before the screen swung wildly open and they all came running out together.

"She's here!" "Anna." "Dear girl." Although she wasn't a girl at all, or so she thought, but a woman.

Richard entered the conversation in his baritone voice, as deep and sure as mountainland water. "This is your staff, Anna." And so they were, standing before her with their tow heads and dark heads and gray, people she should know and couldn't remember, all of them earnest, with arms flailing, telling her things.

"The stove had to be repaired twice while you were gone."

"The new feather pillows came in from Scandia Down."

"We've stored away the old ones in chests for when we need extras."

"Mrs. Collister brought a little dog. She hid it inside her closet until it went to the pond and had a run-in with a skunk."

"We gave it a bath in fabric softener and that helped a bit."

"The Goldstroms came two weeks ago and had their friends for a nordic ski in Yellowstone."

"The Goldstroms asked about you. Dr. Chapman did, as well."

"The guests always ask about you."

"They want to hear—"

But the tiny housekeeper who'd said it stopped, realizing she'd begun to mention something they'd promised not to discuss: Anna's accident, the hospital, the family members who hadn't come home. "Oh, I'm sorry. So sorry." She shook her head as if to clear it out.

Chickadees scalloped through the air, darting from tree to tree in the dooryard. The earth beside the house smelled moist and loamy. "We have guests now?" Anna asked.

A tall, loosely built woman with gray in her faded hair said, "Yes. We do have guests. As always."

Anna said, "It seems they won't hear much from me. I've had an accident and forgotten it all. You'll have to help me, all of you, won't you?" She clutched a knob of burlwood to steady herself, one of the contorted columns standing sentinel beside the steps. She felt a sudden, certain urge to swing around it, to go too fast and lean too far, so far that the sky wheeled and the ground listed and her body succumbed to everything but the dry, cold breeze and the pivoting flight.

At that moment, the very moment she accepted the fluidity of the wood beneath her hand and of the motion, she knew she had twirled on this post as a child. She knew it with her heart, if not with her head, as surely as if someone beside her had tugged upon her sleeve and whispered it to her.

I am close to myself here, she thought.

Richard went to the pickup and manhandled her one small suitcase from the back. The instant they stepped into the house, Anna looked about with keen curiosity. She found the lobby of the inn blissfully warm. A jug of loosely arranged daisies sat upon a desk. Ample flames flared in the hearth, plying light over the walls, even in the afternoon. Beside the daisies, a guest register lay open, a pen propped between its pages.

The eldest woman, the one with graying hair, clasped her hand, taking it upon herself to assist Anna a bit. "I'm Evelyn Noble. Your guest-services manager." Her expression gave Anna a feeling of slight unrest. "We are here to help you, Ms. Burden. You must take over your place again and let us know what you want done."

Another staff member stepped forward, one with a gentle smile, a firm handshake and ebony skin. "I'm

Ginny Ware, the cook. You've always called me Cook Ware. Cook Ware. Like cookware. You know?"

Anna didn't know what to say. Richard took over instead. "She's had a long day, packing things up and moving out of the hospital. Perhaps you'd best get back to your work. Give Anna time to get oriented. Adjusted."

"Yes." Evelyn spoke. "To get oriented. Of course."

As the employees discreetly slipped back to their duties, Richard hung Anna's hat on a peg among a riot of snow jackets, mufflers, and ski poles. She said to him, "I'll take my suitcase." She loosened the toggles of her coat and lay it across a chair. "You mustn't wait on me so."

"You deserve to be waited on, after all this."

She thought it an odd thing for him to say. "I'm not certain of what I deserve anymore." In the mirror over the mantelpiece, she came face to face with her own reflection. An anniversary clock sat on the ledge beside her image, its balance wheel whirling to and fro, its ticking like the sound of water flowing past; one had to listen to hear it. She wondered who had given her the clock. "I'm not certain of anything."

"I'll take your suitcase"—she noticed he diverted the conversation—"so I can lead you to your own bedroom. Otherwise, you might happen in on some unsuspecting guest."

When their eyes met this time, Anna felt dizzy and open, unprotected. She wished for the porch outside, for the zealous staff that greeted and surrounded her, for the sudden, dizzying shelter of Ginny Ware's constant chatter and Evelyn Noble's astounding, inanimate grip. The feeling came that she knew more of Richard than she understood, that she'd happened carelessly upon some dazzling, depthless loss between herself and this man, like jade stones washed forth, then whisked past, as she tried catching them in the creek.

Jade stones. In the creek.

"I've remembered! There's a creek running just past the yard. I've doused myself trying to grab pine cones and whatever else happened to tumble by." She smiled for the first time since she'd left the hospital, a deliberate, wide smile.

"Yes," he said. "There is a creek."

"So I can picture flowers, a creek. But not my own room."

"Doctor Tilaro said it could be this way. Retrograde amnesia. He said you'd remember pieces, that they might not fit together."

"Have I lost my whole life then, Richard?" She'd tried not to be weak, not to feel alone or afraid. But it was too much now, just being here, *belonging* here, not remembering home.

He gave her a quick, significant glance. When he didn't answer her question, Anna supposed he didn't know what to say. "You haven't lost the inn, at least," he said, as if to fill in and make her not notice.

They walked past French atrium doors, beyond which guests lingered over coffee, past tall windows where a heavy curl of snow hung over the little courtyard, threatening to submerge a number of containers and pots when it fell. "I wouldn't want to frighten guests in their bedrooms," she whispered. "Don't suppose that's much good for business, is it?"

"Ah, back to business. That's a girl," he said, his words easy and confidential once they'd gotten upstairs. "Here you go." He held open yet another door for her. "Your room."

My room. My room.

She paused beside the four-poster bed, ran fingers along the forest-green coverlet, as if she were mapping a remarkable journey. She stopped, though reluctantly, the moment she noticed Richard watching. This aloneness, this solitude inside her head, where no man and no memory resided, had become her mantra, the only place in which she solidly fit.

She wanted to prowl around and find drawers where lingerie and hairbrush went, to discover her intimate possessions laid out in their places. She kicked off her boots, sank onto the plaid sofa, and tucked her feet beneath her, resting her head on the cushion as he swung her bag onto a shelf and opened the curtains.

"You want me to help put your things away?"

"No. I'd like to do that myself. It will help me, just spending time and figuring out where things go."

"Feels odd leaving, after sitting with you at the hospital so long." He cast about, as if he hesitated to go. "There ought to be something more for you to read."

"I've read enough, don't you think?" She'd studied everything committed to paper about the inn, the accounting ledgers, the bulk orders of granola, the inventories of bath linens and tiny, tissue-wrapped soaps and Pendleton blankets hidden away inside each chest. "Comes a time to stop reading about an inn and begin running it again."

"Anyone else would be afraid."

"Exactly as I am afraid," she whispered. "I wish the doctors would tell me more. Earl Tilaro has done nothing but stand in my way."

"If not for him"—Richard said, reminding her—"you might not be alive."

She'd relied on Tilaro's instructions in the hospital. He'd told her to find a grip through the everyday operations at the inn, to be patient with herself, to let her own mind reveal her past with the benign, careful serenity of an unfurling bloom. Anything more, he'd warned her, anything different, and she might be set back for months.

"I have my suspicions about your memory," Tilaro'd told her after she'd healed a bit, after they'd first let her leave her bed and go for walks around the winter-gray hospital grounds at St. John's. "The way you've often mentioned a bellman's duties as if you understood them, the way you know how to unfasten your luggage and zip your jacket and braid your hair. This leads me to believe you are suffering from a form of something called retrograde amnesia. Whatever you experienced before the accident could be the impetus to your memory loss."

"I don't understand."

"You don't have to understand for a while. This condition can be caused by many things, Ms. Burden, physical injury as you've had, a disease like meningitis. In your case, the amnesia is caused by an emotional upheaval, as well as by the accident itself."

He'd stopped here and waited for her reaction.

"What are you preparing me for?" she'd asked as she clutched at the blankets.

"For a psychologist to assess you, Ms. Burden. To a point, I see that you haven't forgotten day-to-day tasks. This leads me to believe that we're dealing with something psychological, not physiological."

"I hadn't realized. The zipper on my coat. When I came out here today, I knew how to zip my ski jacket without thinking. I could do it again and again. But I don't remember my favorite color, my favorite food—"

Tilaro smiled. "That's it. You see what I'm saying."

"But I've—"

He interrupted her. "As a physician, I am certain that the trauma you've experienced recently has caused you to react by totally shutting down a portion of your memory."

"It's ridiculous. You're saying I *want* to forget everything? That I've done this to myself on purpose?" She'd thought he'd gone mad. *All I want to do is remember. I want to know who I am.*

"Ms. Burden, I'm not saying your conscious mind wanted to forget anything. But your subconscious has decided you need protection."

"I can't accept that. I won't—"

"You don't have to now," he said. "I tell you only because I want you to know how careful you must be. Anything forced, anything brought out before you are ready to encounter it, and your psychological health will be at critical risk."

Anna hadn't accepted his diagnosis then, and she wouldn't accept it now, as she stood in her room with Richard. "Doctors aren't gods." She propped her chin on her hand, her elbow on the sill, and peered out at the sky beyond the window. "None of them. Although people like very much to think they are."

Richard stepped closer. He was tall, taller than she, his eyes gray as chimney glass on a lantern. "I thought you trusted Tilaro. I thought you believed what he's told you."

She said, "I'm tired of trusting doctors. I want to know how I can trust myself."

From downstairs, the anniversary clock chimed on the mantelpiece. The room fell silent. Richard ended up at the window, staring out. "You can see all the way into the next county from here, can't you? I've always loved this view."

When he said it, Anna sensed he meant more than the words alone. She gazed past him at the cloudless sky, the windswept rocks lace-edged with ice, the wending road where it clung fiercely to high places. Her request came softly, so softly he might not have heard her. "I know I've taken so much of your time, Richard. But will you come back tomorrow?"

"You want me to?"

"I feel a bit shaky, not remembering anything."

Above the tree tops, an eagle soared in ever-widening circles. His lofty presence set willows to jostling. Magpies cawed and fretted from the branches.

"Don't know if I should, Anna," he said. "When you start remembering things, don't know how often I should be around."

$\mathcal{T}wo$

$\mathcal{N}$o one needed to tell Anna that she often rose early.

She lay in the duskiness of her room this morning, listening to the chickadees and lazuli buntings awaken, feeling her heart race, her thoughts more insistent, more troubled than they'd been even the day before. She put back the covers finally and got out of bed, thrusting her feet into slippers she'd left waiting. She stepped softly, afraid of rousing someone.

First thing first. She slid open the top drawer of her dressing table and extracted the brush, taking great pleasure that it lay where, last night, she had left it. She began to brush her hair with long, slow strokes.

She surveyed her reflection in the mirror, taking no particular pleasure in it. As the image of her face shifted and moved behind the glass, it seemed as if another likeness replaced it, a stirring, breathing reflection of someone she'd once been, with the same dark, unruly hair, the same half-desperate smile. *Of*

*course, I've been at this dresser before, have brushed my
hair a hundred, no, hundreds of times.*

She took stock of things to remember the way
Ginny Ware, the cook, might take stock of items in
the pantry. Yes, she remembered twirling on the
porch, leaning her head far back, and feeling the sky
spin. Yes, she remembered the creek in the backyard,
the yellow bells nodding beside the stoop.

What more? What more?

In her memory, she saw the back of an elaborate
silver frame reflected in the mirror, its velvet stand
perched precariously straight atop a little shelf beside the drawer. *It isn't there now,* she thought, and
slowly trained her eyes downward, hoping that the
very deliberateness of the motion might somehow
make the picture, its subject, reappear.

Anna stared at the empty space on the shelf, the
hand-rubbed walnut polished to its high sheen, no
telltale mark in the dust to indicate anything had ever
been set upon it. "What am I being guarded from?"
she asked aloud, of no one. She'd kept a photograph
and an ornate frame in this intimate place. Someone
had removed it. Anna met her own eyes in the glass.
She frowned and laid the brush aside.

When the scratch came at the door, she stood up
from the upholstered stool and went to investigate.
The yellow Labrador waited in the hallway, its amber eyes lifted with hope, its tail switching gravely
upon the carpet. "Hey, girl. You're up early." Anna
bent and rubbed the dog's ears. She kneaded the fur
beneath the dog's woven collar. On the collar, en-
graved in script across a thin brass crest, was the
name "Lily."

"Lily." She stood up and stepped back. "You want
to come in?"

The dog entered Anna's room with her muzzle low, her nails clicking purposefully as she crossed the oak floor. She walked to the armoire, sniffed around the bottom drawer, and sat down heavily.

"What is it, girl? You think something's there?"

Lily whimpered and nosed her way closer, her tail at the same buoyant angle as an aspen branch. Anna opened the drawer. Inside it, halfway hidden by a large pile of panties—some of which she'd restocked last night—lay a worn canvas dog dummy.

"Oh, there you are." Anna got it out and turned it in her hand while Lily began to hop about and tremble with delight. Anna knelt, the thing still in her hand. "I've thrown this for you, haven't I?"

Downstairs, from the kitchen, she heard Ginny vigorously browsing through cupboards, digging out the first trappings of breakfast. The clock chimed. Half past six. No guests would be up and about so soon. Anna kicked off her slippers and pushed sock-less feet into her pac boots. She shrugged into her coat, unwilling to waste time and change out of her nightgown.

They went down a flight. No one heard them. Once they'd gotten outside, Lily bolted across the frozen yard. Anna followed, knowing when she heard the singing rush of water that she was near the creek.

A path began. The stream bed took its turns like an enchanted ribbon, the current glistening and rippling in morning's first rays of sun. Anna hefted the canvas dummy into the air, watched as it sailed gloriously across into a willow thicket and landed.

The retriever surged forth on its haunches, cleared the bank, jostled through the willows, and leapt merrily back, its prize tucked within its jowls. Anna lofted the thing into the air once more, again, again, until she became breathless from throwing and the dog began to trudge back through the water, lapping up drinks.

"Good girl. Good girl," Anna said each time. As she tramped across the grass, she felt young, unguarded, and free, the first freedom, the first youth she could remember.

You will remember, Anna. Soon, if not today. I can promise you that. That's why I've brought you here.

At the very thought of Richard's words, her clarity disappeared. It was as if she was back in the hospital, her mind as blank and restless as an oceanscape; only wanes and swells, no horizon, no land. She pocketed the dummy and began pitching rocks into the water, absently at first, then with gradual, increasing seriousness. During those long, imprisoned days, she had tried to recapture everything, anything, sifting through the nothingness the way one searches for a dream or a name one can't recall, and the only constant presence in her life had been Richard.

Richard. She didn't know where he'd come from or where he'd gone. Richard, who'd said, "When you start remembering things, don't know how often I should be around."

Lily lolled at Anna's feet, pink skin showing through the pale fur on her belly. The sun climbed higher. For the first time, the day felt close and warm.

"How like yourself you are," came a voice from the porch. Anna turned to see Evelyn Noble standing there, leaning out over the railing and giving a meager wave. "Good morning. Didn't expect you out so early. You're out before the guests are up."

"Good morning, Evelyn." The ground frost had started melting in the sun. Wet grass brushed against

Anna's hem, drenching her nightgown until it clung to her legs. She came toward her guest-services manager and smiled thinly. "I see you've arrived and are going at it, too. It's best to get an early start, isn't it? Especially if you've missed many things, as I have."

"You haven't missed too many things. We've done a fine job getting along." Evelyn Noble hesitated a moment, as if she realized she might be giving the wrong impression. She changed the course of her words. "Given the circumstances."

"You say I'm like myself. Then you say you didn't expect it. Why is that?"

"It's a surprise, is all. Your first morning back and already out with that dog."

"Well."

Evelyn knew that to be the way she always said well when she decided to take the conversation back around where she wanted it.

"It's good we've run into each other early. I've a list for you. We'll begin after breakfast."

"A list? You have duties for me this morning?"

"A meeting, mostly. It won't take long and then you can go about your business. We'll discuss the maintenance accounts, how much we've been paying. Something to be reckoned with so we can get back to operations quickly."

It was an authoritative speech to be making on the first morning since she'd left the hospital. Evelyn Noble looked at her with some concern. "I can assure you, Ms. Burden, that your accounting books have been in capable hands since your acci—I mean, your departure. If I've had any questions, I've asked—"

She stopped. Anna could read nothing on her impassive face. "Who have you asked, Evelyn?"

"No one of importance, Ms. Burden. People you've

worked with who would know. The accountant or the lawyer, mostly, when I've been unable to figure it out."

"I am sure the books have been in good hands." Anna rubbed the dog's ears. "Even so, we'll meet at nine."

"Of course. Yes."

"Oh, and Evelyn. I've a question to ask."

"What is that, Ms. Burden?"

"Before I left, I kept an elaborate frame on my dressing table. I kept an important photo in it. Why was it removed?"

"No one removed it, Ms. Burden. You took it with you when you traveled."

"It was in my bags?"

"I've watched you pack it many times."

She sighed, a great, frustrated breath. *Something more the doctors want me to remember on my own.* "It isn't there now."

"Perhaps Richard requested it be put away."

For the moment, Anna felt dazed. "Where might I find Richard this morning?"

"In the next cabin up Heck of a Hill. Across that gully there." Then, twisting the handle of the door as if she meant to hurry inside, Evelyn looked back at Anna curiously, watching her eyes, hesitating before saying more. When she spoke, her voice was quieter even, more than it had been before. "His family owns the adjoining property, you know."

The Labrador, rested and in high spirits, pawed the water and made spray fly. Atop Rendezvous Mountain she could see a lustrous silver latticework formed by the wild, snow-filled gorges, the vertical slash of the aerial tram, the groomed ski runs at Teton Village. Beautiful and complex. Home. She turned from the mountain toward the house, and Lily came along, questing the ground with her damp muzzle. The dog ran ahead, doubled back when she got too far, plopped at the front door, and heralded their entrance with a great thumping of her tail.

Guests, their morning coffee mugs already in hand, filled the lobby. "Good morning," Anna said, becoming painfully aware that she wore a coat but had never dressed. "Hello. Glad to have you at Rockabye Inn." She greeted them one by one as they detained her, listened intently to their various plans for the day. They told her about snowmobile excursions along Togwotee Pass, about nordic ski tours around Jenny Lake, about a dogsledding journey with lap robes provided and lunch set beside the trail.

She leafed through the pile of mail that lay on the polished counter, finding nothing vital or interesting. "They've got me booked for a horseback ride down in Star Valley," one fellow told her. "Only had to pay $125 and I get to herd somebody's cows through the snow all day long."

Anna couldn't resist grinning at this. "Be sure you talk to Evelyn Noble. Have her schedule you a massage for after you return." And, even as she said the words to him, she knew she'd remembered another small, victorious detail of her life as it had been before. "Bet that's something no cowboy did in the old days. A day in the saddle and a professional masseuse to work out the sore."

The back office entrance stood ajar. When Ginny rang the bell in the dining room for breakfast, Anna heard Evelyn's voice on the phone, raised over the din. "It's crazy, isn't it? All this, and she's gotten the idea we'll have meetings." A pause. "No. No. It won't work that way, not for a time, at least."

"Evelyn?"

But Evelyn Noble didn't hear her. She went on. "So you're still the gossip champion, repeating everything you hear. I know, a pity isn't it? All her life, changed in one day. And Anna Burden hasn't got a dog's chance of coming back to full capacity again. Don't care how long she's been studying the books and asking questions. Without Richard's tutelage, she wouldn't remember a thing. Not a thing."

You're wrong! Anna wanted to shout at her. *I remember things. Many things. Jade stones tumbling in the creek. A frame on my dressing table. How to book a massage for a young man who will come in hurting before supper.*

Breakfast dishes passed around the rough-hewn table in the dining room, serving spoons clattering. "It's Richard who is the problem. He won't leave well enough alone, you know. Bringing her home like this, coming around, when she's got no recollection of—"

At that moment, Evelyn pivoted toward the door, wearing a harassed expression, like someone who has got to catch a train. Her face became lifeless. She lowered the telephone receiver. "Why, Ms. Burden. I didn't know you'd come in."

"I've tried to get your attention several times."

"You have?"

Anna kept her composure, making no immediate mention of the conversation she'd overheard. "We have a guest going out on a horse today. He wants you to schedule a massage. I suggest you discuss it with him before he leaves."

"Yes. I will. Of course. What guest is he? Will you tell me his name and the name of his room?"

But Anna hadn't the slightest idea of his name. Nor did she know the names of the rooms. "You can find him. He's breakfasting in the dining room. The fellow with the new red flannel shirt and the bandanna stuck into his rear pocket."

"Of course." The sun that streamed in the window now seemed far too brilliant, far too yellow. A long period of silence fell between them. Evelyn shifted her weight from one foot to another. "Is that all for me, then?"

"I'm not certain. I'm not certain if that's all, or not."

"Anna. Ms. Burden. What you overheard me saying. Just idle gossip, I assure you. People do gossip about this situation, you know. It intrigues everyone."

"Yes. I heard you mention the word gossip before." A subtle message, so Evelyn'd know just how long she'd listened. "I've been wondering how you justify your position here, working for me and saying such things."

"I justify it"—Evelyn squared her shoulders and raised her chin—"because it is true."

"I hired you once. I'd like to trust I made the right choice then." *Surely, surely I can trust myself, the decisions I made before.* "I can fire you, as well, if I decide you've overstepped your boundaries here."

"I have expertise, Ms. Burden."

"I'd rather get along with someone inexperienced," Anna said, "than to make do with someone who would speculate about my capabilities."

When she answered, Evelyn's attitude was deliberate, as if she'd decided to tolerate with peace and steadiness whatever brought on this bewildering behavior. "Just yesterday, you made it clear to all of us, to the entire staff, how much help you needed."

And you told me with great certainty to take my place again. To let you know what I wanted done. But Anna would not voice those words; she would not concede to argument.

As if needing to remind her of her precariousness, Evelyn Noble looked her up and down, making a great show of noting the hastily donned coat, the flimsy, wet nightgown. "You didn't dress before you greeted the guests?"

"No. I was outside with Lily. You know yourself. And I returned to find everyone awake, ready to be served breakfast and depart."

"The back stairs. You've always gone up the back stairs when you've taken the dog out early. You've gone up, dressed for the day, and written letters in your office before anyone had even seen you."

"The back stairs." Anna made a mental note to search them out at once. "I should have used them." At that moment, how she envied Evelyn Noble, the woman's power, her perfect knowledge that asked no questions of the present or of the past. The thought brought pain to her stomach, a sudden sinking. "Next time, I will."

She had no doubt that Evelyn saw through her pretense. The guest-services manager had not been deceived, not for a moment. Anna could lose all hope of having gained respect from her hardy words and her announcement of meetings. Of course, she remembered a frame on her dressing table. Yellow bells swaying beside the stoop on lean stalks. An Alice-blue sky that proclaimed, yes, yes, you have been a child here, you belong here, as do the pines and the morning birds and the mountains.

That wasn't much, not nearly enough, Anna realized. That really wasn't anything at all.

Three

Just as breakfast ended and the guide from Togwotee Adventures began to hand out boots and helmets to the snowmobiling party, Ginny let out a tremendous wail from the kitchen, followed by an expletive that, had the cook intended to offend a boatload of sailors, might've well succeeded. Before Anna could get to the kitchen, Ginny ran into the office instead, twisting her apron with two ample, wet hands. "Dadblasted water pump. I've had enough of this, I say! Well's gone out again, Anna. For the third time since Christmas."

This was not something she'd learned from reading the accounting books and researching through files. "What do we do when the well goes out?" Anna asked.

"I'm standing over the sink, scouring the pots, when the spigot makes a burp and starts dripping down to nothing. Don't know how anyone around this place expects a cook to get the kitchen into shape for lunch without water." She stopped and stared at Anna, the words registering for the first time. Her brown eyes went huge. "What do you *mean*, 'What do we do when the well goes out?' We do what we always do. You get down your tools like your father taught you and you crawl beneath the pump house with a flashlight and have a look around."

A young boy appeared beside Ginny's vast jib of an apron. He poked his head round her and announced, with much trepidation, "My name is Everett James. We're staying in the Black Bear Room. My mother's sent me down to tell you. She's in the shower all soaped up and the water's gone out."

Maintenance records fanned out across the conference table. Anna glanced at the papers only once, glad that an emergency had occurred, that the meeting with Evelyn Noble could not go on as planned. She needed more time, she decided, much more time to remember. "We can't call maintenance in for this?" She turned to Evelyn. The guest-services manager waited just inside the foyer, the clipboard for her room inspections balanced neatly in the crook of one elbow.

Ginny jutted her neck forward at an angle reminiscent of the neck of a sandhill crane. She said, "It takes twenty minutes for maintenance to get here from town. When the water goes out like this, it's always an emergency."

"I'll call maintenance." Evelyn reached for the phone.

"No." Anna raised a hand to stop her. "I'll try it myself."

"You mustn't, Ms. Burden. It's dangerous down there, with electricity. If you aren't certain how to make the repairs, you could be injured."

"Does Richard know how to do this sort of thing? The man who brought me home?"

By the unease she saw in Evelyn's face, Anna knew that her employee objected to this arrangement. Before the conversation went further, the little boy named Everett James ran off to tell his soaped-up mother that help had been found.

"That makes that decision, doesn't it?" A pause. "I suppose the tools are in the shed I saw out beside the yard."

"My, but you *have* forgotten, haven't you?" Ginny moved toward her desk and took Anna's hand inside her plump, still-sodden one, a strange, distinct gesture of protection that Anna did not understand. "Forget phoning Mr. Richard. He's only up the trail. I'll run right over and find him."

"Evelyn," Anna instructed, sensing it best to send the woman on to something useful. "Will you accompany Everett to the Black Bear Room and let Mrs. James know we will have her rinsed off as soon as possible?"

"Yes. Of course."

They got the flashlight from the kitchen. Ginny disappeared past the creek while Anna went out to rummage through the shed. She found the ancient box of tools immediately, waiting on a rickety shelf lined with rolls of baling wire, two or three dozen dented tin cups, and a massive pair of rusty scythes that must've once been used to chop nettles out of the yard.

In the darkness of the shed, she pried open the latch and laid open the box, peering down at the jumble of pliers and screwdrivers, ratchets and hammers. Her father's tools. Tools he'd used when he'd made the repairs. She lay her hands upon all of them and closed her eyes, as if her fingers could help her remember, as if the very touch of the worn implements could topple the wall of secrets that piled one atop each other like stones. "Sure don't know which of these I'll need," Anna said aloud to nobody.

"Why don't you get on under that pump house with all of them?" Here came Richard, striding across the yard. "You'll figure out soon enough which will do." With that, he resumed his quiet whistling.

It wasn't so much the words he said that astounded her, but the certainty in his eyes, his seeming absolute knowledge that she could summon this from within herself. She latched shut the tool box. "I might get lost underneath the pump house."

"There's not space for getting lost in. You want me to go first?" he asked. "Or do you want me to follow you down?"

"You'd best follow me," she said, scooting the toolbox across the floor. "If I get lost, you'll be behind and can haul me out of trouble."

He laughed. "That's the way I've seen this all along."

And so they went, Anna dropping down onto the dirt floor first, brushing webs and rodent nests out of her way. The moment she touched the muddy tank and began to jostle around to find how to remove the casing, she knew as surely as she'd known on the porch yesterday that she'd done this, been here, many times before. She opened her father's old chest and thrust everything around with great noise until she found just the size of wrench she looked for.

"There you go," Richard's muffled voice came from behind her. "I told you. You know exactly which one."

"You were right." And she wondered, as she tugged on the nut to loosen it, how he'd come to know her so well.

She found that she loved working with her hands. They maneuvered of their own volition, feeling along the circumference of the tank. Even without her bidding, they knew the way, naturally. How Anna rejoiced! Richard and Ginny had been right to trust her at this, as if they, too, had known her own hands could search out, grasp onto who she'd been. "Confounded thing. I think it's the pressure switch this time," she announced. Her voice echoed with great certainty from the room above them.

"Switch this time . . . switch this time . . . switch this time."

"I can see it from here. The contactors are burned." She didn't hesitate. She didn't need to. "Got to get to the house and turn off the circuit breaker. This can be fixed in no time."

And, indeed, it was. On a shelf in the tool shed, they found two extra switches still packed in the box from Grand Teton Plumbing. She disconnected the old and reconnected the new, turned on the circuits, climbed back under, and flipped on the switch. Beneath the pump house, in the muck and in the cobwebs, she'd found one more glorious place she belonged.

She talked of nothing else all the time she backed out of the crawl space. "This makes it a much better day. Until now, I've been going around feeling buffeted."

He didn't say, "What do you have to feel buffeted about?" "I expect you're going to feel that way for a while, Anna. But seeing you under there, knowing what to do. Just like old times, when your father used to teach us." He climbed up into the pump house, reached down for her and gave her a lift up when she clambered through the hole.

"I took a walk with Lily this morning. She sat down beside a drawer and wouldn't budge until I found the canvas dummy inside. Before that, I sat at my mirror and discovered something else. I knew that I'd kept a frame there, on my dressing table, with an important picture." Dangerous ground, this. She couldn't be sure how he'd react. But Anna knew to make it casual, as if she mentioned something of no consequence, something he might not find interesting at all. "Do you know anything about the frame on my dressing table, Richard?"

Upstairs, the housekeeper had thrown open several windows. From the Black Bear Room they could hear the sound of Mrs. James in her shower. The water ran loudly. Richard said, "Yes, I know the one," then nothing more.

"I spoke with Evelyn about it. She said no one had removed it from my dressing table, that it was something I took with me whenever I went away."

He let go of her arms at last and gripped her shoulders instead. "Tell me about what you've remembered. The frame on your dresser. And the photograph."

She'd been nodding like a child, pleased with herself, until he said, "And the photograph." The expression in his eyes was horrible, as if he'd become deathly afraid for her. Anna began to shake her head. "No. Not the photograph. It began when I noticed the absence of the frame. I tried an experiment. I trailed my gaze downward as if I could make it appear. I saw the frame, the silver filigree, a blur, nothing more."

"I had no idea," he said, "that this would come so soon."

"Do you have it?" she asked. "Did you remove the frame from my things?"

"Yes." She could scarcely hear him. "I took it from your suitcase long ago."

"Why?"

"Doctor Tilaro thought the photo was something potentially damaging."

"Enough of Earl Tilaro." She made fists, began to pound Richard in the chest with them. She thumped him, heard the precise, hollow echo through his lungs with each sentence. "Enough of everything he's tried to do for me." *Thump.* "He's cut me away from myself." *Thump.* "He won't give me anything to go on and neither will you." *Thump. Thump. Thump.*

During her assault on him, Richard hadn't flinched. Now he caught her wrists and held them away from himself so she couldn't hit. "You don't know what you're saying."

"Someone should sue him. Someone should take away his medical license and run him out of practice."

"He's helping you. If you're going to get better, you've got to accept Tilaro's diagnosis. Anna, please." Richard stopped, seeming unable to go on. As she looked up at him, his sorrow confronted her own. She saw his angry, rasping grief, too. "You've got to fight, Anna, but this time you've got to do it somebody else's way. It's the only way you're going to survive."

"You're angry at them. You're as angry at them as I am."

"I'm not angry at the doctors. I'm angry at"—he stopped and enveloped her fists with his fingers, trying to figure how to word it—"*this.* At the thing that's done this to you, that's made you want to flail out at the world without knowing what you're hitting at."

She relaxed her fingers, opened them into his hands, took a breath. She knew he felt her shaking. "I can't stop being afraid," she said. "I can't stop casting about like I'm in a dark, empty room with no doors, no windows, no way out."

Richard brought her different pictures the next morning, tied securely in a leather pouch. "What are these?" she asked as they sprawled on the dry grass together and he handed them over.

"They're pictures. Of your father. Doctor Tilaro has approved them. The doctors think maybe seeing him will jog your memory."

She was afraid to touch the worn leather. She flipped open the case and held her breath, waiting for recognition to begin. She saw a lithe, elderly man with unkempt white hair and kindness in his eyes. "My father," she whispered. The man in the picture sat upon a pile of logs, peeling away the bark with a chisel. The colors in the photographs had stayed bright, his shirt redder than red, the logs the rich honey brown of pine, the snow on the mountains as white as the white clouds in the sky. "My father," she said again, leafing through the pictures, wanting to love this man's kind face. But she shook her head finally and handed them back to Richard. She might as well have been examining photographs of a stranger.

"Tell me why you are here," she said one day while she threw the dummy for Lily as Richard watched. "Tell me where you've come from, who you are."

He chose his words carefully. "My home is nearby. But I don't stay there often. I travel. I keep busy working at construction sites. I climb mountains in Nepal."

"Did they call you at your house when I had my accident? Did they call and say, A friend has had an accident. Come on down?"

"Not exactly." He pulled a clump of grass out by the roots and shook the dirt free. He glanced up at her, let her see something he hadn't before, a haunted, powerful expression she couldn't comprehend. "They called me in Nepal and said, 'A friend has had an accident. Come on down.'"

"You came from so far away?"

"Yes."

"When I woke up in the hospital and you were beside me, did I recognize my name?"

"Yes, you did." He seemed relieved to suddenly be on safer ground. "I spoke to you, called you Anna, and you turned my way."

"How do you know that's why I turned your way? What if I turned because you said something, and nothing more? I'll never know, will I? If I knew my name was Anna because you said it, or if I answered because I knew my name was Anna."

"You ask funny questions, Anna." He touched her nose when he said her name, like he was playing with a child. *Anna. Anna. Anna.*

"All the same, I'll never know, will I?" She inclined her head toward him, like an innocent bird. "That night you brought me here, Richard, you said, 'When you start remembering things, don't know how often I should be around.' Why did you say that, Richard?"

In a gesture that admitted discomfort more distinctly than spoken words, Richard put up a hand to rub his eyes, and then to smooth back his hair. When the awkward silence went on for too long, he covered it neatly in his baritone voice. "I'm here now because you need me, Anna. We've been friends a very long time. But you've never wanted—" He stopped, watching her with sadness for a moment. "You will remember your own life soon. You will remember the choices you've made."

She sat beside him, feeling wavery, knowing that, while she wanted to rely on no one, Richard's presence in her life overshadowed everything; his inexplicable, gentle power brought her the only strength she'd been able to keep as protection.

Four

"You need to get away from Rockabye some," he said one evening when he'd dropped by to check on her. "Would you mind if I took you out to dinner?"

"I would love to go out," she said, "but I would also be afraid. Getting dressed. Going out in public. What if I see someone I know, someone who starts asking me questions about things I don't know?"

"It's a risk, one you're going to have to take eventually."

She hesitated.

He said, "I'll find some place out of the way. Chances are, no one you know will see us."

He took her to The Granary at Spring Creek Ranch that night, high atop East Gros Ventre Butte. They sat in the dining room and could see far below. Cattle, some of which were ready to drop calves, grazed on ranchland that belonged to a Wyoming state senator. The sprawl of the valley, its ranches, the ski areas and immense new houses, spread below them like an enormous patchwork quilt. The waiter brought them a tureen of soup, a plate of oysters Rockefeller. They held goblets in both hands as they drank wine.

"There are other places I could have taken you, instead of bringing you here," he said with relaxed candor.

"Another restaurant? I like it here."

"No. That isn't what I mean. I'm not talking about this restaurant. Maybe I should've whisked you out of the hospital that day and gotten you somewhere far away. No one would know where we'd disappeared to."

"Why?" she asked. "Why would you take me any place else?"

"I had a choice to make, you see. I could have taken you somewhere where you'd have a new name, a new life. You could leave your old life behind you like a butterfly breaks from a cocoon."

"I don't suppose I would've been happy, doing that sort of thing," she said, thinking about it. "I'd have lost too much of myself if you had taken me away. More than I've lost already."

"Yes," he said. He lifted his glass to the firelight and twisted the stem, watching the play of flame upon chardonnay. "I know that, too."

For a long time, they stared out at the ranches below, the ragged silhouette of the mountains. Then he paid the bill and the tip and left the money in a folder.

Only after they arrived in the yard at the inn did she say at last, "Evelyn Noble doesn't like you much."

Odd that those particular words should be the ones to make him smile. "No. I suppose she doesn't."

"I overheard her talking on the phone the other morning. She didn't know I was there. She said you couldn't leave well enough alone."

Richard poked his hands in his pockets, jiggled his keys. "Let's not talk about Evelyn. Let's talk about something else." He began to whistle a jovial tune she liked but didn't recognize.

"Okay. Places. Let's talk about places you might've taken me, if you hadn't brought me home."

"Tonight? The Cowboy Bar. The Rancher Bar. The Stagecoach. Spirits of the West."

"No. Not tonight. In another life. What you talked about at dinner. Where would you have taken me if you'd taken me to another life?"

An airplane hummed miles above them, its contrail leaving a short wake in the sky. Lily bounded from the door and began to wallow on the grass, arching her backbone against limbs and rocks while her four legs flailed ridiculously in the air. From behind the inn came excited voices, horseshoes ringing against pegs.

"Nepal, maybe. I would've hired a Sherpa mountain guide to climb with us into the Himalayas."

"I wish you *had* taken me."

"Or we could've gotten lost in the markets in Katmandu. Or in Mexico. You could've been a Spanish dancer. You could have danced on the beach with the sea wind in your hair."

She thought about it a long while. "If I had to choose, I'd rather go to Mexico than Nepal. Someplace warmer than the mountains. You make it sound so beautiful. I get tired of all the snow."

On Saturday, by the time Anna had dressed and gotten downstairs to her office, the lobby bustled with departing lodgers. Suitcases, boot totes, and skis in tall, bright bags lined the hallways. Evelyn tallied bills at the desk. The drivers for Buckboard Cab called at the front walk again and again. "Here for Henderson, party of three." "Airport pickup for Atkins, party of five."

"Thank you for coming," she called to the people she'd met. "Have a safe trip back to Chicago." Or Dallas. Or Brooklyn. Or New Jersey. Seemed like she told people good-bye for hours, and they answered, "We had a wonderful time. Our compliments to the staff. We'll recommend this to our acquaintances, to our friends."

She felt lost in a sea of faces, a stranger on a crowded street. "We do this every *week*?" she asked Ginny when she finally sought refuge in the kitchen.

Ginny, with a zucchini in one hand and a knife in the other, stopped slicing and laughed outright. "None of us have been around that long, of course. But you and your father have been doing this every Saturday for eighteen years. Here. Give me a hand. I've got three kinds of cheese to cube before the reception for new arrivals this afternoon."

The last taxi departed just after 11:00 A.M. Before it had completely disappeared down the drive, the housekeepers were stripping beds, shaking out blankets, bringing in ladders, and wiping lemon oil over the rafters. As everyone hurried around her, Anna took a solemn walk through each compartment. The Trumpeter Swan Room. The Buffalo Robe Room. The Wapiti Moon Room. And a child's room made up as if some little girl might come to stay, with a ruffled canopy and a tulip quilt and a crib filled with stuffed antique bears.

Strange, she'd looked forward to this day, when everyone would leave the inn. She'd expected a sense of peace, a silence that would speak to her, a long-awaited reprieve to the days she'd spent trying to find herself, surrounded by people. As long as the inn had been full, she hadn't been able to shake the perplexing notion that she'd been playing hostess the way a little girl plays house. The days kept passing by, filled with people and busyness. She felt left behind.

And today, now that they'd gone, she felt painfully alone.

Each room had the look of being quickly abandoned, sales tags scattered on the floor, unneeded debris jammed into garbage bins. She tried to catch her breath, and couldn't. The inn seemed forlorn and empty without the clamor of the guests it had been built for. Anna stifled the urge to run out into the sunshine with Lily, to go over the hill or down the road without stopping, as if she was leaving, too, without looking back at the roof, the gate, the swinging sign over the porch that said, "Welcome Home to Rockabye Inn."

Ginny, Evelyn, and the housekeepers—an entire staff of them that Evelyn hired in every weekend—kept about their duties with vigor. She felt more in the way than helpful. Each place she went, someone said, "Excuse me, I've got to set this chair in the corner." "Could you step over that rug, please? It's already been shaken." "I need to put these daisies on that dresser, a little to the left of where you're standing."

What did I used to do on these days? she wondered. *I certainly didn't do this, follow people about, make them stumble over me.*

I want to be me. All of me. Only I don't know who that is.

By noon, the maintenance crew arrived from town. Evelyn gave out a list. One man repaired a tear in the carpet, checked the chimney flue, and pounded in a new board on the deck beside the hot tub. Another

checked each fire extinguisher and stretched a new
net across the tennis court. Four hours later, when
those same cabs parked at the front walk, all waited
in readiness. Split logs were stacked beside the hearth.
The brass anniversary clock gleamed on the mantelpiece. Each pillow on every bed lay plump and
smooth.

The newcomers alighted and came up the walk,
the women talking, the men struggling under loads
of luggage, the children wide-eyed and amazed by
the surroundings and the snow. They took turns
standing in line to sign the guest register. Evelyn had
hired a bellboy for the day who tramped upstairs
and down, upstairs and down, with Herculean effort,
lugging enormous assortments of bags.

Lily made her rounds, the pattering feet of the dog
comforting, pleasing amidst the din. Ginny handed
out napkins and presided over the welcome buffet.
She served apples and caramel sauce, cubed cheese
and popcorn, simmering dip and tiny sausages laid
out upon a crystal tray. They conversed in low tones,
ate the refreshments, moved about restlessly, as if
they didn't know what to expect. They jostled into
each other so they could have a seat on the hearth
and admonished their children for running in the
halls. And Anna thought, *I was wrong to want to be
alone. I know I've never been alone here. I'm glad there'll
always be someone coming.*

The last guest to arrive for the day was an elderly
gentleman named Blau who'd chosen to rent a Tau-
rus and drive himself from the airport. He'd gotten
lost coming around the Jackson town square and
called twice en route. When he finally blundered in,
he carried three fishing rods and a pair of hip waders
strung across one shoulder.

"Thought I'd never find this place," he bellowed. One of the fishing poles disentangled itself from the others and plopped onto his head with a loud twang.

Anna hurried to assist him.

"Confounded things. Had them in their cases until we got off the plane. But when we stopped and saw all those fat trout in tanks at the fish hatchery, made us feel better to get the poles together and rig them up."

"Fishing's been good this week." Anna rose to her part a little, got the wayward pole back with the clump. She took the entire array from him and propped it in a corner. "Especially up north of town just below the Jackson Lake dam. You catch enough of them, and we'll convince Cookware Ginny to put together a fish fry before you go home."

Ginny tugged at her sleeve. She whispered, "You called me Cookware Ginny. Did you think of that? You haven't done that since you got home."

Mr. Blau knelt down to the little girl at his side. "Told you we'd have a good time. This whole thing's a lot better than Barbie cars and Nintendo."

"You're probably both tired after being lost." Anna began to fill in the register for him. "Just need you to sign here and add the automobile information. You'll both be in the Coyote Room. I can take you right up, if you'd like."

"Heck, no. Don't take us up to the room yet. We haven't eaten since that box of Post Toasties and that hard brown muffin supposed to pass as breakfast on the plane. It'd be a shame to waste what's left of those fancy sausages."

"Help yourself," Ginny encouraged.

"So we're in the Coyote Room, are we?" He bent down to his granddaughter again. "When me and

Grandma Lulie were here eighteen years ago, we stayed in a room called the Black Bear Room."

Her heart caught in her throat. A return guest. Of course they would have them. People who loved it here and chose to come back for another vacation, a different year. "We still have the Black Bear Room."

"Never caught so many fish in my life, before or after, as when we stayed here. And never had such a good time, either. Did me and Lulie a world of good, coming to a place where the kids could get outside and play and leave us to ourselves."

"You were here eighteen years ago?"—Ginny'd said just this morning, "You and your father have been doing this every Saturday for the past eighteen years."—"That might have been the first year we took over this place," Anna said.

"You know, I'll bet it was. There was this fellow who ran everything, with his little girl. I remember the kids made friends. What was her name? Was it Amy or Annie or Avery—?"

"It might've been Anna. My name's Anna."

"That was it! Anna." He took another good look at her. "Come to think of it, I see a resemblance. Same dark hair, only then it was all arranged in pigtails. You used to work all morning beside your dad. One morning, he had you up beside him on the roof. Another, he had you down in the mud under that pump house over yonder. And one day the two of you laid linoleum together. I hadn't ever seen anything like it. You couldn't've been older than sixth grade."

"The pump house. Even when I was a little girl, he had me under the pump house."

"Your father still around this place?"

"No. I'm afraid he died seven years ago."

I say it so easily. As if I remember him. As if I know his face from my own heart, not from Kodak photographs in a leather-bound album.

"Well, I'm sorry to hear that. I am, indeed. Such a nice fellow, too. Always ready to extend a hand. Got such a kick out of watching you young kids that summer. Once your dad would let you free from the chores, you'd go tearing down that hill there in a rush to bring back those boys who lived next door. Got into all sorts of mischief, you did. You remember them? Like three peas in a pod, you kids were. Inseparable."

"Next door?"

"Well, out here, don't know as you'd call it next door or not. Next house over, within shouting distance. About a quarter mile."

Anna handed him the tray with the last of the little sausages.

He asked, "You want to sit down or something? You look a bit pale, young lady. Maybe it's worn you out, having to take care of old coots like me. I'll bet this sort of thing takes a lot out of you. Getting everybody settled in."

"You don't suppose they live there still? Two boys. Did you know their names?"

"Ashamed to say it, if I did then, I don't now. Hard to describe what it's like, getting old, trying to remember things and having your mind draw a blank. Like coming around the town square this afternoon, thought I'd recognize landmarks and make the right turns. But the wax museum's gone. And I couldn't find the hardware store anywhere. Somebody told me it'd burned down."

"Tell me about those two boys, Mr. Blau. Perhaps one was a Richard. I have dealings with a Richard."

She and Richard had been childhood friends. Perhaps sweethearts, even.

"Kept turning and turning and passed The Gap twice. Whoever heard of a Gap on the town square in Jackson Hole? It's preposterous. Ended up going right out of town the same way I'd come in. Lost as a jack-rabbit in a coyote's den." He winked broadly. "Then I walk in here and find you're checking me and little Melissa into the Coyote Room."

She might've said something humorous to counter him, perhaps suggested she move them to something less predatory, like the Trumpeter Swan Room. But the Swan Room was already taken; a woman named Mrs. Lesley had requested it because she liked the feather throw pillows on the divan. And all Anna could think of were the stories he'd told, the little girl she'd been.

She handed a glass of juice to Melissa. Ginny always served hot cider at these things, and she knew the children would rather have something cool. She prompted him. "You say we played, that we got ourselves into mischief."

Melissa was feeding Lily sausages from her plate. "One poor girl from Kansas City. You told her the wolves got into the house sometimes, that they climbed trees and got into the windows and slunk around the halls when the guests were sleeping at night. Told her they congregated in the kitchen and had to be carried off by the Wyoming Fish and Game Department."

"What an awful thing to do."

"When she insisted she was too smart for that and didn't believe you, you three concocted a scheme, went out to that treehouse your father'd built by the creek and howled for hours at the moon. Kept everybody awake until almost midnight. And the funny part was, when the coyotes and wolves and what-have-you out there in those woods started howling and yipping back, you three came barrelling inside like you'd come close to being eaten yourselves."

"The welcome buffet is all gone, Mr. Blau. We'll be ready with supper in half an hour. And when the moon is full, the trout always bite best when the sun's going down." The sensation had returned, the one that had beset her during the afternoon, when all the rooms were empty, as if she might suffocate from sadness and from being alone. She took a deep breath and took the child's hand, finding a strange measure of comfort in the thin, short fingers that clasped her own. *He knows more about my life than I do.* "Let me get you and Melissa and all those fishing poles up to your room."

"Is the treehouse still there?" Melissa asked. "If it is, I'd like to see."

"Come to think of it, one of those boys might've been named Richard. Seems to ring a bell. Little tough fellow he was, always scrubbing dirt out of his hair and staring up with gray eyes. He was always the one getting left behind, always tagging along after you and his brother. The brother—" He narrowed his brows and shook his head. "Don't remember much about the brother. Gangly kid who'd as soon square off his fists and disagree with you as give you the time of day. The ringleader of trouble, if you ask me. But you idolized him. Followed him around like a calf after its own mama."

Anna led Mr. Blau and Melissa up the stairs. "You've got two queen beds in here," she said as she threw open the door of the room they'd been assigned. "Or I can bring in extra blankets and Melissa can sleep in the window seat." With one arm, she made a sweeping indication of the wide bay window and the bright cushions and the length of coyote skin lining the sill. "This is usually a favorite with little girls."

Melissa climbed up onto it and nodded. "Can I sleep here, Grandpa? Can I?" Without waiting for his answer, she poked her nose against the glass and peered out. "Where's the treehouse? Can you see it from here?"

At the first mention of the treehouse, Anna had pretended she didn't hear. Now, she had no such luxury. They both watched her, waiting for her answer.

She peered out the window, surveying quickly the spruces, the huge lodgepole pines and cottonwoods close to the yard. "It isn't there anymore, is it? Nope." *I'm getting good at this,* she thought. *Asking questions and answering them, all at the same time.* "A shame. Treehouses ought to last."

Not until she'd left them alone and returned with a pile of blankets for Melissa's makeshift window bed did Mr. Blau wink pointedly at her and indicate the span of trees with a slight nod of head.

"Don't blame you a bit for what you told her about that treehouse," he confided so only she could hear. "With the way lawsuits and liabilities are these days, guess it'd be easy to be taken advantage of. It'd be awful if one of your guests got hurt up there. Old wood like that, you never know when it's going to rot through."

"But I looked at the entire yard just now. Couldn't see—"

"Fine idea your father had, building it as far out from the inn as he did. Folks can't find it," he said under his breath, "unless they know exactly where to look." His granddaughter had taken the heap of blankets and was arranging them to her liking, spreading them one by one upon the window bed, paying their conversation no mind. "That's what made your howling that night so frightful. It came from far away, deep in the forest, and high."

The sun settled low atop the massive Tetons and the trees. He pointed past the yard, past the creek, to a particular cottonwood, one standing over the crest of a hill and almost out of view.

"I see it there."

Surrounding this tree was a glen of aspen, graceful and stunning, entwining one another with smooth, white limbs. The cottonwood rose taller than its counterparts, its trunk robust, its bark the peculiar rough grain of a tree well-seasoned and old.

"Of course, the tree's taller than it used to be," he said. "The thing's grown a-plenty over the past two decades. But maybe you wouldn't notice it, the way you don't notice children growing when you see them every day. Bet those boards are still there, too. The ones your father nailed into the trunk so the three of you could climb up."

The cottonwood's branches reached toward the sky like arms lifted in supplication. In the uppermost crook of its skeletal silhouette, Anna could make out the crude platform and a railing several feet wide.

Five

When she set off into the forest, Anna told no one where she intended to go. Lily came with her, trotting nonchalantly across the low grass. Anna stepped across the creek. Lily sloshed through it and shook. The low sun shone on the water where it ran into little pools by the rocks.

They left the trail and stepped off into wheatgrass that stood dense and tall. The dog held her nose high and lifted her ears to attention. Her thick torso parted the weeds with a papery hiss as she trotted.

Anna sloughed through undergrowth that poked smartly into her ankles, entangling her knees. "There must've been a trail out here once," she said. "Can't imagine children trying to make their way through this."

Children. Not just children. *Us. Me and Richard and, and someone. All of us.*

She realized the dog hadn't stayed beside her. "Lily? Lily!" At her calling, she heard the dog leap into the rustling weeds again from somewhere that had—by the silence of it—been clear. Lily nosed the ground, then pivoted, bounding forth confidently the way she'd come. Anna stared up at the tree tops, doing her best to get her bearings. The treehouse could not be seen from the ground. If Mr. Blau hadn't sighted it from the bay window of his room, she might never have known the structure had endured. "You think you know where we're going? Okay. So we'll go your way." Anna changed courses.

With Lily leading, they came upon a copse of willows that had been thinned out recently with clippers or a scythe. The wheatgrass here had been laid low by the passage of feet. Only then did Anna realize that the dog hadn't been guessing at all. Lily knew the way well. She had come many times.

This path followed the creek, too, as it wound its way down from the high ridge that separated the inn property from Richard's. Occasionally, the route was blocked by lingering shelves of ice. Each time Anna stepped upon a shelf, the ice moaned beneath her weight like a fine old floor. The course here was steeper; the water ran faster, gouging into the black soil, dislodging rocks, leaving roots to fend for themselves and to rake like ancient fingers against the water and the open air.

She surveyed the tree tops again. Ah! They'd gotten closer. She could see the old cottonwood now, just across the draw. She tried to swallow, but was stopped by a nameless constriction in her throat.

Anna imagined herself collecting woolly caterpillars. Weaving willow boats and charging them recklessly downstream. Slinging mud balls at two dirt-splattered boys and squealing. Digging up a field mouse and examining its lair with innocent admiration.

This, her childhood stomping ground.

How poignant, how regretful, that someone had told her of this place, that she hadn't known of it until a stranger chanced to direct her.

Anna stood with arms outstretched to the cold evening air. "This is mine," she said to Lily. "My childhood. My life. I'm going to have it." She took a deep breath, glanced toward Heck of a Hill Road in the direction of the inn and saw that the lights had been turned on in the dining room, the low windows glowing amber in cheerful deference to the coming dusk.

Perhaps she should've told them where she had gone.

The tree proved easy enough to find. Once she'd seen it from a distance, she knew in which direction she'd have to travel. But she hadn't known Lily's trail would lead directly to it, that the path of trampled grass and pruned willows would skirt its trunk exactly, and then, only then, begin to wend its way upward through the aspen grove and out of sight.

She leaned against the thick veed trunk for a full thirty seconds, looking straight up. Above her, the limbs, the budding April leaves, formed an irregular canopy against the dusty sky. From here, the platform seemed much too small, much too high for child's play.

The first dilapidated, weather-worn rung had slipped sideways at waist level. The three nails which fastened it to the tree had rusted loose. She lay the backpack she'd brought at her feet and tugged at the old wood, testing it to see if it would bear weight. The step gave way in her hands. A splinter gouged her thumb. She shook her hand, bit her thumb to ease the pain.

"Okay," she said. "We're going to try this again."

She'd brought a hammer, extra boards, and nails, just in case the thing needed renovation. She pounded in a new bottom step, her hammer blows ringing out across the ravine. When she replaced her tools, slung her backpack around one shoulder, and started up, she came eye-level with a surprise. Someone had been here not long before. The third rung had been repaired. The lumber was clearly of a different vintage than the others, evenly shaped on both ends with a saw, its light, pine burnish only starting to weather away.

Anna grabbed it, tested it, found it strong. She hoisted herself to the next step, the next, the next. As she ascended, she found the rungs became sturdier and sturdier, some reinforced with extra nails and some, like the one she'd first discovered, outright replaced.

She counted them down as she went. *Only nine more to go. Just eight. Just seven.* She chanced a look down. Way down. Oblong shadows flanked the grass far below. Lily raced in a delirious circle, first in one direction, then the other. The dog stopped, leapt, barked wildly at the base of the tree. The jagged skyline of the mountains lurched to one side. She stared in fascination as the ground began to reel.

Finally, finally, Anna closed her eyes, pressed her forehead against the rough bark, and clung to the step above her. She took one deep breath, two.

"There. I'll look up. It's much easier, looking up."

Just six more to go. Only five.

Three crows bent their wings and flapped noisily off to roost in another tree. Her hands began to shake. She lectured herself, argued against her fear. She'd done this many times, hadn't she? She'd scrambled up and down easily, accompanied by friends. But, unlike the day she'd replaced the switch beneath the pump house or the afternoon she'd known Evelyn ought to book a massage for a guest, this climbing to the treehouse brought no startling recognition, no warm memory.

When the wind began to sweep across the draw, she hung on, watching it move toward her. The tree boughs began to sway. The grass rippled in waves. Where loose snow remained, it moved forth, never losing rank as it devised shifting, furtive patterns across the ice. The wind delivered Anna's tree a great clout, a gust that caused the branches to stir. The cottonwood groaned, making the same patriarchal sound as someone heavy settling into a chair.

Count them. You're almost there. Three to go. Two. She closed her eyes again, waiting for the motion to subside, then climbed. She grasped the top step with both hands and hefted herself onto the platform. She grabbed the railing. She jostled it. The railing didn't give way. She scaled the last step, grabbed onto a limb, swung up her leg the same way she'd swing it into a saddle. *There. Look.*

The landscape below her unfurled like a hand-worked quilt. From the porch of the house, someone strummed a guitar and sang an out-of-tune chorus to John Denver's "Grandma's Featherbed." The sun had blinded her for a moment, then had all but disappeared behind the craggy gray outline of the Tetons, the globe of light gone, the flexing rays resplendent atop the mountain as they gold-gilded the ragged edges of clouds.

Sunsets were like that, she thought. The sun had to disappear before the sky was lit up and filled with patterns. And maybe her life was that way, too. Maybe the sun had set. Maybe she only had to await the splendor.

From where she sat, she couldn't see the dog. Lily had long-since given up barking at the tree and had gone elsewhere. Anna scanned the creek bottom.

It seemed as if some spirit, some benign and gentle portion of the life she had lived before, reached forth, made itself known, and directed her. Anna's gaze fell upon a clearing below, a spot atop a knoll that would stay sunny beneath the aspens. The trail she had followed ended there.

Brambles and undergrowth, willows and wheatgrass, had all been thinned away. A buckrail fence encircled the clearing and kept it secure. From here, Anna could see a gravestone. Lily lay like a miniature trinket upon the mound, her head and ears flattened along her front paws.

A gravesite! As she crept toward the edge, she felt foreboding and loss, the feeling that she must brace her soul and her heart for this, that she knew more about the stone below than she understood.

The platform shifted. The wood made a shattering sound, gave an inch, two inches, beneath her. She gasped, spread her arms wide, did her best to redistribute her weight. The twilight intensified. For the first time, she noticed she could see the ground through cracks in the boards. The old planking had disintegrated. To the right of the railing, the rotted timber had already broken through.

Anna's stomach pitched. She inched toward the first step, toward the safety of the railing. She felt the wood beneath her begin to crack. She put more weight on her hands, less on her knees.

The plank beneath one knee splintered, fell away. A piece of ancient lumber seemed to loft into the air for a moment, seemed almost to rise as if caught in a draft, before it started to fall. Halfway down, it crashed into another tree and split into fragments. The fragments tumbled to the ground.

Lily sat up and began barking. The crows lifted off again from another tree, joined by others, cawing in alarm. She lowered one careful foot to the first step. She lowered another to the second. Fear and uncertainty stabbed her like a blade.

"Anna!" From far below, she heard the blessed sound of a voice. A grim voice. Richard's. "Anna."

"We u-used to play up here."

"Back down. Back down slow. Whatever you do, don't look at the ground. You used to be fine as long as you didn't look at the ground."

"I looked down before and I was fine. Don't know why you're standing there giving me advice. I made it up here without any t-trouble."

It happened just as she declared the word trouble. Wood splintered. Pine shattered in every direction. The rung lurched free beneath her left foot. Dust spiraled upward like smoke. Dirt fell.

Anna screamed and clawed for a handhold. With one hand, she found the step above her. With the other, she grabbed a knot where a branch had once been. Her legs swung free.

"Anna! Oh, no! Anna."

She quickly glanced down at Richard. He'd been right. She shouldn't look down. She closed her eyes, but not before she saw Richard sitting on the roots at the base of the tree, tying a rope around his middle, his chest heaving as if he'd come from a long run.

"I t-tested the steps on the way up. They s-seemed fine." Her fingers were sticky with tree sap, clammy and warm. She couldn't feel them. "Richard. I'm scared."

"Don't talk. I'm coming up to get you."

"Someone had even f-fixed those steps. Then I got up there and I looked down to find Lily and everything was spinning and I started down too fast because I looked down and saw a grave. I got into a hurry—"

She opened her eyes again. Below her, Richard belted himself with a rope, strapped on his climbing crampons. He yanked the rope back, tugged on it, found it fastened. It encircled his belly, giving him leverage as he kicked in the front points and imbedded his crampons into the soft, old wood. Inch by inch, he mounted, each plunge of the spikes, each scoot of the rope bringing him a small, excruciating distance closer.

Anna looked straight down at his hair. He had two cowlicks, one on either side of the top of his head.

Plink. Scrape. Plink. Scrape.

Bark peeled from the tree, tumbling in pieces to the ground.

Each moment, hallowed moment, passed while he inched closer. When she felt his fingers touch her foot, she squeezed her eyes shut and offered up a silent prayer of thanksgiving. "I'm going to grab your ankles, Anna. That ought to steady you enough for you to hoist yourself higher and get secure footing. Can you do that?"

No answer.

"Can you do that?"

Without looking down again, she nodded.

"Okay. Good. I'm just below you, Anna. I'm right here."

"Don't l-let me fall."

"I'm not going to let you fall, Anna." She heard him imbed the crampons again and knew he'd moved closer. Then she heard him pause no longer than a breath, and utter a gentle, powerful promise. "I'm going to tie you off with this rope. It's going to cut a little under your armpits, but it's the best I can do."

"But we used to p-play up here. That's what Mr. Blau said."

He caught her ankles just as she said it. "There. Good. I've got you. Can you pull yourself up?"

"My arms—"

"Use your arms to pull yourself up. I'm right below you. You aren't going to fall. If you get solid footing, I can rope you off and downclimb behind you so I can keep you from falling."

She groaned with the exertion of it. She didn't think she could do it. Anna pulled herself halfway up. She lost her nerve. She flopped back down again.

"Come on. *Try.*"

Anna leaned her head against the trunk one last time, mustered her strength, bit her lip, and pulled.

"That's a girl. *That's* a girl."

Her foot found the step, slipped away, and found it again. She put her weight on the next rung up and balanced herself.

Richard used the rope and the crampons again to inch his way up beside her. He tied the rope around her waist and yanked again to make certain he'd secured her. "Now. Wrap your arms around my neck."

She did, collapsing onto his shoulder with no more bravado than a Raggedy Ann doll.

"We're going to climb down now. You with me?"

She bit her lip and nodded. She buried her face against his chest.

"Hold on. We're doing fine," he kept saying. "Fine. Here we go. Fine. Fine."

She hung on for dear life until he set her on the ground.

He backed away from her and ran a palm over the side of his neck, a motion bespeaking both terror and relief.

"Richard?" she whispered.

He stooped to unbuckle his crampons.

She said, "After all that, I didn't want you to let me go."

He unlinked the rope and let it drop in a great tumble at the foot of the tree. For the first time, she noticed how thin his face had become during the past few days, how lined and drawn. He had shadows beneath his eyes, as if he hadn't slept.

He said, "Why did you go up there? You've got no idea what might've happened."

"I do, too. I might've remembered something. *Any-thing.*"

"Thank heavens I saw you from the window. Thank heavens I was standing there frying trout and watching the sunset like I always do." His anger, his frustration came out in a rush. "Anna, that was stupid. Plain stupid." For lack of anything better to do with his hands, he gathered the rope into a heavy pile.

She had splinters everywhere. Arms. Legs. Backside. But even gouging splinters didn't hurt as much as the anger on his face. "Richard. Please." He glanced somewhere in the direction of her left shoe and picked up his crampons. He peeled splintered wood off the jagged metal.

Their eyes met.

"Don't you see?" he asked as a breath seemed to explode from him. "You could've gotten killed up there."

The distance between them could have crumbled as surely as the wood had crumbled beneath her feet.

But he wouldn't let it. Despite his words, he stood straight as a plumb line, looking as combative and bristly as a porcupine ready to let loose its quills. *Reach for me,* she longed to say. *Hold me. No matter what I chose before or what I haven't wanted, won't you please reach for me now?*

He didn't move.

"I would rather you not be here to help me, Richard." She backhanded grime off her face. "I would rather you not be here, than to be here to help me and begrudge me of it."

"I don't begrudge you of it, not in the way you're thinking." His face held the raging intensity of a storm. "You don't know what's gone before. Don't draw me into this, Anna."

"Tell me, Richard. Why would you come all the way from Nepal?"

A foot, a yard of the rope fell over his elbow. The thing followed after itself, twisting to the ground like a nylon serpent, askew and unnoticed.

"No." His face had gone white, as white as the ice that still lined the creek bottom. "We haven't been lovers. Ever."

"But you love me." For this, this she knew.

He slung the crampons over his shoulder and went toward the house.

She followed after. "A guest who's come has told me something. When we were young we played together. Inseparable. Like three peas in a pod. We loved each other even then."

Richard bore the countenance of a man haunted, a moth driven to a flame, a man condemned. "You said inseparable. Like three peas. Three. Not just the two of us. Three."

"Mr. Blau said you had a brother. I know there were

the three of us. You make me feel ridiculous. Like a child."

"And what did Mr. Blau tell you about this fellow, my brother?"

"Oh, let me remember. Nothing important. That he disagreed often and was the ringleader. That I followed after the two of you like a calf after its mother. Of what importance is this brother, anyway? If he means anything to us, why isn't he here?"

She saw Richard's jaw square with anger at her words.

"You're angry with him. Is that it? In mentioning him, do I stumble upon some fresh family row?"

"We have all been stumbling for a very long time."

"I'm tired of stumbling. I'm tired of being treated as if I am two separate people. One who I was then, one who I am now."

He laid back his head and surveyed the limbs and the darkening sky, as if the entangled branches above his head might give answer to the entanglement in his soul. "The grave you saw. It is your father's grave. You haven't wanted to see it before."

She wiped her nose on her sleeve. Sweat had left streaks of dirt down her neck. "I thought he'd be buried at Wilson Cemetery. I wasn't up to going to a cemetery. I wanted to remember him alive before I saw the place he'd been buried, dead."

"You don't have to see the place now. You can wait, if you'd rather."

She stuck her hair behind her ears and crossed her arms over her chest in an exquisite motion of dismissal. "Now that I've found it, I don't want to wait any longer, Richard. My father's grave is here. In a place that is alive. Beside our creek and beneath the tree where we've always played."

She started for the little gate she'd seen. Lily followed at her heels. If Anna had turned back, she would have seen him standing by the fence, his breath coming harsh as if it hurt him, as if his entire body ached both to hold her and to hold her back. *It's too late to save her from herself. Perhaps it's always been too late. Perhaps I never should've tried.*

Six

Anna knelt in the clearing, her pulse beating strangely, before the lone monument chiseled from cold, mica-flecked granite. She stared at the name, the dates. Edgar Rogers Burden. Born December 28, 1931. Died May 1, 1990. The letters had been precisely cut, as deeply honed in the stone as they would be in her heart.

In daylight, they would be filled with shadow. She traced each with her finger, as if she could outline her father's face by outlining each letter in his name.

She traced the *E*. She traced the *d*. And on and on. She whispered to him, "I'm here. I'm here." She closed her eyes, mentally browsed the photographs Richard had showed her, and willed Edgar Burden's life, her memories, to come. But they remained firmly out of reach, even here, even now, taunting her like a contender in a game of blindman's bluff.

You can find me. I'm just out of reach. Find me. Find me.

Anna rocked back on her heels and lowered her forehead to the butt of one hand, speared fingers up through disheveled hair flecked with wood chips and moss spores and dust. If she laid upon the ground, if she spread her arms, if she smelled the earth, she would remember him. She'd remember selecting this knoll over others. She'd remember keeping this little hidden lawn. She'd remember planing the logs and stacking them at odd angles for this fence.

She lifted her face from her palm. At the base of the memorial, where the first shoots of frilly spring grass lanced up through last year's dried roots, lay a different slab of rock. It was fashioned of feldspar perhaps, its surface left inclined and rough except for a square area buffed smooth and left for a poem. The poem, which was topped by a delicate engraving of a magpie building its nest, read,

MY HAND
This is my hand,
so tiny and small,
for you to hang upon the wall.
So you can keep watch
as years go by
How we grow,
my hand and I.
No matter how little I am now,
I will remember you, Grandpa, somehow.
This hand of your hand, this heart knows your name.
You are ever beside me, loved always the same.
To Edgar Rogers Burden
Beloved father of Anna Burden
Beloved grandfather of Kelsey Burden Reese
May 4, 1990

One cement square, poured to the size of a stepping stone on a garden walk, lay embedded in the ground beside the marker. Carefully pressed into it was the imprint of one tiny left hand, fingers stretched as wide as could be, the cement smushed up between each digit as if there had been some mess. Above the handprint, meticulous capital letters announced, "Kelsey. Age 3."

She'd helped Kelsey write her name. They'd been holding a stick together, waiting for the cement to stiffen. Kelsey hadn't wanted to wait. She kept yanking the stick away, poking it into the wet cement, leaving holes.

Anna stared down at the handprint and the stone. Her vision blurred. She heard nothing but the sound of the magpies *cheee-chee-cheeing* from the willows and the pounding of her own heart. A dizzying jolt of adrenaline took hold of her at the base of her neck. It curled forward to buzz in her ears, her temple, her forehead. She didn't think she could stand it.

"Richard." She reached behind her blindly, grasping at the empty air. "Richard."

"I'm here," Richard said from behind her. She sensed, rather than felt, his thick hand rounded in the air above her shoulder. She waited for the perfect weight of his fingers to clutch her collarbone in reassurance. But it never came. He said, "You remembering things, Anna? Is something coming back?"

She nodded. The picture in the frame began to come into slow, perfect focus. Light superseded dark. Detail overcame obscurity. A face. A child's face, with eyes the same Alice-blue as the sky.

Things rushed in all at once. She saw a little girl in the picture, with hair the color of wheatgrass, sitting chin to shoulder with Lily, the yellow Labrador. The little girl grinned at the camera with great aplomb and showed two of her bottom teeth gone, one already half replaced by a huge three-pronged adult incisor, the other a saddle gap in the gum that looked as if it had just been vacated.

Anna turned to him and tried to rise to her feet in slow motion, but stumbled back to the ground. "The photograph, Richard. The one you told me to try hard to remember."

"You seeing it?"

"It's a picture of Kelsey. The little girl that put her hand here. I keep it in the silver frame on my dressing table. And Lily's in it, too."

At her name, the dog came over and began to lick Anna's hand. "Raked up here this past week," Richard said, as if raking made any difference, thinking maybe the mention of something commonplace would give each of them a mooring. "I thought with springtime coming on and all—"

But Anna was staring at the imprint of the little hand again. He might as well have been talking to the four winds. Nothing, nothing could have prepared her for this. When she closed her eyes, tears came at the corners of them. Before long, they spilled down her cheeks. She didn't try to hide them or wipe them away. She let them roll down her jawline unwiped, unchecked, until they dangled on her chin like raindrops on eaves and rolled freely to wet her shirtfront.

For the picture in the ornate frame had come alive for Anna. She remembered not only a photograph; she remembered also a little girl. Kelsey, who cuddled deep against the pillow whenever Anna swept her bangs away and kissed her forehead. Kelsey, who smelled like a nosegay when she'd had a bath and been sprinkled with Yardley powder and like a foundling orphan when she hadn't.

Kelsey, who'd watched for Santa Claus through breath-misted glass and who'd fought to grow her bangs way past her nose and who'd learned to ride her two-wheeler despite the rutted driveway of Rockabye Inn and who'd been grounded because she'd belted a fifth-grade boy at school.

Kelsey, who'd said, "You know what, Mom? When I grow up, I'm going to be a princess and eat Twinkies and you can't stop me."

She turned to Richard, the newfound joy and the tears and the sense of possibility lustrous in her eyes. "I have a child, Richard. I have a daughter."

And his sad reply was, "I know."

"She's grown up at the inn, just like I did. And when my father died, we made this monument together, and she couldn't understand why he had gone. 'When Grandpa died,' she asked me the day of the funeral, 'did he go up to heaven and get wings?' 'You make it sound like pilot school,' I told her. 'No. I don't think Grandpa got wings.' 'Why not? Isn't he an angel now?' she asked. 'No,' I told her. 'Grandpa would not make a good angel. I think God made angels to be angels. And people to be people. He needs different sorts of beings to accomplish different things.' 'What's heaven like then?' she asked."

And here Anna shrugged her shoulders and said to Richard, "Such questions for a three-year-old, don't you think? I told her, 'I don't think I'd like to live where everything's gold and people are gowned in white. Heaven is life, but so much more life than what we've understood before. Maybe ruttier roads, nubbier sweaters, crisper mornings, colors too brilliant to fathom.' 'Maybe more chocolate,' Kelsey put in. 'Yep,' I said. 'Maybe more chocolate. And all better somehow, because hate is gone. There's nothing to do except just love God and love each other. No more competition with anybody about anything.' "

Richard rose, walked to the fence, and leaned out over it, his elbows on the buckrail, his body the angle of a pocketknife two-thirds open. He said nothing, only gazed at the pale starlight and the line of bluffs across the broad sagebrush meadow.

She didn't understand his somberness. "Pretty good of me, isn't it? An hour ago, I didn't know anything. And now I'm remembering heaven."

"It's what's in between that's going to give the problem, Anna."

"For me, heaven would be having things around here the way it was when I was a little girl, with Dad directing guests up the walk and me helping serve in the dining room, knowing, when we're finished, that I can run over to your house to get you and—" A pause, and faint color came to her cheeks. "Richard. Where is she? Where is my daughter?"

"I'll go up to the house and get the picture. And I'd best call Doctor Tilaro. He'll want to see you in his office."

"I don't want the picture. I've remembered the picture. Where is Kelsey?"

Pounding fear drove Anna to her feet.

"Where is she?"

Before he could stop her, Anna began to run. She flung open the gate and it banged back hard on its hinges, catching Richard in the groin. Lily ran, too, thinking it a game, crashing through the underbrush in the darkness. "Kelsey!" she cried. "Kelsey!" She sloshed through the ice that lay in the trail, stumbled over willow roots, felt limbs slash her face. She ran faster, faster still, past the old tree and its treehouse, past the creek. She dared not slow, dared not let her body stop, for, where her body stopped, her mind would take over with its swift, dismal revelations. *"Where is she?"*

Richard crashed through the willows and the branches and the ice behind her. He prayed as he ran, to the same power and presence that had always been beside him as he'd left home, left her behind to go climb mountains in Nepal. *Help her survive this. I know she made her choices long ago. But, dear God, help her live through them now.*

She bolted onto the porch and slammed in through the front door, dodging past the bewildered guests who'd come to sit at the fireside. "Where is Kelsey?" she screamed. She pounded up the stairs.

Evelyn had just slung a coat around her shoulders and gotten her keys from her satchel, ready to drive home. She threw her hands into the air in dismay. "She's disrupting the guests," she shouted at Richard when he bumped in through the door behind her.

"Let her disrupt them, Evelyn. This is something much more important."

"But I am in charge of the guests. Hired to make certain they have a pleasant time."

"The guests can go to Timbuktu tonight, for all I care. Now get out of my way. I've got to get to her."

She stood in his path for a second too long. "It's the way it's always been with you, isn't it? You've always been the one to go to her. You've always been the one meddling."

"Excuse me." He got her out of the way and took the stairs two at a time. Ginny had already heard the ruckus and had crept up before him. She followed Anna up the hallway, wringing her apron, while Anna banged open the doors to every room. The Wapiti Room. The Trumpeter Swan Room. The Buffalo Robe Room. Five different rooms before she had come to this one. The child's room, made up with a ruffled canopy and a tulip quilt and a crib filled with stuffed antique bears.

"This is it, isn't it? This is her room."

Ginny nodded.

"I thought it was a guest room when I looked in. I wondered why it had no name. It's Kelsey's room," she said. "Richard, why isn't she here? *Where is she?*"

Ginny buried her face in her apron. "That little girl loves you, Anna. She loves you and she'd never've chosen to go. I know that much, Miss Anna, I do. If we'd've known what he was doing, we would've tried to stop her."

Richard led Anna into the child's room and set her on the tulip quilt. After Ginny left, he handed her a box of tissues and stooped beside her on the floor. "Anna, listen to me. There are other things you've got to remember. Kelsey's father, for instance."

"Of course. Kelsey has a father. She would have to have a father." Anna blew her nose and lifted her huge, dark eyes to him.

"You don't remember Kelsey's father?"

She shook her head, then asked the question he'd feared, and been ready for, for so long.

"Do I have a husband then? Someone I have loved besides you?"

He steepled his fingers over his mouth, his expression filled with pain, saying nothing and, in the nothingness, everything.

Anna held on to her composure, but barely. "Who is he?"

He shook his head.

"Dear God, Richard. If I do have a husband, if I have a complete family, where are they? Won't you please tell me?"

He rose, sat beside her on the bed, and doubled forward, elbows to knees. "They called me back from Nepal when you had the car accident. I flew into Jackson Hole late the next day. Before I arrived, I couldn't imagine why anyone would've needed to send for me."

"You came from so far."

He would have come from the ends of the earth for her, but he couldn't tell her that now. Especially not now. "When I got to the airport, I hired a taxi and went straight to St. John's. The sheriff told me they hadn't found anyone else to call, that your husband was not at home, that he could not be reached.

"The deputies told me the details of the accident as best they could. They had found your appointment book. All they knew was that you were driving on Spring Gulch Road, headed into town for an appointment with a lawyer."

"A lawyer? I don't remember having had an appointment with a lawyer."

"If I'd chosen to take you away from Jackson, to the Caribbean, perhaps, I could have kept you to myself. I could have kept you happy and free. It's the butterfly story, Anna, the story of the cocoon. You could have been a very different person, a person who had never remembered running an inn or climbing a tree or having a daughter. Maybe no one would have found us. And you might not have ever known. It was, in its own way, a means of saving you. You might always have thought that you had chosen me."

Recognition began to dawn. "He's taken Kelsey away, hasn't he?"

"Yes. That's what the deputies say."

"I had an appointment with the lawyer. I was going to get a restraining order or something. I'd asked him for a divorce." She leapt from the bed, began stalking back and forth. "He said I couldn't do anything to stop him because he had as much parental right to Kelsey as I did." She picked a good-sized bear from the crib and squashed it against her bosom. "I have to find my little girl, Richard. I have to find her *today. Now.*"

"Is she in danger from him?"

"No. He's her father, after all. But she's . . . she's"—Anna scrubbed her temples with eight fingers, pleading—"she's all I'm certain about anymore. She's the only thing that's *real.*" Even now, she could smell Kelsey's cottony hair, could feel life warmth as she lay her cheek against the girl's eiderdown skin. Memories of the child pursued her on every sensual level, poignant and crushing. "She won't understand what's going on between him and me. She'll just want to be home."

So this is what my mind has closed away from me, that my husband has run away with my child.

"There's no telling where he's got her."

"How long has it been since my accident?" She tried counting back, hating herself for the amnesia, berating herself because she'd lost track of time. "How long since all of it?"

"If the sheriff's reports are right, three-and-a-half weeks since the day you filed a complaint and Deputy Lindsay advised you to meet with a lawyer. Three weeks since the accident. Nineteen days since I left Nepal."

"You've got to help me find her, Richard. It's been three weeks. Almost a month. She'll think I haven't tried to find her or see her. She'll think—Oh, heaven only knows what she'll think."

"Why are you divorcing him?"

"I'm not," she said. "He's divorcing me."

Richard touched her hand. "Anna, are you ready for this? Are you ready to remember?"

"Every time he had an affair, I stood by him. We never even told our families, I was so set in protecting our marriage. Every time the counselor helped us make new commitments to each other, he would lie. Four times, four different women, and I stayed."

The details came to her, blow by devastating blow. "He never wanted me, I don't think. He just wanted to *have* me. Our whole lives, he's treated me like the only reason he wanted to be married to me was so someone else *couldn't* be."

With one hand, Richard smoothed the dark hair from Anna's cheek and ran his fingers beneath her chin so she'd lift her face. "He made a *choice*, Richard. He knew what he'd be giving up if he gave up on me."

"I've been looking for them, Anna. Every day since I've gotten to Jackson."

"Have you been to her class at school? Fourth grade at Jackson Elementary? Did he take her out? Did he pick up her records or anything?"

Richard shook his head. "It's been spring break. And they've marked her absent every day since. If they're still in this valley, I have no idea where he could have taken her. I've checked his regular haunts, his favorite places. I've talked to friends who might have heard if he's nearby."

"How could you know so much, Richard? How could you know about his friends, his favorite haunts?"

"That's why the sheriff called me, Anna, when they

could find no one else. Ginny Ware gave them my number so they could notify me as next of kin." He tented his fingers and dangled them between the *v* of his legs. "I've stayed away from you all this time, Anna, because you chose him first. You have been married to my brother."

Seven

That night, Anna dreamed of a wedding party, a couples' party where everyone came and brought gifts and good wishes and toasted with fine Merlot wine. She sat on the floor amidst heaps of lavishly appointed packages, her spine against the cushions, her fingers interlaced over a knee. The wrappings shone, iridescent in the firelight, silver and gold holograms, glitter-edged bells, hearts and birds, flowers.

"Which should we open?" she asked everyone around her. And then a laugh, joyous, wholehearted, that she could still hear. "Are there always so many to choose from?"

He sat behind her on the couch, this man she would marry, the crisp-ironed crease of his trousers possessively close beside her ear. "Open Richard's first," he said. "Let's see what Richard's got to give us."

She leaned forward and took a gift in both hands, hoisting it high so everyone could see. "This one?"

A camera flash went off. Then another. "That's it."

Richard sat across the room alone, elbows on knees,

chin steepled on fingers. "Hope you like it, both of you. It's awful being a man and shopping. Wanted you to have something you'd keep, something to remember me by."

She shook one finger at him, the exact way she'd always teased him since they'd been playmates. "I know you wrapped this yourself, didn't you? It's just like you, these nut hatches and pine cones and a satin bow."

He pointed to the embossed emblem fastened on the corner. It said, "Vandewater's." "I had it done up at the store. Bow and all."

She broke the tape with her thumbnail. He swallowed and leaned farther into his knees. She felt his eyes on her hands as she pried open the box, and she knew with vast certainty that she loved him, that he loved her. She flipped open layer after layer of thin, brittle tissue, joking, as most giddy brides do. "There's nothing in here for us, is there? It's only paper. Thank you so much for the paper, Richard. Something to remember you by."

She'd never imagined being married to one of the brothers and not having the other. The three of them had been like the plaits of a rope, their friendship becoming stronger with time and weather. But Richard had been the younger, the follower, never the one to say, "Let's get our bikes. I'll beat you down Heck of A Hill" or, "Don't tell your father, Anna. He'll think I've made you give me your skis" or, "If you kiss me with your tongue, Anna, you'll know what it feels like to French kiss a boy."

Inside the tissue lay an anniversary clock, polished brass workings encased inside beveled glass, its balance wheel set and ready to whirl. "Look. Oh, look what he's done." Anna held it up. The clock's glass corners caught the light and threw rainbow prisms across the room. "It's beautiful. Oh, Richard."

He left the hearth and came toward her. He took the clock from her hands and placed it on the mantel beside the mirror, where it had always remained. "May it tick off many happy memories for you both," he announced in a voice that bordered on the dramatic. "Happy hours. Happy days. Happy years."

They threw wadded wrapping paper at him to make him sit down and be quiet. After what seemed like a hundred more boxes, ribbons, explosions of tissue, she caught him as he left down the walk. "The clock is too much. You shouldn't've done it," she said, wondering why he focused somewhere past her left earlobe instead of on her face.

"Nothing's too much. You know that."

"I wish you wouldn't talk about going away, about giving us things to remember you by. It makes me too sad."

"Comes a time to go on with what you know is right. To move on alone, no matter about your old chums."

"Is that why you've given us a clock? To remind us that 'there comes a time'?"

"Maybe. Maybe I wasn't even thinking of it, but that's what I meant all along."

"When do you leave for Nepal?" she asked.

"Three days after your wedding."

"Why so soon?"

"Just want to get out of here is all. Doesn't make much sense, hanging around."

"It won't seem like home without you."

He wore a brown University of Wyoming baseball cap with a caricature of Cowboy Joe. He took it off his head, dusted it off on his leg, and held it in both hands, turning it slightly, the way he'd turn a steering wheel. "There's not much chance of that. This place not seeming like home to you. This inn. The land. It's everything you *are*."

"Not without you," she said quietly. "Home isn't a landscape, Richard, or even a building. It's a place in our hearts." Then, even softer, she said, "How I'm going to miss you."

He swallowed once, twice, as if he needed to work up the courage for something. "Ought not to even be out here with you," he said.

And, in her dream, which she knew wasn't a dream, but more of a memory, she told him, "That's the craziest thing I've ever heard you say."

"Yes. I'm saying it. And I'm asking it. I've got to know something, Anna. If I'd been the older one, or if I'd done the asking first, would you have married me?"

A tattered cloud wove its way across the moon. Their faces were lost to one another in the darkness. She waited a long time before she answered him. At last, she said, "No, Richard. I wouldn't have married you if you'd asked me first."

He slapped his hat back on, puffed out his cheeks, and gave a little nonchalant whistle, as if he didn't care. "Just wondered, is all."

"Some other things happened first, too. You should know the whole of it. I'm pregnant, you see," she said. "No matter who's done the asking, I can't do anything different."

Richard did not sleep in the wee hours of the morning. He stood over open drawers, staring down at a pile of mismatched socks, a shirt too lightweight to be worn in the mountains, an assortment of boxers.

Nineteen days he'd searched for his brother and his niece, Kelsey. Nineteen days, sitting in the Stagecoach Bar listening, visiting friends—and he had found nothing. Nineteen days he had watched over Anna while she remembered and began to heal.

Every time it got damned impossible not to go to Anna and tell her he loved her, he made himself remember that, ten years ago, she'd chosen his brother over him.

A tapping came at his door, soft but insistent. He glanced out the window. The moon hung thin, transparent as an opal over the buttes. A great horned owl called from the distance. *Whoo-whoo. Whoo-whoo.* It would be a good hour before dawn took hold in the eastern sky.

The tapping came again, softly, urgently. "Mr. Richard," somebody whispered. "Came down here because I saw your light on. Are you awake?"

He unfastened the deadbolt and peered into the darkness. "Who is this? What's wrong?"

"It's me. Ginny Ware. Oh, everything's wrong."

She stood on his stoop wearing a pair of jeans beneath her nightgown and a crocheted shawl draped around her neck. She twisted the ends of the shawl in her hands. It occurred to him that she twisted everything with her hands, constantly, tea towels, aprons, bread dough.

"Come in, Ginny. What time is it?"

"Only four in the morning. But I've been laying in my bed all night staring at the ceiling and flipping like a pancake on a hot griddle. Couldn't stand it any longer being flat on my back with my chest pounding, I just couldn't. And when I looked out the window up there and saw lights on in this house, I knew that was my sign from the good Lord to get down here fast and tell you what's going on."

"Suppose you tell me. I suppose I'd better know."

Ginny wiped her eyes with the corners of her shawl and went on. "When a person cooks in a household as long as I have, you learn to wash dishes and listen. You watch families, or what should be families, around a table, and you figure things out you probably have no right to even figure out."

Richard offered Ginny a tissue, which the woman gladly used to replace the shawl and to mop up liberally around her nose. She sniffed. "I've been watching that family gather around the table for a decade. And I can tell you this, she honors her vows, but that brother of yours, he don't stay around much. She hasn't been happy for a long time. He takes and takes and takes. And when she won't agree to follow him, he takes some more.

"When he got Kelsey, he planned it just right. He waited until the middle of Saturday afternoon, with all the guests checking in and everybody watching him drive away, and never guessing we wouldn't see her again. We could have called Anna out of the office and told her they were going off somewhere. Instead, we were all waving goodbye."

The woman had started twisting the tissue by now, and it had come apart in feathery shreds in her hands. "Watching her fight to remember things has been like watching a swimmer try to surface to get a breath. I want to do something to help, Mr. Richard. I've been laying awake all night trying to figure out how to find Miss Kelsey."

"I'm afraid my hopes are down, Ginny. If they've gone from the valley, there's no way to get them back without Anna's restraining order and a legal battle for custody. The sheriff won't have any legal authority to bring Kelsey back until then."

Ginny clutched her shawl around her breadbasket. She lowered her eyebrows and thinned her lips, as if she'd been appointed detective on a case involving the crown jewels and the British royal family. "I've got my suspicions about something, Mr. Richard. Big suspicions."

"What is it, Ginny?"

"Makes sense, doesn't it, that if he's holed away, he's got to stay somewhere close. He hired Evelyn himself, four years ago. She's loyal to him, much more than she is to Anna."

She stopped talking. Their eyes met.

Ginny said, "If I was wrong, if I'd falsely accused someone, I'd feel horrible. But she's been acting so strange lately. She answers the office phone before any of us get a chance. She didn't worry about the bookkeeping while Anna was gone. She'd get stuck on a column and she'd leave it until the next day and she'd come back confident about the figure she needed."

Richard gripped the cook's hands. He said, "Evelyn Noble."

Ginny nodded.

Eight

$\mathcal{E}$velyn stood before the mirror in her bathroom and adjusted the bow on the collar of her blouse. She closed her powder compact. *Snap.* She fluffed up her hair one last time and grinned widely. She examined her teeth in the mirror. Not bad for an old lady. She poked a wand of mascara into her pocketbook and blotted her lips.

Ah, peace and quiet. She found it nice to have the house to herself. She shouldered her purse and patted it fondly. She needed to stop by Jackson State Bank this morning to deposit a hefty sum. Her employer had paid her well, and in cash. Untraceable.

On her way out to the garage, she saw a nerf dart sticking out from beneath the sofa. She bent down, picked it up, and tossed it into the trash can. Wouldn't do for anyone to see something like this laying around. One of the many toys he'd bought to keep Kelsey quiet and happy. She tore the top piece of notepaper from the pad on the kitchen cabinet. On it was the phone number in St. George, Utah, where they could be reached. She folded it carefully once, twice, three times, and hid it between two cookbooks.

She'd just swung onto the street with her small yellow Subaru when she saw Richard's Jeep pull up behind her. She steered to the curb, cut the engine, and got out. He vaulted out, too, leaving the Jeep's engine running in the middle of the street.

"I don't have to ask what you're doing here," she said in a judicial, deliberate manner. Her purse swung to and fro, to and fro, on her arm. "But you're too late. *Too late.*"

"What do you mean, too late?"

"Poor little Kelsey. You know what he told her? That her mom had an accident and had to go to the hospital. Seemed like a logical thing to do, didn't it? Tell her that, and that she had to come to my house and stay with me."

"You've had them all along."

"I've had them until this morning. But I told him Anna remembered everything yesterday. He knows she'll be coming after them now. So he's gone to the airport." She shaded her face and peered overhead as if she expected the flight to soar overhead any minute. "They're traveling on the first flight out."

The Sky West ATR sat perpendicular to the runway at Jackson Hole Airport. Its hatch lay open, its steel stairs sprawling out onto the tarmac. Behind the wing, a gate agent crammed clothes bags and last-minute suitcases into the hold. Another agent announced over the intercom, "This is your final boarding call for Sky West Flight 263 to Salt Lake City. All passengers should be on board at this time."

Richard parked in a five-minute loading zone. He ran through the automatic doors before they'd fully opened and gripped the edge of the counter. "I've got to talk to somebody on that plane."

"I'm sorry, sir. No one is allowed on board without a ticket."

"You've got to get somebody off then. Please." He pivoted and jutted his chin at the ceiling in frustration. "You don't understand."

"We've already made the final boarding call, sir. We have to secure the hatch so the pilot can start the propellers. We cannot ask anyone to exit the plane."

Richard stared around him with the sickening conviction that he had come close and missed them. He ran a hand over the side of his neck.

The intercom began again. "This is your final boarding call for Flight 263 to Salt Lake City."

From the direction of the airport restrooms came a man and a little girl, each of them lugging a huge backpack and wrapped in a massive winter coat. "Hurry up," the man said, dragging his daughter. "They called the flight a long time ago. I can't believe it took you so long in there."

"I couldn't help it, Dad." The little girl sniffed. "The strap broke on my backpack and I couldn't get it back together. I can't"—here she flopped the pack higher on her arm—"carry all this."

"Just come on. Please."

"I don't want to go. I don't want to leave Jackson without Mom."

"Mom can't come right now. She's sick, you know."

Richard boosted himself away from the counter. He took one step toward the man and child, then another. He tried to holler, but the call stuck somewhere below his Adam's apple. He cleared his throat and tried again. "K-Kelsey!"

She stopped when she heard her name. "Uncle

Richard?" The backpack slid down her arm and fell to the floor. She wrenched free of her father. "Uncle Richard!"

"Kelsey!" He went down on his knees and held his arms out. She ran to him and plastered her arms around his neck, knocking the breath clear out of his lungs. She'd grown a good foot since he'd seen her two Christmases ago. He had to look up to see her straight-toothed grin, her clear-sky blue eyes.

She put her chin on top of his head and squeezed him tight again while her father looked on, helpless.

"We're on our way to Utah," she said. "What are you doing here?"

"I've come to talk to you." He adjusted one leg and set her on it, his words measured and wise. "I've come to ask you to make a choice. Not an easy choice, Kelsey, and maybe one that doesn't have a right answer."

She picked up her backpack and slid it over one shoulder. "What is it?" She listened with wide, serious eyes.

"You know your mom and dad aren't living together anymore. Your dad wants you to go with him to Utah. Your mom wants you to stay here in Jackson. I think you should know both those things before you fly away."

"But Mom's sick in the hospital. And maybe she doesn't want to see me. Dad told me that. I haven't talked to her in a whole month."

"She's feeling better, and she's home." Oh, blessed way to explain it to a child who'd been stolen and hidden and taken away! Richard wouldn't make enemies of a child and her father. He wouldn't uncover a lie. Today would be Kelsey's choice—until the courts could decide.

"Your mom and dad have equal rights to you,

Kelsey. You are a part of both of them and they are both a part of you. And I think they owe it to you to decide where you can be while they work out where *they're* going to be, don't you think?"

She nodded and glanced back and forth between them.

"Do you want to fly to Utah with your father?"

"Yes, but . . ." She glanced at her father woefully. "No. I mean, I want to be with both of them, but I want to be at home, too."

"Sometimes moms and dads do better if they're apart, Kelsey." Richard glanced behind her at his brother. "Sometimes it's hard for moms and dads to remember how to play fair. My Jeep's right out that door"—he motioned toward it—"if you want to go home."

"Dad? We don't have to go. We could go back and see Mom. Will you come?"

Her father shook his head like a whipped dog. "No. I don't think so." The man didn't stoop. And he didn't hug his daughter. He swatted her behind and tried to keep his voice steady. He'd lost a great war when Richard had found them, but he couldn't let Kelsey comprehend. "Maybe you'd better, though, since your Uncle Richard has found you. Sounds like your mother's feeling better. You run and get in the Jeep, okay?"

She squeezed her father tight around the stomach. Then they both watched her go, skipping across the terminal, her hair bouncing, the huge backpack clunking along behind her. Only after she'd disappeared outside did they square off, shoulder to shoulder, man to man, brother to brother.

Richard said, "I'm not sure which one of us should throw the first punch."

"It should be me. I've always been first at everything."

"Maybe this time you'll be the first to get punched."

They both made fists. They both breathed hard and thrust out their jaws. "I was always the one getting us into trouble, wasn't I? And you were always the one who came around to clean up the mess. Well, you've cleaned up this one, too. Richard to the rescue."

"Sir." The gate agent approached them. "You've checked in for this flight. Are you going to take it? We're waiting on you so we can fasten the hatch."

"Yes. I'm taking it. Yes." The brothers began to walk side by side, then to run. "You're going to be around to pick up the pieces, aren't you? With Anna, too."

"I'd decided to leave, to stay out of the way while you two worked out your differences and sorted out your lives. But I've always loved her," Richard said. "I always will." Then, "Play fair with Anna during the divorce. She's trusted you a long time."

"She hasn't trusted me as much as you might think."

They came to the security gate, and Richard couldn't go further. "What do you mean?"

The backpack and the coat began their slow journey along the conveyor belt. "It's you she's always thought of," he said with fierce resentment. "She hasn't told you? Maybe she hasn't remembered. In the long run, she didn't choose me. Not about anything that mattered. You were her choice to get the land, even though she and I were married. She's had papers drawn up, Richard. New deeds for the property. She did it a long time ago, right after Kelsey was born. If anything happens to her before Kelsey can run that old place, she's got the inn signed over to you."

* * *

Anna worked at the front desk, her brows drawn, a pen in her teeth, two three-ring binders open and stacked one upon the other. She handed three vouchers for a wildlife-viewing excursion to the gentleman next in line and took the pen out of her mouth.

"He'll have you snowshoeing some up in Grand Teton National Park. Last week on this trip, they tracked radio-banded pine martens. You should also see elk and moose. And the big-horned sheep are out this time of year."

"Thank you."

She turned to the next guest in line. "The southern entrance to Yellowstone won't open to cars for two more weeks. But if you'd like to get in to see Old Faithful, you can drive to the west entrance"—she brandished a highlighter and a photocopied map— "by going this way."

The front door rattled loudly, and everyone started. As Richard came in, Ginny entered from the opposite direction, looking distraught, touching her apron to her eyes. "Oh, I thought it was Evelyn. We're all waiting for Evelyn. She never arrived to work this morning, Mr. Richard."

"It isn't Evelyn," Richard said. "Just me, and someone you'll be glad to see."

"She hasn't missed a day in four years. Anna's filling in for her, with the guests. Can't figure out what's going on."

"You ought to be able to figure it out, Ginny." He touched her on the shoulder and gazed down at the cook gratefully. "You can say it aloud now. To everyone. You were right, you know."

"Right about what?" Anna laid down the pen and came around a wall of brochures.

He gazed down at her, but didn't touch her. He leaned against the wall and folded his arms, cocking his head a little to one side. "It's possible you may want to hire a new guest-services manager." He waggled one hand behind him, glanced over his shoulder, and grinned. "She won't be coming back to work for you, if she knows what's good for her. Besides, she's got a nest egg now. Your husband probably paid her a handsome sum to hide them both away."

Anna's hand fluttered uncharacteristically to her breast, then to her mouth. "They were at Evelyn's. *Both* of them?"

"Until this morning."

Richard unbent a little and a blonde head protruded from around his left sleeve. "Mom? Remember me?"

Just during this past month, her face had acquired that particular lankiness of upcoming adolescence. But she was all Kelsey, with a grin as wide as Wyoming, her mangy bangs pulled back with a scrunchee, and a hundred questions in her eyes.

"Uncle Richard came to find me. He said you felt better. We were at the airport. About to leave. I wanted to come back and see you instead of going to Utah with Dad."

It took two seconds, perhaps, while Anna stood transfixed, her arms lax at her sides, before she uttered a low cry of joy. They halved the distance between them. Their arms intertwined. They pressed against each other for dear life, their hearts clattering.

"I missed you," murmured mother to daughter.

"I missed you, too," Kelsey murmured the other way around.

"I love you," said the mother.

"I love you, too," Kelsey said the other way around.

Lily, who'd bounded downstairs, her body atremble with delight, bumped their elbows with her nose.

"Don't have any of my things," Kelsey said at last. "They're all in a suitcase that got checked on the plane."

Anna cupped her daughter's ears, one palm on each side of Kelsey's head, and drank in every detail of the precious face. "That doesn't matter. Nothing matters except that you're here."

"Dad won't come back," Kelsey said with frank sadness. "I don't think he ever will."

Anna leaned her forehead to touch her daughter's. "I don't think so, either. Not to stay, anyway."

"I wanted to be with him. But I wanted to be with you, too."

"There are different kinds of love, Kelsey. Sometimes even grown-ups don't understand that until life has hurried past and bowled them over. One thing I know about love"—she glanced over Kelsey's bangs, toward Richard—"is that it isn't fragile. It doesn't break or end. When it has to make a choice between two people, it doesn't divide and become weak. It just grows and changes and becomes what it needs to become to survive. Sometimes something new and better, sometimes something different. But strong. Unbreakable." Mother's eyes to daughter's eyes. "Can you understand that, Kels?"

"I think so. Now, can I get my stuff up to my room?"

Anna hugged her. "Sure. You'd better. I know some bears up there who are going to be very glad to see you."

"Can I help Cookware Ginny serve lunch?"

"Oh, my goodness!" Ginny mopped her face roundly

with her apron and threw up her hands. "Lunch is coming, isn't it? I'd better start simmering the broth."

Kelsey kissed Anna and traipsed off, dragging her backpack upstairs. The guests went their separate ways. Ginny disappeared into the kitchen and, almost instantly, came the sound of *bang, bang, bang,* which could only be the meat tenderizer having its way with a sirloin. Richard stood at the window looking out, his hands behind him, his head inclined.

"You can see all the way into the next county from here, can't you? I've always loved this view."

"Thank you, Richard," she said as she waited by the desk. "For bringing Kelsey home. For bringing me home."

Still he did not turn around. She crossed the room, reached out for his hand, his thick sun-browned hand, and laid it against her cheek. She kissed the back of it, and then the fingers one by one.

He turned, put his arm around her, and pulled her to him very close. She stood with her face against his shoulder.

"I've been wondering"—when he spoke, she could feel the rumble of his words inside his chest—"if you meant what you said to Kelsey about love divided, choices, changes."

Her reserve was broken. "Different kinds of love. It's what I needed to learn when I was younger, what I didn't know."

"He told me about the land," he said, "about the deed, about you signing the inn over to me if anything should happen."

"It seemed the safest thing to do, for Kelsey, for the property. I set it up that way a long time ago."

Richard heaved a great sigh. "He was always convincing you to try things you oughtn't to have tried."

"And now there are new things I'd like to try. Traveling to Mexico for one. We may need some time, Kelsey and I, getting through a divorce and healing. But I want to be who I am and who I was before. Someone who's run an inn, and had a daughter and shared trouble, but who can dance on the beach. It's not too late for that, is it?" she asked swiftly.

"No, it isn't too late." He traced the outline of her mouth with one gentle, certain finger. In the motion of his hand, the depth of his expression, he revealed a need for her as potent and honest as a thirst or a hunger. In her mind, she became a child again, toes dabbling in creek water, hands closing around jade stones. She drew one quick breath. And, with that, he began to kiss her, the first time he'd ever kissed her, whispering of the hope that could now be between them, murmuring her name.

DEBORAH BEDFORD

Deborah Bedford's many novels have been published
in a dozen countries and fifteen languages. Along
with winning Romance Writers' Award of Excellence,
her work has been a finalist for the prestigious RITA®
Award, the Reader's Choice Award, and *Romantic
Times* Reviewer's Choice Award. Check out her new-
est books, *Remember Me*, *Only You*, and *The Penny*, co-
authored with Joyce Meyer.

www.deborahbedfordbooks.com
P.O. Box 9175
Jackson, Wyoming 83001

paperback format,
t to carry and easy to read.

S BELIEVING!